El Camino Drive

A Novel

By

Edward Izzi

El Camino Drive

ISBN: 979-8-6703-23048

AUTHOR'S DISCLAIMER

"El Camino Drive" is a complete work of fiction. All names, characters, businesses, places, events, references, and incidents are either the products of the author's imagination or are used in a fictitious manner to tell the story. Any references to real-life characters or events are used purely as a fictitious means of reciting a narrative, for enjoyment purposes only.

The author makes no claims of any real-life inferences or actual events other than to recite a fabricated story with a fictitious plot. Any resemblance to real persons, living or dead, or actual events is purely coincidental or used for entertainment purposes.

For Quindina, Gloria & John

About the Author

Edward Izzi is a native of Detroit, Michigan, and is a Certified Public Accountant with a successful accounting firm in suburban Chicago, Illinois.

He is the father of four grown children and one lovely granddaughter, Brianna.

He has written many poems and stories over the years, including the following fiction thrillers:

Of Bread & Wine (2018)

A Rose from The Executioner (2019)

Demons of Divine Wrath (2019)

Quando Dormo (When I Sleep) (2020)

El Camino Drive (2020)

His novels and writings are available at www.edwardizzi.com.

He currently lives in Chicago, far away from El Camino Drive.

...His lifeless body, soaked in blood,
from a battle, he couldn't survive.
His spirit now one of many ghosts
...of El Camino Drive.

CHAPTER ONE

DETROIT – HALLOWEEN, 1978

It was a warm, balmy evening on Halloween, 1978, as Antonio 'Tony' Valentino had just completed the night shift at the Ford Assembly Plant on Twenty-Three Mile Road and Mound. He punched out his timecard at eleven o'clock and walked toward his red and white Ford pick-up truck parked outside the plant parking lot. As he walked toward his vehicle, his girlfriend, Joni, was patiently waiting for him. She immediately flicked her cigarette as Tony approached her, standing next to his truck.

Joni kisses him as they warmly greet each other.

"How did your day go?" she eagerly asked.

"Not bad. I didn't see you on break," Tony replied.

Joni Williams worked in the sewing and upholstery department of the Ford Plant department adjacent to his. Tony Valentino was a forklift operator on the night shift's assembly line at the Ford Plant in Sterling Heights, Michigan, about twenty-three miles north of Detroit.

"I was outside, having a cigarette with my girlfriend, Gina. She wanted to talk."

Tony unlocked his pick-up truck, and Joni got in from the passenger side. She put her lunchbox on the floor of his vehicle and gave Tony a hot passionate kiss.

Joni was a pretty, platinum blonde with big blue eyes and a sensual figure. She was very voluptuous, close to five feet, five inches tall, and carried herself as though she was walking onto the movie set of a Marilyn Monroe movie. In her late twenties, Joni was married for almost ten years, with eight-year-old twin boys at home.

"Are we going back to your place tonight?"

"Yes," as Tony was getting excited. "Does your husband know you're working late?"

"No, but he said he would be out tonight bowling with his friends and won't be home until very late. Don't worry, Tony. I've got a hall-pass," she smiled. Tony smiled to himself as Joni opened his three-button blue Polo shirt and ran her fingers up and down his chest.

'Going back to his place' meant going to his house in Sterling Heights, just off Schoenherr Road. Tony had just closed on it about six months ago, which was still vacant and was in the process of renovating. He hadn't moved his wife, Isabella, and their three children into the house yet, as their home in Warren, Michigan, was on the real estate market and had been for sale for a few months. Tony's wife knew that he regularly visited the house after his late shift at the Ford Plant, but of course, she had no idea that he was using their second home as a meeting place for him and his married girlfriend after work.

"I'll meet you at the house," Tony quickly said, hoping that he would still be anxious and excited to amorously hook up with Joni at their usual, discrete location.

Joni quickly got out of his pick-up truck and climbed into her 1972 blue Mustang. As they began to exit the Ford Plant parking lot, another vehicle, a white 1970 Oldsmobile, parked two rows away, started its ignition. As the car's rear brake lights turned on, the car filled with three men immediately began to follow the red and white Ford pick-up truck.

Howard Williams had been stalking his wife at her place of work for the last two weeks and became well aware of the torrid affair his wife was having with Valentino. He had carefully planned this evening with his two friends, Jack Hansen and George Johnson. Williams, who was a pipefitter by trade, was small in stature but very quick-tempered. He was an abrasive, vicious alcoholic with a checkered past, and police record the length of his arm. He had done time for armed robbery, counterfeiting, extortion, and assault and battery. Howard Williams was an ex-convict who seemed to have something to prove to everyone and anyone who challenged him. He also ran one of the bookmaking operations on the East Side for the Licavoli Family, and Jack and George were into him for over a 'G-note' a piece.

When he finally saw his wife, Joni, making out with Valentino in the parking lot two weeks ago, he decided on an evening where he would violently do something about it. And that evening would be on Halloween.

Howard brought two of his former prison friends along with him. His friend Jack brought along a .25 caliber pistol he had borrowed from a friend.

The white Oldsmobile quickly followed the red and white pick-up truck that Valentino was driving, going southbound on Mound Road. The three men must have been following Valentino too closely, as he had immediately taken notice of them while sitting at the traffic light on Fourteen Mile and Mound Roads. When the light turned green, Tony accelerated his truck and began dodging the late-night traffic going southbound. Because it was Halloween and was close to midnight on a weeknight, the Mound Road traffic was almost empty. He sprinted his truck, quickly changing lanes and trying to lose the three men.

At some point, Joni must have noticed the ensuing chase between her boyfriend's truck and her husband's white Oldsmobile. She turned off of Twelve Mile Road, making a left-hand turn on a red light and going eastbound, hoping that her husband didn't see her.

The chase continued down Mound until Tony approached Eight Mile Road. As the light turned yellow, he quickly accelerated his truck and went eastbound down Eight Mile, hoping that the white Oldsmobile would get held up at the traffic light. Since Howard Williams was driving and had no respect for traffic laws, he stepped on the gas and made the left-hand turn onto Eight Mile, again following Tony's truck closely. This chase continued for another fifteen more minutes until Tony turned his vehicle into a side street off the main, four-lane highway. He tried to lose the three men, turning off of different side streets, trying in vain to lose the white Oldsmobile. Finally, Valentino turned off a side street that he didn't realize was a dead-end...a street called El Camino Drive.

When Tony recognized that he was on a dead-end street, he decided to foolishly park his truck and confront the three men following him. He suddenly remembered that his young six-year-old son, Johnny, had left his green water gun in the glove box of his truck when he was playing in it over the weekend. Valentino grabbed the toy squirt gun and put it in his right jacket pocket. With his truck still running, he opened his door.

The white Oldsmobile parked adjacent to the pick-up truck, and the three men got out.

"What the hell do you guys want?"

"You know goddamn well what we want. You're fucking my wife, you asshole!" Howard Williams immediately replied, with his two men backing him up and standing behind him.

Although Howard was only 5' 4" tall and significantly smaller than Valentino's almost six-foot frame, he had brought along his more enormous 'gorillas' with him, both over six feet, four inches tall. Jack Hansen grabbed the .25 caliber pistol hidden underneath the seat, wrapped in a white towel. When he saw Valentino come out of his truck with his hand in his right jacket pocket pointed at the three of them, he immediately believed that Tony Valentino had a gun in his jacket.

"Stay away from my wife, you fucking dago-greaseball," Howard said, getting within several inches of Tony.

"I'm not with your wife," he lied.

At that point, the three men together shoved Valentino up against his truck. Still pointing the squirt gun in his jacket pocket at the three men, Tony continued to maneuver his hand to look as though he was about to shoot at Williams.

Hansen, holding the unwrapped pistol in his pocket, immediately pointed the gun at Tony's head. As the scuffle continued to ensue, Hansen pulled the trigger, firing the weapon three times.

Two of the bullets pierced the left side of Valentino's head. As his body began to slump down against his truck, the third bullet hit his shoulder. The three men stood still as they watched Tony Valentino slump down from the side of his vehicle and fall onto the hard, concrete pavement of El Camino Drive. As he laid face up under the opened truck door of his truck, his right hand fell out of his pocket, along with his son's green toy squirt gun, onto the middle of the street.

The three men stood there, watching Valentino lay dead in a pool of blood under his red and white Ford pick-up truck.

"You were only supposed to scare him with that gun, you asshole!" Williams immediately blamed Hansen for firing the pistol.

"I thought he had a gun in his jacket, and he was pointing it at you!" he immediately responded. Because residential houses surrounded the street, they immediately climbed back into the Oldsmobile and backed up, then quickly drove off onto Eight Mile Road. It was still dark, past midnight, and no one on the street seemed to hear or see what had just happened. In the middle of the road, laid Tony's body, his head face up in a pool of blood. The lights of the truck were still on, and the motor was still running.

Located less than a foot away was little Johnny's green toy squirt gun, lying in the middle of El Camino Drive.

It was soaked in his father's blood.

Chapter Two

A Therapy Session – Forty Years Later

Fall, 2018

"Detective? Detective?"

Someone was loudly shouting.

"John, wake up, please."

"Huh? What?"

I was abruptly awakened by the police department psychologist, as I had probably dozed off during our therapy session.

"Oh, I'm sorry. I must have dozed off again."

I was sitting on the black leather couch in the office of the Detroit Police Department psychologist, Dr. Elaine Trafficanta, on that late October afternoon. I was put on a two-week suspension by my precinct commander for a physical altercation with my detective partner.

"John, this is the third time you've dozed off. Perhaps we should postpone the rest of our session. You seem to be more interested in sleeping rather than talking." She was obviously annoyed.

I looked at her attentively, trying to keep my eyes open and stay awake for the rest of that therapy session. I had stopped at the Crazy Horse Lounge on Eight Mile Road for lunch a few hours earlier. My turkey club sandwich went well with the five Corona beers and two Johnny Walker whiskey shots that I had enjoyed along with it.

I always had to have a few drinks before going into therapy, as I was forced to confront my feelings and emotions that I tried to avoid and dreaded talking about. I was fortunate that I could drive my unmarked squad car to the psychologist's office on Harper Avenue in an inebriated state.

"No, Elaine. That's okay. I haven't been sleeping much lately, so I have been dozing off."

"Yes, I can tell," she looked at me suspiciously.

I could tell the young, shapely psychologist was humoring me, probably smelling the alcohol on my breath when I immediately walked into her office. The Precinct Commander had ordered me to check in with the police psychologist twice a week to help me get over my anger issues.

"Look, John, we need to talk here."

I looked at her again, struggling to keep my eyes wide open.

"This is the second time you've come in here drunk on your ass, John. How are we supposed to have a productive therapy session if you spend more time sleeping on my couch than talking?"

"I only had two beers, Elaine. I'm okay." I lied.

A few moments of silence.

"Look, Doc, coming here and spilling my guts out to some stranger isn't easy for me. I'm a copper, not a crybaby." I defended myself and made another excuse for drinking, especially before my therapy sessions.

"Where did you go?"

"I met a few buddies over at the Crazy Horse on Eight-Mile, where I always go for lunch."

Another lie. I was there by myself.

"Crazy Horse? Isn't that a strip club?"

I looked at her and smiled.

"Well, if you call a bunch of ugly women dancing topless with pasties on their breasts on a dilapidated dance floor, well, yes...eh, I guess it is."

She looked at me, somewhat anxious, for several long seconds.

"John, why do you feel the need to go to strip clubs? Is this something we need to elaborate on here? You've been sent here by the department to discuss your anger issues. I'm struggling to find the correlation here. Do you have anger issues with women?"

Dr. Elaine was trying to find a connection between my drinking, my explosive temper, and my recent divorce from my wife of twenty-two years, Marina.

We had been married and had two boys, Anthony and Dario, who were both students at Notre Dame High School. We had just paid off our small, three-bedroom house in Harper Woods and was in the process of erecting a new two-car garage in the back before my wife sprung me with divorce papers over a year ago.

"No, Doc. My anger has nothing to do with women," I explained, although my anger was probably more centered on just one woman rather than all females.

"Do you have issues with your recent divorce with Marina? You just signed those papers, right?"

I was trying hard to keep my eyes open and listen to her questions.

"Well, yeah, Doc. I do have issues with Marina. What the hell do you expect? I married my high-school sweetheart and thought I was in a happy marriage for twenty-two years when she springs these divorce papers on me from her Southfield, Jewish lawyer." I angrily replied.

"Maybe you should have stopped drinking years ago," she curtly answered.

"Our issues had nothing to do with my drinking," I loudly responded, feeling my infamous temper coming on.

I was obviously in denial. I can't remember how many times Marina came over with the boys sleeping in the car to fish me out of the bar. I had a bad habit of stopping at the corner lounge on Kelly Road after my shift with the guys from the precinct, and I always lost track of time. It seemed like I would order my first drink at six o'clock, and the next thing I knew, it was one o'clock in the morning.

"What else are you angry about, John? Is it your kids?" she asked.

Anthony was a junior at Notre Dame and had just started driving. He was a good, responsible kid who played first-base on the baseball team and came home with straight-A's.

Dario, a freshman, was my troublemaker. He seemed to inherit my quick temper and had been suspended twice for getting into fights with the other kids in school. I was always holding my breath with him, hoping that he wouldn't get permanently kicked out of the all-boys Catholic high school.

"No," I replied. "My boys are fine."

She looked at me quickly after looking at her watch, a gesture that I noticed all shrinks have a terrible habit of doing.

"Then what else is troubling you, John? You seem to have a lot to be angry about. You've been drinking more since you've signed those divorce papers."

Several silent minutes passed without either of us saying a word.

I looked at her again, still struggling to keep my eyes open. I had not had a good night's sleep the night before, and I had bad dreams again. It seemed as though my bad dreams and nocturnal demons were centered around my childhood.

"Is it your father?"

My psyche was suddenly awakened and went into high alert. The death of my father was a subject that I never liked to talk about. This was only the second time she had brought up the issue, whom she had learned about from a crime report volunteered by my precinct commander.

Besides drinking and getting angry, I wasn't sleeping very much and was starting to have nightmares again.

Bad dreams about the same thing, over and over.

Truth be told, my nightmares were always about my father, who was murdered when I was only six years old. My forty-one-year-old father's sudden death in 1978 was an incredible shock that I don't believe I ever got over. I remember waking up to the sounds of two Detroit police officers in our kitchen in Warren, telling my mother and my older sisters that my father had been shot and killed.

It seemed like after that Halloween night in 1978, the rest of my childhood was a foggy, forgettable daze. I barely remember the rest of my upbringing and teenage years after that shocking morning following trick-or-treating with my friends.

I remember copiously crying for hours on end. I remember burying my face into my wet pillow, holding my breath, and hoping to die too so that I could immediately see my father again. I remember being in art class in the second grade and getting in trouble for drawing violent pictures of my father being shot in a truck by some evil men. I remember standing in front of my father's tomb many times at Mount Olivet Cemetery as a teenager, crying and drunk, pounding my fists until they would bleed against the marble crypt out of frustration and anger.

I was an angry kid. I had my first cigarette when I was only twelve years old and started drinking soon after that. Between the booze and the drugs in high school, it was a miracle that I survived.

This was all of his fault. I blamed my father and his irresponsible death on how difficult my life has been. After that horrific morning and that incredible shock, my life was never, ever the same.

"Why do you keep bringing up my father?" I curtly asked.

She gazed at me again, thinking very intensely before answering my question. Her big brown eyes and well-combed, auburn hair complimented her shapely figure for a single mother of two children. She was very sexy, in a nerdy, librarian sort of way. She had a bad habit of taking her horn-rimmed glasses on and off while talking, which only distracted me even more. She liked to wear those conservative, Anne Klein business suits that did a terrible job of hiding her amazing, thirty-something figure.

"You still have issues with the sudden loss of your dad as a young boy. Maybe his sudden death has been the root of all of your problems."

"The root of all my problems?"

"Well yeah, John. Your anger issues, your temper, your consistent drinking, your sleep issues, which explains why you can't keep your eyes open right now," she explained.

"You're tormented. And now, you're an alcoholic."

I started counting to ten under my breath.

As a forty-eight-year-old sergeant detective with the Detroit Police Department, I had been on the force for almost twenty-five years and had more than a few reasons for drinking.

Being a veteran policeman, I had seen more than my share of gruesome murders, dreadful car accidents, and slaughtered young, innocent victims. All of these terrible, horrifying incidents that were part of my job description as a police detective were enough of an excuse for me to drink and quickly get angry. After a long day of Detroit felony and crime investigations, I needed to have a few drinks after work to calm myself down and keep from choking the shit out of every asshole who got on my nerves.

"First of all, my father's death doesn't have anything to do with my issues here," I loudly denied.

"And secondly, I'm not an alcoholic."

She probably believed that for about three seconds, as the sexy shrink glared at me.

"My father's death is not up for discussion here, Dr. Elaine."

She looked at me even more intently.

"John, think about it. Your dad was suddenly taken away from you when you were a little boy. Your mother and the rest of your family has never discussed or talked about it with you. You grew up without a father-figure, only adding to your depression and your bitterness, which you take out by drinking and losing your temper."

"You grew up in an old school, Italian family, where nobody ever talks about their problems. You were the only boy, with two other sisters, and where everyone hid their feelings under the rug."

She paused for a moment.

"I know this, as I was brought up in the same kind of family."

She took her glasses off, trying to make a point.

"And now, you've just signed your divorce papers."

I looked at her, struggling very hard not to get angry and say the wrong thing. If she weren't so sexy and so damn beautiful, I probably would have lunged at her and choked her after our first session.

"Wow, Doc, you've got all the answers today, don't you? Imagine that," I answered sarcastically.

Dr. Elaine put her glasses back on and then looked at her watch for the seventeenth fucking time.

"Well, John, our time is up. You've been ordered to come back here three more times by your precinct commander next week. I believe Monday is our next session, correct?" she mentioned while looking at her Apple iPhone.

"I guess, whatever you say, Doc," I casually answered. I didn't want to tell her that our therapy sessions were a colossal waste of her time and weren't doing me a damn bit of good. The only reason why I continued to show up for therapy, besides keeping my job, was to stare and fantasize about her with her clothes off.

I must have undressed her with my eyes a thousand times.

"I think we're making progress, Detective. You will have to make me a promise, though."

"What promise would that be?"

She looked at me, putting her glasses back on, then pulling them down to the tip of her nose.

"You won't directly come over here from the Crazy Horse Lounge again," she casually suggested.

I smiled. "Are you banning me from Eight Mile Road?"

Everyone in Detroit knew about all of the numerous, sleazy lounges and strip clubs on Eight Mile. Many of my copper friends hung out there, especially at the Crazy Horse Lounge.

"Yes, or anywhere else on Eight Mile," she reprimanded me. "Don't make me report you to Commander Riley."

Dr. Elaine was required to send a detailed report to my precinct commander, Lieutenant Joseph Riley, after every therapy session. She had done me a favor and left out my inebriated state of mind these last few sessions but threatened to 'rat me out' if I came into her office drunk again.

I smiled at her, still struggling to keep my eyes open. My greatest fear of any of our therapy sessions, especially after having a few drinks, is that I would lose control of my mouth and emotions and make a pass at her. I could tell that she was one of those professional types that didn't mix her personal life with her patients. She probably followed those prohibitive 'doctor-patient' rules, and my asking her out would only be a total waste of time. Besides, she looked way too uptight and was probably lousy in bed.

"Thanks for everything Doc," I said as she extended her hand towards me.

"I have you marked down, "as she looked at her phone. "Detective John Valentino; Monday at three o'clock...see you then."

I put my jacket on and walked out to the professional building's parking lot in Grosse Pointe Woods. It was a brisk Friday afternoon in October, as the maple leaves from all the trees were starting to change and carelessly fall onto the ground. Because I was still on suspension with pay, I didn't have to be at the police station at work and had nothing but time on my hands.

I was spending a lot of time at the Crazy Horse, sitting around the bar drinking eight-dollar beers and enjoying twenty-dollar lap dances, which was starting to get very expensive. I needed to start paying attention to my checkbook and credit cards, as I was practically spending all of my paychecks at the Crazy Horse and was worried about paying the rent this month.

I had just moved into my two-bedroom, nine-hundred-dollar-a-month apartment on Nine Mile Road and Kelly, two miles away from Marina and the boys. I wanted to live close to them since I had custody of my sons once a week and every other weekend. Living close by in the same town as Harper Woods made a lot of sense, even though I ran the risk of seeing my ex-wife and her new boyfriend in and around the neighborhood.

When Marina served me with those divorce papers a year ago, she used my 'excessive drinking' as an excuse. In all honesty, she didn't waste a whole lot of time going out with her girlfriends and eventually finding my replacement.

Even though I could stay in the house until the divorce proceedings were settled, it was painful watching my wife move on with her life. I couldn't have been out of the house more than a week before her new boyfriend, Tom Pratt, who worked at the Chrysler Auto Plant, moved into my cozy, paid-for bungalow and my king-size bed.

But there wasn't a damn thing I could do about it. Marina got the house in the divorce settlement. I wasn't required to pay her alimony, only child support, and college for the boys. She was an elementary school teacher at St Jude's, a parochial school nearby, so staying in the area made sense.

My only fear was that I would run into her shopping at the nearby grocery store with her new boyfriend, as I knew I would friggin' lose it.

I missed being a father, a husband, and a family man. I missed having my sons in my garage, talking with them, and handing me my tools while I fiddled around with my nearly restored 1966 Corvette Convertible.

I missed waking up in our bed, in our house, having morning coffee on our patio. I missed watching TV and sharing popcorn when I wasn't at the bar drinking.

I missed my wife.

And after all of these years, I still missed my father too.

I continued to struggle with getting a good night's sleep, as images of my dad sitting with me, helping me build things with my toy Lego blocks, or throwing me a baseball when I was a little boy came to haunt me every evening.

My demons, my sleep issues, my depression, and my constant drinking were taking an incredible toll on me, as my life was steadily falling apart.

Maybe, the sexy police psychologist in the Anne Klein suit was right. I was tormented, and I felt like I was a time-bomb, ready to explode.

It seemed as though everything was coming to a climax as I pulled my squad car into the parking lot of the Crazy Horse Lounge.

CHAPTER THREE

CRAZY HORSE LOUNGE

I locked my squad car in the Crazy Horse Lounge parking lot and walked very gingerly into the dark, forecasted doorway. It was almost four o'clock, and the Happy Hour specials, along with the ten-dollar lap dances, were still going on.

My usual chair next to the stage was vacant, but I decided to sit at the bar instead as I found my way through the darkness. My eyes adjusted to the dark as I navigated myself to a barstool and waited very patiently for the bartender's attention.

The blaring sounds of the modern rap music seemed to overtake the darkness of the drab, topless bar, as some young dancer that I didn't recognize was on stage.

I sat down and stared at her for a minute or two, wondering who she was. The announcer's voice stated her stage name was 'Veronique.' She was dark-haired and skinny, with the left side of her body scattered with tattoos and red pasties on her breasts. The dancer was attractive, in a skanky sort of way. I continued to stare at her when the bartender finally came over and got my attention.

"Hey, Johnny…the usual?"

"Yeah, Dolores…thanks."

The bartender was an older blonde lady, probably in her late sixties, who had worked at the Crazy Horse for as long as I can remember. The make-up on her face was always over-done, and she had a hard time covering up her aged skin, even in the dark. The red blush and excessive blue eye shadow looked like over applied war-paint on her wrinkled face.

Dolores was wearing a short-sleeve blouse and had various colorful tattoos posted over both of her arms.

"Lime with that, Hon?"

"Yeah, sure."

Within less than a minute, she had my Johnny Walker on the Rocks with a splash of water and lime sitting in front of me, as I focused again on the new, unknown dancer on stage.

Veronique must have noticed my gazing intently at her while she was dancing, as she started to make eye contact with me while twirling herself around the dancer's pole. I must have fallen into a hypnotic trance when I suddenly was brought back into reality with the sound of a familiar voice.

"What's up, Johnny?"

"Hey, Frank...what's going on?"

"Same shit. How was the 'shrink session?' Did you get to nail her yet?" he jokingly said with a laugh.

I stood up and hugged him, as I hadn't seen him at the Crazy Horse in a long while.

Officer Frank Partridge was my old partner over at the Detroit P.D. Third Precinct before transferring over to Intel on the West Side. Frank had called me earlier in the week, and we planned to get together that Friday night at the Crazy Horse. We were still good friends and maintained a great relationship over the years, even though we weren't partners anymore.

We had arrested more than our share of gangbangers, drug dealers, and murderers over the several years when we were partners, and we always seemed to get along well.

Truthfully, Frank was the best patrol partner I ever had. There were many times when I felt myself losing control in a toxic or violent situation, and Frank was always there to calm me down.

Frank lived on the West Side of Detroit past Livernois. He had a beautiful wife and three daughters and always seemed to be relatively happy.

Frank was a twenty-year veteran detective with the Detroit P.D. at the Eighth Precinct and was well adept in violent homicide investigations. Partridge was a certified explosives specialist and long-range marksman expert in the Marines after high school. He was an extremely talented marksman. Frank was the partner you wanted at your side if there ever was a shoot-out with the 'bad guys.'

This guy was Detroit P.D.'s version of Chuck Connors of the 'Rifleman.' When it came to using any weapon or a rifle, Detective Partridge was in a league all his own.

Frank was rather tall, perhaps six feet, two inches, and carried a stocky, muscular body that would envy any former Marine. He was rather good-looking, in a Marlboro Man sort of way, with a square jaw and piercing blue eyes. Partridge looked like he could play a believable stunt man to any Hollywood action movie.

Partridge didn't have the bad habit of taking his job home with him, as most coppers did. Although he was a few years younger than I was, he was an 'old soul.' Frank seemed to understand the emotional problems and personal tortures that were actively going on in my life.

"No, Frank, I haven't nailed her. Nor do I want to."

"Why? I've heard she's smoking hot."

I looked at him and smiled.

"She's too uptight for me. No, thank you," as I took the first sip of my drink.

Dolores came over and greeted Frank.

"Absolut Vodka and Cranberry with a Lime, right?"

"You've got it, Dolores," Frank joked, as he made himself comfortable sitting next to me.

"Why is she too uptight?"

I looked at him, feeling the necessity to explain myself.

"She gets way too deep into my shit. I don't need that. If it were not for Riley and his goddamn orders, I would have blown off these shrink sessions altogether."

Frank's face turned serious.

"This suspension was probably the best thing that could have happened to you, Johnny."

"Why?"

Frank chuckled. "Why? You're a fucking time bomb, waiting to go off and explode, that's why," he said. "

"You're so damn intense, John. It doesn't take a Harvard shrink to figure out what's going on with you. You've just finished a bitter divorce, for Christ's sake. The ink is still wet on your divorce papers."

Frank paused to finish his drink.

"You've got a lot of shit going on right now, and Riley did you a favor."

I looked at him and only shook my head. I wasn't sure I wanted to hear what he had to say.

"Johnny, he suspended you with pay. Now, what precinct commander would do that? Especially after you beat the living shit out of Hacker," Frank explained.

Last week, my violent outburst with my partner, Detective Andrew Hacker, was juicy gossip within the Detroit Police Department.

Hacker was assigned to be my partner three months ago, and we were the 'odd couple.' Riley must have thought I would be an excellent mentor to this kid. But he was not an eager student willing to learn. Hacker was a young teenager in an adult body.

Detective Andrew Hacker was a twenty-seven-year-old, 'Mister Rodgers' millennial born with a gold spoon in his mouth. He grew up in a very affluent family on Grosse Pointe Shores' ritzy side and graduated from Liggett Academy.

His father was a prominent lawyer and a state senator in the Michigan Legislature in Lansing. He was an influential, old school politician who made his money and fortune the old-fashioned way: bribes, payoffs, and local corruption.

The Honorable George Benjamin Hacker had his hand in everybody's pockets, and everyone on the East Side of Detroit was indebted to him in one way or another. There were rumors that he had intensive ties with Detroit's organized crime and was on the Licavoli Family payroll.

In my opinion, George Hacker was a very shrewd, corrupt politician. He was sharp enough never to get caught with his hands in the cookie jar. It was no wonder that he was able to get his spoiled, entitled, languid son onto the Detroit Police force as an upper-level detective after immediately graduating from the police academy.

Most entering the police force have to put in their time on patrol streets before being promoted as a detective. But 'Junior' came out of the academy and became a detective right away.

Having to babysit this kid on my patrols and investigations was a considerable stretch of my patience. I found myself controlling my terrible temper while he was either playing with his cell phone or talking or texting to one of his many girlfriends. He spent a lot of time playing online video games at his precinct desk when no one was looking.

Hacker was pretty much neglecting his job duties, leaving me to hold the bag. I was getting no help from him, writing up and handling all of the case reports and crime files that I needed to follow up on.

I complained to Commander Riley, letting him know that this partnership wasn't working out at all. He told me to be patient, figuring it would be a good distraction since I had two boys at home and was going through a divorce. Showing this millennial the ropes would be a good thing, according to my commander.

Big mistake.

After about three months of this shit, I asked him one day last week to get off of his 'precinct computer-turned-play station' and assist me in a homicide case that needed closing.

"Get off my back, you Dago-drunk," were his exact words.

Huge mistake. I saw red.

"I only slapped him, Frank. He cried like a little girl," I recalled.

"Are you kidding me? Do you not remember what you did to him?"

I shook my head. Seriously, I didn't recall or remember. My outbursts had gotten so bad that my mind would go blank whenever I would lose control, and I would completely go berserk.

"You sent him to St. John's Hospital, with ten stitches on his head and face. You beat him up so badly that it took three other detectives to pull you off of him. You're lucky you still have a job and that you're not in jail."

I looked at Frank, then took another long swallow of my Johnny Walker on the Rocks.

"Yeah, well, these therapy sessions are a huge pain in my ass."

Frank Partridge laughed and pointed his drink glass at me before making his point.

"You need to thank Riley. You should be kissing his ass, Johnny. Considering who this kid's father is, you're lucky to have a job still. Riley had to go to bat and defend you when Old Man Hacker wanted to crucify you," Frank replied.

"You owe him, big time!"

I had to admit it. Commander Joseph Riley had my back on several occasions during my tenure at Detroit's Third Precinct. I often wondered why Riley was always defending and looking out for me. More so, it seems, than the other patrolmen and crime detectives within the precinct.

But why? Why was he so good to me? I felt as though I was his 'special boy.' Why was I his favorite? Did he just feel sorry for me?

"I don't need Riley's sympathy, Frank."

"Remember that old saying 'don't look a gift horse in the mouth'? If Riley's got your back, if Riley's is going to bat for you, just be thankful."

"Yeah, but why?"

"Who cares? You can use all the angels you can get," Frank replied.

We continued to order another round of drinks when Veronique came over to ask me if I wanted a lap dance.

"No, thanks, baby."

"Are you sure? I've never danced for Richard Gere before," she flirted, running her hand across my shirt.

I appreciated the compliment, but I didn't take it seriously. My increased drinking and smoking had taken a toll on me, and I was starting to look old for my age. I had lost almost twenty pounds since the divorce began last year. At five feet-ten and 170 pounds, my gaunt frame and grey hair was anything but flattering.

She smiled. "I'll be back, baby."

She continued to walk around the bar, wearing only a see-through black lace gown, hustling other customers.

Frank and I ordered another round of drinks and continued to make small talk. He had mentioned that my scuffle with Hacker was all the rage of the Detroit P.D., and every detective was talking about how I gave that spoiled, 'Sesame Street' detective the beating that he so much deserved.

As we were enjoying our second drink, I decided to confess to one of my best friends.

"I received those police investigation reports on my father's homicide the other day."

Frank looked at me, looking confused.

"You mean your father's murder forty-something years ago?"

"Yeah," I took another long swallow of my drink, which was going down very smoothly.

"Why, Johnny? What's the point?"

"I don't know. It's been haunting me for years, and I could never get a straight answer from anyone in my family. I was never told who the killers were or why my father was even killed for that matter."

Frank took a long swallow from his crystal tumbler.

"I'm still not sure why you would want to go there. Nothing is going to bring your father back."

"Maybe not, Frank."

Another long moment of silence.

"Maybe I need some closure. Maybe I need to see for myself what happened to these killers and why they were never punished for the crimes they committed."

Frank Partridge, knowing my personality and my temper way too well, made a very demonstrable observation.

"Johnny, you've got enough problems. Hunting down the past isn't good for you right now. You've just gotten divorced, and you're holding on to your job by a thread."

"Frank, I'm only curious…"

"Bullshit! I know you better," he said with a smile.

"You're looking for an excuse to hunt those bastards down and give them your own brand of justice," he said, smiling. "I know you too well."

I looked at my former partner.

"Maybe."

"Don't do it, Johnny. You don't need this in your life right now."

I looked at him, almost starting to get annoyed.

"Johnny's Justice," he smiled, raising his glass.

"Get it out of your head," he then said, putting his glass down on the bar.

"Must you always be the voice of reason?"

"Someone has to. You're very angry with your life right now, and you're looking to take it out on someone. Who else would be better than the bastards that took away your father?"

I looked at him, trying to pretend he was wrong about his presumptions.

"I'm just curious."

Another long minute of silence, as we were both staring at Veronique, doing a lap dance for some old bastard at the other end of the bar.

"Just let it go, Johnny. You've got enough problems right now."

We then changed the subject and made small talk about his wife and kids and how his girls were now in high school volleyball and basketball. I could tell that Frank truly enjoyed being a husband and a father, which made me momentarily envious.

We were sitting together talking when an older, bald man sat down two barstools away from us. He was very short, no more than five feet, four inches tall, wearing a white windbreaker jacket and dark slacks.

The bartender greeted him immediately.

"How are you doing, Howard?"

"Great, Dolores. Give me a Jack Daniels, please," he said with a very thick, Southern accent.

The older man sat at the bar and enjoyed his drink while a few of the girls approached him, trying to get him to pop for a lap dance. He continued to sit there and watch the stage entertainment when he received a phone call. I usually wouldn't have paid attention. But his phone ringer was so loud; I couldn't help but overhear him.

"Williams speaking," he said as he loudly answered his phone.

"Yeah, yeah, I'm here," he said to whoever he was talking to.

I looked at the old man and studied him, as I was beginning to put two and two together. My suspicious mind was always working, trained ever to be aware of my surroundings. I learned to be distrustful and wary of everyone and everything.

Williams? Howard Williams? Why did that name sound familiar?

Frank and I had a few more drinks together until it was almost ten o'clock. I would have usually stayed later, but I was having a hard time keeping my eyes open.

"You're falling asleep at the bar, Johnny. Besides, I have to get home. Patty is waiting for me."

"You're a lucky man, Frank. Take care of that pretty wife and those beautiful kids of yours," I said.

Dolores, the Bartender, was probably on break having a cigarette, so another bartender gave me the bar tab when I asked for it. I promptly gave her my credit card.

"Thanks, Johnny. We need to do this more often."

"I agree, Frank. Call me again next week."

"I will," he said when the cute little bartender came back with my credit card, my receipt, and a ballpoint pen.

"Thank you, Detective John Valentino," she smiled, reading my name off of my Visa credit card.

As I was signing my receipt, I noticed that the older man was staring at me. He suddenly got nervous when he heard I was a detective. He quickly placed some money on the bar and nervously began to leave.

Howard Williams, Howard Williams, who was this guy? And why did he get so nervous when he heard my name?

Frank was getting ready to leave and about to walk towards the door when I decided to go with him, keeping my sight on the old man.

His name sounded so damn familiar. But where did I hear it before?

The older man was walking over to the Crazy Horse Lounge's parking lot while Frank and I were walking ten feet behind him. I kept turning his name over in my head several times.

Suddenly, it hit me like a ton of bricks.

"Oh, shit!" I said to myself, immediately remembering where I had heard his name before.

"Hey there! Police! Stop!" I ordered the old man as he continued to walk quickly to his car in the parking lot.

"Johnny, what are you doing?" Frank inquired, but I ignored him.

"Hey, old man! Stop! We need to talk to you!"

Now the older man started to run away towards his car. I began to run after him, with Frank following close behind me.

"John, what the hell are you doing?" he screamed at me.

I didn't respond. I only sprinted faster until I was able to stop the old bastard as he was ready to open his car door.

I grabbed him by his arm, and I pinned his little old body against the driver's side door of his black Cadillac CTS.

I had him by his collar, and Williams just looked at me, trying to look clueless.

"Let me see some identification?"

"Go to hell! Who do you think you are harassing me? Let me go and leave me alone," he said in a cocky, arrogant voice.

"John, what are you doing?" Frank asked again.

I still had the little bastard by his collar.

"Why did you leave so quickly when you heard I was a detective?" I asked him.

"Go to hell, you asshole! Leave me alone!"

He struggled to break free from my grip on his shirt. I only glared at him as he starkly looked directly into my eyes. For a split second, I felt as though I was staring into the eyes of Satan.

Finally, Frank pulled my arms off of him, allowing Williams to get into his Cadillac quickly. He kept his window closed and locked his door while I stood there, helplessly watching him pull away.

As Howard Williams was driving out of the parking lot, he slowed his car just enough to look at me and smile. He was laughing and shaking his head as if to mock me. He then stepped on the accelerator, spinning his back wheels as he sped off, eastbound on Eight Mile Road.

"Johnny, what the hell are you doing? You can't go around shaking up strangers in the parking lot without cause. Are you getting goofy?"

I tried to compose myself, waiting for my sudden anger to calm down before answering him.

I remember recently reading the police reports regarding my father's murder. I had looked up the files and made copies of them, remembering all the details of the crime reports and police investigations. To this day, I still have those files in the bottom drawer of my desk.

When the older man heard my name at the bar, he knew exactly who I was. At that moment, he quickly left the Crazy Horse Lounge.

"Who was that old man? Do you know him? What did he do?" Frank asked.

I looked at him, and I felt cold, freezing ice water going through my veins.

"He killed my father."

CHAPTER FOUR

ONLY ON OCCASIONS

I was fast asleep in my bed that October evening when I suddenly woke up to the sound of sirens. It was just past two o'clock in the morning. My new apartment was off the main, busy street of Kelly Road, and all of the loud, bustling traffic continued to make distracting noises that I wasn't used to. I woke up from the mattress on my floor and looked out of the window, see what it was. There was some sort of police chase going on as several loud Detroit squad cars went whizzing by my apartment.

I hadn't been in my apartment any more than a week and had minimal furniture. My bed consisted of an old, single mattress that I took from home that my dog used to sleep on and a dilapidated leather couch that I had grabbed from my mother's damp basement. I stole the television from my son's bedroom that he used for video games. In the kitchen, I had precisely one fork, one knife, three plastic plates, and two spoons.

When I got a little more money, I promised myself that I would go shopping for some furniture. But at the rate I was going, that wasn't going to happen anytime soon. My credit card bills were practically 'maxed out,' and I was living paycheck to paycheck. One would think that with all the financial problems that I was currently experiencing, I would have the sense to stay away from the bars and especially the Crazy Horse Lounge.

I laid back down on my very used mattress, using whatever blankets I had to make myself comfortable. To say that Marina had sent me away with very little more than my underwear was an understatement. I was in a rented apartment, with no money for the next month's rent, using my credit card to buy whatever meals I could afford and, of course, managed always to find the money for the strip club.

I laid down, with my eyes open, wondering how I ever let my life get this bad. Was it my childhood? Was it the sudden loss of my father? Was it my uncontrollable temper? The words of Dr. Elaine were ringing loudly in my ears that whole night.

She bluntly called me an alcoholic. Do you believe that bitch? An alcoholic is someone who lets alcohol take over their lives and, eventually, ruin it. I had met and arrested enough of those alcoholics to know that I wasn't one of them.

I had a drink only on occasions...

Only on occasions...

Only on occasions...

I said that phrase to myself several times. For me, 'only on occasions' was becoming a habit of having drinks at mid-day during lunch and in the evenings, consisting of several beers with each meal and whiskey shots after that.

Only on occasions...

I said to myself again. I was angry at myself for letting that uptight Anne Klein shrink call me an alcoholic without getting angry and upset with her.

She had no idea what she was talking about.

I laid awake until it was almost six o'clock in the morning. It was now early Saturday, and I realized that I wouldn't have my boys that weekend. I had nothing planned for that day. Usually, when I was at home, I would go into my 'man-cave' in my garage and tinker with my Corvette. Because I had to put it in storage, I could only go there and take it out on occasions, as I had to pay a security entry fee of five dollars whenever I went into my one car storage unit.

I turned on the television but soon realized that those days of 'Bugs Bunny' and Saturday morning cartoons had long gone away with my childhood.

I was depressed, bored, and hungry. I wanted to go to the party store down the street and pick up a bottle of Johnny Walker Black. But when I looked in my wallet, I only had three single dollar bills. I knew that my credit cards were almost topped off, and I didn't want to use what was left to buy more liquor. I had to choose between getting something to drink and putting something into my stomach.

I took a shower, got dressed, and climbed into my squad car.

"Welcome to McDonald's. May I help you?"

"Eh, yes, could I have an Egg-McMuffin and an orange juice, please?"

"Okay, that will be $5.87. Pull up to the next window."

I suddenly went into shock as I slowly pulled up to the next window. I started looking for any change lying around in my car. I was looking on the floor, the ashtray, or in the front seat. There was nothing.

"Excuse me…I don't have enough money. Could I just have some hash browns, please?"

The young African American girl glared at me, knowing that it would be a pain-in-the-ass to void out my breakfast order and amend it only for some hash browns and an orange juice. She looked at me in frustration, then abruptly closed the window. She must have gone off to talk to her manager. I then heard her say, 'pull up to the second window, please,' over the intercom.

Confused, I pulled up to the next pick-up window when another older lady answered. Smiling, she suddenly handed me a bag that felt reasonably heavy, and I knew there was more in that bag than just some hash browns and a small orange juice.

The older lady smiled.

"Have a nice day, officer."

As I looked into the bag, I suddenly had tears in my eyes.

There inside were two Egg McMuffins, a Sausage McMuffin Sandwich, two hash browns, and a large orange juice.

I waved to her, barely being able to focus as my eyes were full of tears.

I was thankful, knowing that I had enough to eat for not only breakfast but maybe lunch as well. I pulled my car off to the side of the McDonald's parking lot and began eating my breakfast. As I was enjoying my meal, I was extremely grateful.

I wanted to say 'grace' to myself but realized that I couldn't. I hadn't been to church in so long, and I had forgotten how to pray.

The hunger pains were slowly going away as I was eating my Egg McMuffin in my squad car in the parking lot. I started to think again about what Dr. Elaine had said to me the day before.

Here I was, accepting food handouts from the local McDonalds, with barely enough to eat and with no money. I was less than a month away from being homeless, and I was holding on to my job by a shoestring. It had suddenly dawned on me, and I now believed that maybe...she was right.

I needed to do something about my problem. But I didn't know where to start or who to turn to. For some odd reason, I decided to drive back to the Third Precinct. Not because I wanted to work or needed to get anything done, but only because I had nowhere else to go.

At that moment, I realized that I was an alcoholic.

CHAPTER FIVE

MORNING OF THE MURDER – NOVEMBER 1, 1978

It was almost four o'clock in the morning when the telephone next to Ross's bed loudly rang, waking up the whole house.

"Hello?"

"Ross, it's Isabella. Something happened to Tony."

Ross rubbed his eyes to awaken to the unusual sound of his sister-in-law's voice at such an early hour.

"Ross, you need to come here, quickly. The police are here."

Ross was still rubbing his eyes.

"Isabella, Cos'è successo?"

He immediately demanded to know, asking her in his native Italian. He suddenly realized how serious it must have been to have his sister-in-law calling him at such an early hour. He knew it had to be extremely serious.

"Vieni qui subito. Tuo fratello è stato sparrato," exclaiming that his older brother, Tony, had been shot.

Ross immediately went into shock, thinking that this was suddenly some kind of bad dream. He immediately put his pants and shirt on, threw on his shoes and jacket, and quickly drove from his house in Sterling Heights to his brother's home in Warren. It was usually a fifteen-minute drive, but Ross was able to make it in less than ten minutes. Every fearful thought was going through his mind. He wondered where, how, why, and what could have possibly caused his older brother, Antonio, to be shot.

Rossano 'Ross' Valentino was two years younger than his oldest brother Antonio. They were from a large family of four brothers and two sisters, who lived within proximity of each other and were a very close, tight-knit family. Having all immigrated from Casalvieri, Italy (near Rome) in 1957, they struggled together to embrace their life in their new world of Detroit, Michigan. They all got jobs working in the automotive factories in Detroit. The Valentino brothers married young and started families. They all worked hard, purchased homes in the suburbs, and fulfilled the American dream.

Of all of his siblings, Ross was the closest to his brother Tony. With less than a two-year spread between them, they relied on each other for moral and financial support. They usually had breakfast together once or twice a week and always had each other's backs. Their two younger brothers, Alberto, and Paolo, with two sisters between them, were several years younger and had their own close relationship.

In all, the Valentino's were a tight family, indeed. They all got together as a family for their children's birthday parties, summer picnics, all the holidays, and especially Christmas Eve.

Ross admired Tony's ability to work hard and save his money. Tony was frugal, still driving his first car, a red and white 1959 Oldsmobile Super 88 convertible, still in his garage with only 30,000 miles. He had saved enough money to pay cash for his second house in Sterling Heights and was debt-free. Tony helped Ross buy his first house, lending him the money for the down payment.

But Ross was well aware of Tony's faults too. The Valentino brothers were tall, good looking men who never had any trouble with the opposite sex. But they all knew their limitations and their essential responsibilities as respectable, married family men.

Except for Tony. Women seemed to be his ultimate weakness. Tony openly philandered and played around on his wife. He always seemed to have a sexual, romantic fling or two on the side.

This bothered Ross, who admonished him on several occasions to discontinue his selfish, reckless behavior. But of course, Tony never listened to his younger brother. He seemed always to be involved in various extramarital affairs.

Deep down in his stomach, Rossano Valentino knew precisely what had happened to his older brother.

As he pulled his new Lincoln Continental into the driveway of his brother's house, he noticed two Detroit police squad cars parked on the driveway. He also saw two familiar Ford, turquoise pick-up trucks.

It seems that Isabella had called her brothers to come over as well.

Ross walked into the side door, and Isabella immediately hugged her brother-in-law.

"Tony è morto," she cried in Italian, exclaiming that her husband was dead. They both embraced each other, as Ross began crying uncontrollably in Isabella's arms.

Mario and Aldo DiVito, Isabella's brothers, were sitting at the kitchen table with two police officers, while Tony's two daughters, Rosanna and Lucia, were sitting in the living room, crying to themselves and sharing a box of Kleenex.

One of the Detroit police detectives, Detective Sargent Joseph Riley, expressed his condolences to Tony's brother.

"I'm sorry for your loss," after he introduced his detective partner, Sargent David Miller.

"What happened?" Ross asked.

"Your brother was found dead, face up next to his truck with three bullet wounds just after midnight. His vehicle was parked, the engine was stalled, and it had its lights on. His body was next to the truck with the driver's door open.

"Where?"

"Just off of Eight Mile Road, on a dead-end street named El Camino Drive," Detective Miller said.

Rossano began sobbing as everyone in the kitchen was utterly silent. For five long minutes, no one said a word, as the shock of Tony's death was slowly sinking into everyone's heads.

"Why? How could this happen? Didn't Tony go to work last night?"

"Yes," Detective Riley answered. "We don't know a whole lot of details right now, but we do know that he worked his shift at the Ford Plant."

"Someone was following him after work and confronted him, based on the position of the body and the fact that the truck was still running," Detective Miller stated.

They all looked at each other, not understanding how any of this could have happened.

Detective Riley pulled out his notepad and began taking down notes.

"Did your husband have any enemies that you are aware of?"

"No," Isabella immediately said.

"Did you and your husband have any issues or problems in your marriage?"

"No," Isabella quickly responded.

"Did your husband ever receive any threats from anyone?"

"No, not that I'm aware of."

Suddenly, a voice came out of the living room.

"No, Mom, that's not true," Lucia said while sitting on the couch, still sobbing.

Everyone's eyes suddenly focused on the nine-year-old little girl and turned their attention to her.

"Someone called the house about a week ago, and I answered the phone. It was a man's voice, and he asked for Dad."

"Really? What did he say?"

"I told him that he wasn't home, and he said to tell your father to stay away from my wife, or I'm going to kill him," she recounted.

Isabella looked at her daughter. "Why didn't you say anything?"

"I told Dad when he came home, but he just laughed and shrugged it off. He said it was a prank call."

Both detectives looked at each other, knowing that this could lead to a motive in this case. At that moment, Detective Riley got a call from his radio, which he took outside. After several moments, he came back into the house.

"Your husband's body is at the Wayne County Morgue on East Warren Boulevard. We will need someone to identify the body."

Mario, Aldo, and Rossano all nodded their heads. One by one, they all hugged and kissed Isabella and got into their respective vehicles.

In the corner of the kitchen, little six-year-old Johnny was sitting on the floor, sobbing, and crying his eyes out. He had just gotten out of bed and told that his father had been killed.

Detective Joseph Riley stopped and stared at the little boy crying in the corner.

At that moment, the detective's heart was broken.

In a parade of cars, they followed the two Detroit patrolmen to the Wayne County Morgue on East Warren Boulevard. As they entered the morgue, Dr. Michael Huspen was waiting for them to arrive. He expressed his condolences to the brother and two brothers-in-law and then led them to a steel door cabinet where Tony's body was shelved. As the doctor opened up the white body bag, Ross Valentino immediately broke down, as Mario and Aldo tried to comfort him.

"Is this your brother, Antonio Valentino?" Detective Riley asked Ross.

"Yes, it is," he sobbed, wiping his eyes with a handkerchief.

Dr. Huspen then described the bullet wounds and the belongings which had been placed in a plastic sandwich bag. There was a silver Timex watch with a black band, a brown and white handkerchief, and a small, green plastic change purse with 48 cents inside. Dr. Huspen then handed Ross another plastic bag with another item.

Covered with dried up blood was a green, plastic water pistol.

"This was recovered at the crime scene, about six inches away from the body," the coroner stated matter-of-factly."

One of the brothers-in-law, Mario DiVito, questioned the coroner.

"Why would there be a plastic water gun at the crime scene?"

Detective Riley speculated. "We think the victim found the plastic water gun in his truck and tried to fool his killers into believing that he had an actual weapon in his pocket."

The three relatives looked at each other, unsure how a plastic water pistol would have ended up in Tony's truck.

"That's probably little Johnny's toy gun. He liked to play with it in his father's truck," Ross conjectured.

"He probably left it there, and when Tony saw that he was in trouble, he tried to use it as a ruse to fool his killers," Detective Miller replied.

Tony Valentino's lifeless body was only partially exposed, with his face clearly showing the dried-up blood stains from the gunshot wounds.

Tony had been shot three times, twice on the left side of his forehead and once in the shoulder. The coroner explained that the initial wound entered his left eyebrow and exited out of his right eye. The second shot came in from the top of his forehead and exited out of his mouth. The third shot hit his left shoulder. All three bullet wounds were caused by what looked like a small .25 caliber pistol.

“It looks like the victim was slumping down as he was shot at close range,” Dr. Huspen stated, describing the details of Tony’s mortal wounds and how he was killed.

Ross kept shaking his head. He knew that his older brother had brought all of this on himself.

Tony was a player and a ladies-man. He proudly flaunted his extra-marital flings and relationships to anyone interested in listening. He especially enjoyed bragging about all of the details of his sexual escapades to his brother Ross. But the younger Valentino warned his brother several times about the consequences of having extra-marital affairs, especially with other married women.

Ross also remembered what his niece had said back at the house. Someone had called the home and left a warning to Tony to stay away from his wife, but his brother didn’t listen.

Unfortunately, Ross knew his brother was blessed with handsome, movie-star good looks and an extreme, cocky arrogance to match. Tony felt impregnable and was beyond being lectured by anyone, especially by his younger brother.

Antonio Valentino’s body was laid out at the Frank J. Calcaterra Funeral Home on Seven Mile Road and Kelly on that following Tuesday. There were throngs of people coming into the funeral parlor to pay their respects to the young, fallen husband and father.

It didn’t take long for the whole Italian community to learn about what had caused Tony’s mortal fate. There was media coverage by the local television stations and the newspapers, flagrantly mentioning Tony's alleged affair with a married woman and how he had become the victim of a jealous husband's revenge. Inside the dark, wooden coffin laid Tony Valentino's ashen body, his hands still stained with his own blood.

As friends and family came to pray and pay their respects throughout the day, there were distinctive whispers in the hallway, all asking the same question: Why?

Why would Tony risk his own life to be involved in an extramarital affair with a married woman? Why would he jeopardize the well-being of his family?

Why didn't Valentino heed the warnings, knowing that he had found the wrong married lady to fool around with? Why wasn't Tony more conscious of his family and the effects such a dangerous affair would ultimately have on his wife and children? Why would he risk the chance of his three young children growing up without a father?

In the far back of the funeral chapel, there was a young blonde lady silently sitting on one of the steel folding chairs, alone. She did not go up to the casket, and she did not pay her respects to Isabella or the family. She was wearing a black, sleeveless dress and was holding a long, black leather coat. Although she was visibly grieving, she did not say a word to anyone.

Ross Valentino, who was standing next to the casket along with his brothers, noticed the platinum blonde sitting alone in the back. She looked familiar, but he couldn't place her and couldn't recognize who she might be.

With many people going through the reception line, Rossano thought about the identity of the mysterious woman. After an hour, he planned to approach her and introduce himself, as he was curious as to how she was connected to his slain brother. When the opportunity finally came for him to move towards her, she was gone.

As Fr. Dominic Rossi said the rosary at seven o'clock that evening in the funeral chapel, they all prayed for the eternal repose of Antonio Valentino's soul.

"May his soul, and all the souls of the faithful departed, rest in peace," the Catholic priest concluded.

"Amen."

In front of the dark wooden casket, Isabella and her three young children continued to mourn and cry.

The widow had fainted several times in front of her husband's casket, overtaken with grief. They were inconsolable, knowing that their husband and father was now forever gone.

They were the only one's weeping.

CHAPTER SIX

CATCHING THE KILLERS – NOVEMBER 1978

Detective Joseph Riley was sitting at his desk, eating a sandwich at the Twelfth Precinct on Seven Mile Road. It had been a slow Monday morning, and he was finishing up some prior case paperwork when he got a phone call at 12:23 pm.

"Detective Riley speaking."

He was trying to answer his desk phone with his mouth still full of the last bite of his turkey sandwich.

"Joe? It's Jim Karas, from the Sterling Heights Police Department," said the voice on the other line.

"I don't know if you remember me, but we worked together on a homicide a few years ago."

The detective thought for a few long seconds.

"Oh yes, that homicide on Dodge Park Road; the suspect was an Eight Mile gang banger…yes, I remember."

"How are you doing?"

"Great, Joe, but we've got a little problem here. We have a suspect who walked into our station and demanded a paraffin test done on his hands. He says he was involved in a homicide on El Camino Drive the other night."

Paraffin was used at the time to test for gun residue on anyone who had used a firearm. The test is conducted by applying melted paraffin wax to the back of a suspect's hands. With a brush, the back of the hand is coated with paraffin wax, which upon cooling, solidifies and can be peeled off the hand. The detection of dark blue spots is indicative of the presence of nitrates from a firearm.

The Detroit detective was silent for several long seconds.

"He just showed up at our station and confronted one of our detectives, requesting the test," Karas stated.

"I was told you're the one handling this case."

"Yes," he said slowly, still thinking about that little boy crying in the corner of his mom's kitchen.

"We're holding him here. You may want to come down and pick him up."

Detective Riley had been working on this homicide case over the weekend but was getting nowhere. They had interviewed several employees at the Ford Plant where Valentino worked, but no one had seen or heard anything. The only thing they were able to verify was that he was a 'ladies' man.'

Detective Miller had gone from house to house on El Camino Drive, but no one in the area was able to mention anything helpful. The few residents who live on that dingy street were accustomed to being questioned by the police and conditioned never to volunteer any information.

El Camino Drive was a dead-end street located several blocks west of Eight Mile Road and Gratiot Avenue. It had been misnamed for years, as it was a long boulevard that was cut off by some commercial and industrial buildings back in the 1960s. That area had been developed at the end of the road, blocking its thorough-way path to Seven Mile Road.

The street was never correctly labeled with a dead-end sign. It was a constant turn-around for unassuming drivers, unaware of its abrupt end. Because it has several boarded up and abandoned houses on the street, it had become a crime-infested, violent area within the edge of the city. It is a seedy, secluded area where drug-deals and brutal murders continually take place.

"Don't end up on El Camino Drive" has been a famous catchphrase on the East Side to anyone wishing to stay away from the gangbangers, sleazy street hookers, and violent drug deals.

Although the area is well patrolled, it always seems to cough up dead bodies from drug deals or sex tricks gone bad. It has become one of the most dangerous areas on Detroit's East Side, and Tony Valentino couldn't have found a more dangerous place to park his truck and confront his enemies.

By 2:30 pm, Detectives Riley and Miller were at the Sterling Heights Police Department on Dodge Park Road.

"Detective Karas, please."

"You both must be from the Twelfth Precinct. Come on back, he's expecting you," the desk sergeant said.

The desk sergeant was an older lady with thick horn-rimmed glasses and dark, dyed jet-black hair with a tinge of blue. She buzzed them into the door and led them to Detective Karas' office cubicle.

They all greeted each other and made small talk, as Karas then led them to the interrogation room, where the suspect was waiting.

Howard Williams was a short, scrawny little man, no more than five feet, four inches tall, balding, and in his late twenties. According to Detective Karas, they had run a background check on him and had several prior offenses, and had done some time at the Jackson State Prison. His abrasiveness was apparent as he insisted on having the paraffin test done.

He wanted to immediately prove to the police that he wasn't the one who pulled the trigger. Williams had a volatile, criminal past and had done time for various offenses, including extortion, robbery, and assault.

The three detectives walked into the interrogation room and greeted the ex-convict.

"Mr. Williams, I'm Detective Riley, and this is Detective Miller from the Twelfth Precinct. You met Detective Karas," as they all shook hands.

"I understand you have something to tell us."

"Yeah," he replied in a loud, cocky voice. "I need to get that paraffin test done to show you guys that I didn't do it."

"Do what?"

"You know...kill that dago-grease ball that was fucking my wife," he said in an irreverent voice.

Still remembering that little boy, Riley started to raise his voice.

"That dago-greaseball that you probably helped kill had a name. He also had a wife and three young children, Mr. Williams."

"Do you know his name?" Detective Miller asked.

"I don't know...Tony Dago-Valentine-something," he said in an arrogant voice.

At that moment, Detective Riley got up from his chair and lunged at Williams, grabbing him tightly by his throat and pinning him up against the wall.

"His name was Antonio Valentino, asshole!" as he was tightening his grip around Williams's scrawny little neck.

"And he had three little kids who now don't have a father, thanks to you, you little rat son-of-a-bitch!"

"I didn't do it! I didn't do it!" he tried to scream as Riley's colossal hand was around his neck.

Detective Joseph Riley was a six-foot, four-inch, 275-pound former college football player. He played linebacker for Brother Rice High School and was a first-string defenseman for the University of Michigan before he got his degree in criminal justice. He had just joined the Detroit Police Department after graduating from the academy two years ago and was still considered a rookie in his precinct.

Riley towered over Williams, almost lifting him by his neck. He couldn't get that six-year-old little boy crying in the corner of his kitchen out of his head and wanted to take out his anger directly on Williams.

Detective Miller and Karas sat there and watched the show, only verbally telling Riley to try 'not to kill him.'

The angry Detroit detective put down the perpetrator and sat back down.

"Okay, asshole...let's try this again," Riley said.

The three detectives stared at Williams as he tried to get his bearings straight after almost being choked to death by the detective.

"Now, Mr. Williams, would you care to tell us what happened last Friday night?"

Howard Williams went on to recite the specific events that had transpired over the last two weeks. He talked about how he had discovered his wife was sleeping with Tony Valentino. Williams described how he had spied on them in the parking lot of the Ford Plant and how he had enlisted his two friends to help 'roughen' him up after work on Halloween night.

He gave up their names, Jack Hansen and George Johnson, both residents of Detroit. Williams had known both of them from his stint at Jackson State Prison two years ago. It turned out that Howard Williams was a bookmaker for the Licavoli Family, and Hansen and Johnson were into him for over $1,000 bucks apiece. He said he would cover their marker in return for the favor of helping him rough up his wife's boyfriend.

Williams talked about how they were following Valentino down Mound Road to Eight Mile Road when he abruptly turned his truck onto El Camino Drive.

"This guy then gets out of his truck and confronts us, with a gun in his jacket," Williams described.

"One of the guys I was with, Jack Hansen, gets out of the car and shoots him. I didn't even know he was packing," he recited.

"So," Miller repeated, "You didn't get out of your car and confront him first? And how was it that you didn't know that he was carrying a gun?"

"I told him to come with me and help scare this guy. He owed me a favor, and I needed the muscle," Williams said.

"And you never touched him? You never had any intention of killing him?" Miller asked.

"No," Williams insisted. "We only wanted to talk to him and convince him to stop seeing my wife."

"Convince him?" Riley repeated. "Do you call chasing him from the Ford Plant to Eight Mile Road a gentle method of convincing? You probably scared the shit out of him."

Williams started to smile. "We only wanted to talk to him."

"Really? So, you bring along two gorillas packing a gun to only gently persuade him to stop seeing your wife?" Riley sarcastically asked.

"Well, yeah. I never had any intention of killing him. I didn't have the gun, I didn't pull the trigger, and I didn't kill him."

"Okay, so who did?"

"Jack Hansen did. Jack was the one who killed him."

The three detectives looked at each other.

"You didn't know that Valentino wasn't armed?" Miller asked.

"Hell no! We saw him coming out of his truck with his right hand in his jacket pocket, shaped like a gun."

"Yeah, asshole...a squirt gun!" Riley commented.

Williams looked shocked.

"How the hell did we know? He came out of his truck with his hand pointed at us."

Miller pulled out his notes.

"The victim was shot at point-blank range. He was found face up against his truck with his door open as if he had been pulled out of it. His blue shirt was crumpled and looked as though someone had grabbed him by his collar," the Detroit detective read from his notes.

"Sounds to me like you went after him and hunted him down like an animal, Mr. Williams."

"No!" Williams said, almost yelling.

"It was self-defense!"

"Do you call shooting someone who was pointing a green, water-pistol at you fucking self-defense?" Riley screamed, ready to grab the 'perp' by the collar again.

"The victim had a water-gun in his pocket!"

"How the hell did we know?"

Williams looked at the three detectives in shock. His face turned ashen white upon knowing that Tony Valentino was unarmed.

Detective Miller looked at his watch and noted that he had to be back at the Twelfth Precinct in an hour.

"I suggest that we all finish this cozy little conversation back at the station, wouldn't you agree, Joe?"

At that moment, Detective Riley handcuffed Williams, read him his rights, and they both escorted him to their squad car parked outside of the Sterling Heights Police Station. They then returned to their precinct on Seven Mile and locked up the prisoner.

Detective Riley then took several patrolmen along with him to apprehend the other two suspects.

Jack Edward Hansen was a union electrician who worked for a local contractor on the West Side. He lived on Hamburg Street off of McNichols Drive near Gratiot Avenue, in the Von Steuben neighborhood. Three of the patrolmen staked out of his house until he arrived home at 6:00 pm.

Hansen was confronted and then arrested. His house was searched, finding a .25 caliber Pic-DeCauter automatic pistol, blue in color, stuffed in a white sock in a dresser drawer in his bedroom.

George Johnson lived alone on St. Patrick Street, just off of Gratiot Avenue. Detective Miller and two other patrolmen waited for Johnson to come back before he was arrested. His house was searched, but no weapons were found.

Hansen and Johnson told quite a different story. They stated that Williams had planned to murder Valentino all along and wanted to make sure that Hansen had brought along his gun that evening.

They both recounted that evening, stating that they intended to 'rough up his wife's boyfriend until he pointed what appeared to be a gun in his jacket. At that point, Hansen withdrew the weapon, but it had misfired, firing three rapid shots at the victim. A paraffin test was conducted on all three suspects, and Hansen was, indeed, the triggerman in this homicide.

The three suspects were locked up and arraigned for the following day in front of Judge Robert O'Conner, to which the three men were advised to stay mute. They pleaded 'not guilty' to the first-degree murder charges. They were held at the Wayne County Jail without bond.

Three weeks later, a preliminary hearing was conducted in the Wayne County Court. After the prosecution and their defense attorneys presented the evidence, the charges of first-degree murder were dropped entirely against Howard Williams and George Johnson, and they were immediately released from prison.

Their attorneys stated that while their clients intended to scare Valentino, that they never touched him. Their attorneys argued that Williams and Johnson never fired the weapon that ultimately killed him.

Then first-degree murder charges were downgraded to second-degree against Jack Edward Hansen, a burden that carried fifteen years to life in prison. This was based on the fact that Valentino had in his hand what appeared to be a weapon and that Valentino drew his gun first.

Hansen, stating that he had no control over his weapon, pointed three inadvertent bullets into Antonio Valentino as he was slumping down against his Ford pick-up truck, leaving him to die to face up in the middle of El Camino Drive.

He continued to plead that the borrowed .25 caliber Pic-DeCauter pistol had jammed when he inadvertently fired the gun by accident. The original owner of the firearm testified on Hansen's behalf, stating the weapon had a long history of jamming and was the reason why he was unable to sell it.

When the prosecutor asked them why they didn't call an ambulance instead of fleeing the scene of the murder, they stated that they were 'scared.'

"So scared that the three of you went to have drinks at the Blue Pony Lounge on Van Dyke and Ten Mile afterward?"

"We needed to calm down," was Hansen's excuse.

The prosecutor, several days before the trial, offered a plea bargain to Hansen of involuntary manslaughter, a mandatory sentence of seven years in federal prison. But Hansen was advised by his attorneys to go to trial, pleading self-defense.

On March 20, 1979, after a long, three-day trial, Ross Valentino bore witness to the American justice system in the murder of his brother Tony. Along with him were Mario and Aldo DiVito, Tony's two other brothers, his two sisters, and several friends that were there to give them support.

Seated next to them was Isabella Valentino, the slain victim's widow, who was only there to see justice in the death of her husband of seventeen years.

Isabella held her breath as the verdict on second-degree murder charges was read against one of her husband's killers, Jack Edward Hansen.

"We, the jury in the charges of second-degree murder against Jack Edward Hansen, find the defendant...not guilty, Your Honor."

Isabella began to cry uncontrollably as her brothers hugged her in comfort.

The defendant was able to successfully prove self-defense, believing that the victim had a gun.

Jack Hansen jubilantly smiled at his attorney as he was released and escorted by his family out of the courtroom.

Although George Johnson was not implicated, he was asked to testify as a witness in Hansen's defense. Howard Williams, the one who planned the whole violent episode on that Halloween night, was also asked to testify. But while cross-examined, he pleaded that he had no idea that Hansen had a gun. This testimony should have brought him perjury charges. Of all the suspects in Valentino's homicide, he was the one who truly got away with murder.

Hansen smiled at Johnson as the three former murder suspects congregated in the hallway of the courtroom. While the three of them planned their bar celebration, Rossano Valentino, escorted by his brothers, walked within three feet of the former suspects. He gave them a long, dark stare, as his eyes were seething with a vengeance.

Rossano then said aloud, a cursing proclamation against his brother's killers. It was a curse that he had heard his mother say only once, a curse only used to cast death and the evil eye against one's mortal enemies.

"*Che il diavolo diamine i vostri mente cattiva cuori e li dia da mangiare ai lupii affamato. Possa lei e le sue figli morire millemorti,*" he said out loud at the three of them.

Everyone in the back of the courthouse was startled, all wondering what he had said.

He was then escorted by his brothers out of the courthouse, along with Isabella, who was still crying profusely.

While Mario DiVito lagged behind, Williams yelled out to him in a cocky voice:

"Hey, what did that dago just say?"

Mario glared at them; his eyes filled with anger.

"He just gave all of you an evil curse," he replied.

"A curse?"

"Yes, in Italy, we call it a 'maloccio.'"

As the three of them laughed, Mario translated:

"May the devil gauge out your evil hearts and feed them to hungry wolves. May all of you and your children burn in hell and die a thousand deaths."

CHAPTER SEVEN

COMMANDER RILEY-FALL, 2018

The traffic on West Grand Boulevard was rather light on that Saturday morning, as I pulled my squad car into the Third Precinct of the Detroit Police Department. I pulled into the parking lot and walked into the side personnel door, which was reserved for patrolmen only. As I found my way to my desk, I greeted a few of the detectives who were working on their case files and catching up on their paperwork.

One of them, Detective Mike Palazzola, was shocked to see me on that Saturday morning, knowing that I was suspended.

"Hey, Johnny, what's up?

"How are you, Mike?"

"Good…are you back from your suspension already?"

"No... I'm here on the sneak. I've still got another week."

Detective Palazzola was holding a fresh donut and a cup of coffee as he walked over and greeted me. The aroma from his coffee quickly began to hypnotize me.

"I'd hug you, but my hands are full," he said as we both smiled.

Detective Palazzola and I had worked on a few cases before together, and we got along reasonably well. Because he and I were only two of three Italians within the precinct, we would get into some playful battles about whether homemade 'sugo' should be called gravy or sauce. My mother, Isabella, raised me to call it Sunday Sauce, while his family called it gravy.

"So…you gotta be pretty bored to be coming in here on a Saturday while on suspension," as he was talking with his mouth full, enjoying his fresh, Dunkin' Donuts chocolate eclair.

"Why aren't you home watching Saturday morning cartoons?"

I smiled. "You're showing your age, Mike. Bugs Bunny stopped doing Saturday morning reruns a long time ago."

Palazzola walked closer to me, making sure no one was within earshot.

"So glad you gave Little Boy Blue what he had coming last week. You gave him quite a few stitches."

He then started to laugh, "Salute," as he held up his cup of coffee.

"He had it coming, big time. As far as I'm concerned, you took one for the team. Somebody was going to clean his clock sooner or later," he mentioned.

"Yeah, well...I'm stuck now in therapy with the copper shrink all week."

"Huh? Are you kidding? I heard she's smoking hot! Your punishment can't be all that bad," Palazzola laughed.

Staring at his donut and coffee made me want some for myself.

At that moment, I decided to walk back into the precinct kitchen and help myself to a hot cup of fresh Mrs. Folgers coffee. As I entered the small cafeteria, I realized that the angels on that Saturday morning were smiling down on me.

There on the table were a dozen or more freshly baked sesame seed bagels, some chocolate eclairs, and some newly baked lobster tail pastries.

Being that I was still kind of full of my McDonald's breakfast, I put a few bagels and a couple of pastries into both of my coat pockets. Suddenly, the sound of a familiar voice unexpectedly shocked me.

"What are you doing here?"

I felt like a little boy caught stealing candy from a party store.

"Thought I would stop by and make sure I still had a desk and chair," I meekly replied.

Commander Joseph Riley was the current Chief of the Third Precinct within the Detroit Police Department. He was an old school Irishman in his middle sixties, and he had been on the force for over forty years. Chief Riley probably should have taken his exit plan and retired with his exorbitant pension years ago.

"What am I going to do? Stay home and plant tomatoes?" I remember him telling everyone in the office when asked why he hadn't retired yet. He had been assigned as the Commander of the Third Precinct several years ago. Top brass probably figured that giving him a lovely, cushy desk job at the Third Precinct would be a good swan song to ending his career.

Commander Riley was a widower who lived alone on the West Side of Detroit. He lost his wife to breast cancer several years ago, but he still blamed himself for her illness. He and his wife, Elena, were married for over thirty years, and she tolerated his many years of drinking and alcoholism.

"My boozing pushed my Elena over the edge," he would often tell friends.

Joe Riley took anti-depression drugs to battle his extreme anxiety issues and was once a hard drinker. He and his wife never had any children. Riley eventually got help for his problem and, after her death, became a devout

Catholic. Riley rarely missed daily mass at 7:00 am at St. Casimir's Catholic Church and found time to volunteer at the Capuchin Monastery's Soup Kitchen once a week. There was a small statuette of Blessed Solanus Casey sitting on one of his bookshelves.

Joe Riley was also a voracious reader. He read two to three novels a week and took adult literature night classes once a week at the University of Detroit on McNichols. He also met up with a few book clubs every month, with one of them reading and sharing poetry from literary greats like Robert Frost, E.E. Cummings, T.S. Eliot, and Walt Whitman. Riley spent a lot of time checking out books from the library and often went to the Detroit Library on Woodward Avenue.

"Really, John? You have no idea how close you came to losing it," he said.

Riley was staring at the bagels sticking out of my pocket as I realized the white sugar from the pastries was scattered over my dark jacket.

He shook his head and laughed.

"Come into my office, Valentino."

I eagerly followed the commander to his small office near the other side of the police station.

As I nervously sat down, I was more concerned about squishing the stolen pastries in my pocket than what Chief Riley had to say.

I noticed a Detroit library book, "Selected Poems by E.E. Cummings," sitting on the corner of his desk, which he said he had probably checked out the week before. Whenever Riley's door was often closed in his office, he was usually destressing himself from all the pressures of overseeing the Third Precinct with his face in a book.

“Johnny, do you have any idea what kind of shit-storm you left me in last week?

“I told you, Chief. I’m sorry for what I did to that Hacker-kid. I had been babysitting him for three months now, and I can’t tell you how many times I wanted to clean his clock due to his childish behavior.”

“Try telling that to one of the most powerful politicians on the East Side, Johnny. I had to put my balls on the line to keep you from losing your job.”

A few moments of silence.

“I’m sorry again, Chief. I didn’t mean to put you through this.”

“I got a phone call from Dr. Trafficanta yesterday,” he mentioned matter of factly.

“She revealed that you have been arriving at your therapy sessions drunk.”

I shook my head. That little bitch shrink ratted me out.

“She also says you’ve been spending a lot of time at the Crazy Horse Lounge,” sounding like an angry father reprimanding his son for breaking his curfew.

“How are you supposed to get anything out of these therapy sessions and control that terrible temper of yours if you show up stoned?”

“Chief, I only have a drink or two,” I heard myself saying. “Besides, how am I supposed to spill my guts out to some strange, copper shrink that I don’t even know?”

Commander Riley then made eye-contact with me.

“Suck it up, Johnny. This is your last chance to fix your temper and your life. I promised a lot of the top brass that you were going to clean up your act."

I obediently sat there, trying to absorb his every word.

"It's time to grow up, John. You've got to stop trying to choke the shit out of every person that gets on your nerves."

Another silent moment.

"And stop drinking."

"I'm not drinking that much, Chief."

Riley looked at me; his dark eyes felt as though they were piercing right through my soul.

"You're an alcoholic, John. Enough is enough. You need to do something drastic about your drinking. You're getting out of control."

A moment of silence.

"Why don't to go to a library and pick up a book once in a while? Instead of drinking and staring at strippers on Eight Mile Road? Reading is a great pastime."

For about five seconds, he sounded like my mother. I looked at him, feeling like a humiliated little boy. I knew that he was right, as much as I hated to admit it. My drinking had ruined my marriage, my finances, and now it was jeopardizing my job and wrecking my life. Deep down inside, I knew that I had to fix my drinking problems and get my life on track. But I seriously didn't know where to start.

"Did you have breakfast?"

I looked at him. "Eh, yes. I went to McDonald's"

I didn't want to tell him that I had received my breakfast begging like a homeless person.

"I am going to call up Dr. Trafficanta this morning. I will have her set you up with an

Alcoholics Anonymous class close by in the area next week."

I was a little shocked at his forwardness.

"You're a good cop, Valentino. You remind me a little of myself years ago when I was a detective on the street."

I thought for a moment.

"Is this the reason why you're so good to me? It seems as though you've had my back since I came here from the tenth precinct four years ago."

Commander Riley smiled at me. For a few moments, he could have passed for Father Flannigan from Boys Town.

"Let's just say I have my reasons."

He smiled at himself, shaking his head.

"I remember when I was on the street, I never took any shit from anyone. And I used to go off to some 'gin-mill' after my shift and suck down on the bottle."

Then he looked at me straight in the eye.

"You can't keep living a hard life like that and not have it take a toll on you. I know what you're going through."

"You need to fix your life, Johnny. You need to stop drinking."

He stared at me for a few moments, expecting me to give him an argument. I was already coming to the same conclusion that he was. Still, it was painful to hear it come from someone else, especially from my boss.

"How is your new place? Are you getting settled in?"

"Getting there, Chief. Not much furniture."

"Where did you move to? Nine Mile and Kelly?"

"Eh, yes," I nervously answered. I didn't remember telling him where I had moved to when I was thrown out of my house after the divorce.

He then reached into his desk drawer and pulled out the precinct checkbook. It was used on rare occasions when office expenses had to be paid out directly from the precinct by the Chief himself.

He wrote out a check and ripped it out from the long, black check binder. He then passed it over to me from across his desk.

It was drawn in my name for five thousand dollars.

"This is an advance on your salary. Use it to buy some furniture for your new place. Go to Art Van or Ikea and get something cheap that you can afford. Bring me back the receipts."

I was in shock but grateful. Riley didn't have to do this. It was like he was going out of his way to be kind to me and to help me out. For a moment, I felt embarrassed accepting his assistance.

I took the check, knowing that I could look forward to sleeping on something other than an old mattress on the floor.

"I'm going to send some patrolmen over to your apartment next week to check your place out. It better have some furniture inside," he warned.

I looked at Commander Riley, trying to keep myself from getting emotional.

A few silent moments passed between us.

"Is there anything else, Chief?"

"That will be all, Detective. Go home and enjoy those pastries," he smiled.

I got up and gratefully shook his hand.

"Thank you."

I was getting very teary-eyed. He nodded his head, looking down in the other direction and trying not to make eye contact with me.

"Call Dr. Trafficanta this afternoon," he reminded me.

As I was walking out of his office, he yelled out his last directive:

"John? Don't let me hear that you're still drinking. And stay away from the Crazy Horse Lounge."

I silently nodded my head as I walked back to my desk. I wondered if Riley was doing all of this because he felt sorry for me. Who knows what his real motives are? Maybe I did remind him of himself.

I sat there for several moments, shuffling some papers around and trying to look busy. I then remembered that I had acquired some files and the old police report from my father's murder forty years ago.

I opened the bottom drawer of my desk and pulled out the four large, old manilla envelopes. I had ordered the documents from the records department several weeks ago. I only glanced at them at the time. I wasn't emotionally ready to go through them in detail. I figured when I acquired the emotional strength inside; I would meticulously go through them.

It was far too painful for me to go through those old reports from 1978. I wasn't ready to learn about all of the mistakes my father had made that cost him his life and robbed us of a father.

The four large manilla envelopes were marked:

Detroit Police Department:
Valentino, Antonio
Homicide, November 1st, 1978 –
12260 El Camino Drive

Each sealed envelope was marked with the numbers one through four. The last container enclosed five pictures of my father's dead body lying face up underneath his pickup truck. I had only briefly glanced at them before, not having the mental fortitude to study those photographs and the rest of those police reports.

If nothing else, bringing them home and reading them in detail might give me some long-awaited answers and refrain from doing something foolish.

I had frequently asked my mother, Isabella, to tell me exactly what had happened to our father. She would either not answer me at all or get emotional and run into the bedroom crying. Although I had the right to know, I didn't want to make my mother and my sisters cry anymore.

One day when I was a teenager, I asked my Zio Rossano one evening how Dad died. We were all having a family barbeque over at his house. I had waited to get my uncle alone, away from the rest of the family.

"Your father was doing something he wasn't supposed to be doing. He was running around with a married woman," he vehemently said.

I looked at him, puzzled.

"Why? Who killed him, Zio?"

He looked at me, and his face completely changed. His dark brown eyes enlarged and became filled with anger as if he were ready to swiftly kill someone.

“Some goddamn hillbillies!” he managed to say.

I grabbed a large plastic grocery bag from the precinct kitchen and put the large manila envelopes inside.

I had no clue what I would find in those reports.

CHAPTER EIGHT

ANOTHER NIGHTMARE

I had been sitting on my dilapidated couch on that autumn Wednesday night, looking for the remote control. The program '*Chicago Fire*' on TV was a rerun, so I wanted to change the channels as soon as I could find the remote control.

I came straight home from the Third Precinct and bought a bottle of Johnny Walker Black from the party store on Kelly Road. I had been beating myself up all day, and I couldn't take it anymore without having at least one drink.

I kept thinking about my wife Marina, sleeping and spending time with her boyfriend in my house. I kept thinking about my boys, Anthony, and Dario, watching their mother playing house with this strange bastard that she had only been dating for a few months. I kept thinking about what a terrible example she was giving my boys, living with someone in our house that she wasn't married or engaged to.

Marina DiBernardo was the only girl I had ever been in love with. I remember meeting her in freshman English class at Cousino High School in Warren. I would continue to stare at her when she wasn't looking, or at least pretending not to. I always had a feeling she could see me from the corner of her eye.

She had dark brown, curly hair and huge brown eyes. She had a voluptuous figure, and her sensual lips were parted perfectly. Marina had the most alluring smile, and when she finally looked over at me, smiling at me from the other side of the English class, my heart must have melted. She reminded me of Jaclyn Smith from 'Charley's Angels' and had a bubbly, joking personality that could make any guy laugh out loud.

We started eating our lunch together in the cafeteria and would hold hands in the hallway between periods. Even though I was drinking, smoking, and doing weed periodically at a young age back then, Marina was attracted to my charms. All of her girlfriends in school tried to warn her about me, telling her what a 'burnout' I was and that I would never amount to anything.

But Marina saw something in me in the ninth grade that I didn't even see in myself. She helped me gain the confidence that I couldn't find anywhere else.

"Close your eyes and make your dreams come true," she used to say to me all the time. Even though I was only fourteen years old, I realized that I couldn't spend my life without her. At a very young age, I was head over heels in love.

We would often meet out in the parking lot after school. Marina and I would then walk to the football field and sit on the bleachers and make out when the weather permitted. Sometimes we would walk to the coffee shop on Hoover Road, and we would pool what few dollars we had to buy coffee for the two of us. I used to ride my bike to her house during the summers and sit on her front porch talking for hours. Sometimes we would meet at Paul's Party Store on Schoenherr Road and hang out drinking lemonade frozen Slurpee's. Her parents didn't know about us, and we kept our relationship a secret until our senior year.

We had to wait until she was seventeen years old before we could start dating, and even at that point, we were subjected to being chaperoned by her mom, little brother, and later, another couple.

We never actually went out alone until our senior prom. We went to the Hillcrest Country Club in Mount Clemens, spending most of the time dancing, then making out on the veranda of the country club looking out of the lake. We had a fantastic time, and I promised her that she would be the one with whom I would spend the rest of my life.

Marina went to Madonna College after high school and got her teaching degree. My Uncle Ross got me into the police academy, and I got a job as a street patrolman with the Detroit P.D. We both waited until we were securely employed before buying a house in Harper Woods and getting married.

Unfortunately, my drinking progressively got worse, and after many years of hitting the 'gin mill' and burying my problems into my drink glass, it finally destroyed my family.

On that Wednesday night, my heart was utterly broken. I let the ghosts of my fractured childhood take over my life, and I faithfully turned to a whiskey bottle to ease my pain.

Marina desperately tried everything to get me help, to no avail. I was coming home drunk almost every night, and my wife and children were suffering tremendously. My wife had no choice but to file for divorce, which was bad enough.

But to allow some stranger into her life that she had met at a bar with her bitchy girlfriends? She had barely been dating this bastard for two months when she allowed him to move into our house, happily showing me the door.

Here I now was, barely holding on to my life, only having a whiskey bottle and my mother's dilapidated couch to show for it.

At that moment, I was in complete and total emotional pain, and I was physically sick to my stomach. I realized that she was totally gone from my life and that the only girl I had ever loved was never coming back.

I thought about my father, who had been dead for over forty years and had abandoned me as a little boy, alone to face this rotten world.

I was also bitter for being placed on suspension for taking out my anger on my former partner, Andrew Hacker. I was wondering what kind of retribution his powerful politician father was going to take out on me and my possibly losing my job as a detective.

I guess I was angry at the world. I was extremely down on myself and totally depressed. I finished my shift on that day and ran for the only thing that has always helped me deal with my stress.

I didn't even bother picking up or making dinner. I just took off my pants, my white shirt and tie off and laid down on the couch in my boxer-briefs, sucking down the juice.

My half-empty bottle of Johnny Walker Black was sitting on the floor next to my half-filled drink glass. I wanted to be careful that I didn't accidentally knock it over, as I was searching for the remote control under the couch.

I pushed the remote from underneath the couch. Then I got up to grab it, but somehow, I tripped and fell on the floor, hitting my head pretty hard.

After drinking a half bottle of whiskey and hitting my head, I must have passed out.

Wherever I was, I was entirely out of reality.

We were sitting in a booth at our favorite Italian restaurant, Villa Ristorante, on Van Dyke and Fourteen Mile Road, when the waitress came to our table.

"Can I get you something to drink?"

Marina, who was sitting across from me, gave me a dirty look.

"I'll have a diet coke, please."

"I'll have the same," she said.

We had just gotten engaged, and we were discussing our wedding plans that evening. We had both just turned twenty-five, and we were both anxious to start our lives together. Marina was teaching at a local high school while I had just gotten on the Detroit Police force at the Tenth Precinct. We were both saving our money to buy a house, and we were looking at Harper Woods.

Halloween was a few days away, and we were invited to a costume party on that Friday night. We were talking about our outfits that we were going to be wearing.

I had ordered linguini with clam sauce, while Marina had ordered veal parmesan. Our entrees had just arrived at our table when I noticed someone walking in the door with some other people. He was a taller, handsome man in his early forties, sitting in the booth with a platinum blonde, another dark-haired lady, and a younger man who was tall and lanky.

I kept staring at the man, as he had an uncanny resemblance to my father. He was even wearing the off-white jacket that he used to wear all the time. I then overheard the platinum blonde talking to the man in a very thick southern accent.

"Oh, Tony…you're so damn funny!"

I then realized that the man sitting in the other booth was my father. I had to adjust my eyes as I couldn't believe what I was seeing, as my father at the time had been dead for almost twenty years.

"What's wrong?" Marina asked.

"That man sitting at that table is my father!" I exclaimed loudly.

The four of them continued to laugh and joke loudly, as the waitress had brought them over a large plate of spaghetti to share.

I always remembered how much my father loved spaghetti. I remembered being a little boy at a church picnic. My dad entered the spaghetti eating contest with ten other men sitting at a very long table. They started playing Italian music, and my dad was sitting there, his hands tied behind his back, shoving his face into a large pasta dish.

My sisters and I were all loudly cheering when he was the first one to finish and won the spaghetti eating contest that day.

"No, Johnny…that's not your father."

"Yes! I'm telling you, honey. That is my father! And those women he's sitting with are strangers that I've never seen before."

My father was only sitting there, periodically making eye contact with me, while he and the others were eating spaghetti and laughing.

I finally got up and approached them at the table.

"Dad? What are you doing here?"

He only looked at me, totally clueless.

"Do I know you?"

"Why are you sitting here with this lady? She's married, and her husband wants to kill you! You need to get out of here!"

The man resembling my father laughed at me.

"Who the hell are you? And I am not your father!"

"Dad," I pleaded with the man.

"Please listen to me! You need to run away from this lady! Someone is going to shoot you in a few days and take you away from us! You need to get out of here and get away from this lady!"

At that moment, the platinum blonde started to laugh hysterically.

"Oh, Tony! Don't listen to this guy. My husband would never kill anyone. He doesn't even know about us!" she said in a very thick, southern accent.

"Dad! You need to leave this woman and get the hell out of here!"

At that moment, the four of them looked anxious and annoyed, knowing that I was bothering all of them and interrupting their meal.

"You need to leave us alone!" the other younger man said. I could tell that they had just gotten off of their shift at the Ford Motor Plant as the other man's shirt was blue and dirty and had the Ford Motors emblem on it.

I kept pleading with my father, telling him to leave the restaurant and to run away from the platinum blonde who would eventually have him killed.

Finally, both men put some money on the table and began to leave, all of them giving me a dirty look as they were exiting the restaurant.

I went back to sit at our booth, and Marina gave me a dirty look.

"Was that necessary?"

"Marina, that was my father! And that woman he was sitting with was his girlfriend, not my mother! She is going to get him killed!" I loudly insisted.

Marina only looked at me, probably thinking that I was losing my mind.

As we finished our dinner, I paid the bill, and we both decided to get up and leave. It was late at night, and we both had to get up early for work the next day.

We were holding hands, exiting the restaurant, when I noticed my father's red and white pickup truck still sitting in the parking lot. It looked like there were two people inside, as the windows looked as though they were getting steamed up.

I walked over to the truck and began loudly banging on the driver's side of the door.

"Dad, Dad…" I kept pleading.

"Get out of here. This woman is going to have you killed!" I kept shouting.

My father turned on the light in the truck. His hair was messed up, and the front of the blonde's blouse was unbuttoned, openly exposing her black bra.

"You need to get the fuck out of here, you bastard!" the lady yelled.

"No! My father is married and so are you! You need to leave my Daddy alone!" I replied loudly.

She suddenly pulled out a green toy water pistol and pointed it at my father's head. She pulled the trigger, and there was a loud noise.

Blood was suddenly splattered all over the windshield.

I woke up on the floor of my living room with a massive bump on my forehead. The television was still on, and the bottle of Johnny Walker was spilled all over the hardwood floor.

I had another very horrific, very bizarre dream about my father.

It wasn't the first dream I had about him. My father had become a regular nocturnal demon who constantly invaded my sleep.

I had dreamed that I was an adult, trying to stop my father from having an affair with that woman who would eventually have him killed. I had dreams about him sitting in his truck while being shot by three large men.

I had vivid thoughts about his being abandoned in a dark street, left face up dead, next to his truck in a pool of blood.

I had terrible nightmares about him throughout my life, and his death haunted me since I was six years old. They were always images of my murdered father while his perpetrators laughed out loud, shooting a gun at him, and knowing that they would get away with murder.

I laid there on the floor, groaning at the pain in my head and grasping the empty bottle of Johnny Walker.

The horrific images of my dead father continued to haunt me; his demons were disrupting my sleep for so many, many nights.

There was no more 'juice.' The booze was gone, and my father was still dead. I couldn't stop him from getting killed. I couldn't stop him from making a wrong decision that would change all of our lives forever.

No matter how much I tried to stop him from being shot in my dreams, he always ended up the same.

Dead, with his wide eyes open…face up in a pool of blood on El Camino Drive.

CHAPTER NINE

A MEETING WITH THE UNDERBOSS-FALL 2018

Howard Williams was sitting at the Crazy Horse Lounge on that Friday night, waiting for an old acquaintance, Caesar Giordano, to show up. They had known each other for over fifty years since meeting at the Jackson State Prison back in 1975.

Williams had recently moved back to the Detroit area from Hermitage, Tennessee, after abruptly leaving in 1979. Williams still had many friends and relatives here living in the Detroit area.

Since coming back to Michigan for the funeral of his older brother that past April, Williams decided to uproot from the South and come back here and stay with his remaining brothers and sisters.

"Family is family," he would continue to tell his siblings and local friends after being away from them for over forty years. Howard was still grieving over the loss of his brother Harold, who abruptly died from pancreatic cancer. He was 69 years old, only two years older than Howard.

After his death, Howard Williams decided to pass what few remaining years he may have in his life and spend them with his two brothers and sister, along with their families.

At the age of 67, Howard Williams was still in good shape for his age. Other than taking his Lipitor medication, he was in excellent health. He also faithfully did his two shots of Jack Daniels every evening before going to bed. He had just purchased a double-wide, two-bedroom trailer on 26 Mile Road and had finally resettled into his new life back in the Midwest. He collected his monthly pension from the Plumbers and Pipefitters Union Local 43, along with his social security, and could now afford to splurge on the brand-new Clayton, two-bedroom double-wide manufactured home in Chateau Estates for $45,000.

Howard was in a celebratory mood that evening. He had just come back from the estate attorney's office, having been informed that he had inherited $77,000 from his deceased brother's estate.

"What will it be, Howard?" Dolores asked.

"How much is a shot of your Louis XIII? I'm ready to party!"

"Are you sure you wouldn't like a girl to party with?" Dolores asked.

"No thanks, honey. I'm waiting for a buddy of mine to show up."

"$75 bucks a shot."

Williams smiled, showing several missing teeth as he placed a hundred-dollar bill on the bar.

The bartender poured him a shot from the coveted Remy Martin Louis XIII Cognac bottle, which was stored on the backroom shelf in a blue velvet cover. Williams drank a toast to himself in front of the bartender.

"Here's looking at ya, beautiful," as he gulped the smooth cognac in one gulp.

He slammed his empty shot glass on the bar counter.

"Wow," was all he managed to say, as Dolores watched in amazement.

"Was it good?"

"Honey, you have no idea!" he smiled.

The bald, lean little man was ready to celebrate regarding his newly acquired, inherited fortune.

Since moving back to the Detroit area, Williams was reconnecting with many of his old friends. Years ago, when he was living in Detroit, he was a bookmaker, running the numbers for Don Pellegrino Licavoli and the powerful Licavoli Family.

The Licavoli Family is one of the most formidable, organized crime families in Detroit and the suburbs. They are connected with the city's casinos, strip clubs, and the gambling operations on Detroit's East Side and the suburbs. Williams had made a lot of friends within the family but was especially close to Caesar Giordano, the family's underboss.

"Hey Howard," a classy, older gentleman exclaimed as he sat at the barstool next to Williams. He was of average height, wearing a light gray sport coat, black dress slacks, and shiny black Venetian loafers. Giordano looked very upscale and was distinctly overdressed for that strip club that evening.

"Hey Caesar, how's it going," as the two shook hands. The two of them had not seen each other since Caesar abruptly left Detroit in 1979.

"You haven't changed much," Caesar exclaimed after ordering a scotch and water.

"Yeah, well, I have fewer teeth now since living in the South," Williams smiled.

"Must be all that roadkill you guys eat for dinner," Giordano snickered.

They both grinned as the two of them toasted to each other's good health. Caesar Giordano was an older gentleman in his early seventies, seldom seen in public without a cigarette in his mouth. He smoked three to four packs of cigarettes a day and, other than a nagging cough, was in good health.

It was a warm autumn evening on that Friday night, and there were more than the usual number of patrons at the Crazy Horse. The rap music seemed louder than usual that evening, as Caesar was having trouble hearing Williams talk, even though he was sitting right next to him at the bar.

Caesar Giordano was the controlling underboss of the Licavoli Family. He oversaw the slot machines, betting parlors, strip bars, and the illegal gaming operations within the city. Since Don Pino was now in his middle eighties and in failing health, the day-to-day operations fell upon the shoulders of the family underboss Caesar Giordano.

Giordano and Williams had been friends since being cellmates at the Jackson State Prison, where Giordano was doing time back in the early seventies for extortion and armed burglary.

"I just had a shot of Louis XIII," Williams proudly bragged.

"Oh, really, what's the occasion?"

"My brother left me $77,000 in his will. I can sure use the money."

Caesar smiled at Howard, now suddenly remembering what he was dealing with. Caesar was slowly recalling his relationship with Howard Williams and the manner of how he was running the street gambling operations for the family. He recalled that, although Williams was a good soldier and did what he was told, he was rather hot-tempered and tended to get himself in trouble.

He remembered the incident, which involved his wife and another man she was sleeping with while she was working at the Ford Plant in Sterling Heights back in 1978. Williams had approached him back then and requested the family to help him 'take care' of his wife's boyfriend.

But Caesar had refused, suggesting that Williams only 'rough him up' a bit and to convince this man to stay away from his wife. It was not the style of the Licavoli Family to get involved in marital disputes, no matter who was involved. Caesar recalled Don Pino becoming extremely angry when he had heard that Williams had murdered his wife's boyfriend.

The two of them made small talk for a while as they were finishing their drinks and admiring the young pole dancers on stage.

"So, Howard, are you still married?"

"Joni and I got divorced after we moved back to Tennessee forty years ago. She never forgave me for killing her boyfriend," he smiled, displaying his missing teeth.

"Neither has Don Pino," Caesar replied.

A moment of silence as Williams stared at the underboss.

"Oh, come on, Caesar, are you trying to tell me that Don Pino is still angry with me after all these years?"

Caesar made eye contact with Williams.

"You took a man away from his wife and three young kids."

Williams tried to make light of it.

"Oh, Caesar, I know better. Don Pino was angry because we killed a greaseball dago!"

Caesar glared at the older hillbilly from Tennessee. At this point, the underboss was trying very hard to control his temper.

"Yes, Howard, that too!"

Caesar recalled that when Don Pino heard and read in the papers that the man Williams and his friends killed was a young Italian named Antonio Valentino, he was heartbroken. Caesar remembered Don Pino angrily reaching out to Williams, telling him that he should have never brought along a gun that Halloween night with his friends. Don Pino Licavoli admonished him, saying that he was washing his hands of Williams and his hillbilly friends.

"You were only supposed to rough him up, not kill him."

"Things got out of hand, Caesar. I told you that. We thought he had a gun."

Caesar then raised his voice, pointing his drink glass at Williams.

"At that moment, you should have walked away."

Williams got angry.

"How the hell was I supposed to walk away when I had brought along two guys to beat him up. I didn't know Jack had a gun."

"Don Pino never believed that story. You and your friends were fortunate that you got off."

"Yeah," Williams smiled. "Thanks for sending us that sharp attorney, Mark Abdo. It turned out that he was good friends with the judge."

"The judge owed Don Pino a favor, and the fact that the man had a toy pistol in his pocket saved you," Caesar replied.

Williams took another sip of his drink.

"I know. It turned out that Jack's borrowed gun had a history of jamming up, too." Williams bragged, ordering another shot of Jack Daniels.

"We asked you and your friends to leave town and never come back. Why are you here?" the underboss asked.

"I came back to my brother's funeral. I thought I would move back into town to be with my family since I have no one else down south," Williams replied.

Caesar was now starting to get extremely aggravated with the hillbilly. He was sorry that he bothered to even meet up with this old, southern hick loser.

"You should have never come back here, Howard. You were supposed to stay down south. Your life is in danger here."

Howard smiled at the Licavoli Family underboss.

"Come on, Caesar. It has been over forty years. My life can't still be in danger anymore. Besides, after all of these years, you guys can't possibly still be mad."

"Just because you're ballsy enough to come back to Detroit and you're still walking around doesn't mean that your life isn't in danger," the underboss replied.

"And yes, Don Pino and the family are still angry with you."

Caesar glared intently at the older man with a distinctive southern accent.

"Don Pino doesn't forget things. We told you to leave town forty years ago for a reason. Had that boyfriend's family not killed you out of revenge, Don Pino would have murdered you himself. You recall how angry he was."

Williams smiled, still trying to make light out of the whole incident.

"Come on, Caesar, that was over forty years ago."

The underboss shook his head.

"Italians never forget," Caesar reminded Williams.

The two of them sat there at the bar in silence for several minutes while they stared at the pole dancers on the stage floor.

"You know, Howard, you have other problems right now," Caesar mentioned.

"The son of the man you murdered is now a detective with the Detroit P.D."

Williams looked at the underboss.

"I think I saw him sitting here the other night with another copper. I overheard his name mentioned by the bartender," he casually said.

Caesar looked at him straight in the eye before commenting.

"His name is John Valentino. One of our boys knows him pretty well. I've also met him, and he's a standup guy. He's with the Third Precinct."

Williams nodded.

"I would be careful if I were you. I certainly would not stay in town. There are a lot of people that still remember that hit. You and your buddies got away with that murder."

They were silent for a moment.

"With Valentino's son as a detective on the police force, I would watch your back if I were you."

Williams suddenly got angry.

"He was fucking my wife, Caesar. He got what he deserved."

Caesar's eyes started to bulge out of his head, now displaying his anger.

"Listen, you asshole. From what I heard, Valentino wasn't the only one sleeping with her. She played around with a lot of guys at that Ford Plant. You were married to a hillbilly slut!"

A few silent moments as the conversation was starting to get tense.

"And no, Howard. That man didn't deserve to get killed."

At that moment, the bartender approached the two men.

"Another round, boys?" Dolores asked.

"I'll take another," Williams quickly replied, but the underboss shook his head.

"No, thanks, I've got to get going," Caesar answered, finding it difficult to be polite.

The underboss was now anxious to leave that bar quickly and to get as far away as possible from this old, arrogant hillbilly. He then reached into his pocket and pulled out a hundred-dollar bill, and set it on the bar counter.

Williams quickly swallowed down his Jack Daniels on the Rocks.

"That was one for the road," the old man said.

Caesar was momentarily distracted, staring at the new, young stripper on the dance floor. He then looked at Williams.

"Well, Howard, it was nice seeing you again," the underboss lied, now wishing he had have never agreed to meet up with this old bastard from the South.

"Caesar, I was wondering if you needed any help. I thought if you needed someone to help you out with the numbers, you know, or with street collections or something, you know, like the old days."

The underboss smiled, shaking his head.

"A lot has changed since you left Detroit, Howard. Unless you are 'made man' and in the family now, we don't farm that out anymore," Caesar replied.

Howard Williams had worked for the Licavoli Family running the numbers and taking bets back in the 1970s after he was released from Jackson State Prison. But he always knew that not being an Italian would work against him in the Licavoli Family. After killing his ex-wife's boyfriend, he was forced by the Licavoli's to leave town and was told that his life was in danger.

They had also been tipped off by someone in the Detroit P.D. that one of the murder victim's brothers had vowed to take revenge for his sibling's murder and had gone as far as to begin following and stalking Williams.

They left the bar and began walking outside together into the parking lot. Caesar shook hands with Williams as he began fumbling with the keys to his black, new model Chrysler 300. He then pulled out a pack of Marlboro Lights from his coat pocket and lit a cigarette.

"Take care of yourself, Howard. Remember what I told you tonight. If you're smart, you'll go back to Tennessee."

Williams laughed, shrugging off the underboss's warning.

"I'm not worried, Caesar. I've got a brand-new double-wide on Twenty-Six Mile Road in Marine City now. Nobody is going to bother me out there," he confidently replied.

The underboss smirked at the older man, now remembering that this old hillbilly was never known for being very smart.

"Take care, Howard," he said.

As Caesar started walking towards his car, he loudly turned around.

"Do me a favor. Lose my number and don't call me again," he sternly replied as he walked back to his parked car.

Howard Williams was shocked. He stood there in the parking lot of the Crazy Horse Lounge and snickered at the underboss. It had been over forty years, but the grudges and hard feelings that he had left Detroit for in 1979 had not changed with the Licavoli Family. Don Licavoli was still extremely angry that the man that they had murdered was a fellow Italian with a young wife and three little kids. He had also learned that he and his friends had gotten lucky beating that murder rap with the judge. Caesar did him a favor forty years ago, demanding that he leave town before his luck ran out.

Now, with his recent encounter with Detective Valentino the other evening in the Crazy Horse parking lot, Williams was starting to think twice.

Maybe moving back to Detroit may not have been such a good idea.

That crossed his mind for all of about three seconds.

Howard Williams then laughed out loud to himself, dismissing Caesar's advice. The old hillbilly had no conception about how Italian 'maloccio's' work and how seriously personal revenge contracts are taken in this town.

He didn't realize that the family vendetta against him had never expired.

CHAPTER TEN

ANDREW HACKER-FALL, 2018

Detective Andrew Hacker was in the reception area of St. John's Hospital, waiting to be picked up by his father. He had been recovering for the last several days from injuries that he received by his former partner, Detective John Valentino.

Because of the ten stitches and acute head injuries that he endured from the fight last week, the doctors suggested that he stay in the hospital for a few more days after being transferred from intensive care. All the doctors were concerned about any long-term effects of the head injuries which Hacker had suffered.

Besides the intense blows to his face and head, Valentino had slammed his head a few times on the hard, concrete floor before three other detectives pulled him off.

The severe head trauma and the forceful beating initially knocked Hacker unconscious. When he arrived at the hospital by the paramedics, the doctors were worried that the intense head trauma would make it difficult for him to regain consciousness again and, most of all, survive. Such severe head trauma can often cause long term brain damage and possibly, disable any person suffering from that kind of beating.

He was under twenty-four-hour intensive care at St. John's for four days before he regained consciousness and was moved to his hospital room where he could fully recover from his injuries.

As Hacker sat in his wheelchair at the reception area of the hospital on that autumn day, he was extremely bitter. He was upset with the whole Third Precinct for allowing Valentino to get in several hard punches into his face and head before running to his aide. He was angry with Commander Riley for sticking up for Valentino and only giving him a full, two-week suspension with pay.

But most of all, he was outraged and resentful towards Detective John Valentino. He had no right to attack him, even though he called him a 'dago-drunk' in front of the whole precinct. The beating he received from Valentino was severe, and Hacker now realized that the beating he got almost cost him his life.

The nurse wheeled him in front of St. John's Hospital as his father, former state representative George Benjamin Hacker, pulled up in his black Lincoln Navigator.

"Thanks," he gratefully said to the African American nurse, who had helped him climb into the front seat of his father's car. The nurse gave some written instructions to the older man regarding the care of his son's stitches and making sure that his son didn't immediately fall asleep and back into unconsciousness. His bandages were wrapped tightly around his head as he was careful to rest himself into the front seat of the car.

"How you feelin', son?" the old man loudly asked.

"Like shit." he only responded.

Andrew closed his eyes as his father pulled out of the hospital driveway and onto Moross Drive.

He wanted to close his eyes, not only because of the pain he had endured but for another, more important reason:

Andrew Hacker was embarrassed. He knew that he humiliated and shamed his father.

George Hacker went through great lengths and pulled a lot of strings to get his son onto the police force as a rookie detective. He called in a lot of favors with the superintendent of the Detroit Police Department and several city council members to get his son bumped up to an investigative detective in the Third Precinct.

Andrew now realized that his childish, immature behavior at the precinct was the cause for the critical beating from Valentino, and he knew that he had utterly embarrassed his father.

As the old man was driving, he was silent. George Hacker didn't say a word to his son as they made the twenty-minute drive from the hospital to their expansive mansion in Grosse Pointe Farms.

When he pulled his Lincoln Navigator into the driveway, three servants were waiting to assist Andrew with getting out of the car and into their mansion. They helped and supported him upstairs to his bedroom, where he could rest. They assisted him to undress and get into his comfortable pajamas, where he could sleep in his bed and recover from his head injuries.

Andrew Hacker laid in his bed that whole afternoon, wide awake. His emotions were mostly keeping him from closing his eyes. Andrew was angry, bitter, and hurt. His mother, Florence, came into his bedroom and tucked in her twenty-seven-year-old son into his bed in the same manner that she did when he was a little boy.

"Welcome home, Andrew. How are you feeling?"

"Terrible," he replied. "My head is pounding, and I feel like my stitches are bleeding. I'm afraid to close my eyes."

"Just close your eyes and rest, honey. I will be here next to you until you fall asleep," the mother said while holding his hand.

Florence Hacker took extremely good care of her only child, pampering and spoiling him at every opportunity. She went into mild shock when she had learned of her son's work-related injuries last week. Florence refused to believe that her only child may have instigated the fight that caused his life-threatening wounds.

Andrew fell in and out of sleep that day, resting as best he could while trying to settle his mind. One of the servants brought him up some homemade chicken soup, and Florence helped her son try to eat. She sat next to his bed and read a book while Andrew tried to sleep. He asked for his father several times, and Florence reassured her son that his father would be up shortly.

But his father never came upstairs.

Finally, Florence went down to the study to check on her husband.

"Do you plan on talking to your son now that he's back home?"

George looked up from his desktop computer on his expansive oak desk. His extensive study was lined with bookshelves filled with law books, court cases, and various other reference materials which the older man often read. His study was a very small, expansive law library, which George Hacker often referred to while he practiced injury and corporate law from his home office.

"When I'm ready," he coldly responded.

"George, he's our son. We need to deal with this and help him to heal. He's very emotional that you're upset, and you both need to make peace with this."

"Florence, your son, has humiliated this family. When I heard how he was neglecting his job duties as a detective at the third precinct, I was totally embarrassed. To have to be admonished by the precinct commander of how he called his partner a 'dago-drunk' and how he was playing video games from his desk at the precinct has wholly embarrassed me. I had to go through great lengths to get him hired as a detective and keep him off the streets as a patrolman."

Florence stood there in the middle of her husband's study with her arms crossed.

"He was neglecting his job duties, Florence. He was constantly fooling around at his desk, talking and texting his girlfriends on his cellphone, and not assisting his partner in their crime investigations. Do you know how that makes me feel to hear this from his commander?"

"George, he's our son. You need to talk with him," she begged.

The older man, in his late sixties, glared at his wife.

"As I said, ...when I'm ready."

Exasperated, Florence stormed out of the room.

It was several hours later as George continued to work in his study. It was past ten o'clock at night when there was a knock on the study's door.

"Come in."

"Dad? Can I interrupt you for a moment?"

George Hacker looked at his twenty-seven going on twelve-year-old son. He was wearing light blue pajamas and a dark Macy's velour bathrobe, and dark slippers. His wide bandages were covering his head and part of his left eye, and he had dark bruises on both sides of his face. His left jaw was still extremely swollen.

"Sit down, son," he directed him to sit in one of two black leather chairs facing his oak trimmed wooden desk.

Andrew slowly sat down at the chair, and the two of them glared at each other for several long seconds.

"Dad, I just wanted to say how sorry I am. I know I've embarrassed and humiliated you in front of the whole Detroit Police Department."

George loudly responded to his son's apology, as if he had already memorized the verbiage that he was about to say.

"Do you have any idea what shame and disgrace you have brought upon our name and this family? Do you have any idea what I had to go through to get you onto that force, especially the Third Precinct?"

"I know, Dad, I know. I am truly sorry."

"And to think you let a fifty-something-year-old drunk beat the shit out of you in front of the whole precinct? You didn't even defend yourself."

"He blindsided me, I..."

"If you're going to insult someone, be ready to defend yourself. I raised you better than that, Andrew."

There were several long minutes of silence as the two of them sat there staring at each other.

"May I ask you a question? Why did Valentino only get suspended for two weeks, with pay no less? Riley only slapped his wrist with a two-week vacation. How is that punishment fair? Why does Valentino still have his job?"

"Because if I were to pressure Riley and go to the Superintendent, there would be some skeletons brought out of the closet by Riley that I prefer not to deal with. That goddamn bastard has me over a barrel."

George Benjamin Hacker did not want to bring up the time two years ago when he was arrested on a drunk driving charge with two hookers in his car. He had to beg Riley to keep the arrest quiet and to release him quietly without the incident hitting the media. Commander Riley threatened to bring it up and call up the reporters if Hacker forced Riley to terminate Valentino.

Commander Riley had other incidents and various police reports regarding George Hacker that he knew he had on him. He did not want to take the chance on Riley going public with his 'files,' especially when his son was the direct cause of his precinct beating.

"Is that why he wasn't arrested on assault and battery?"

"Exactly."

More silent moments.

"So…now what?" the son asked.

"I've talked to the commander at the Tenth Precinct, and he said he would initially put you on street patrol until you ‘earn your stripes,’ so to speak.”

“Street patrol? Are you kidding?”

“Would you rather be cleaning toilets or writing parking tickets on Woodward Avenue? Cause that can be arranged too.”

Andrew looked at his father, clearly defeated.

Another quiet moment.

“Presuming that by the end of next week, you feel better, you will start there next Monday.”

“But Dad, what if I…”

“We’re done here, Andrew. I hope that you have learned your lesson.”

Andrew Hacker slowly got up from his father’s study and retired to his bedroom. He was being demoted by his father, starting as a rookie patrolman at the bottom of the food chain. Andrew Hacker wanted revenge against Valentino. He could taste it in his mouth.

And he knew he would have a hard time doing it from a patrol car on Livernois Avenue.

CHAPTER ELEVEN

EASTER SUNDAY 1979

It was a warm, spring Sunday morning as the Valentino family was leaving the church, having just finished attending Easter mass. The sun was blinding as the worshippers were exiting San Francisco Catholic Church in Clinton Township. Isabella Valentino was holding the hands of her nine-year-old daughter, Lucia, her six-year-old son, John, along with her oldest daughter Rosanna as they left the church. They had attended a special Easter mass that Sunday and prayed together in remembrance of their beloved husband and father, Antonio.

Her brothers, in-laws, and their families were escorting the immediate family as they were all leaving the small, quaint little church on that Easter morning. It had been five months since the untimely murder of her husband, and Isabella was still grief-stricken.

Isabella Valentino had loved her husband deeply, despite his frequent infidelities. Since eloping together and arriving in Detroit from Casalvieri, Italy, Isabella knew that her husband was often unfaithful to her.

She knew that she could not hold him. Tony, with his movie-star good looks and undaunting charm, knew how to manipulate any lady who gave him the time of day. No one ever thought that his reckless infidelities would eventually cost him his life.

Almost everyone in his family was aware of his blatant betrayal. Most everyone who knew him wondered if there was anyone on the East Side of Detroit that he hadn't sleep with. His reckless affairs and self-centered, narcissistic behavior would have been enough for any normal housewife to file for divorce.

But Isabella DiVito Valentino, who married her husband when she was only eighteen years old, was utterly devoted to her egotistical, self-centered spouse. The thought of her ever leaving him, despite his numerous acts of adultery, had never been considered.

Even after his death, she was still devoutly dedicated to his memory. She went to his crypt at Mt. Olivet Cemetery three times a week with red roses in hand. She did prayer rosaries with her church group once a week and had perpetual candle lit next to his picture in her living room.

His clothing and his unwashed work clothes were still folded on a chair downstairs, the same way he had left them on the day before his death. His 1959 Oldsmobile Super Eighty-Eight Convertible was still in the garage, undriven and untouched since the day he died.

Her family and especially her brothers thought that she should move on, especially after the trial of her husband's murderers. But Isabella could not let go. Her husband's wardrobe was still hanging in their closet. His toothbrush was still in the master bathroom that they shared. Isabella always slept on her side of their king-size bed, always hoping that her husband would come home in the middle of the night.

She hoped that he would miraculously appear lying next to her. Isabella was hopelessly still in mourning, and her family wondered if she would ever recover from his death.

Rossano Valentino, on the other hand, was mourning his brother's loss in a very different way. He vowed revenge against his brother's killers and especially Howard Williams, the man who initially planned the whole plot to kill him.

Ross began following him recently after work. He parked for hours in front of William's house in Mt. Clemens, following him wherever he went. Rossano Valentino had gone to the gun shop on Sixteen Mile and Van Dyke and purchased a Beretta 9mm handgun. He kept it loaded with the safety off, keeping it in the glovebox of his Lincoln Continental. Ross hoped that he could stalk him the same way Williams and his friends stalked his brother. Ross dreamed of mercilessly assassinating Howard Williams when no one was around.

He made it clear to everyone that Howard Williams, the man who planned his brother's homicide, would not get away with taking his brother's life. He had come to realize that the American justice system was cruel and unfair.

Ross Valentino wanted to get even. He wanted to avenge his brother's death in the same tradition as was done in the old country, back in his hometown in Italy.

In Casalvieri, it was always "un occhio per un occhio."

An Eye for an Eye.

As the whole family had left church that morning, they arrived at Rossano's house in Sterling Heights to celebrate Easter as a family together. Ross and his brothers had gone to the brother-in-law Mario's farm in Marine City to slaughter several baby lambs on that previous Good Friday. They had butchered the fresh lambs as sliced lamb chops and were getting ready to prepare them on the grill.

As the children and wives prepared the long table downstairs, set for thirty people, Mario DiVito had brought over several gallons of his homemade red wine that he had made in the fall. They were pouring glasses of their precious red nectar for everyone to enjoy.

It was fair to say that everyone in the Valentino and DiVito Family wished to move ahead and recover from Tony's sudden death on that previous Halloween night.

Everyone in the family except Ross and his brother's grief-stricken widow. They just could not move on.

They finished their Easter dinner of barbequed lamb with lemons, honey baked ham, and homemade spaghetti. The men and children then went outside to enjoy their cigarettes and cigars while enjoying more of Mario's wine. Afterward, coffee, biscotti, and Easter baked goodies were on the table for all to enjoy.

As all the men were called back downstairs to the table, Isabella pulled Rossano on the side, grasping his hand, and pulling him over to the living room.

"Voglio parlare con te'," she said, asking him to sit down and talk.

As they sat down, Isabella immediately confronted him.

"Ross, what are you doing?"

"What do you mean?" he immediately responded.

"You know what I mean, Ross. Why are you following those guys around? Haven't we had enough tragedy in this family?"

"I don't know what you're talking about," Rossano lied.

There was a brief moment of silence.

"One of the detectives called me the other day. He said that your Lincoln was spotted by another Mt. Clemens patrolman the other day, parked in front of that man's house."

Rossano was surprised.

"How did they know it was my car?"

"Someone must have seen you and reported your license plates to the Mt. Clemens police," she explained.

"When they realized who you were and what you were probably doing there, they called the Detroit Police Department, and Detective Riley called me."

Ross looked at his sister-in-law in silence. The last thing that he needed was for anyone to know of his plot to take revenge against her husband's killers.

"They're on to you, Ross. They have been watching you while you have been watching them, stalking that bastard," Isabella revealed.

Rossano suddenly became defensive.

"How do you want me to handle this, Isa? Do you want to let these 'bastardi' get away with murder? Because that is precisely what the justice system has allowed to happen!" Ross thundered.

"I cannot sleep at night, knowing that these sons-of-bitches killed Tony in cold blood and got away with it."

Ross now had tears in his eyes, as the hatred for these three killers had overcome his disposition and whole demeanor that Easter Sunday.

Isabella lovingly grasped her brother-in-law's hand.

"Ross, my children no longer have a father. With Tony gone, my kids and especially Johnny, look up to you as their dad," she explained.

"If something were to happen to you, that would be another loss that we all could never bear," the widow stated.

They both looked at each other as tears were streaming down Isabella's cheeks.

"We can't bear to lose you. We all need you in our lives, Ross."

Another long moment of silence.

"Per favore, non farlo," she pleaded with him not to do this.

Ross looked at her, now grasping her hand with both of his as they silently looked at each other.

"Okay, Isa. I promise you that as long as you're here on this earth, I will be here for you and the kids."

"Don't take your revenge against them, Ross. They will come back to our family, and someone else will die. This whole killing cycle will never end."

Ross looked at Isabella in the eyes.

"Yes, Isa, you're right. I will not do anything to hurt you or the children."

He kissed Isabella on the cheek as he rose from the couch.

"No, I will not take revenge...*for now.*"

Isabella looked at him.

"If you are going to do this, do it when my children are all grown-up. Do it when I am no longer here. I do not want to answer to God for this."

She wiped her tears away as she spoke. Isabella had always been a very religious, devout Catholic.

"It is God's will, not to take revenge, but to love and forgive your enemies. I could not live with myself, knowing that I allowed you to kill them for what they did to Tony."

"But they got away with murder, Isa!" Ross exclaimed loudly again.

"Ross, my husband was no angel. As much as I hate to admit this, he brought this on himself and all of us. Had Tony only done the right thing and put his wife and family first, this would have never happened."

At that moment, her brother Aldo came upstairs to look for both of them. He had overheard part of the conversation.

The two of them abruptly stopped talking and looked at Aldo DiVito as he walked into the living room. Aldo was the closest of Isabella's brothers to her husband. He briefly stared at the picture of Tony with the lighted candle and a small statuette of the Blessed Mother next to his picture frame.

"Ross," he quietly suggested. "Let it go."

A moment of silence.

"Let it go. This is not the time. The kids are too little, and my sister needs all of us together as a family. We cannot be wasting our energy trying to bring justice to these ruthless, hillbilly bastards. We have to let it go," Aldo explained.

And then he followed up his sentence,

"...for now."

Ross looked at Aldo. As they made eye contact, Ross knew precisely what Aldo was trying to say.

Now was not the time to take them out and make all of them pay for taking a husband and father away from his wife and young children.

Besides risking his whole life and putting himself in the line of fire, Ross
knew that the police would immediately suspect him if anything happened to Howard Williams and his despicable friends.

Now was not the time to implement 'An Eye for an Eye.' Time had to pass. Time for the children to grow up. Time for Isabella to get over her grief. Time for Ross to heal from the pain of losing his older brother.

They all rose and went downstairs to have espresso, biscotti, tiramisu cake, and other Easter goodies with the rest of the family downstairs.

As they all sat down, Aldo and Rossano made eye contact again. It was as though they had silently made a pact.

There will be another day when 'An Eye for an Eye' would eventually come.

CHAPTER TWELVE

DETROIT'S GREEK TOWN-SPRING 2019

Pappy's Bar and Grill on Monroe Street in Detroit's Greek Town was a happening place that Thursday night, as I strolled into the front door.

My drinking habits since my joining Alcoholics Anonymous six months ago had to be very different now. I had to learn to enjoy the social settings of being in a bar or restaurant without having an alcoholic beverage in my hand. I have to say, it took some getting used to. I missed my Corona Beers and my Johnny Walker Whiskey shots. Going out and partying without an alcoholic beverage in my hand was going to be very different.

It was a Thursday night during the middle of April, and everyone had a spring fever. It was like every calm, warm night that spring was a celebration of life, of spring, and was an annual rite of passage.

The evening hours in Detroit's downtown Greektown were bustling with business executives from all of Detroit's surrounding business districts. People flocked everywhere from Jefferson Avenue, the Penobscot Building on Griswold Street, and the General Motors Renaissance Center. There was a baseball game between the Detroit Tigers and Chicago White Sox at Ford Field that night, so fans were flocking after the ball game to Pappy's as well.

As I walked in, I couldn't have looked better. I had on a light blue button-down shirt, and dark blue Ralph Lauren sport coat, and a new pair of dark designer blue jeans that went with my reasonably new blue suede shoes. As I strolled into that bar, I felt like I could play the part. For the first time since my devastating divorce, I felt extremely good about myself. Greektown could have been Rodeo Drive that evening, and it wouldn't have made a difference.

I was out that evening, by myself, to rediscover my new identity. I was no longer interested in drinking my sorrows away in front of some sleazy pole dancers. I was ready to revive myself without any booze or depression.

That night, I was prepared to show off the new John Valentino.

As I approached the bar, I had learned to ask for a drink without actually drinking alcohol. When the bartender approached me, I made sure no one was listening.

"What will it be, sir?"

"Seven-Up, with a lime, please."

He looked at me a little phased but threw several ice cubes into a tall glass with a few limes. I then gave him a ten-dollar bill for what was literally a glass of soda.

The bar section of Pappy's was crowded with people, as the jazz music was playing loudly with a piano player, a drummer, and a saxophone player in the corner of the bar.

I hadn't realized at the time that I was being watched by someone that I didn't even know. As I was sipping my Seven-Up with Lime, I noticed that a beautiful brunette was staring at me, standing next to one of her girlfriends, trying not to look too obvious.

As I moved toward the opposite direction, I heard a voice next to my right ear say:

"Very smooth."

I looked around and noticed that the beautiful brunette was standing right next to me, staring at my drink.

"Excuse me?"

"I said, 'very smooth.'"

I looked at her for a second.

"Are you complimenting my dress jacket or my blue suede shoes?" I bantered back with a smile.

"No," she giggled, "Your drink."

I looked at her for a few vacant seconds.

"Do you always come to the bar to drink Seven-Up?" she asked.

I looked at her, and I tried to lie.

"This is actually a Vodka and Sprite with a splash of lime," I tried to say.

She looked at me and laughed, knowing that she caught me in a bald-faced lie. Then, without even asking first, she grabbed my drink from my hand and took a sip of it.

"Just as I thought...Seven-Up."

At that moment, I was a little perturbed.

"Do you always go around taste-testing other people's drinks?" I asked her.

She smiled. "Only the ones drinking Seven-Up and pretending that it's Vodka."

This stunning but very forward girl came across a little too hard for me that evening, and I didn't know what to make of it. I hadn't spent a lot of time trying to pick-up women during or after my marriage, and I was initially at a loss for words. Other than the dancers looking for a twenty-dollar lap dance at the Crazy Horse Lounge, I had not spent a whole lot of time talking to other ladies or working on my dance-club one-liners.

At that moment, I thought about just getting out of her way to another part of the bar. I only wanted to enjoy jazz music and my Seven-Up and Lime when she suddenly extended her hand.

"I'm Olivia," she said, in a soft, very demure voice.

"Hi, I'm John," I replied as I shook her hand.

She was a stunning, beautiful brunette with long, curly dark brown hair, adoring brown eyes, and a very shapely figure, probably no more than five feet, five inches tall. This attractive stranger was wearing a light beige jacket, matching skirt, and a bright blue blouse, which complimented her semi-dark complexion. The lady was wearing light red lipstick and a stunning smile. She looked like one of those classy, Hollywood actresses that you often see posing for one of those glamour magazines, displayed next to the cashier at the supermarket. She was drop-dead gorgeous.

"So," trying to make conversation, "Is this your Thursday night watering-hole?"

Olivia smiled. "I usually come to Greek Town with my girlfriends on Thursday nights. Most of the time, we either come here or the Firebird Tavern, depending on who is the entertainment."

Olivia looked around for her girlfriend, who was talking to another gentleman.

"This is my girlfriend, Cindy. We work together," she mentioned.

"Oh? Where do you both work?" I was trying to talk over the loud, jazz piano music.

"Great Lakes Life Insurance Company. We're on the thirty-sixth floor of the Renaissance Center."

She paused for a minute. At that moment, her friend Cindy jumped in.

"She's the boss," she interjected as she was giggling while holding her Stella Artois beer.

"Really?" I managed to say.

"I'm the chief financial officer there."

"Interesting," I mentioned. By that moment, I was noticing how sensuously shaped my new friend was. She looked to be in her middle forties up close, but I wasn't sure. She carried herself very well, and I could tell her tight abdomen didn't come without putting a lot of intense time into the gym.

"How about you?" Olivia asked.

I paused for a moment.

"I work for the City of Detroit," I said, not wanting to be too informative. Most people freak out when I tell them I'm a cop or a police detective right away.

"Oh," she said.

A few more moments passed, as her gin and tonic drink was practically empty. I called over the bartender and ordered another round for her and her girlfriend.

We hung out and noticed there was some room on the dance floor. The jazz band was playing a slow song from the 70s, a song that I recognized but didn't know the name of.

"Would you like to dance?" I asked.

"Sure."

We walked over to the dance floor and held each other rather close. I could smell the fragrance of her perfume, which was quite distinctive.

"What is that cologne you're wearing?" she asked. "You smell so good."

"Creed Aventus," I remembered. It was an expensive bottle of cologne that I hardly wore anymore. I managed to sneak it out of my house, along with my only shaving kit. It's the same cologne my wife Marina loved and bought for me a few years ago for Father's Day.

"How about you?"

"Channel Mademoiselle."

"Very nice," I said.

By then, we were dancing extremely close.

"Do you like Earth, Wind, and Fire?"

"Yes."

I could feel her hand going up and down my back.

"This is a great song."

"What's the name of it?" I asked.

"' After the Love Is Gone,'" she replied.

We danced close to that song and another slow song after it. Then she asked the question that I knew she would eventually ask.

"So, John, what do you do for the City of Detroit?"

I decided to play a guessing game.

"Would you believe me if I told you I worked in the sanitation department?"

"Really? What do you do there?"

I smiled. "I clean up shit!"

Olivia laughed. "You look too polished to be cleaning up anyone's shit," she said.

A few more moments passed.

"I'm a detective," I finally blurted out.

We stopped dancing for a few moments, and she looked at me at first. She then smiled.

"I should have guessed," Olivia said.

"Why?"

"I must be attracted to detectives. My last boyfriend was a police detective."

"Really? Where?"

"Chicago," she quickly replied.

I didn't want to ask too many questions.

We continued to dance together until a very fast, upbeat song came on that neither one of us was interested in dancing to. We then went back to the bar and finished our drinks.

By that point, I thought I would be bold and take her someplace where we could have a quieter conversation without the bustling crowds of the loud bar.

We decided to leave together, and we walked to a small coffee and Greek pastry shop three blocks away.

As we sat down, she gave me a little personal history lesson about herself.

Olivia Laurent was an accountant by trade. She received her accounting CPA certificate after graduating from Albion College. She went on to get her law degree from Wayne State University, with the hope of having a career in taxation law and forensic accounting. Olivia instead took a temporary job while in law school as an insurance adjuster with the life insurance company. She climbed the corporate ladder over the last twenty years to her present executive position within the corporation.

Olivia was an intelligent, beautiful insurance executive who had never been married, and at this point in her life, had no desire to do so. She explained that she had been in a few intense relationships over the last few years, which included her detective boyfriend from Chicago.

Olivia also revealed that she had taken a long leave of absence for about three months and lived in the Caribbean, on a little island called

Labadee. She had returned to her executive job in Detroit several months ago.

"So, what inspired you to go off to a secluded Caribbean Island?"

"I went there to stay with a friend," was all she said. I got the impression that her friendship with whoever was on that island was not a platonic one.

"How about you? You've only mentioned that you were once married and now divorced."

"Yes," I said. "Twenty-two years to a girl I had been dating since high-school. I've known her since the ninth grade and have never dated anyone else. We have two boys, Anthony and Dario. They're both students at Notre Dame High School."

"I'm sorry," she said. "What happened?"

"It was my fault," I meekly said.

I gazed at her, somewhat ashamed to finish answering her question. A few silent moments passed. She then looked at me intensely.

"Does it have something to do with your drinking Seven-Up's tonight?"

I nodded my head.

"I see."

We had ordered two Greek coffees and some baklava, and the waitress was readily bringing refills.

We talked about both of our backgrounds. Olivia explained that her law and accounting degrees were valuable tools for which she utilized in her career. She was able to use her forensic accounting techniques, along with her excellent understanding of the law, for the company's various life insurance claims. Olivia signed off on all the requests for which the Great Lakes Life Insurance Company was liable.

We then finished our coffees, and I walked her back outside, where she needed to take a taxicab home to her condominium on Jefferson Avenue.

"Would you like my number?" she volunteered, probably figuring I was too bashful and shy to ask her outright.

"Absolutely," I said.

She dialed my number into her cell phone and then called me. I appropriately labeled her new contact on my phone list.

It was just after midnight, and as the taxicab arrived, I kissed her on the cheek, opening the cab door.

"You're cute," she managed to say and planted a ten-second wet kiss on my lips.

"Call me," she said.

As the taxicab sped off down Monroe Street, I wondered if my heart was ready for someone new in my life. I pondered if I could ever move on from the heartache of walking away from a wife, the only love that I've ever had in my life, and the loss of my two children. I questioned if I could ever start a new life with a new love and not ever look back.

I wanted so much to do so.

CHAPTER THIRTEEN

OLIVIA LAURENT

The line of people at Starbucks was almost to the door as Olivia Laurent arrived for her usual morning cappuccino, for which she preferred Grande, Extra Wet. It was a beautiful April spring morning in downtown Detroit, as the temperature was starting to climb to 68 degrees. She was suffering from an intense migraine headache first thing that morning and was skeptical as to whether a fresh cup of her usual cappuccino was going to do her any good. The young business executive had just gotten off the bus from her downtown Jefferson Avenue condo to her office at the Great Lakes Life Insurance Company, where she was the chief financial officer. Olivia grabbed her coffee that morning and walked over to her office on the thirty-sixth floor of the Renaissance Center across the street.

She had just settled into her office when her associate brought in some documents, and some insurance claims to review.

"Good morning, Olivia," greeted her associate.

Cindy Jankowski was a sharp, heads-up claims accountant who had been with the insurance company for over several years. Olivia considered her "the extra pair of eyes and ears" within the company.

She should have probably gotten herself a glass of tomato juice and some aspirin to soothe her throbbing morning headache, or perhaps, her hangover. She had gone out with some girlfriends to Detroit's Greek Town for dinner and drinks the night before and didn't get home until one o'clock in the morning.

"Cindy, do you have any aspirin?"

Cindy noticed her bloodshot eyes upon closer inspection and realized that her usual Starbucks grande cappuccino, extra-wet, wasn't going to do the trick. She quickly went to her office and brought back two Excedrin aspirin for her boss a few minutes later, along with a small cup of water.

"How late were you out last night?" Cindy asked as Olivia swallowed the two Excedrin.

"Until one in the morning. I'm getting too old for this shit," Olivia replied.

She had just celebrated her forty-fifth birthday last week, and although she looked phenomenal, she was starting to feel the effects of her ripe-old middle age. She followed a vegan diet, watched her waistline, and invaded the local gym and Zumba classes four nights a week. Other than her periodic cravings for cheese fries and her usual gin and tonics, Olivia lived a reasonably healthy lifestyle. She was also single.

Although Olivia had her fair share of past relationships, the insurance executive had never been married and had no children. She had given up on her biological clock, realizing that her lucrative corporate career was far more rewarding than all that overrated hype regarding kids, marriage, and motherhood.

Olivia had been back at her job as the chief financial officer for several months now at the Great Lakes Insurance Company. She had recently taken a brief leave of absence for three months, deciding that she needed to go away.

Far, far away.

Eighteen months ago, her company had processed some very lucrative life insurance claims for some pedophile priests who had been brutally murdered in Chicago. With the suspicious circumstances of their murders and the Archdiocese of Chicago as the beneficiary of their policies, Olivia was compelled to get involved in the investigation.

Maybe she got a little too personally involved. Olivia was mentally recuperating from the emotional devastation of two very personal relationships.

Olivia ended up having a very personal, romantic affair with the Chicago detective who was in charge of the 'Pedophile Priest Murder' investigations. Detective Philip Dorian was a divorced, middle-aged veteran policeman with the Chicago P.D.'s Sixteenth District. He displayed a tremendous amount of generosity and kindness towards her that she hadn't experienced in a very long time with anyone else. Dorian went out of his way for Olivia, wining and dining her in Chicago. Before long, she became passionately involved with him. After dating him for a few months, and she had fallen head over heels in love with Philip Dorian.

But at that time, she also found herself involved in another emotional relationship that she probably should have never gotten herself into. Two years prior, she had met a gentleman at a Catholic Pro-Life Seminar she was attending at her Guardian Angels Parish in Detroit by the name of Joseph Kilbane. He was an older man in his early sixties, and she certainly wasn't initially attracted to him. But they sat together at the day-long seminar, and they immediately hit it off, discussing very intellectual subjects and conversations regarding pro-life issues, biblical old-testament topics, and the current sexual abuse scandals in the church. Being that Laurent was a devout Catholic, she realized that Kilbane was a very religious intellectual with an extremely educated background.

She became smitten with his intelligence, his kindness, and his old-fashioned charm. He was very old-school and was always a complete gentleman. They started meeting for coffee, then dinner dates, and they became intimate after a few months.

One faithful weekend, Olivia decided to surprise him with a visit to his Chicago home in Lincoln Park. It was then that she found out one of Kilbane's many hidden secrets that completely shocked and devastated her:

Her new boyfriend was a Catholic priest.

But not just any priest. Kilbane was a very influential Catholic official and a high-ranking cleric within the Archdiocese of Chicago. He held the title of Monsignor, with the position as chief of staff to Chicago's Cardinal Markowitz. Kilbane was a well-known cleric within Chicago media circles and ranked second only to the Chicago cardinal himself.

Olivia was devastated, and she immediately broke off the relationship. But Kilbane wouldn't take no for an answer. He continued to call and text her, inundating her with love letters and emails. He swore that their love and that their involvement together was a 'gift from God.' With her help and her love, he claimed, he would eventually leave the priesthood. They would retire to a 'desolate island' somewhere together in the Caribbean and live happily ever after.

By that time, Kilbane had realized that her insurance company had underwritten the lucrative life insurance policies on an innumerate number of defrocked pedophile priests. With Olivia being the chief financial executive, Kilbane hatched a plan where four of the multi-million-dollar policies would be cashed in on four of those pedophile ex-priests that had been brutally murdered in Chicago.

Monsignor Joseph Kilbane also had another dark secret. He was the Grand Knight of a covert, religious secret society of hooded killers, known as the 'Society of the Rose Crucifix.' It was through this secret society that he was able to supervise the murder of the four pedophile ex-priests. He was able to cash in on their lucrative life insurance policies that were taken out on them years prior when the church initially defrocked them. With Laurent being an executive with the Great Lakes Life Insurance Company, his having a close relationship with her assisted him in getting these high dollar policies converted into cash.

Olivia Laurent finally acquiesced and went through the motions of conducting an independent investigation on behalf of the life insurance company. She eventually signed off on twenty million dollars' worth of settlement claims, payable to the Chicago Archdiocese. Kilbane, with his connections to the Chicago underworld, was able to siphon off and divert the insurance money away from the archdiocese by way of the IWR, or the Vatican Bank, using blackmail against the Pope and the Holy See. Kilbane ended up personally receiving half of those insurance proceeds or ten million dollars.

Monsignor Joseph Kilbane abruptly left Chicago and permanently moved to the Caribbean Island of Labadee, a remote paradise located not far from Haiti. He kept his word to Olivia and left the priesthood, retiring to the far-off island. Kilbane had successfully escaped and moved far away from the Chicago Archdiocese, the pedophile priest murder scandals, and the Chicago authorities.

But while all of this was going on, Olivia began getting involved concurrently with Chicago P.D's Detective Philip Dorian while conducting her independent investigation into those murdered pedophile priests in Chicago.

She found herself in two profound, emotional relationships. Kilbane, who was almost twenty years her senior, represented the intellectual side of her personality that she wasn't able to fulfill with Dorian or any other past relationship. She enjoyed their deep, scholarly conversations regarding religion, politics, art, and culture.

But Dorian, who was only a few years older, was fun, energetic, spontaneous, and down to earth. She found herself having a wonderful time with him throughout their relationship. Although she was also involved with Joseph Kilbane, she realized that she was indeed in love with Philip Dorian.

When Detective Dorian found out about her independent investigation for the life insurance company behind his back, they quarreled and broke off their affair. Olivia was emotionally devastated. She avoided Dorian's calls for three months afterward, trying desperately to forget him and their intense, emotional connection.

Olivia ran into Dorian at a Blackhawks vs. Red Wings hockey a few months later in Chicago, and she tried to make amends. But by that time, Philip Dorian wanted no part of her or her hidden agenda. She then assisted Monsignor Kilbane in settling up with the life insurance company and eventually met up with him on the island of Labadee.

But their beautiful life in paradise did not last very long. After a few months, Olivia got tired of Kilbane's possessiveness, his excessive mood swings, and his sometimes-violent temper.

After being a Catholic priest for over forty years, Joseph Kilbane had extreme behavioral problems and psychological issues. He was clueless about how to conduct himself in a relationship and avert his intensely selfish, self-centered behavior. Their hot and heavy affair in paradise eventually collapsed.

By the following spring, Olivia Laurent was back in Detroit, back at her job at the Great Lakes Insurance Company. She had nothing to show for either failed relationship, and she fell into an intense, dark depression. Olivia went into psychological therapy after her associate and good friend, Cindy Jankowski, found her at home unconscious. Laurent had taken one too many sleeping pills, and she was hospitalized at Bon Secours Hospital for a few days. Besides her failed Chicago relationships, she also found herself in another precarious predicament:

Olivia Laurent was broke.

Even with her chief financial officer salary of $235,000 a year, she had an excessive amount of personal bills, credit cards, car payments, and home mortgages. After years of spending beyond her means, she was struggling to stay above water financially. Even after receiving a 'cash stipend' of $50,000 from Kilbane, all of her money and savings were gone. When she moved to Labadee, she had hoped that Joseph Kilbane would financially take care of her, especially since she had greatly assisted him in cashing in those insurance policies.

But Joseph Kilbane turned out to be a very selfish man. He was not about to share his wealth with Olivia, despite her help. Laurent was far too embarrassed and financially strapped to file for personal bankruptcy. She needed to make some quick money, enough to pay off her more than one million dollars in personal debts. She needed to make a big score.

As the chief financial officer of Great Lakes, Olivia supervised the internal audits that were periodically conducted by her accounting department. For years, the insurance company kept a large reserve for paid off life insurance policies that had very high cash surrender values but went unclaimed by the beneficiaries. It was the standard policy of Great Lakes that, after several years of inactivity on the insurance policy, that the cash surrender values of these policies be written off and recorded as additional income to the insurance company.

Olivia Laurent, through her legal and accounting abilities as an attorney and CPA, had devised an elaborate scheme. She realized that, if she acquired the death certificates of these insured policyholders and was able to obtain signed police reports associated with their deaths, she could divert these payoff policies to their 'beneficiaries.' She would then create trusts on behalf of these beneficiaries for which the funds would be deposited.

These funds would then eventually end up in Laurent's offshore accounts. With the intricate help of the authorities, she would become an identity thief. She could acquire the stolen identities of these policy beneficiaries and then authorize the payoff of these abandoned insurance policies with their high face value amounts. She estimated the company had over twenty million dollars of abandoned or expired insurance policies, waiting to be written off and recognized as income to the insurance company.

But this wasn't a scheme that she could do on her own. She needed the help of a police detective. Only a detective with security clearance to acquire very personal information would be able to assist her. She needed someone who could aid her in acquiring all of this stolen personal information, signing off on false, filed police reports, and creation of these fake beneficiary claims. She needed social security numbers, social media passwords, dates of birth, addresses, and other personal information in helping her to file these claims. Laurent needed the aid of someone of authority who could support her in getting this private information of these deceased policyholders and file these claims for her benefit.

She needed the help of a dirty detective who was as financially desperate as she was.

CHAPTER FOURTEEN

FAMILY JUSTICE – APRIL 1979

Don Pellegrino Licavoli was sitting outside, overlooking the sizeable expansive estate of his Farmington Hills Home. As was usually his routine, Don Pino was enjoying a cigar and a glass of his favorite bourbon whiskey. It was a warmer spring day in April 1979, and after a long, hard Detroit winter, the middle-aged crime family boss was enjoying the beautiful spring weather.

His father, Vito Licavoli, had long been an integral part of the Detroit Mafia. Their organized crime family had been actively involved with the prevalent bootlegging that was going on during the 1920s. During Prohibition, illegal whiskey and alcohol were being smuggled between Detroit and Windsor, Canada, and the Licavoli Family had an active role in that criminal activity. During that period, 'rumrunners' were used to cross the Detroit River with their illegal stash from Canada. The Licavoli Family provided the muscle to make sure that its illegal, unauthorized inventory was safely guarded and adequately distributed to other parts of the country.

Their family success during Prohibition did not come without the high costs of blood and violence. The Tocco and Zerilli Families were also involved in that same illegal activity, and the crime wars between those of the 'Purple Gang' and the 'Cosa Nostra' continued up until the Second World War.

But now, despite the organized crime violence that was going on in New York and

Chicago during that period, the three powerful crime families of Detroit were enjoying a long period of peace. It was his father, Vito Licavoli, who was credited with instigating the meetings between all of the crime families in Detroit and Toledo. The elder Licavoli created a 'Board of Directors' of sorts, where the heads of the crime families, along with their underbosses and consiglieri, would have monthly meetings and vote on various issues and problems that were impacting their combined Detroit empire. Unlike the other Mafiosi in other cities, there was no Capo dei Capi. There were only board chairmen, who were voted in by the other members for annual terms. Each crime family took turns as the dominating board of directors' chairman, with the other members of each family holding prevalent positions within the board.

Since the board of directors' creation, the Detroit Crime Families have successfully been able to avert the jealousies and betrayal that other crime families in other cities have not been able to avoid.

And thus, Vito Licavoli rightfully earned the reputation as the 'The Peacemaker.' He acquired the status of being extraordinarily reasonable and logical and tried to avoid violence amongst members of his own family and the other families at all costs. He had engineered a successful peace treaty between all of the Detroit Mafiosi since the early 1950's that crime families in other parts of the country only envied. With the separation of territories and illegal business activities, there was now newfound respect and tranquility amongst the Detroit underworld.

When his father died in 1975, the Detroit crime family bosses looked to Pellegrino Licavoli to assume his father's reputation as a peacemaker and continue that long-standing peace.

As Licavoli sat in his chair, smoking his cigar that afternoon, something was definitely on his mind. His underboss, Caesar Giordano, was keeping him apprised of a small situation that was now brewing and getting out of control.

One of his street bookies, Howard Williams, was involved in a murder several months ago involving a love triangle between his wife and her boyfriend. In most cases, Licavoli would not get involved in such minuscule matters involving his 'associates.' But in this case, that particular situation and the ensuing murder that followed had more than angered and upset the family capo.

When Williams approached his underboss for assistance in correcting his marital situation last October, Giordano directed him to have a serious talk with the boyfriend, to advise him to end the affair with his wife. At no point was Howard Williams encouraged to kill him.

But when Williams and his friends were being held in a Detroit precinct jail cell without bail, the Licavoli Family washed their hands. They no longer wanted any part of Williams or his crude, irrational hillbilly temper. It was a mistake to follow the advice of his underboss in allowing Williams to participate as a street bookie for the family. When Don Licavoli realized that the wife's boyfriend he and his friends had murdered was a fellow Italian and a family man, he became enraged.

“Let them rot in jail,” was Don Pino’s angry advice to his underboss, refusing to exert any influence on any of the judges or the district attorneys and prosecutors involved in that murder case.

But somehow, through the legal savvy of the accused individual’s attorneys, the three of them were able to get the homicide charges acquitted.

In Don Pino’s mind, Howard Williams was a low life scumbag and didn’t deserve to be exonerated for that crime.

Even though Williams was only a small-time street-bookie working part-time for the family, Licavoli knew that Williams was a bad seed. He was a lousy example to not only the other Licavoli family members but to the other crime families as well.

Word had gotten out to the Tocco and Zerilli Families that a Licavoli street bookie had killed a fellow Italian in cold blood, and everyone was furious about it. Furthermore, there was word that an Italian, old country ‘vendetta’ had been placed on the heads of those three killers after the murder trial.

This small, minuscule marital problem that Williams was told to reasonably handle on his own had escalated out of control. And now, Don Pino Licavoli was being asked by the other crime families to do something about it. He could no longer close his eyes, wash his hands, and expect the judicial system to dispense justice accurately.

He now had to take the law into his own hands, and he needed to do it swiftly.

"Buon Pomeriggio," his underboss greeted, wishing The Don a good afternoon. The man kissed him on both cheeks as he approached the beautiful, stone-clad courtyard of the Licavoli estate.

Don Licavoli nodded his head as he sat back down on his chair, taking a long drag from his Cohiba cigar. He had asked his underboss to come over and discuss some pressing matters, and the Valentino murder trial was one of them.

Caesar Giordano was a trusted underboss of the Licavoli Family. He moved up the ranks of the family hierarchy over many years since being a street tax collector from the Cavalupo neighborhood, near the Eastern Market. Giordano had been keeping the family Capo apprised of the developments of the recent murder trial of Tony Valentino, and he knew of the Don's anger and disappointment.

The two of them sat there in silence for several long minutes, as one of the servants had brought over two espresso coffees for both of them to enjoy.

Breaking the silence, Giordano then immediately spoke, "You wished to talk to me?"

Don Licavoli, wearing a casual, beige windbreaker jacket and light khaki pants, could have passed for one of the servants that day. The head of the crime family enjoyed keeping a casually low profile, and he seldom enforced his family authority unless it was necessary.

"We need to address the situation of your friend," Don Licavoli started the conversation.

"Regarding Williams? Yes, I know."

"The other families are looking to us to admonish your friend for what he has done. It's quite obvious that the legal hands of justice were not properly served in court last week."

"I know," Caesar agreed. "But what do you wish to do?"

Don Licavoli shook his head as if to be without an answer.

"Would you rather we take them all out?" the underboss asked.

"No," he immediately responded,

"Even though that is what the three of them so greatly deserve."

The Don took a long swallow of his bourbon from the crystal glass tumbler.

"Besides, it would be too obvious," he noted.

"You heard about what happened at the end of that trial, yes?"

Licavoli looked at Giordano.

"The victim's brother loudly proclaimed a vendetta against Williams and the others in the middle of the courthouse after the trial," Giordano said to The Don.

Licavoli shook his head.

"I heard. But if an outsider were to take out one of our own, even if it is only a scum-bag street bookie like Williams, we would be obligated to avenge his death."

Another long puff of his cigar.

"This is all we need right now. Somebody else taking revenge against one of our own."

The two of them were silent for several long minutes.

"I'm sorry I got him involved with us, Don Pino. He seemed like a great guy who was willing to take orders when I met him in the joint."

The Don puffed on his cigar, looking at his green, expansive lawn.

"We were both wrong, Caesar."

The two of them sat there in silence for several long minutes as the underboss finished his expresso.

"What do you wish for me to do?"

"Get them out of town, Caesar. I want those three son-of-a-bitches out of my fucking sight. I don't want to hear any more about this hillbilly bastard, his 'puttana' wife, or any of his fucking friends."

The underboss nodded his head to Don Pino Licavoli. He now realized what he ultimately had to do.

The gloomy, abandoned warehouse parking lot was located just west of Mt. Elliot Avenue and Caniff Streets. It was almost dusk, as Howard Williams was sitting alone in his blue Monte Carlo. He was told to arrive at the parking lot at eight o'clock that Monday evening, as there would be a meeting between only himself and Caesar Giordano.

Williams, since being released from jail, had heard about Don Licavoli's reaction to the murder of his wife's boyfriend. Although his wife denied the affair, Williams had justified his actions on that Halloween night. He had used Hansen and Johnson in that situation several months ago, and he felt that Valentino was warned. He had it coming.

Howard Williams was unapologetic. He felt vindicated after he and his friends had been able to get exonerated for that murder in court.

Two more cars pulled into the parking lot, and Williams immediately knew that the others had been asked to meet Giordano for this meeting as well. He had not spoken to the others since the murder trial at the Wayne County Courthouse, and he was well aware of their anger towards him.

Williams had now become concerned, initially thinking that this meeting would only be a one-on-one encounter with his friend Caesar. Now he was starting to get scared, realizing that he was totally and completely unarmed.

With Hansen and Johnson still sitting in their cars, they all waited for the underboss, Caesar Giordano, to arrive. It was a little after 8:15 pm when a black 1977 Lincoln Mark V pulled in.

Everyone got out of their cars in unison, as the family underboss and two very large henchmen came out of the late model Lincoln.

As they got out and met in the middle of the parking lot, Giordano made no mistake of his animosity towards the three of them.

"We have a little problem here, gentlemen," as Giordano put a Lucky Strike cigarette in his mouth and then calmly lit it up, taking his time to exhale the first drag.

"You three assholes are supposed to be rotting in jail," he coldly said to the other three former convicts.

"You guys were not supposed to beat that murder rap. You, rotten bastards, were supposed to be sentenced for a very long time and pay the price for what you all fucking did," he sternly said while holding his cigarette.

The two men next to him stood at attention, waiting for any wrong move by either Williams, Hansen, or Johnson.

Howard Williams was the only one who had the guts to respond to his former friend.

"That dago bastard got what he deserved," he loudly exclaimed.

At that moment, one of Licavoli's men grabbed Williams by his neck and severely pistol-whipped him in the middle of the parking lot while Hansen and Johnson looked on.

After several long minutes of watching the former Licavoli street bookie get severely beaten, the others stood quietly, knowing that evening could very well be their last.

Williams was now lying on the ground, bloodied throughout his face and barely conscious.

"Do any of you other hillbilly assholes have anything else to say?"

Johnson and Hansen stood there silent as Williams laid there on the ground, struggling to move.

"We understand that there is a vendetta against the three of you," he stated.

"I'm here to let you all know that if this Valentino guy doesn't take you guys out, we will."

Williams had now managed to get up off of the ground, struggling to stay on his feet as the others stood silent. It was as though they were now standing silently in front of a judge. But this time, it was a street judge, acting on behalf of a higher order of justice.

"The Don has asked me to inform the three of you that you are no longer welcome in this town," he loudly exclaimed.

"You've got one week to pack up your shit and leave. We don't care where you go. But we strongly suggest that the three of you get as far away from Detroit as possible."

With that, Caesar lit another cigarette and then stared down at the three of them. There was a long moment of silence as the three of them looked at each other.

"Don't let me ever see the three of you again. Or the next time, there will be more than just one of your faces being slapped."

With that, Caesar got back into his Lincoln with his henchmen. Within minutes, he pulled quickly away from the abandoned warehouse. The three of them, still standing alone, stood there in shock. But neither of them said a word to each other. They all silently and quickly got into their vehicles.

Each one of them now hoped that neither would ever have the pleasure of ever seeing the other again.

CHAPTER FIFTEEN

A MOTHER'S PASSING-SPRING 2019

The sound of my very loud cell phone abruptly went off as I was trying to negotiate myself through another terrible nightmare.

"Hello?"

It was my oldest sister, Rosanna, calling me at 3:37 in the morning. I was glaring at the timeclock, illuminating bright, red numbers from my nightstand.

"Johnny, I'm sorry to wake you."

I stood up from my wet, soggy pillow as I was rubbing my eyes, wondering if my sister's late-night voice was only an extension of another bad dream.

"Rose? What's wrong?" I was still groggy.

"Lucia and I are here at St. John's Hospital. They rushed Mom over here around midnight."

My 72-year-old mother had been undergoing breast cancer treatments for the last four months. She was diagnosed with stage four breast cancer just after the Christmas holidays, and the intense chemotherapy and radiation treatments did not seem to be slowing down her very aggressive disease.

"She was having chest pains and was having trouble breathing. Lucia and I were going to wait until the morning to call you, but we're not sure if she's going to make it through the night."

"Okay," I responded, still sleepy. "What's the room number?"

"7-431, Bed 2. They admitted her about a half-hour ago. She's on the seventh floor," Rosanna replied.

A moment of silence, as I was rubbing my eyes.

"I'll be right there," as I pushed the END button.

I was still staring at the desk clock, as its bright red numbers were the only light in my bedroom. It was so weird, as my terrible nightmare was about my mother.

In my dream, she was in my car with me, giving me directions as I was driving her to Mt. Olivet Cemetery to visit my father's grave. This was a chore that I always did with her on Sunday afternoons. But what was so weird about this dream was that I couldn't find the cemetery nor my father's crypt.

I quickly got dressed, deciding at the last second to brush my teeth just before running out the door of my apartment. This was so strange. I was still trying to comprehend my terrible nightmare while I was driving to the hospital in real life.

My mother, Isabella, had found a lump on her breast a few days before Christmas but decided to wait until after the holidays to tell us about it and get a digital mammogram. I recalled the doctors over at St. John's Hospital telling my sisters and me that her form of breast cancer was an unusually aggressive one. Had she been more diligent about getting her annual mammograms, the doctors said, they would have been able to treat her cancerous disease before it had metastasized. They did a mastectomy of her left breast and removed all of her lymph nodes, of which fourteen out of sixteen of them were infected.

What was worse, the oncology doctors said that it had metastasized to her liver, and they did not believe that the radiation and aggressive chemotherapy was going to slow down its progress.

I kept talking to myself as I was driving my squad car southbound down Kelly Road to Seven Mile and Harper, wondering if this was going to be the very night that I would lose my mother.

"*She might get her to wish tonight,*" I said to myself.

It had been a long-standing belief for my sisters and me that my mother couldn't wait to pass on and be with my father, who had been dead for over forty years now. My mother, despite the way my Dad had suddenly passed away, was utterly devoted to his memory. She went to his crypt every Sunday afternoon. Mom always insisted that I always take her to Mt. Olivet Cemetery on Sundays after picking up several roses from Mancuso's Flower Shop.

I was suspicious when the doctors finally diagnosed my mother's stage four cancer. I had asked her several times if the lumps on her breast were the first time she had noticed them. Mom always insisted that they were.

But the unusual thing about all of this was that my mother wasn't fighting. She wasn't expressing any desire to fight this very aggressive breast cancer disease.

It was as though she was ready to die.

As I arrived at St. John Hospital, I took the elevator to the seventh floor to the hospital room where the doctors and nurses were trying to make her comfortable. There in the room was my two sisters and my Zio Rossano. We all hugged and kissed each other as my mother was stoically lying there. Her state of mind floating in and out of mental consciousness.

I hadn't seen my Zio Rossano for a long time, and he hadn't aged very well. At 79 years old, he was slowly walking with a cane, and I had heard that he had cardiac problems. He still had a full head of grey hair but looked almost gaunt, still struggling to get around.

He and his wife had a vacation home on Marco Island and spent six months of every year between their homes in Florida and Sterling Heights.

"Mom," I said as I kissed her on her cheek.

"Johnny," she faintly said. Her eyes lit up, and she smiled at me. She continued to hold my hand tight as if she were trying to tell me something important in a very soft voice.

"I'm going to see your father this morning," she said in a near voiceless whisper. She then faintly smiled.

"No, Mom, you're still with us. Dad and the angels can wait," I reassured her.

"No, Johnny, no," she insisted. "It's time."

There were a few long moments of silence next to her hospital bed.

"I'm so very proud of you, John. You've had such a hard life without your father. I'm so proud of the way you turned out," she whispered.

"My detective," she smiled, kissing my face as I held my ear next to her mouth, making sure I can hear her every word.

The doctor came into her room and then explained that she had a heart episode and that it was beating very faintly, the result of cancer spreading into her heart and lungs.

"She has the most aggressive breast cancer there is. Other than making her comfortable, there isn't anything else we can do," the doctor told us outside of her room.

I looked at my two sisters, who were already crying. Rossano was stoic, looking at my mother on her death bed as if he had something to say. Finally, after a few hours of all of us watching my mother with her labored breathing, my uncle went over to her and kissed her on her cheek.

"We made a promise to each other many years ago," Ross said to my mother.

She nodded her head. "Yes, Ross, you have kept your promise."

There were several moments of silence as we all stood around and watched my mother continue her labored breathing.

She then looked at Ross.

"Fai quello che devi fare."

I did not understand Italian nor what she had meant by the comment she had made. Ross just stood there next to her deathbed, tears welling up in his eyes. It was almost nine o'clock in the morning when my mother took her final breath. Within minutes, the heart rate monitor flat-lined.

My mother had passed away.

As we were all emotional with my sisters crying, the nurses came in to take my mother's body away to the morgue downstairs and to call the funeral home. My uncle was sobbing as they took her body away. My sisters signed some papers by the nurse's station, and then we slowly made our way to our cars parked in the hospital parking lot. We all knew that we had to meet at the funeral home on Fifteen Mile Road in a few hours to comply with the funeral director and plan her services.

There were crowds of people beginning to gather inside of St. Malachy Catholic Church on Fourteen Mile Road in Sterling Heights. We had arrived early at eight o'clock on that warm Saturday morning in May for my mother's funeral. We decided to allow visitors to view my mother in her oak, wooden casket three hours before the funeral mass, rather than have a viewing at the funeral home. By the time it was ten o'clock that morning, there had to have been over three hundred or more people who had already passed my mother's casket sitting on a bier in the vestibule of the church.

Calcaterra Funeral Home had done an excellent job in preparing my mother for her viewing, wearing a black satin dress and her dark hair combed up in a bun. She indeed looked as though she were sleeping. My uncles and my only brother-in-law stood next to me in the receiving line, as everyone had complimentary things to say about what a wonderful person my mother was. But I just wanted to get this over with.

As the funeral mass began, my mother's casket was escorted to the front of the church. The hymn "How Great Thou Art" echoed and reverberated across the magnificent, grand stone walls of the old Catholic Church, with its intricate stained-glass windows and old carved woodwork. I tried to control myself as the eulogy about Mom was made by my sister Rosanna, who said she 'was an incredible pillar of strength to the family.'

"Mom never forgot where she came from and never stopped being a loving mother and a loving wife. She is up in heaven with the man she always loved and all the angels who looked over her while she was here on Earth."

Rossano Valentino and his wife, Elvira, were completely beside themselves as I assisted my sister Lucia from almost completely collapsing from grief. Rosanna had broken down a few times while giving the eulogy, while Mom's brother Mario stood there stoically and without emotion.

Mom's nephews and my sons, along with my Uncles Mario and Uncle Rossano, put on the white gloves and stood next to the casket as the pallbearers at the end of the funeral mass. They dutifully followed her remains toward the outside of the church, while the canter sang an operatic rendition of the "Ave Maria" at the end of the funeral requiem. The traditional song seemed to reverberate from the magnificent walls of St. Malachy Church, with its ornate statues of Jesus and his twelve apostles. The emotional Italian lyrics transcended its sacred sounds for all those who came to witness the ascension of my mother's soul. As the crowds of people exited the neighborhood church, everyone stood at the front of its ornate wooden doors.

Everyone watched the pallbearers load the casket onto the black hearse and climbed back into their cars. As we closed the hearse door and walked to our respective vehicles, I noticed someone standing next to her black Lexus ES 350 in the parking lot.

I was shocked to see her, as I did not expect her to be here for my mother's funeral. The lady was waiting along on the black fence near the sidewalk. She was next to the long foray of parked cars, ready to leave for the cemetery.

"Hey John," the familiar brunette said, wearing a black dress and Zanotti high heeled shoes. She looked beautiful, dressed in black.

It was Olivia.

"Hey Olivia, what are you doing here?"

She looked at me intently as I looked at her for several long seconds. She finally walked towards me.

"Johnny, I'm so sorry for your loss," she gently said, in almost a faint whisper. I could tell she was fearful about approaching me.

"Thank you, Olivia," as she kissed me on the cheek and gave me a brief hug.

We both stood there in the church parking lot, feeling awkward and not having a lot to say to one another at that moment. We were both silent, struggling to make conversation.

"How is your abstinence going," she suddenly asked, referring to my being sober.

"Good," I proudly replied. "It's been almost six months. I still go to AA meetings on Wednesday nights."

"Congratulations," she smiled. For some odd reason, her approval meant so much to me at that moment.

"Did you want some company? We can take my car and drive together if you like."

Since my sons, who were the pallbearers, were riding with my sister Rosanna, I figured riding with her wasn't a bad idea. Besides, my sisters were so grief-stricken, I wasn't in the mood to be in the funeral procession in the same car with them from Sterling Heights down to Mt. Olivet on McNichols and Van Dyke.

"Okay," I agreed.

I had only seen Olivia Laurent a few times before the day of my mother's funeral, so I was pleasantly surprised that she had taken time off from work to come to the funeral service and pay her respects. We began walking towards her car and left with the funeral procession departing towards Mt. Olivet Cemetery.

As I got into her Lexus ES 350, I noticed the black rosary that was wrapped around her right hand as she was starting her car.

"Do you know how to pray with that?"

I asked.

Olivia smiled. "You're not a church-goer, are you?"

"No. Since losing my father when I was a little boy, I haven't been too fond of God or the Catholic church."

She looked at me while she was driving and maneuvering her car.

"Are you an atheist?"

I thought for a moment. "No. I do believe there is a God. I'm just not sure how He would allow such intense suffering and so many injustices to exist in this world."

"You're very bitter about losing your father, aren't you?"

I was silent for a moment.

"It was tough growing up without a father. Thank God for my uncles and especially my Uncle Ross. If it weren't for them, I don't know if I would have survived."

I looked out the window, trying not to make eye contact with her.

"I was drinking, smoking, and doing drugs by the time I was fourteen years old. I barely graduated from Cousino High School."

A silent moment.

"If it weren't for my Uncle Ross and my mother's loving patience, I would have been dead, face down somewhere years ago."

"Well, it looks like you straightened out your life," she complimented me.

"All except for the drinking. The alcohol has only gotten worse over the last several years, and it finally cost me, my family. I sometimes blame God for that."

Olivia looked at me and smiled.

"It's not God's fault. We are all put on this Earth, and we all have the freedom to live our lives the way we choose to live them. The Lord can only guide us through love, forgiveness, and prayer. He cannot fix all of the wrongs in this world when humanity has the power to choose, the power of free-will to decide right from wrong."

We were both silent for several moments.

"You're pretty religious, aren't you?"

Olivia looked at me and smiled.

"I'm not the best Christian in the world, but I've learned to find peace within the Church."

A few silent moments.

"I try to attend Mass every Sunday. And I say my prayers every night like a good little girl."

"Your mother taught you well," I smiled.

I thought about what she had said for a moment.

"Maybe that's what's missing in my life."

"What would that be?"

I didn't immediately answer her.

"Peace," I finally responded.

We followed the long motorcade down Fourteen Mile Road towards Van Dyke, past my mother's house in Warren, where the black

Cadillac hearse momentarily stopped on her street. It then proceeded past all of the red lights, along with several patrol cars escorting the procession to Mt. Olivet Cemetery on McNichols Road.

Olivia was fumbling through the radio stations, asking me several times what music I liked. I wasn't feeling very particular, as she selected an oldies station that was playing 1970s music. I then decided to be noisy.

"So, what Caribbean island were you on again?"

"A small island called Labadee. It's a small private island off the coast of Haiti. There are only a few hundred occupants there that have their secluded residences. It's quite isolated."

"Was that where your boyfriend lived?" I boldly pried.

She smiled but was initially silent for several long seconds.

"My boyfriend used to work for the Chicago Archdiocese. He came into quite a bit of money and purchased a large villa there off of the ocean."

I immediately saw right through that explanation.

"Your old boyfriend was a Catholic priest?"

She was quiet for a moment.

"For a time, yes."

Another silent minute.

"Oh, I see."

She was dating a Catholic priest. What the hell was that all about?

Olivia started nervously playing with the radio.

"Was this after your relationship with the Chicago detective?"

"Eh, yes," she said. I could tell she was getting somewhat nervous, answering my questions.

I looked at her for several moments from the corner of my eye, trying not to stare. Things weren't adding up in my head, and I was getting suspicious.

Perhaps it was the detective in me. I got the impression that Olivia Laurent had quite a checkered history regarding her past, previous relationships, and I wondered how all of it fits together. But I didn't want to judge her. God only knows that I had more than my share of personal issues and a checkered past as well. The fact that I was a recovering alcoholic was more than enough to scare anyone away.

More questions for another time, I thought to myself.

The funeral hearse finally pulled up in front of the many aisles of neatly arranged marble crypts towards the newly developed section of the cemetery, each row named after an obscure saint. We both stood there, outside of the mausoleum, as the pallbearers carried the coffin to Mom's final resting place. There was an open marble crypt at the third row from the bottom, whose stone slab had already been removed, awaiting the arrival of my mother's body.

The Catholic priest mumbled a few more prayers as each of the gatherers placed a red rose on top of the oak, wooden casket. All the mourners, including my family, stood silent as the special forklift raised the coffin, with two undertakers alongside it, and slowly pushed Isabella DiVito Valentino's body into the empty marble crypt, waist level in the third row.

At that moment, Olivia decided to leave me alone with my family as we said our final good-byes to my mother.

"Johnny, call me later, please," Olivia said as she quickly kissed me on the lips.

As I watched my mother become forever entombed, I said the Lord's Prayer to myself (what words I could remember), wishing eternal rest for her soul. With my face drenched with tears, I silently waited for the rest of the mourners to leave until I was the very last one facing Mom's gravesite...alone.

"I'm sorry I wasn't a better son, Mom," weeping to myself. I stood there in front of her crypt, her name, dates of birth, and death now already marked on her marble stone. I was there for at least fifteen minutes or more, left alone to grieve.

As I departed, I noticed Zio Rossano waiting for me, standing outside in the cemetery parking lot in front of his black Cadillac CTS. He gave me an intense hug, and we briefly cried together.

As we got into his car to drive to the funeral luncheon, I decided to ask him the question that has been on my mind since my mother's death. It had been bothering me, but I hadn't had the chance to approach my uncle alone until that moment.

"What did Mom say to you in Italian before she died?"

Ross Valentino just looked at me straight in the eyes.

"Do what you have to do."

CHAPTER SIXTEEN

MY MOTHER'S ATTIC-EARLY SUMMER 2019

It was a glorious Friday morning in June as I took my 1966 Corvette Stingray Convertible out of my storage unit and brought it over to the car wash on Nine Mile and Gratiot. Even though the classic car needed a paint job, I enjoyed keeping my car clean. The Blue Carriage Car Wash always had a special place in my heart, and it had been there for years. I remember my father taking me with him to that car wash on Sunday mornings to get his 1959 Oldsmobile Super Eighty-Eight cleaned and waxed as well. For me, taking my vintage car to that car wash was a weekend ritual, and I always thought of it as the beginning of a relaxing weekend ahead.

After spending a half-hour or more at the car wash, I drove over to my mother's house over on Twelve Mile and Schoenherr. Mom had died almost a month ago. I was to meet my sisters there to help them clean out and fix up the house that weekend. We were going to put it up for sale in the next few weeks. I was dreading all of the painting, repairing, and all of the improvements that needed to be done. There had been nothing fixed or replaced in that house since my father was alive over forty years ago. Her home on Doreen Drive had gotten dilapidated after all these years, and we were forced to do most of the work ourselves.

We had spent all of that weekend repairing and cleaning out the house and had all of the rooms painted by that Saturday evening. The furniture had either been donated to goodwill or sold outright at a low price to anyone interested. My sisters had a giant garage sale on that prior weekend, and we were able to get rid of most of my mother's belongings that none of us wanted. I had taken a few things for my apartment. Between my shopping spree at Art Van Furniture six months ago and some of my mother's dining room furniture, my home was finally furnished.

That Saturday, I dreaded going up into my mother's attic to clean it up and go through all of the boxes of stored clothing, tools, old tables, and chairs. As I finally went up there with my sister Rosanna, amidst all of the old junk, we found in the corner of the attic an old wooden trunk. It was loosely locked, and it only took one swing of the hammer to break it open.

There in the trunk were a lot of bags labeled with sentimental items that my mother was storing. There was a folded, plastic garment bag holding my mother's wedding dress, several shoeboxes of old letters and photographs, and three stapled paper bags labeled 'Detroit Police – Evidence Department.' The bags were written in black marker with the date of November 14, 1981, when the evidence bags were turned over to my mother. On the other side of each bag was a white label with the typed information:

Evidence – Homicide:
Valentino, Antonio – November 1, 1978.

"Are these what I think they are?" I said to my sister Rosanna.

"I remember when Mom got these from the detectives. She refused to open the bags and immediately locked them in the wooden trunk in the attic. She never wanted to go through them," my sister replied.

We took the three evidence bags and brought them downstairs to open with my sisters. At that moment, I felt myself having an uncontrollable meltdown. Against everything I had learned in Alcoholics Anonymous classes and with all of the positive encouragement of my family and friends, I lost all self-control. I hadn't had a drink in nine months but decided to reach for a bottle of Jim Beam Whiskey, which my mother had stored in the liquor cabinet. I knew I would need something to calm my nerves while I went through the evidence from the night of my father's murder.

"Johnny, I thought you stopped drinking," Lucia observed.

"I need something to help me get through this," I replied.

I poured myself a shot, took a long swallow, then I opened up the first bag. In that brown sack was my father's clothing, which included a blue Polo shirt, a pair of dark slacks, a brown belt, and a brown pair of shoes and socks with some very faint bloodstains. There was also a beige London Fog jacket that was stained with blood. In the next bag was his wallet, which contained a blood-stained payroll check from the Ford Motor Company for $167.31, a green change purse, and some blood-stained Fruit of the Loom white underwear.

My sisters began sobbing.

"Johnny, just stop. I can't do this anymore," Lucia said.

I poured myself another shot of whiskey, ignoring my sister's plea.

As I opened the last paper bag, several more personal items were inside, including a silver Timex watch with a black band, a little black phone number book which my father kept with him, and a white and brown handkerchief with more bloodstains. Lastly, there was a clear plastic bag containing an unusual item:

It was a green toy water pistol, which was stained with my father's blood.

I looked at my sisters, "What is this?"

"That's your toy squirt gun, Johnny. Dad used that toy pistol to try to fool the men who killed him that night."

I stared at that green, blood-stained water pistol, barely recognizing it from my childhood.

A million thoughts were going through my head. I started imagining what that object must have felt like in his hand, as it was the only thing that my father had as self-defense against his murderous killers.

An extensive foray of emotions began to envelop and overcome me. They were feelings of sorrow, anger, rage, but mostly revenge.

I took another shot of Jim Beam.

"Johnny, you stopped drinking. Please do not go off the wagon for this," Rosanna pleaded.

"Shut up, Rose," I yelled at her in my abusive tone of voice. I felt myself losing all control of my senses.

"Those bastards are still running around out there, while Dad's lifeless, cold body is lying in a marble condominium at Mount Olivet Cemetery. Those bastards deserve to die for what they did to Dad, to Mom, and all of us," I angrily shouted.

"Stop it, Johnny," Lucia yelled loudly.

"Nothing is going to change what happened to Dad and us. Let it go!" she emotionally begged.

"Nothing is going to bring him back," Rosanna also tried to reason, her black mascara running down her cheeks.

I poured another shot of Jim Beam. As I took another long swallow, I felt myself getting angrier and angrier. My sisters started copiously crying even louder.

We all stood around the table sobbing, staring at the brown paper bags from the evidence department of the Detroit Police. After about ten minutes of weeping and drinking the rest of that Jim Beam bottle, I looked at my sisters.

"What do you want to do with this shit?" I finally asked them.

Lucia, who was now still visibly upset, grabbed the three evidence bags from the kitchen table and went out to the garage with them. After several long minutes, I looked out of the sliding door in the family room and onto the backyard.

Lucia had stuffed the three evidence bags into a steel garbage can. I watched her pour some gasoline onto the contents and then light them on fire.

My sister and I went outside to watch Lucia finish burning the contents in the middle of my mother's backyard.

"You know, there are ordinances against backyard bonfires in Warren," I casually mentioned.

"Johnny, when are you going to let all of this shit go?" Lucia screamed.

"It's all because of Dad's death, right? It's Dad's death that screwed up your life? It's Dad's death that made you do drugs in high school? It's Dad's murder that made you start drinking?

And it's Dad's sudden passing that ruined your marriage and losing your family, right, Johnny?"

I felt my temper explode.

"Those hillbilly assholes are still walking around, Lucia! They took Dad away from us! They took Dad away from Mom. And those damn bastards got away with murder! They pleaded self-defense and got away with it because Dad had my fucking squirt gun in his pocket!" I yelled out at my sister while Rosanna was still crying.

"Really fair, huh, Sis? Those bastards never paid for what they did to Dad and us. Nice justice system! Somebody probably paid off the judge, and those three bastards got away with killing Dad. They ruined our lives!"

"Life isn't fair, Johnny! Get over it!" Lucia screamed.

"Yes, Lucia, life isn't fair! But it will be fairer after I put a bullet into the heads of those hillbilly bastards that killed Dad in cold fucking blood!"

"Stop it!" Rosanna demanded.

Rosanna finally came over and grasped my hand.

"Aren't you tired of being angry, Johnny? You're almost fifty years old. Aren't you tired of drinking and hating and making yourself so bitter over this?"

She looked at me, trying to calm me down.

"All of this bitterness and hatred takes way too much energy. You're wasting your whole life on anger and resentment. It's pushing you over the edge, Johnny."

She paused for a moment.

"Dad isn't coming back. It's been over forty years. You need to let this go."

"Sure," I retorted loudly. "While no one has given them the justice they so rightfully deserve?"

A moment of silence as the three of us stared at the impromptu garbage can fire in the middle of the back yard. I then confessed my confrontation with that Howard Williams at the Crazy Horse Lounge a few months ago.

"I saw the evil bastard that killed Dad at a bar on Eight Mile. I know it was him. He had the same name, and he fits the same description. He even had a hillbilly accent. When I tried to confront him, he pulled away from me. Then he laughed in my face as he was pulling out of the parking lot. It was him. I just fucking know it!"

I had worked myself into an intense, uncontrollable rage of fury. My two sisters then looked at me, now concerned. There was more silence as we stood around the fire.

"Let it go, Johnny. Please, let it go. All of this rage and revenge is going to kill you," Lucia pleaded.

I glared at my sisters as if venom were coming out of my pores.

"Not if I kill them first."

At that point, I was furious. I hastily grabbed my car keys and jumped into my Corvette. I began speeding down Twelve Mile Road, swerving from lane to lane, blowing off stoplights. Within about ten minutes, just as I was approaching Gratiot Avenue, a Roseville patrolman was behind me with flashing blue lights.

As he pulled me over, I showed him my Detroit police badge, along with my license and my insurance card.

"Common courtesy, right officer?" expecting the young patrolman to release me after a few minutes. I was sure at that moment he could smell the liquor on my breath.

The Roseville patrolman walked back to his squad car and, after being on the radio for several long minutes, walked back to my car.

"I need to ask you to step out of the car, Detective. I need you to take a sobriety test for me." He then pulled out the alcohol test kit.

"Could you blow into this for me, please?"

Now any good copper knows to never blow into a breathalyzer when pulled over, especially after having more than one drink. It wouldn't take a genius to figure out that I was over the limit for being under the influence of alcohol.

"Sorry, Officer, I can't do that. Can't we just let this one go?"

The very young patrolman, who looked old enough to be my son, put his right hand over his loaded gun holster and stepped back away from my Corvette. He looked like he was getting ready to draw his weapon.

"I need you to get out of the car, sir," the Roseville copper loudly demanded.

At that point, I knew this was going to get ugly. Realizing that I did not have my gun with me, I knew he was going to follow the book and bring me down to the station. For some reason, I was more worried about leaving my vintage car parked on the side of Twelve Mile Road than I was for myself.

"Can I at least put the top up and lock up my car, please?"

"Give me the keys, and we'll have it towed," he loudly said.

At that moment, I knew this young copper was going to be an asshole.

I got out of the car, and he ordered me to put my hands on the trunk of the vehicle. He then handcuffed me to put me in the back of his squad car.

I knew that it was going to be a very, very long night.

CHAPTER SEVENTEEN

ROSEVILLE POLICE DEPARTMENT

The drab, gray walls of the ten by twelve-foot Roseville prison cell were dreary and dilapidated as I sat on the single mattress situated within the middle of the room.

I had been there overnight, and I was understandably upset with not only the arresting officer but mostly with myself.

I had been doing so well since joining AA classes, and I just couldn't understand how I allowed myself to falter and suck down a bottle of Jim Beam last night. I let the haunting memories of my father's murder overcome me while going through his personal belongings from the night of his death.

It was as if his ghost had immediately assaulted me, and I had an emotional meltdown. All the sorrow, all the anger, and my intense need for justice and reprisal had become mixed into a deadly cocktail of mortal revenge. I wanted so much to pursue my father's killers last night while looking at the bloodstains of his old clothing, and I become overwhelmed with emotion. I had a total meltdown, and grabbing a bottle was the only way I knew how to cope.

I also could not understand why I wasn't allowed to have a hearing in Macomb County Court on a Sunday when I knew the courts did weekend arraignments. They insisted that I would not be able to bond out until Tuesday, as the courthouse was jammed with other criminal cases. Therefore, I had no choice but to spend the rest of the weekend at the Roseville Police Station.

Roseville Detective Al Iacobelli had come into my jail cell to visit me, and I told him that I was a Detroit Police Detective with the Third Precinct. He certainly wasn't amused or impressed. It appeared that there was no love lost between the Roseville and Detroit police departments. Getting pulled over in Roseville and informing them of my Detroit P.D. affiliation was like letting the Palestinians know that I was a Jewish special-ops agent from Tel-Aviv.

The Roseville Detective glared at me, and I could tell he was only interested in a large piece of my ass.

"Detective John Valentino, right?"

"Congrats," I sarcastically answered. "You can read a rap sheet. I'm impressed."

The extremely tall detective glared at me, as I could tell he didn't appreciate my unusual sense of humor.

"What were you doing driving drunk on Twelve Mile Road last night?" Detective Iacobelli curiously asked me. It was as though he was looking for a criminal case against me on what should only be a simple DUI case. I later came to find out that there was a long line of hatred and animosity between the Detroit and Roseville Police Departments.

"I don't think I need your permission to drive around Twelve Mile Road after a few shots of Jim Beam."

Detective Iacobelli smiled as he sat on a chair on the other side of my jail cell.

"Well, needless to say, you were under the influence, so you will pay the price for driving your vehicle so recklessly last night. I hope you're not too attached to your driver's license."

I looked at the detective.

"What is it with you guys? I feel like I'm being held against my will in some down south lockup with Sheriff Buford and his good old boys, Cletus and Bubba."

The detective scowled at me, not at all amused with my prison analogy.

"Which one are you," I point-blank asked him.

At that moment, I wondered if this guy had the guts to try and physically take a piece of me while I insulted his integrity and his backwoods, draconian police department.

"You city coppers think you can drive around drunk and assume all of us little police departments around Detroit are always going always to cut you guys a break," Iacobelli said.

"We take DUI's very seriously here in Roseville, Valentino. You're gonna wish you weren't on Twelve Mile Road last night."

I then started getting angry.

"Where am I again? Is this Roseville, Michigan, or Butcher-Holler, Arkansas?" I said with an angry, sarcastic voice.

Detective Iacobelli, who wasn't less than six feet, five inches tall, was massive and towered over my five-foot, ten inches, 170-pound frame. He was so tall that he probably got nosebleeds whenever he reached down to tie his shoes. Iacobelli was a big man, and my talking smart to him may not have been the best idea.

"It's too bad you don't have a Southern accent, Detective," I said. "You'd make a great Sheriff Buford," referring to the Smokey and the Bandit movie.

The towering Roseville detective only smiled.

"You're going to love it here in Roseville, Valentino. Because it certainly looks like you're going to be here for a while."

"Absolutely, Detective," I smiled. "Being that this is the white-trash capital of Michigan, I can't think of a better place to spend my time while waiting for my hemorrhoids to heal," I said.

One would have to admit that I was pretty good on my feet, and I most certainly wasn't going to take any shit from this asshole detective.

Iacobelli only smiled at me as he got up from the luxurious, plush wooden chair within my jail cell.

"Enjoy your stay at the Roseville Hilton, Detective. If you need room service, just clang your tin cup on the bars," as he left my prison and locked the door behind him.

Butcher-Holler, Arkansas indeed.

It was probably later in the afternoon when one of the prison guards came in to interrupt my long sleep on one of their uncomfortable prison cots.

"Valentino, you have a visitor," he only said as I quickly jumped up from my cot.

It wasn't ten seconds before a familiar voice was insulting me before he even walked into my prison cell.

"Well, well, if it isn't Detective Dumbass. Look who decided to start drinking again and fuck-up my Sunday afternoon?" he loudly said.

It was Commander Riley.

"Hey, Chief. What are you doing here?" I was surprised and shocked to see him of all people.

"No worries, Valentino. I had nothing else better to do on my day off than to fish you out of this Roseville shithole."

"How did you know I was here?"

"The day-shift sergeant, Sergeant Reynolds, used to be a patrolman in my precinct years ago, and he owed me a favor," Riley described.

"I'm holding your get out of jail free card," he said.

I couldn't tell if he was mildly amused or just totally aggravated.

"Man, Johnny, you couldn't catch a DUI in Clawson or Madison Heights? You had to get busted here in goddamn Roseville?"

"What's the story on Roseville, Chief? These guys are total assholes. I feel like I'm locked up in Stalag 13," I naively asked.

The Commander smiled and explained while he made himself comfortable in my plush, prison cell living room.

"One of our patrolmen in the Twelfth Precinct busted the Roseville Chief of Police coming out of a strip joint on Eight Mile Road a few years back. He was driving drunk and had two prostitutes in the back of his squad car. The Detroit News got a hold of it and splashed the story all over the papers. It eventually got on Channel Six ABC Eyewitness News. The Roseville Police Department was embarrassed and displeased about the charges, especially because the Twelfth Precinct didn't cut him a break," Riley recalled.

"The Roseville Chief of Police has since sworn vengeance against the Detroit Police Department. It's been open season here on city coppers ever since."

I smiled to myself and nodded my head, which explains why the little prick patrolman would not even consider letting me go last night.

It has always been an unspoken courtesy within all of the police departments in the Detroit metro area to assist and help each other out when busting another police officer in their field of jurisdiction, especially when a DUI is involved. I had personally played 'catch and release' to several area policemen when I was on patrol years ago, and I knew for a fact that the practice was still being done today. This is why I was so surprised that the Roseville Police were holding me on a Saturday night without having the chance to bond out.

"Sergeant Reynolds called me this morning as a courtesy call when he learned you were a Detroit copper," grinning from ear to ear.

"I promised him you wouldn't be driving again on Twelve Mile Road anytime soon."

"Well, that's going to be tough, considering my mother's house is on Twelve Mile and Schoenherr," I mentioned.

"Take I-696 to Van Dyke, then go east to Schoenherr. Stay out of Roseville, John. They're not very happy that I'm springing you out of here."

I thought about it, realizing that Commander Riley had, again, had my back, and went out of his way to help me out. I thought about how Riley had been overly vigilant in making sure that he had my back. It was like he was my guardian angel, always looking out for me.

"Oh, and in case you're wondering, your Corvette is here in the police parking lot," he mentioned.

"I thought they were gonna tow it?"

"They did. It was in some impound towing lot on McNichols Road. I had them bring it back on their dime," Riley said.

"How did you manage to do that?" I asked.

Riley was smiling, totally pleased with himself.

"I told Sargent Reynolds to put aside their little chicken shit grudge and start playing nice with the city coppers. I reminded him that our department was ten times bigger than theirs and that they needed to stop fucking with us."

He then paused with a smile.

"Or the next time we bust any of their boys in the city for as much as jaywalking, we would crucify and staple their fucking testicles together."

I started laughing.

"You've always been good at the art of negotiation, Chief," I complimented.

Riley's face suddenly became serious.

"Would you care to explain to me why you were drinking again? And then speeding down Twelve Mile Road no less?"

I looked at him, somewhat embarrassed, as I didn't want to go into the specifics.

"My sisters and I had been cleaning and fixing up my mother's house yesterday, and we got into a little disagreement," I explained.

The Commander looked at me, wanting to be more specific.

"You were doing so well, Johnny. I'm very disappointed."

"It won't happen again, Chief. I had a meltdown last night and found a bottle of juice in my mother's liquor cabinet."

"Well, you need to get back on track, kid. I'm getting tired of being your personal Father Flanagan. It seems like I'm bailing you out of trouble all the time," the old commander said.

We walked together to Sargent Reynold's front desk, where he had me sign some papers and gave me back my cell phone and car keys.

"Besides, I was in the middle of binge-watching 'Chicago P.D.' this afternoon, and I didn't appreciate having to get up off the couch," Riley continued.

"I was watching the part where Sargent Hank Voight kills the guy who murdered his son."

I chuckled as we were walking towards the exit door. I then became curious, as we were in the process of leaving the Roseville Police Department on Gratiot Avenue.

"Why are you doing this, Chief? It seems that whenever I get into trouble, you're always there," I curiously asked.

Riley looked at me, dismissing the question immediately.

"I like you, Johnny. You remind me of myself many years ago."

He then reprimanded and gave me a directive.

"Your penance is to check in with Dr. Trafficanta tomorrow morning before your shift and figure out how we can avoid this from happening again."

"Really?"

I didn't want to have to face that Anne Klein shrink again and have to stare at her prancing around her office, shaking her ass.

"Really," he repeated as he got into his squad car.

Within minutes he drove away, going southbound on Gratiot Avenue.

I was back at my apartment later that Sunday evening. I was rather hungry, so I decided to boil some water and a can of Contadina tomato sauce in a pot and make myself some pasta that night. As I was waiting for an hour for the sauce to cook and water to boil, I decided to pull out the old police reports from way back in November 1978. I wanted to familiarize myself again with all the parties that were involved in arresting my father's assassins as I was going to try and locate these killers. I took out a sheet of paper and started taking notes when I suddenly went into a mild state of shock.

While going through the police files, I found out the name of the arresting officer and the lead detective who was in charge of the investigation into my father's homicide.

His name was Detective Joseph Riley.

CHAPTER EIGHTEEN

THE LEGAL ASSISTANT-EARLY SUMMER 2019

A black Lexus ES 350 pulled into the parking lot of the busy retail center located on the corner of Fourteen Mile Road and Van Dyke. Several cars were trying to maneuver their way in and out of the various parking spaces that were sparse on that late Thursday afternoon in June.

A pretty, dark-haired lady in her early fifties closed her car door behind her after she grabbed her purse. She had just gotten off of work, as she worked as a legal assistant for a law firm in Mount Clemens. She had been gainfully employed there for the last twenty years, and her employer, Benedict Segesta, was very appreciative of the fine job she did for his law firm. Not only was she an excellent legal assistant, but she was also a great office manager. She did everything for the three-partner law firm of Segesta, Alesia, and Viviano, P.C., which included billings, collections, accounts payable, and various drafts of different contracts and real estate closings.

There were five retail stores located within the strip mall in Sterling Heights, which included an Italian Deli, a Palestinian restaurant, a Seven-Eleven convenience store, and a small lady's shoe boutique. But it was the store discretely located at the far end of the strip mall that she was interested in visiting. That store was almost hidden from public view and was hard to see from either Van Dyke or Fourteen Mile Road. The store remained locked at all times, and each customer had to be buzzed in before being allowed to enter.

The pretty, middle-aged brunette pressed the doorbell, and she was allowed inside. The store was stocked with display cases holding various and expensive inventory that one needed a firearms card to possess and buy legally.

Second Amendment Guns and Ammo has been located on Van Dyke for the last fifty years. They enjoyed a steady stream of loyal customers, ranging from first-responder police and security officers to the deer and game sportsmen.

The legal assistant had previously received her FOID card and had her background checks by the state police before that day.

A store employee immediately greeted her.

"May I help you?"

"Yes, I'm the person who called earlier regarding the purchase of a Beretta handgun."

"Oh, yes, I remember talking to you," the helpful, older gentleman said. He then immediately guided the legal assistant over to the gun case with the handguns she was specifically looking for. He brought her over to the detailed display case, which had an extensive inventory of the particular handguns that she was interested in purchasing.

"You mentioned something about Beretta handguns, yes?"

"Yes," she replied.

She had heard that the Italian made handgun was an excellent quality weapon, handcrafted, easy to fire, and never jamming or malfunctioning.

"We have an extensive inventory of Beretta's here in this display case. We sell more

Beretta's here at this store than any other gun shop on the East Side."

The display case was filled with several different models of the Beretta handgun. Their models ranged from M92 and .22 caliber pistols to Neos .22 and Magnum automatic weapons.

The legal assistant held a few of the different models of Beretta handguns in her hands, as the salesman explained to her which one would be the most accessible gun for her to maneuver with the least amount of recoil, or 'gun kick-back.' After several demonstrations of the unloaded guns, she chose the Beretta 92X Centurion Semi-Auto Pistol. There seemed to be the least amount of short-recoil, and the vertex-style grip panels made it comfortable to hold in her hand and fire the weapon.

The salesman took her to the front desk and began filling out the paperwork.

"Could I have your name, please? I will also need some identification."

"Of course," as she tendered her driver's license and her FOID card.

"Lucia Valentino," the salesman read her identification out loud.

Lucia had just had her driver's license changed back to her maiden name, having just gotten divorced from her husband of twenty-six years. She had three grown children, Silvana, 25, Adrianna, 23, and Dominic, 21 years old.

Her oldest daughter, Silvana, was an airline stewardess for United Airlines. She was engaged to be married to her fiancé Peter next summer. Her middle daughter Adrianna was an ICU nurse at Beaumont Hospital in Royal Oak and lived with her boyfriend, Scott. Her youngest son, Dominic, was still living at home and finishing his final year at Michigan State. He would be attending Wayne State Law School next year.

Lucia and her husband, Gino Bavaro, had a very tumultuous marriage. Her husband had a ferocious temper, and she had him arrested several times. After twenty-six years of constant fighting, physical abuse, and his continuous philandering, Lucia had endured enough. Her husband was a cement concrete contractor and, although he was able to provide a very nice lifestyle for her and the children, she could no longer tolerate the physical and emotional abuse.

Her husband, Gino, even though he was a lousy husband and father, was very much against the divorce. He did everything in his power, including physically threatening and abusing her, to keep her from divorcing him. She had gotten a court order of protection against him from the Grosse Pointe Police Department on several occasions. Lucia had to beg her hot-tempered and protective brother, Johnny, from getting involved in keeping her husband from physically harming her. She had to get in the middle of a physical altercation between her brother and her husband, where Johnny had severely beat him up within an inch of his life.

When the two-year divorce proceedings were finalized, Lucia kept the house in Grosse Pointe Woods and one of their rental properties in Boca Raton, Florida.

Along with her legal assistant job in Mount Clemens, Lucia was now financially and emotionally, much better off than when she was married.

She was now working out, doing Yoga and Zumba classes four times a week, and taking a creative writing course at Macomb Community College. Lucia was starting to take control of her life, doing the things that she wanted to do and not having to worry about answering to anyone else.

But she needed security. She needed peace of mind. She needed protection.

And the only way Lucia was going to be able to acquire that was by being able to protect herself. She had been on the wrong end of her husband's temper way too many times and did not need him showing up angry and unannounced to her home and making any more violent threats against her.

Lucia Valentino was not without her faults. As the middle of three children, she was barely nine years old and in the fourth grade when the front doorbell awakened her on that early morning of November 1, 1978.

She remembers that horrific morning as if it were yesterday, as two Detroit detectives appeared at their home in Warren to tell them that their father had been murdered. Lucia was the one who had to wake up her six-year-old little brother Johnny and say to him that Daddy would not be coming home again.

Like her siblings, Lucia grew up very bitter with the loss of her father, and as a result, she was especially close to her mother, Isabella. Lucia clung to her loving mother incessantly as a young child after the loss of her father, always fearful that she would lose her mother as well. Lucia was still at her mother's side, from the time she was little until her mother's recent death from breast cancer.

By all accounts, Lucia grew up to be a very emotionally strong adult and somewhat unapproachable. She had a reputation of being the 'ice bitch' in high school and appeared to be extremely cold and aloof to her few close friends.

"Is this gun for home security, Ms. Valentino?" the salesmen asked.

Lucia thought for a moment.

"Eh, yes. I live alone now."

"As you know, we have to process your FOID card. But once you have clearance, you can come in and pick up your gun and ammunition."

"That would be great," Lucia replied as she tendered her VISA card for the $679.67 invoice for the firearm and ammunition.

"I gave you three firing range sessions for free that you can use anytime between now and the next six months," the salesman said as Lucia was signing her credit card receipt.

"That will be great. I'm sure I will need the practice."

Lucia Valentino thanked the salesman and walked out of the gun and ammo store and back to her Lexus parked in the strip mall parking lot. Before she started her car, she sat there with both hands on the steering wheel, thinking.

There were other reasons for her to buy that Beretta firearm. Besides the potential threat of her ex-husband, there was a more important reason. Lucia had not been able to sleep very well since finding out from her Detroit P.D. detective brother that the man who had instigated her father's murder was back in town.

Lucia was privy to the promise that her Uncle Ross had made to her mother, to not take retribution against any of her father's killers while she was alive. She was more than aware of the 'maloccio' or vendetta that Rossano Valentino had placed on her father's murderers on the day of the trial when they were exonerated.

Lucia asked her mother a lot of questions over the years, as she was extremely close to her. Because of her religious beliefs and being a devout Catholic, her mother would never allow anyone in the family to take revenge against the men who had so abruptly taken their father and husband away from them.

But Lucia had her problems growing up without a father as well. She never got over the bitterness of growing up without a father-figure that she could love and trust.

It took her a long time to accept the fact that her father had been not only murdered but had been killed by the jealous husband of a lady with whom he was allegedly having an affair. It was difficult for her to grow up without a father figure, without a male role model that she could look up to while growing up.

She never had the chance to be a 'Daddy's Girl,' to be spoiled by a dad who would splash her with love and affection throughout her life.

Little Lucia would spend many nights sitting in front of their picture window, imagining what it would be like to watch her father come home from work and spend time with the family. She recalled the family dinners they used to all enjoy together, especially on Sundays.

It was a beautiful life at home that Lucia remembered. She would watch every red and white pickup truck that would go by, hoping that one of them would pull into their driveway and her father would magically appear.

She spent many parent-teacher conferences during her grade school years, watching all of her friends bringing their fathers to school to meet their teachers. She even recalled her freshman year at Regina High School, when all of her girlfriends got to go to the father-daughter dance except her. All of her girlfriends learned to drive with their dads, and she would recall all of the doting fathers taking pictures of their beautiful daughters in their prom dresses.

It was during her years in high school that she could not comprehend the emotional distress that came with missing her father and not understanding why he died the way he did. It was a blessing from heaven when her high school counselor, Sister Giovanna, intervened and helped her to control and understand the many emotions that came with growing up without a father.

She was always eternally grateful to 'Sister Joanne' for the guidance she had given her. After graduating from Regina, she wrote and continued to correspond with her.

Lucia Valentino was mildly upset when her brother Johnny told her and her sister that he had approached one of their father's murderers in the parking lot of the Crazy Horse Lounge. She was well aware of the adverse effects that growing up without a dad made on her brother's life.

And now, with her mother gone, her brother was drinking again and vowing revenge against their father's killers.

Lucia continued to sit in the parking lot of that strip mall on Fourteen Mile and Van Dyke, mulling over her terrible childhood and her miserable marriage.

Yes, she thought to herself. This new Beretta firearm was going to come in handy. It will give her the protection and the security she needed now in her life. But once she had the practice of using the firearm, she knew that this gun would be useful for another reason: It will keep her brother from doing something stupid while being in a drunken, angry state of mind.

Perhaps this Beretta will be useful in assisting her in controlling her brother's violent temper while he attempted to fulfill their Uncle Ross's vow of revenge.

Perhaps this new firearm would keep her little brother from taking out that old hillbilly, the man who plotted and murdered their father. This gun, she hoped, would give her the power to protect Johnny from himself in attempting to take revenge against that murderous bastard that ruined their young lives.

With the grip of that gun in her hands, no one was ever going to emotionally hurt her or her family ever again.

CHAPTER NINETEEN

THE THIRD PRECINCT

It was eight o'clock on a sunny Monday morning in June when I pulled my squad car into the parking lot of the Third Precinct on West Grand Boulevard. It had been a long weekend, spending part of it painting and fixing up my mother's house and part of it in a Roseville jail cell. The parking lot was full, and I was tempted to double park my police car as I pulled up in front of the Third Precinct. But I thought better of it, knowing that I would probably be sitting at my desk most of the day. I patiently waited for another police patrol car to pull out before grabbing the next parking space.

My detective pallie, Mike Palazzola, was already sitting at his desk, waiting to greet me as I walked in the door. He had his usual cup of coffee in his hand and was eating what looked like a stale donut from the weekend.

"What's up, Johnny? How was your weekend?

"Great, if you like bonding with Roseville coppers."

"What happened?"

"I got pinched on Twelve Mile Road after a couple of drinks. The little prick copper wasn't playing 'catch and release'".

Mike looked surprised. "Those bastards! Do you know how many of those assholes I've busted for drinking and driving over the years? Especially on Eight Mile Road! How many times I would only shake their hands and let them slide?"

I nodded my head in agreement.

"I know. Me too."

Mike was still shocked, "I wonder what that's all about?"

"Something about a grudge against city coppers. Somebody in the Twelfth Precinct busted their commander coming out of one of those strip joints on Eight Mile Road, all juiced up with two working girls in the back seat last year," I eagerly answered while walking into the kitchen to get a cup of well-deserved coffee.

Detective Palazzola was walking carefully behind me as if he had nothing else better to do that morning. When it came to Detroit P.D. juicy gossip, Palazzola was our precinct 'Mrs. Kravitz'."

"Those sons-of-bitches! Just wait until I catch one of those Roseville coppers on Eight Mile Road again."

I smiled and shook my head, finding my way back to my desk. I had some burglaries and some auto theft reports that I needed to finish up, so I had more than enough work to keep me busy. As I was getting up to go to the kitchen and get a coffee refill, Commander Riley called me into his office.

Right away, I knew I was busted. I found my way to one of the chairs in his office.

"Valentino? Weren't you supposed to be at Dr. Trafficanta' s office this morning?"

"Yeah, Chief. I called her office early this morning, and she wasn't in," I lied, figuring that getting an eight o'clock appointment with the police psychologist on a Monday morning was going to be next to impossible.

I noticed a few library books sitting on the other side of his desk. One of them was titled 'Leaves of Grass' by Walt Whitman.

"You need to get in there today," he demanded. "We can't have you getting another relapse. You've got to get back on track."

"I understand, Chief. I will call her again this morning," I dutifully answered.

Sitting down on a chair in front of his desk, I decided to confront Commander Riley about something that had been bothering me for a while. It was especially troubling me when I found out that he was the lead investigator in my father's 1978 homicide investigation.

"So, Chief, I was going through the police reports for my dad's homicide over forty years ago," I started the conversation.

"Yes," he nodded his head.

"You signed off on those reports. You were the lead investigator."

Commander Riley looked at me, trying to control his reaction to my question.

"Yes?" he nodded.

"Well?" I was trying to prompt him for a reaction.

"Well, what?"

"Why didn't you ever say anything to me about it, Chief? I had no idea that you were involved in that investigation."

Riley looked at me, almost stunned at my even asking him. He briefly looked out the window of his office behind him, practically turning his back on me while he attempted to answer my question.

"I've been on the police force for almost forty-five years, John. I had never seen such a travesty, such a miscarriage of justice as when we investigated the murder of your father," he started.

As Riley was beginning to explain, he kept staring out of the window as if he couldn't make eye contact with me while talking.

"We handed those three bastards to the Wayne County Prosecutor all tied up and wrapped with a nice little red bow. It was very obvious to us that it was a blatant, premeditated murder. Those three bastards should have gotten life in jail, and perhaps even the death penalty. We knew that the lady's husband had planned every detail of that murder. He set up his friends, even got them drunk before following your dad from work that night. He made sure that he wasn't the one handling the gun."

"You mean Howard Williams?"

"Yeah, that's him. He had made sure that those other men were the only ones that were roughing him up and doing the shooting. The fact that there was a plastic toy gun involved, carried by the victim, should have never played into that case."

Riley was now talking in a loud, angry voice.

"He made sure the others were doing his dirty work."

Riley continued to stare out the window, still shaking his head.

"Those guys were into Williams for some money. Williams was a mobbed-up bookie for the Licavoli's at the time, and those guys knew that if they did a good job roughing up his wife's boyfriend, that he would cover their markers."

He was silent for a few moments.

"He set those guys up to kill your father that night. Then the Wayne County judge on the case let them all off on some stupid self-defense charge. That murder was anything but self-defense."

I sat there silently listening to his every word.

"Those rotten bastards planned to kill your father in cold blood. It's bothered me for over forty years."

We were both silent for several long minutes. Riley's face then changed as he looked directly at me.

"What are you doing, going through those police reports? Why are you rehashing all of this shit?"

At that moment, I felt that I needed to confess.

"We were at my mother's house cleaning her things and getting ready to put it on the market. My sisters and I found the evidence bags up in the attic with all of my father's belongings on the night of the murder. One of them was the green squirt gun that was at the scene of the crime."

"Is that why you were all juiced up, driving down Twelve Mile Road the other night?"

"Well yeah, Chief. All those unpleasant memories and bitter issues were going through my head."

Commander Riley then looked at me straight in the eyes, as if he already knew what was going through my mind.

"Forget it, Johnny. Get it out of your head."

"Get what?" I innocently answered. It was as though he had read my thoughts.

"Everyone in the department at the time knew and heard about the vendetta your Uncle Rossano swore on those murder suspects after their trial. We all heard it at the courthouse."

I sat there, trying to look like I didn't know anything.

"In fact, one of the patrolmen was assigned to tail around your uncle for several weeks after the trial because we were all convinced that he was going to take Williams and his buddies out himself. We have detailed surveillance reports on him."

At that moment, I said something that was totally from my heart, and I was candid with the Commander.

"You should have let my Uncle carry it out, Chief. They would have never gotten away with Dad's murder."

Commander Riley looked at me, startled at my statement. He was silent for several moments.

"He probably would have been out of jail by now," I pointed out.

Another moment of silence.

"That wouldn't have brought your father back. Besides, with Williams' deep, dark connections, you don't know if it would have stopped there. That's probably why he was strongly encouraged to leave town after the trial."

I tried to get him to look directly at me.

"Who did the arm twisting?"

"Don Licavoli, probably. The rumor around town was the Licavoli Family wasn't pleased when they found out that the man Williams and his friends killed was a fellow Italian with a young family. Everyone felt terrible about it, especially the other coppers within our precinct."

"Is that why you've always looked out for us?"

The Chief then made direct eye contact with me.

"Johnny, isn't your birthday at the end of July?"

I nodded my head.

"Do you and your sisters remember getting a birthday card with cash stuffed inside on your birthdays for several years after your Daddy died?"

"Yes."

I recalled getting birthday cards until I had graduated from Cousino High School, signed by the Detroit Police Department and stuffed with variant amounts of money ranging from twenty to fifty dollars in cash. My sisters would get birthday cards from the police department as well during their birthdays. Those birthday cards were part of the many reasons why I wanted to be a cop. I always thought that it was so impressive that the police department would remember my sisters and me after my father died.

"Who do you think was sending out those cards?

I looked at him as he nodded his head.

"I still remember that morning when Detective Miller and I went to your house in Warren to tell your mother about your father's murder. I can still see you as a little boy, sitting on the floor of the kitchen, crying in the corner."

He paused for a moment.

"I remember it as if it were yesterday. It broke my heart."

The Commander became very quiet and melancholy.

"I would always take up a collection with the other coppers, and we would all chip in a few dollars so that you and your sisters would have a nice birthday."

"So, that's why you've had my back, huh, Chief?" I smiled.

It was apparent that Riley was very fond of me ever since I was transferred to the Third Precinct.

Riley smiled. "Don't let it go to your head, Valentino. One of these goddamn days, I'm going to let the hungry wolves eat your ass up alive."

As I was ready to get up, he repeated his initial warning.

"Forgetta' about it," Chief said in his fake Italian accent.

"Forget what?"

Riley looked at me with that serious look on his face.

"We all know that Howard Williams is back in town. Forget about enforcing your uncle's vendetta, Johnny. It's been over forty years, and nobody is going to believe that you're not involved if anything happens to him."

I got up and looked at him, winking my eye.

"I'll make sure I have a good alibi, Chief," I kiddingly smiled as I got up to leave his office.

"Johnny, don't do it. Let it go. Think about your boys. You still have to lead a good Christian example for them. Enforcing an old, family vendetta against your father's killers is not going to bring your dad back. Besides, he's a harmless old man now. He's just not worth it."

I tried to make light of it, trying not to tip my hand about what was really on my mind.

"Don't worry, Chief. I won't be on the six o'clock news anytime soon."

"Call Dr. Trafficanta," he loudly and sternly repeated. "Don't let me find out you're sucking down any more bottles."

I left his office and went back to my desk, trying to concentrate on the various police reports that I needed to finish on that day.

Throughout the whole time, I kept thinking about all of the nice things Riley had been doing for me since revealing that he was the one behind those birthday cards while I was growing up. I remember my mother starting to cry every time she would give me one of those cards from the Detroit P.D.

She thought so highly of the Detroit Police Department. I remember my mother being so honored and excited when I told her I was going into the police academy and would eventually join the Detroit police force.

My mother always spoke to others about me with so much pride, informing everyone who would listen about what an honorable profession I had chosen. She was so proud of my being a first responder and looking after others within the community.

Maybe it was for that reason that my mother didn't wish any vengeance against my father's killers. She only wanted peace. And she knew that as long as she was alive and my uncle was intent on fulfilling his grudge against Williams, that she would never have peace in her life.

But Commander Riley also knew that now, with my mother's recent passing, everything was from this moment forward was about to change.

From now on, all bets are off.

CHAPTER TWENTY

JONI WILLIAMS HARPER-SUMMER 2019

Howard Williams was driving eastbound on Marine City Highway that muggy July evening, about to make a left-hand turn into his trailer park in Chateau Estates. He just had dinner with his sister at her house in New Baltimore and was struggling to keep his eyes on the road. Williams had a few shots of Jack Daniels earlier that evening. He was looking forward to relaxing and passing out again on his couch watching 'McMillian and Wife' and 'Columbo' reruns on MeTV.

As he pulled into a single parking space in front of his trailer home, he noticed a red Mercedes SL Convertible with Tennessee license plates parked in the area next to his, and his front door was wide open. Williams was perplexed, wondering at first how some unknown person from Tennessee had gotten into his new trailer home.

He then groaned, realizing who it was.

"Oh shit," he said to himself as he opened the door.

"Surprise, baby," a familiar voice loudly exclaimed as she was sitting on the couch with the TV on, holding a glass tumbler with a drink in her hands.

It was his ex-wife, Joni.

"How did you get in here?" he asked.

"Oh, c'mon, honey. Bad habits are hard to break. You always leave an extra key under the doormat. You've always done that since we were married," Joni answered.

Howard had always kept an extra key under the mat of his home so that when he arrived drunk, he wouldn't have to fumble with his keys and struggle to get into his own house.

Joni was smoking one of her Virginia Slims, holding a cigarette and her drink tumbler with her right hand as she got up to hug her ex-husband.

"It's been so long, Honey," as she tightly hugged Williams, making sure that she didn't spill any liquor or cigarette ashes on his new carpeting.

Joni Williams Harper was a frumpy, older lady in her late sixties, with dyed, Elvis jet-black hair and overdone make-up. She was significantly overweight but always managed to squeeze her size sixteen figure into her size twelve pants. She was wearing a black, short-sleeve sweater to cover her over-sized breasts and several pieces of cheap, gold necklace jewelry.

Since the two of them divorced almost forty years ago, Joni left Detroit and moved back to her hometown of McMinnville, Tennessee, with her sister. She eventually remarried a wealthy real estate broker, and they remained together until his recent death from lung cancer over three years ago. After many years of hatred and animosity, Joni had recently reconciled with her first husband.

Williams was more than surprised to see his ex-wife in his trailer home that evening. Since moving away from Tennessee, he was looking forward to living a quiet life away from all of the drama that had besieged him down South. His twin sons had grown up to be drug addicts, with one dying from a drug overdose and the other doing eight to ten years for armed robbery and dealing drugs at the Bledsoe County Prison in Pikeville, Tennessee.

It was never a secret as to why the two of them originally divorced back in 1979. Howard Williams was always known for his violent, jealous rages in his younger years. Joni liked to play the game of making her husband angry and resentful in their rocky marriage.

She would openly go out and sleep with other men, cheating on him whenever their marriage hit a rough patch. Williams had always threatened to do something drastic whenever she played her dangerous, stupid little games. But Joni never took her crazy husband's jealous rages seriously.

That is until he and his friends hunted down and killed one of her boyfriend's one evening after work.

Never blaming herself for her boyfriend's murder, she tried to get as far away as she could from her violent, raging husband. She realized too late that Howard Williams was capable of doing anything, and she was rightfully very bitter. Williams and his friends had no right to take the life of a family man away from his wife and children on Halloween, 1978. She was only having fun, and her affair with Valentino wasn't serious.

Joni later married a wealthy real estate broker named James John 'Jimmy-John' Harper. They settled down in Hermitage, Tennessee, and lived a charmed life for thirty-six years, far away from her horrific Detroit past.

Harper doted on his wife, showering her with cash, gifts, pre-paid credit cards, and extravagant vacations. There was always a new

Mercedes parked in the garage of their lavish, 6,500 square foot mansion, and Joni never had any limitations to how much money she could spend on herself and her friends.

Of course, being married to a real estate tycoon didn't slow down her sexual appetite. Joni continued going out to the bars, picking up and sleeping with different men. She would always raise the volume up on the radio whenever she heard the seventies song 'Lyin' Eyes' by the Eagles, figuring that the song was probably written especially for her. Her second husband, who was significantly older, would always turn a blind eye to Joni's philandering, figuring that he was way too old to get a divorce and start his life over again.

When Harper died of lung cancer at the age of 78 years old, Joni was shaken into a very cruel reality. Jimmy-John Harper had left the bulk of his multi-million-dollar estate to his sister and nephews, leaving her practically penniless. Being forced to sell their home to pay the back taxes, she was left with no other assets and very little money to live.

Joni was now struggling to survive on her $880 per month social security check. She was back living with her sister, trying to sell and make whatever occasional real estate deals she could on the side.

Howard Williams, however, was in a far better position to retire. Having been in the Plumbers and Pipefitters Union for almost forty years, he had a comfortable pension. He was now on the receiving end of a distribution from his brother's estate and was now living in a new, paid-for mobile home in Marine City.

It did not take a Wall Street genius to figure out why Joni was suddenly nice to her ex-husband again. It was quite apparent to everyone that Joni Williams Harper was now broke. Other than her used red Mercedes Convertible and her cheap costume jewelry, she didn't have two quarters to rub together.

After over forty years of being blindly in love with Joni, Howard finally started to see the truth about his ex-wife. Williams finally figured out that his once glamourous, Marilyn Monroe look-a-like wife had not aged very well and had very little to show for her selfish, evil, gold-digging ways. Joni was now a 68-year-old alcoholic, trying to pretend she was still thirty. Joni even went out almost every evening to the local bars and lounges, hoping she could again bait the same men to satisfy her sexual appetite that she did over forty years ago.

While Williams spent most of his life trying to win back the heart of his beloved ex-wife Joni, he was now only interested in getting as far away from her as possible. Howard, until recently, never considered being with another woman. He always held out a flame for his ex-wife, hoping that she would eventually come back. But now, things have significantly changed.

For Howard and Joni, their relationship fell under the '*Be Careful What You Wish For*' category.

Howard Williams moved back to Detroit to be with his surviving siblings, to be around their families, and to get as far away as possible from his ex-wife and all of her toxic, selfish, narcissistic drama.

Joni Williams Harper was the last person he wanted to see in his mobile home on that summer evening.

"Joni, what are you doing here?"

"Oh, c'mon now, baby...that's no way to treat your ex-wife," as she planted a few wet, bourbon flavored kisses on his cheek.

"Aren't you excited to see me?" as she moved her hand up and down his crotch.

"Not really, Joni. The last time we talked, you were pretty drunk. You started rehashing some past shit that I didn't want to talk about anymore."

Joni smiled at her ex-husband Howard, pretending that she didn't have any clue concerning what he was talking about.

But Joni remembered their last argument quite vividly. During their previous fallout, Joni had blamed him for her poor financial condition, the death of one of their drug addict sons, and the imprisonment of their other son. But the one subject that always continued to come up and create animosity between them was the murder of Tony Valentino.

"You had no right to kill him!" she would always say.

"You were cheating on me," was Howard's usual response.

"He was just a friend," she would always retort, using the same description that she still used for all of her numerous past lover boyfriends.

Although Joni felt terrible for the way Tony had died forty years ago, she never assumed any blame for his murder.

"I killed for you, baby," was Howard Williams's standard excuse when his wife would bring up the subject of Valentino's murder many years ago.

But now, in his older years, Howard Williams had finally seen his ex-wife for what she really was.

Joni Williams Harper was now an old, drunken sex-addict who was too narcissistic to accept the blame for any of the problems that she so boldly created.

"Baby needs another drink," she cooed, planting another wet kiss on Williams's cheek.

Howard, being buzzed himself, had neither the strength nor the energy to throw her out of his trailer home. Williams had been sleeping alone since his last girlfriend had left him several months ago, so he figured that he would take advantage of the situation and allow her to spend the night with him.

Williams walked over to his kitchen cupboard and pulled the bottle of Woodford Reserve Bourbon. He then refilled her glass tumbler with three-fingers full and two fresh ice cubes, followed by a splash of water and lime.

Just the way this fucking bitch likes it, he thought to himself.

Joni went over to Howard and cautiously approached him from behind, unbuttoning his red flannel shirt and rubbing her hands up and down his chest.

"Did my baby miss Mommy," she whispered into his ear as he gave her the beverage. She had a thick, Southern accent that was quite distinctive. Joni was very difficult to understand when she was drunk and slurring her words.

Williams only smiled, figuring that for one evening, he would play along with his ex-wife-turned-devil-woman and happily allow her to have her way with him.

She continued to rub his crotch up and down repeatedly for several minutes until he began to react to her mild teasing.

"Does my baby need a magic pill?" she asked.

"Maybe later," he said as he broke from her embrace and walked over to the couch, carrying a bourbon drink of his own.

As he sat down and began fidgeting with the remote control, Joni unzipped his pants and started orally teasing and stroking him.

After several long minutes, Williams could not take it anymore. They both rose from the couch and walked into the master bedroom.

As all of this was going on, neither one of them bothered to look out the window of William's trailer home. There was usually so much activity taking place at the Chateau Estates that Howard never really paid much attention to all of the nearby noise and commotion that was going on in the vicinity.

The trailer park was filled with over a hundred other trailers, and the transients that moved in and out of that mobile home park were continuous. One never knew who their neighbors were, as new occupants seemed to move in and out of their mobile pads frequently.

It was now very dark outside, as there were only a few streetlights sparingly scattered throughout the trailer park.

Parked a hundred yards away from Howard Williams' trailer was a black, late model Ford Escape, with tinted dark windows and black, alloy wheel rims. The car almost looked mysterious, as if a hooded cape crusader were lurking and waiting in the darkness.

A very old vendetta was about to be fulfilled.

CHAPTER TWENTY-ONE

SUZANNE CARLETON – JUNE 1978

The last day of June 1978 was a hot one indeed, as Tony Valentino walked into the Georgian Café on Twelve Mile Road and Hoover to meet his brother Rossano for breakfast. The temperature was already 85 degrees, and it was barely ten o'clock in the morning. He had parked his red and white Ford pickup truck in front of the parking lot so that his brother would be able to find the restaurant easily and that he had already arrived. He had gotten off of work at midnight at the Ford Assembly Plant and had intended to get a few more hours of sleep before reporting for work again that afternoon at four o'clock.

Tony sat down at the booth near the window, and a very pretty blonde waitress approached him with two menus.

"Coffee?"

"Yes, please."

The waitress poured the freshly brewed black coffee into Tony's cup as he started acquainting himself with the breakfast menu. The young waitress was studying the new customer while he read the daily specials.

"Are you expecting anyone?"

"Yes," he said. "My brother should be here anytime."

She smiled at him after he winked at her with his response.

"Okay, Hon...I'll be back."

About ten minutes had passed when his brother Ross finally strolled into the small restaurant. They smiled at each other as Ross immediately sat down across from Tony. The waitress immediately assaulted him with her coffee pot.

"Coffee?"

"No, it's too hot for coffee. I'll take a nice cold Coca-Cola, easy ice, please."

"Of course," the waitress replies, still gazing at Tony while he wasn't looking.

"What took you so long?"

"I had to pick up a few things for Elvira at the store. I rushed here as fast as I could."

Rossano's wife, Elvira, didn't drive, and he took his wife everywhere she needed to go, which also included errands and grocery shopping.

They made small talk after ordering breakfast from the menu, both having scrambled eggs, sausage, and hash browns. Tony requested an English muffin, while Ross asked for a sesame seed bagel and cream cheese on the side.

They both talked for several minutes when Rossano pulled a large white envelope out of his back pocket and handed it to his older brother.

"Che cosa è questo?" he asked, inquiring what it was.

"Dead presidents," Ross immediately responded with a smile.

"What?" Tony looked bewildered, never hearing that term or description before.

"It's the money I owe you," he said in a loud whisper. "It's all there."

Tony opened the envelope and eyeballed the bundled cash currency, neatly and tightly enclosed in the white, manilla envelope.

It was five thousand dollars in cash.

"We should be squared up," Ross said.

Tony looked at his brother and winked his eye.

"What about the interest?" he joked.

"Your ass!" Rossano responded.

He was thankful to his brother for lending him the money for the down payment of his new house in Sterling Heights.

By then, their breakfast entrées had arrived, and it was apparent that they both were hungry. Tony hadn't eaten since getting off of work at midnight, and Ross didn't usually have breakfast unless he was meeting his brother, which they routinely did once or twice a week.

The waitress continued to watch Tony as he was finishing his breakfast with his brother. The restaurant was a small place with about twenty tables, and they were not very busy during that time of the morning.

As they both finished their breakfast, the waitress approached the table.

"Can I get you anything else?"

"No thanks, Suzanne. Just bring me the check, please," Tony said, reading the nametag on the waitress's long, brown apron.

He started studying the young lady who was serving them as she turned toward the kitchen to prepare their breakfast check. She was a cute blonde, probably no more than thirty years old, with an adorable figure. Ross noticed his brother staring at the waitress.

"Do you ever stop?"

"She's a cute girl," Tony said, making sure that his voice didn't carry. He was studying her while she sauntered around the restaurant, shaking her butt.

The waitress quickly returned as she handed the breakfast check to Tony.

"You two have a wonderful day," she said as she winked her eye at Tony.

Tony smiled as he looked at the bill. It was for $10.44, but she wrote something was on it that amused him.

The waitress had written her name and telephone number on the check, along with a smiley face and a message:

'Call me – 264-4902.'

Tony looked up at the waitress who was standing by the cash register, smiling and winking her eye.

Rossano looked at his older brother.

"Let me guess. She gave you her phone number, right?"

"Ross, we were just sitting here, having our breakfast. I didn't say anything to her. She just gave me her telephone number," Tony laughed.

Ross was used to his brother getting 'hit on' when they were together. At times it was almost embarrassing.

Tony never wore his wedding ring, which may have been part of the reason why he was always being hit on. There were many occasions when they would go out for dinner or to the movies, and Tony would have some strange lady talking or making a pass at him. Ross would feel bad when Tony would begin flirting back with them, especially in front of his wife.

Isabella learned to tolerate it, and she would seldom mention anything about it to her husband. His 'Adonis' good looks and his narcissistic, arrogant personality was a cross of her marriage that she had to bear. But she always took comfort knowing that whatever or wherever Tony would go, that he always came home every night to her. No matter what he did every evening after work, he always spent the night in their bed together.

As Tony went up to the cash register and paid the bill, Suzanne continued to look at him, steadily making eye contact.

The good-looking married man then nodded his head to her in acknowledgment.

"We'll see you later," Tony said, conceding that he would probably take advantage of her telephone number.

As they walked out to the parking lot, Ross admonished his brother.

"Tony, quando smetterai?" he angrily asked his brother, wondering when this will ever stop.

"What are you talking about?" he replied, trying to play stupid.

"Come on, Tony. That poor lady waits at home for you every night while you're out fucking around with every goddamn broad who makes a pass at you. When is this shit going to stop, Tony? Why in the hell do you bother staying married?"

Tony looked at his brother.

"We were both married too young. We started a family while we were still kids."

"That's still no excuse. You need to stop this."

Ross then looked at him with an angry, contorted look on his face.

"One of these days, you're going to find the wrong girl, and she will destroy you," he warned.

The way Rossano said it was as though he was predicting the future for his older brother. Antonio Valentino had always dismissed his brother's warnings, and he had no reason to take him seriously now.

He kissed his brother on the cheek and then got into his red and white Ford pick-up truck, driving away down eastbound Twelve Mile Road.

Later that afternoon, Tony had gotten dressed for work and began to leave his house for his shift at the Ford Assembly Plant. He kissed Isabella good-bye and got into his truck. As he was driving west down Twelve Mile Road, he stopped at a Seven-Eleven convenience store, where there was always an available payphone.

"Hello, Suzanne?" he said after inserting a quarter and dialing her number.

"This is Tony, from the restaurant this morning."

"How you doing, honey. I was hoping you would call."

They continued to flirt with each other over the payphone while Tony was looking at his Timex watch, making sure that he still had time to get to work.

"What are you doing tonight? I get off at eleven o'clock. Would you like to meet up for coffee later?"

"Sure," Suzanne replied, as they planned to meet up at a late-night restaurant on the corner of Van Dyke and Fourteen Mile Road.

Tony punched into work at the Ford Plant at 3:57 pm to start his shift as a forklift operator for the auto assembly division. He looked forward to meeting up with his new blonde conquest and hoped that he would have some fun after work.

After finishing his work shift, he was at the parking lot of the Villa Lounge by 11:15 that evening. The waitress from the Georgian Cafe was already there waiting for him in her blue 1977 Pontiac Grand Prix.

They went into the restaurant together. After enjoying some coffee and a quick meal, they were both sitting in his truck. The two of them were kissing, mashing, and grabbing each other like two high school kids in his Ford pick-up.

Suzanne Carlton was a thirty-year-old divorcee who had been married for a short time and had no children. She lived in a small apartment in Madison Heights and went to the community college part-time. Suzanne was taking general education classes as she was hoping to acquire her nursing degree someday and work for a large hospital.

Tony and Suzanne continued to get together for several nights after work until they finally decided to get a room for twenty dollars at the King Richard Motel on Van Dyke Road. They continued to meet up, as Tony occasionally called her from his favorite payphone at the Seven-Eleven store on Twelve Mile Road.

Suzanne had no issues with Tony being married with three kids at home. He had assured her that there were problems in his marriage and that Tony would be filing for divorce soon.

It didn't take long for Suzanne to realize that she had fallen deeply in love with Tony. Even though he was married, she was willing to share him with his family and would do anything to have him. Suzanne was ready to continue the relationship, even if it were for just a few stolen hours at night after his shift. They went to the King Richard Motel a few nights a week, staying there until almost three o'clock in the morning.

By now, Isabella was getting suspicious, as her husband was coming home later and later. Tony only lied to her, telling her that he was meeting up with friends after work or stopping at their new house, which they had just purchased on Schoenherr Road.

By that time, Tony was rehabbing and fixing up the house, hanging up drywall, and updating the kitchen. They had put their home up for sale in August. He was spending a lot of time there before and after his shift at the Ford Plant.

By the time the Labor Day weekend had come around, their intense, romantic affair was over. Tony had simply stopped calling her. Suzanne went to the Villa Lounge at 11:15 for several nights, but Tony never showed up. She knew that she couldn't call him at home and only knew that he worked at the Ford Plant on Twenty-Three Mile Road and Mound.

By the end of September, Antonio Valentino had a new girlfriend, Joni, who worked in the sewing department of their Ford Plant. Tony was no longer interested in his old flame from the Georgian Cafe. Although Joni was married for several years, she had no problem meeting up with him after work. By now, they were spending hours together at his new house on Schoenherr Road in Sterling Heights.

Suzanne had not seen or heard from Tony. She then decided to track him down at the Ford Plant one night after his shift.

As Tony was exiting the plant, arm in arm with his new girlfriend, Suzanne Carlton, was waiting for him at his truck.

"Hello Tony," she eagerly said.

Embarrassed, he excused himself from Joni and angrily approached his distraught old girlfriend.

"Suzanne?" he said in an aggravated voice. "What are you doing here?"

"We need to talk, Tony. You disappeared, and I haven't been able to contact you."

Tony, totally embarrassed, only looked at Suzanne.

"I'm sorry, but I don't want to see you anymore."

"So, you used me, you fucked me, and you tossed me aside. Well, we now have a little problem, asshole."

Tony looked at her, now bracing himself for what she was about to say.

"I'm pregnant, Tony. And yes, it is definitely your baby."

A moment of silence.

"Are you sure?"

"Yes, Tony. I'm sure."

Tony Valentino was speechless, and the two of them didn't say a word to each other. There were several long minutes of silence.

"How could this happen, Suzanne? You said you were on the pill."

"I was on the pill, Tony. I must have forgotten to take it a few times. I don't know what happened."

Tony was trying to hold his temper, wondering if Suzanne had successfully entrapped him.

"So? What do you want to do?" Tony asked.

The two of them sat there quietly in his pick-up truck.

"I don't know, Tony. I'm not ready to have a baby right now, and you're married. I don't want to do anything to ruin your life. But you're a real asshole for not calling me anymore and not letting me know that you no longer wanted this relationship."

There was more silence.

"How far are you along?"

"Twelve weeks. I haven't had my period in two months, and I just took the pregnancy test the other day. I have a doctor's office appointment tomorrow."

Tony Valentino looked at Suzanne, trying to look sympathetic. He knew that he couldn't have another baby to care for at this point in his life. He was about to turn 41-years-old in a few weeks and did not need the burden of bringing in and taking care of an illegitimate child besides his wife and three children.

He immediately thought about his options. He knew that no matter what was decided that his loving wife Isabella would never divorce him. She needed him, and for personal and religious reasons, would never entertain the idea of a divorce.

"You can't keep this baby, Suzanne."

"You can't go around killing things either," Suzanne immediately replied.

"Well, if you abort this baby, I will pay for it and give you the money. That is all I can do. I can't afford to take care of you and another family," he reasoned.

Suzanne began to lose her temper.

"You should have thought of that before!"

Now Tony was angry.

"You should have told me, and we would have used protection!"

"Tell you what? That I forgot to take the pill a few times?"

"That would have helped."

Tony then tried to control himself.

"I'm sorry, Suzanne. Paying for an abortion is the best I can do. Let me know what you decide," Tony coldly said.

Suzanne looked at Tony with tears in her eyes.

"Why can't we have this baby, Tony? I can't kill something inside of me that belongs to you. I love you, Tony. I don't want to abort this baby."

Tony looked at her, completely surprised and unsympathetic to his old girlfriend.

"That is out of the question, Suzanne. You need to do the right thing for both of us, and having this baby is not going to work."

Suzanne, now with tears in her eyes, opened the door and exited the truck. As she was leaving, she looked at Tony with her big, blue eyes.

"I don't think I can kill something inside of me right now," she said, as she loudly slammed his truck door.

"I'll call you," he yelled out the open window as she stood there with the truck door closed.

"And don't come here to my place of work anymore."

Valentino started his truck and put it into drive, pulling away from Suzanne, who was walking towards her car parked elsewhere in the Ford Plant parking lot.

This was a problem he didn't need right now, and he knew that, at the very least, this was going to cost him a lot of money. Tony was worried. He didn't need her showing up at his front door and letting his wife know what was going on and that she was pregnant. He didn't need her coming over to his place of work, hanging around, and badgering him with her problem.

Suzanne being pregnant was the last thing he needed right now. He guessed that he would convince her to abort the baby.

He assumed he would take her to some medical clinic in downtown Detroit somewhere that does abortions.

Yet still, Tony was worried.

He had no idea what Suzanne had on her mind.

CHAPTER TWENTY-TWO

VALENTINO'S GHOST-JULY 26, 2019

Howard Williams was lying awake in his bed that warm Friday night, unable to fall asleep. It was almost eleven o'clock, and he had just made love to his ex-wife Joni, who arrived unexpectedly at his trailer home that evening. She had driven over eight hours from Hermitage, Tennessee, to visit him that night. Joni honestly thought that her ex-husband would be more excited to see her.

Williams, in recent years, had become very cold to his once revered ex-wife. Where he once worshipped and honored the hallowed ground she walked on, he had now realized what a narcissistic, promiscuous gold digger that she genuinely was.

Williams was somewhat drunk when he found Joni waiting for him in his trailer home. But Howard decided to take advantage of her and her situation. He hoped that the booze and the mindless sex would allow him to have a good night's sleep.

That did not happen.

While Joni was lying naked on the other side of the king-size bed, sound asleep, Williams was still wide awake. He got up, noticing that the clock on the nightstand said 11:14 pm.

He put his pants on and decided to turn on the television in the living room, flicking through the channels, finding nothing interesting to watch.

It was turning out to be a hot, muggy summer evening, and Williams realized that he was thirsty. After looking in his refrigerator and noticing nothing cold to drink, he decided to jump in his truck and run out to the party store on Marine City Highway to buy some beer. Because it was a Friday night, he knew the store would be open until midnight. The trip there and back would not take any longer than thirty minutes. It was precisely 11:29 pm when he started his red pickup truck and left his trailer home.

At approximately 11:35, a stranger entered Williams' trailer. The intruder was wearing a black mask, black leather driving gloves, a black T-shirt and jeans, and dark Nike shoes with plastic shoe coverings over them. The front door of the trailer was locked, but the cheap aluminum locks on those mobile home doors were easy to pry open with a large, flat screwdriver.

The invader walked softly into the master bedroom, where Joni was sleeping, naked on the left side of the bed.

Assuming that it was Williams, Joni immediately turned over, still half asleep.

"What are you doing out of bed, baby?"

At that moment, the intruder covered her mouth and pressed a sharp, serrated knife up against her throat.

"Who are you?" Joni managed to scream.

The intruder, who was carrying a large plastic bag, shoved a large piece of meat into her mouth, forcing her to choke on it while he continued to jab the knife into her throat.

In a deep low voice, the intruder only said:

"Valentino's Ghost."

Joni began to squirm, trying to fight off the intruder while the knife was quickly used to surgically cut her throat from the right side of her ear all along to the left side of her neck.

Blood began spewing everywhere as the intruder continued to stab and cut up Joni Williams Harper. She began making loud, uncomprehending gurgling noises as blood began spewing out of her mouth. The intruder continued to stab her naked body, jabbing it twenty or more times into her torso, arms, neck, and abdomen. The killer then took the knife, inserting deep inside of her vagina, and tore up her inside tissue, cutting her body vertically from her genital area up to her already severely sliced throat.

Blood was splattered everywhere on the bed, the floor, the walls, on her pillows, and all over the intruder's clothing.

The killer then pulled out a white envelope along with a token gift for Williams. The intruder then quickly left the trailer home undetected in the darkness and pulled away in the black Ford. The stranger had carefully covered the license plates of the car as it pulled away from the murder scene.

It was 11:49 pm.

At 11:53 pm, the black Ford Escape pulled down the dark, dirt road of Hessen and Marine City Highway and into an abandoned farmhouse. There, the killer changed out of all the bloody clothing and placed it into the trunk, with the intention of burning the clothing somewhere else later. The serrated, ten-inch hunters' knife was cleaned and sterilized, put into a plastic bag, and hidden in the trunk of the car underneath the spare tire.

By 12:05 pm, the black Ford Escape had sped westbound on down Marine City Highway, unnoticed and completely undetected.

At 12:11 pm, Williams had arrived back at his trailer home. He immediately noticed that the door was unlocked but attributed it to his forgetting to lock the door as he hastily left for the party store.

Carrying his twelve-pack of Miller Light, he immediately deposited the beer into his refrigerator. He didn't turn on any lights as he didn't wish to wake up his ex-wife from her deep sleep.

He sat on the Lazy-boy chair, turned on the television, and watched a rerun of 'Blue Bloods' for a half-hour, drinking several beers in the dark. At about 1:15 am, Williams decided he was sleepy enough to return to bed. With the lights still off and the bedroom pitch black, he removed all of his clothing, including his underwear, and unknowingly jumped into the right side of the bed, never noticing Joni's condition on the other side.

After about twenty minutes, Williams rolled over to the other side of the bed where Joni was lying.

Howard Williams suddenly was startled, as his hand and part of his body was now soaked with her blood.

At that very second, Howard Williams screamed at the top of his lungs, and he went into total, complete shock.

He ran up to the light switch and turned on the bedroom light.

The ghastly, horrific murder scene suddenly unfolded before his very eyes, and Williams began to yell and loudly scream uncontrollably.

Joni Williams Harper's naked body was covered entirely in blood, with over two dozen stab wounds to her face, neck, shoulders, arms, and abdomen. Across her body was a large gash going from her vagina upwards toward her neck, as if she were about to be surgically dissected. Blood was splattered all over the walls and floor, with a large pool of blood on her side of the king-size bed. Howard's naked body was now also covered in her blood as well.

Joni's mouth was opened, and a large piece of meat was protruding out of it. Next to her head was a sealed white envelope.

Then on the bedroom nightstand was a green toy water pistol.

Williams became psychologically jolted, yelling and screaming as he ran out of his trailer home, loudly banging on the neighbor's door next door.

"Call the police! Call the police!" the naked man screamed, completely covered in her blood.

As Williams continued to shriek at the top of his lungs, between all of the alcohol he consumed and his elevated heart rate, he passed out in front of his trailer home.

His naked, blood-covered body was spread out unconscious, across the pavement next to his red pickup truck.

CHAPTER TWENTY-THREE

DETECTIVE RONALD SINCLAIR

Ira Township Detective Ronald Sinclair was fast asleep on that muggy day in July when his cell phone loudly went off at 1:45 am. It was the police dispatcher, who seldom ever called his cellular phone at such an early hour. He was still groggy, letting the phone ring several times until he finished rubbing his eyes. It was probably another car accident on Marine City Highway. With the speed limit an excess of sixty-five miles an hour, fatal car accidents on that one-lane highway were quite common, especially in the summer months.

"Sinclair here," he answered.

"Sorry to wake you, Detective," apologized Sergeant Trudy Garrett from dispatch. "There seems to be some kind of horrific accident at 477 Chateau Lane there in the trailer park. A naked man is lying on the ground there, full of blood. I've notified a couple of squad cars as well."

"Thanks, Trudy," he said, still rubbing his eyes.

The dispatcher's reference to 'a couple of squad cars' meant that the whole Ira Township police department, including the commander, would all be there. Their very small police department consisted of one dispatcher, three patrolmen, one detective, and one chief of police-commander. Sinclair figured everyone would be snooping around at the scene of the crime.

Detective Ronald Sinclair was a tall, slightly overweight man in his late fifties, who had been on the Ira Township Police Department for the last seven years. He had initially been with the Detroit P.D.'s Eighth

Precinct for twenty-two years before he and his wife, Annette, moved out to Marine City. Their three children had grown up, married, and were now out of the house. Sinclair and his wife had always dreamed of having a brand-new home, some acreage, and a horse stable, far away from their cramped little house on Ten Mile Road and Gratiot. They bought ten acres several years ago on Palms Road and built a new, four-bedroom house, and had several horses for the two of them to enjoy.

Sinclair, at the time, was too young to retire, so he joined the Ira Township Police Department to finish up his career and his lucrative police pension. He enjoyed being a detective for that rural township near Lake St. Clair in Eastern Michigan. Up until that early morning, their most recent, serious crime was a shoplifting incident at the party store on Twenty-Six Mile and I-94. There just wasn't a lot of crime or criminal cases in the Marine City area, and his job as a detective there was sometimes a rather quiet, boring one indeed.

But he didn't miss being a Detroit copper. Sinclair wanted to get as far away as possible from the kinds of horrific city crimes and murders that he was now encountering on that early Saturday morning.

He quickly got dressed and jumped into his squad car, leaving his house on Palms Road. The detective raced over to the Chateau Estates, which was right down the street on Marine City Highway.

As Detective Sinclair pulled his squad car into the trailer park and in front of the mobile home, three other patrol cars were parked there, and a crime scene tape was already wrapped around the property. An ambulance had just arrived, and Williams was being loaded on a stretcher.

"Denny, what do we have?" Sinclair asked Patrolman Dennis Henderson, who was the first on the scene.

"You don't want to go in there, Ronnie. There's a lady who has been brutally stabbed to death."

Sinclair was mildly astonished, as there hadn't been a murder in Ira Township in several years. His heart rate started to rise rapidly.

"Who is the victim?"

"Her name is Joni Williams Harper, from Hermitage, Tennessee. That's her Mercedes car parked over there. She's the ex-wife of the homeowner. The man in the ambulance is Howard Williams. He still seems to be in shock, but no apparent wounds."

"Is he the perp?"

"Ronnie, I'm not sure what he is. This guy is still in shock and drunk on his ass. He's been rambling and mumbling ever since we put him in the ambulance. He's was covered with blood but has no wounds to speak of."

Detective Sinclair looked perplexed.

"It looks as though he fell on top of the bloodied, dead body."

He then looked at the patrolman.

"Is he that drunk? How the hell do you fall on top of a dead body, especially when it is covered in blood?" the detective asked, shaking his head.

Henderson smiled, "Maybe he was trying to have sex with it."

"Oh, God, I hope not."

Sinclair grabbed his facemask along with his flashlight, putting on his rubber gloves as he entered William's mobile home.

"I've never seen anything this brutal before," Henderson said, as he escorted Sinclair into the home and to the master bedroom.

There on the bed was an older, naked lady in her late sixties, completely covered with blood from head to toe. She was lying on the bed in a large pool of blood. It was splattered everywhere on the floor, the wooden headboard, and the surrounding walls. There were at least two dozen stab wounds throughout her body, starting from her face and shoulders throughout to her abdomen. There was a large, vertical wound going from her slit-opened throat to her genitals, which displayed more stab wounds. There was a large piece of flesh protruding from her mouth as if she was forced to choke on it while being stabbed to death.

"Dear God," Sinclair loudly exhaled, grasping his gold crucifix, which he always wore around his neck. He was a devout Catholic his whole life and said a quick prayer as he examined the crime scene. As a DeLaSalle High School alumnus, he grabbed his 18-karat gold cross often.

"What the hell happened here?"

"Looks like she was stabbed up pretty good. There is a white sealed envelope and a green water pistol on the nightstand," Henderson recited.

"A green water pistol?"

"Yeah. What the hell does that mean?"

Sinclair then shook his head.

"Wow."

He knew that the green squirt gun had a lot of symbolism, along with the knife wounds and the method in which the victim was killed. He wondered out loud what this kind of crime scene symbolism would mean.

"Denny," he said a directive to Patrolman Henderson, "Have one of the patrolmen go around the neighbors nearby and see if anyone heard or saw anything."

Another patrolman handed the sealed white envelope to Sinclair. He hesitantly opened it up with his pocketknife. There was a short note, which looked like it was typed, and had a simple message:

A warm dark night, All Hallows Eve,
a hunted man went there.
A small toy pistol was all he had,
because his hands were bare.

"Looks like our killer is a poet," Sinclair read it out loud several times, then handing the message over to his patrolman.

"All Hallows Eve?" Henderson had a blank look on his face.

"Yes, Denny. That's the old-fashioned word for Halloween. You weren't paying attention in grade school."

The detective continued to study the mutilated, bloody corpse on the bed.

"What do you estimate as the time of death?" he asked the patrolman.

"A few hours ago, probably around 11:30."

He looked closer into the mouth of the victim, trying not to touch the body.

"What's in her mouth, Denny?"

The patrolman looked at the detective.

"Good question. Looks like some protruding piece of meat of some kind."

They both glared at the victim.

"If I had to guess, I would say it's the genitals from some kind of animal," Denny observed.

Ron Sinclair stared at the patrolman. "You mean, like the penis from a horse? Like the 'Godfather' movie?"

Henderson smirked. "Yep, exactly."

Still holding the white envelope with the killer's poem, he handed it to another patrolman at the crime scene, giving him a directive.

"Give this to CSI when they get here. We will need to run this and the squirt gun for prints."

Detective Sinclair walked around the mobile home, looking for any more signs of blood, evidence, or forced entry. He walked over to the door.

"Looks like the door was jammed open."

The detective continued to walk around the mobile home carefully and then went outside and thoroughly inspected the outside of the trailer with his flashlight, noticing nothing else unusual.

"What's the story on our naked man?" he asked Henderson.

"He's still recuperating in the ambulance. The paramedics are cleaning him up and attending to him. One of them went into the house to get his clothing."

Sinclair walked over to the ambulance, asking one of the paramedics about the condition of the victim's husband.

"How is he?"

"He's still in a bit of shock. We started an IV on him and have been giving him some fluids.

Right now, he's on diazepam to calm down his anxiety."

Sinclair stepped inside the ambulance to speak with the husband, who was lying in the gurney.

"How are you doing?" he asked Williams.

The man didn't say anything but only shook his head.

"Can you tell us what happened here tonight?"

At first, Williams didn't say much. He only began to ramble about how he should have been the victim to be killed instead of his ex-wife.

"It was a vendetta," Williams softly replied.

"Why do you say that, Mr. Williams? What's going on here? What can you tell us?"

Still emotional, Williams didn't say anything for several long seconds. He then looked at Detective Sinclair, replying in a loud whisper:

"It was that dago-vendetta."

The detective tried to press the subject with the shocked man wrapped in a blanket as he started to cry.

"What vendetta? What are you talking about?"

Howard Williams was silent as the detective started to grow impatient.

"Look, Mr. Williams. You need to help us catch whoever did this to your ex-wife. You're not injured. And from what the paramedics tell me, you were found drunk and passed out outside, covered in blood. It looks like you fell on top of your wife's murdered body."

Williams only glared at the detective.

"It's a vendetta. Those dago-bastards are out to kill me!"

The detective looked at Williams.

"To what are you referring? What's with the green squirt gun? And why the envelope with the poem about Halloween?"

Williams was silent, not saying a word.

At that moment, Sinclair was done playing around, as he was exhausted and impatient. The veteran detective was in no mood to play any games with some drunken, babbling idiot from the trailer park.

"Let's get him dressed, and we'll take him down to the station. We'll need to get a statement out of him," he directed the Ira Township paramedics.

As the paramedics got Williams dressed and out of the ambulance, two of the officers assisted him into the back of the squad car, still wrapped in a blanket.

The crime scene investigators had by now arrived at the trailer home, and a large black van from the St. Clair County Morgue had come to take the deceased victim to the coroner.

As one of the patrolmen was getting ready to bring Howard Williams to the police station, Henderson approached the detective.

"How do you want to play this?" he asked.

"I'm going to need your help with some of the leg work on this homicide, Denny. There's some deep shit going on here, and I have a feeling this old drunk knows a lot more than what he's telling us."

As the big, dark van from the morgue pulled away, the detective went back into the house, looking around again. At the same time, the photographers from the St. Clair County crime investigations unit were busy taking pictures and samples from the bloody bedroom.

He kept thinking about the poem, the squirt gun, and the brutal method of how the victim was killed.

Detective Sinclair stood there at the doorway of the mobile home, turning the facts of this gory homicide over in his head. He figured that whoever the killer or killers were, they were very angry with the victim, taking an extreme amount of anger with the knife onto her body. But why? What had this victim done to cause this kind of crime, with these kinds of stab wounds? For what reason?

Why was there a horse's penis inserted into the victim's mouth? And why the green squirt gun? What the hell is that all about?

The detective kept shaking his head, totally perplexed.

A vendetta? What the hell is this drunken old man talking about?

Detective Sinclair walked back to his squad car and left the crime scene. It was now almost five in the morning. He was in dire need of his regular Dunkin' Donuts coffee, which he faithfully got every morning from the drive-thru on Marine City Highway.

"Good morning, may I help you?"

"Large coffee, a splash of cream, no sugar."

The employee over the loudspeaker recognized the detective's voice.

"No chocolate éclair today, Detective?"

"No, thanks, honey," he replied. "My stomach is a little queasy this morning."

Just leaving that bloody crime scene left the Ira Township detective void of any appetite. He then drove his squad car directly over to the Ira Township Police Station, balancing his hot beverage between his legs while maneuvering his squad car.

Sinclair was anxious to get back to the Ira Township police station to interview the victim's ex-husband.

He couldn't wait to hear all about this 'vendetta' against Howard Williams.

CHAPTER TWENTY-FOUR

A NEW LIFE– THANKSGIVING 1978

Suzanne Carleton couldn't get out of bed on that Thanksgiving morning. It had been a long, rough night, where she had been awake throwing up several times. Her morning sickness had continued to worsen, as she was now approaching the end of her first trimester.

As she managed to continue to work her waitress shift at the Colonial Café on Twelve Mile Road, the symptoms of her pregnancy were now getting more aggravated. She had called in sick the day before, and she was thankful that it was a legal holiday on that day. Her mother and father had invited her to come over to their house for Thanksgiving dinner at one o'clock that afternoon, and she had a full three hours to get herself ready and make herself presentable.

Except for Tony and her doctor, no one else knew that she was pregnant. She had already been to the doctor on two occasions before she made the decision that would now wholly change her life.

Before that faithful night of Halloween, she was unsure about keeping the baby. Suzanne had been enrolled at Macomb County Community College part-time, and she only needed fifteen more credit hours before transferring over to Madonna College to complete her nursing degree. When she met Tony Valentino that previous summer, she was utterly smitten with him. She was head over heels in love with Tony and couldn't get him out of her mind.

But when she told her boyfriend at the end of September that she was expecting his baby,

Tony was less than pleased. His only reaction was that he would be willing to pay for the abortion. Because he was a married man and had his own family to think about, he wanted to no part of being a father to another child.

Tony had lied to her. He had mentioned to her several times that his marriage was extremely rocky and that he would be filing for divorce very soon. When she got pregnant with his baby, she assumed that he would happily get divorced and make a new life with her.

But Valentino didn't see it that way. Suzanne then realized that Tony had used her and that he would coldly pay for her to get an abortion and nothing more. He had warned her at their last meeting not to 'show up' at his place of work ever again.

'Let me know how much,' was all he had to say. She finally realized that all of his empty words of love and affection were untrue. At that point in her life, she had no choice but to abort the baby.

And the deadline to have that abortion was soon approaching.

But Suzanne Carleton wasn't raised that way. Having been raised a devout Catholic in Warren, she went to St. Edmonds Grade School and graduated from Regina High School in 1965. She was the only child of Raymond and Elizabeth Carleton, and she always felt like she was a complete and total disappointment to her parents.

She had enrolled at the University of Michigan after high school and began her studies as a pre-medical student. But she had gotten caught up in the Vietnam anti-war protests on campus and had then fallen in love with her now ex-husband, Brian Trombley.

Brian was a long-haired, hippy love child who spent more time doing drugs and acid than going to class. Since he came from an affluent Grosse Pointe family, his father was able to get him a student deferment from the draft, and he avoided going off to Vietnam.

Instead of attending class, they would trip out together listening to Beatles and Rolling Stones music for days at a time, some days never getting out of their bed. Her lack of commitment to her studies cut her time in Ann Arbor short, and they both flunked out. Her parents begged her to break it off with her 'love-child' boyfriend, but Suzanne wouldn't hear of it. She claimed that she was deeply in love with him, and they ran off to Florida and eloped together. It wasn't long before she realized that marrying Brian was a huge mistake, and she returned to Michigan alone.

She attended the local community college on and off for several years while waitressing, and she was now at the point of her life where she was independent of everyone and could now pursue her dreams.

But now that she was carrying Tony's baby, her life would now be different. At the age of thirty-years-old, she already had a failed marriage on her hands. Suzanne was very apprehensive about diverting her life away from her dreams. She had worked so hard to get to the current point of her life. Suzanne was making decent money in tips at the restaurant and was able to afford her apartment in Madison Heights.

She hadn't seen or heard from Tony in several weeks when she saw the television news broadcast on the evening of November 1, 1978:

"A Warren man was violently shot in Detroit today. Antonio Valentino, 41-years-old, had just worked his shift at the Ford Assembly Plant in Sterling Heights when he was found dead of gun-shot wounds to the head," the newscast said.

Suzanne went into total shock. She had meant to touch base with Tony again, hoping that they could come to a favorable decision regarding the baby. But that never happened, and Tony Valentino was now dead.

She attended Tony's wake, trying to get some closure on his death and the cruel means by which he had abandoned her.

She didn't approach his family. She didn't approach his casket. She didn't want to. She only knew now that she was entirely on her own, no thanks to Tony.

On that Thanksgiving Day, Suzanne needed to inform her parents of her situation that she was pregnant with another man's baby. A man, she had to describe, that was not only married but was now dead. She was nervous about approaching them but knew that she couldn't have this baby on her own.

Her mother and father lived in a modest little house off of Common Road, near Schoenherr. As she walked in the door, her mother had the dining room table already set up for the Thanksgiving holiday.

"Can I help you with anything?" a smiling Suzanne eagerly asked her mother.

"Yes, could you put the sweet potatoes into the oven for me? The turkey and the stuffing have been cooking since six o'clock this morning."

Suzanne obediently prepared the sweet potatoes and continued to assist her mother for their elaborate Thanksgiving dinner. They usually had her aunt and uncle come over and attend their holiday celebrations as well at their home, but they had other made commitments on that November holiday.

Her father Raymond was reading the newspaper in the family room, with the 'Hudson's Thanksgiving Day Parade' loudly blaring from the TV set.

She approached him on his Lazy-boy chair and kissed him on the cheek.

"Happy Turkey Day, Daddy."

He smiled and kissed her back as they both made small talk about politics and the anticipated football game that afternoon. As was their tradition, the family would have Thanksgiving dinner and then watch the Detroit Lions play football.

The day progressed, and the three of them enjoyed their Thanksgiving Day dinner together. Suzanne helped her mother clean up, and then they all enjoyed her mother's freshly baked, always firm pumpkin pie. They all then sat in the family room and watched the football game. It was almost five o'clock on that day when Suzanne decided to spring the news on her parents.

"Mom, Dad...we need to talk."

"What's wrong, honey?" her mother eagerly asked.

Suzanne took a long, deep breath.

"I'm pregnant."

Mr. and Mrs. Carleton looked at each other in total shock and disbelief. The two of them were utterly speechless. The family room was quiet for almost ten minutes.

"Who is the father?" her Dad finally asked, trying hard to control his famously uncontrollable temper.

"His name is Tony Valentino, and he's dead," she replied.

Suzanne then went on to describe her relationship with him and how he had abandoned her when she had informed him of their problem. She then explained the circumstances of Tony's death and how he had left his family without a husband and father.

Raymond Carleton grabbed his pack of Camel cigarettes sitting on the kitchen counter and walked outside onto the patio.

He needed to be alone. The weather on that November day was misty and mild, having rained all of the previous night. It was nearly fifty degrees outside, and he stood there all alone on the concrete patio, smoking his cigarette without a jacket.

Suzanne and her mother only sat there, discussing her serious situation.

"You are going to have this baby, correct?" her mother asked.

Suzanne only nodded her head silently.

"I think so. As mean and as cruel as Tony was to me, I know that deep down, he loved me," she lied to her mother. She didn't want to paint the picture of her baby's father any worse than he really was.

"This baby is the only thing that I have left of him."

Her mother looked at her.

"Does his wife know?"

"No, Mom. I saw them when I went to Tony's wake. She looked so frail and so broken from the circumstances of his death and all. The last thing I want to do is make even more problems for them."

At that moment, Mr. Carleton came back inside the house and sat down in his comfortable chair.

"You need to gather your things and move back home. You're going to need some help."

Her mother looked at her father and smiled.

"I guess we're going to be grandparents," he said, as a shadow of a grin came over his face.

They all looked at each other and smiled. A complete sigh of relief came over Suzanne Carleton. She knew that her parents loved her and that their unconditional love would get her through all of this.

"I only have one condition," her father requested.

"I want this baby to carry our name."

Suzanne smiled and nodded her head.

"Okay, Daddy."

With the help of her parents, Suzanne moved back home and continued to work, waitressing, and living with her Mom and Dad while continuing to take two classes that winter semester.

During that early Spring of 1979, Suzanne was still waitressing at the Georgian Café one Sunday morning when Rossano Valentino walked in with his wife for breakfast. At that time, Suzanne was six months pregnant, and Rossano immediately recognized who she was. He remembered that summer day when she had met his brother during breakfast. He recalled

Tony bragging about how he was sleeping with her during the prior summer. They both made eye contact while Suzanne waited on another table. She tried to ignore him.

Rossano and Elvira finished their breakfast and paid at the counter. As they both left the restaurant, Ross and Suzanne made eye contact again.

As he gazed at her with her enlarged stomach, Suzanne only looked at him and nodded her head. Ross then turned around and left the café with his wife.

The very next morning, Ross was back at the restaurant. This time, he walked up directly and approached Suzanne while she was still holding a fresh pot of coffee.

"Weren't you at my brother's wake?"

She only looked at him and nodded.

"Why didn't you say anything? I've been in here so many times...why didn't you say anything about your being pregnant?"

"I didn't want to hurt you or his wife. You have all been through enough. Besides, what the hell are you going to do about it?"

Ross looked at her.

"If you're carrying my brother's baby, we at least have the right to know."

Suzanne gave Ross a dirty look.

"Really? If it were up to your brother, I would have had an abortion. He wanted nothing to do with me or his baby."

Ross gazed at her for several long seconds as they both stood there in the middle of the little restaurant. He didn't want to start a public scene with her.

"I'm in here often. Let me know if you ever need anything."

Suzanne smiled and thanked him as he abruptly left.

On April 15th, 1979, Suzanne had a healthy baby boy. He was eight pounds, four ounces at St. John's Hospital in Detroit.

At the last minute, Suzanne decided to name her child after his biological father:

Anthony Valentine Carleton.

As she was recuperating from her delivery, she received several flower arrangements from her many friends on the beautiful addition to her family. One flower arrangement of lilacs and white roses arrived at her hospital room.

The attached card only said:

Auguri.

Love, Tony.

She asked one of the nurses, who told her that 'Auguri' was Italian for congratulations. She then immediately realized who had sent them.

With the help of her parents, Suzanne went on to get her nursing degree from Madonna College and was hired as an emergency room nurse at Beaumont Hospital in Royal Oak. The three of them happily raised the baby boy in their home in a healthy family environment. Two years later, Suzanne eventually met a young man named Jeff Peterson, an X-ray Medical Technician who had worked at that hospital along with her. They eventually married and settled down in Clawson, and her new husband accepted and raised little Anthony like his own son.

Little Anthony grew up to be a fine young man, having the love and support of his adopted father, his mother, and his loving grandparents. He couldn't have had a more stable childhood.

He went to Catholic grade school, like his mother, and attended Brother Rice High School in Birmingham. He then went on to attend Central Michigan University, graduating cum laude with a bachelor's degree in accounting in 2001. He passed the CPA exam on his first attempt and was hired as a field agent for the Internal Revenue Service.

Anthony was already married with a child of his own when he was promoted as a federal treasury agent almost twenty years later. His mother had always told him that his real, biological father was killed before they could get married and that his unplanned conception was a 'gift from the angels of heaven.'

He never knew the actual circumstances of his biological father. He never knew that Tony Valentino was a married man with a family of his own and wanted nothing to do with his mother. He never found out the truth about how he acquired his name, his biological father's real name, or his mother's past relationship with him. His mother had always told him that he was named after St. Anthony and that his middle name was from St. Valentine.

It was during a subsequent investigation years later that he would discover some interesting facts about his biological father and his family.

Anthony would one day cross that path.

CHAPTER TWENTY-FIVE

INVESTIGATION-IRA TOWNSHIP POLICE-JULY 27, 2019

As Detective Ronald Sinclair pulled his squad car into the Ira Township Police Department parking lot, Commander Paul Nelson was waiting for him by the door.

"Nice of you to bring me some coffee," as Sinclair was juggling his keys while trying not to spill his hot beverage.

"I didn't want to get roped into buying you breakfast."

Commander Nelson was a tall, older man in his sixties, with a sizeable protruding waist that probably better resembled a wine barrel. He buzzed cut what few hairs that he had left on his head and had one of those thick, burly mustaches that made him resemble a sheriff from the Wild, Wild West show, minus the cowboy hat.

"Are you ready to hear about 'the vendetta?'" Sinclair chuckled to his amused commander.

"Yeah, right. I can't wait for this one. This drunken bastard has been watching too many 'Sopranos' reruns."

The two of them walked back towards the other side of their small police station, which wasn't larger than two thousand square feet. It only consisted of a small conference room, which doubled as an interrogation room. It also had several steel desks, a reception area, two small bathrooms, and two very small lockups. The jails were complete with wrought-iron gated doors, a single cot, and a toilet and sink that looked too clean and shiny to be in a prison cell.

As Commander Nelson and Detective Sinclair made their way to the interrogation room, Howard Williams was sitting by himself at the table, wearing a gray blanket around his shoulders and a styrofoam cup filled with water. He was fully dressed, thankfully, wearing an old pair of jeans and a gray, worn-out, oil-stained sweatshirt.

Sinclair held his breath as he carefully opened the door.

"Mr. Williams? This is Commander Nelson, and I'm Detective Sinclair. We would like to ask you some questions."

Williams was emotionless, still staring at the plain, blank wall with the one-way window.

"Could you tell us about what may have happened to your ex-wife?"

Williams took a long swallow from his styrofoam cup. He then again said only one word:

"Vendetta."

Nelson and Sinclair looked at each other.

"Could you elaborate a little more about this vendetta? What is this all about? Why are you making such a statement?"

Williams continued to stare at the walls, not having any reaction.

"It's a vendetta that was put on me many years ago by some dago bastards."

Commander Nelson, who had brought along a writing pad, began to scribble down some notes as Williams started to elaborate.

Howard Williams began to discuss the murder on El Camino Drive in Detroit that occurred in November 1978 against his alleged victim, Tony Valentino. He talked about the details regarding how Valentino had been seeing his wife and how he and two other men had 'accidentally' shot him after attempting to rough him up. He talked about how he and his associate, George Johnson, were released on murder charges. Williams mentioned the trial of his other companion that night, Jack Hansen, and how he was acquitted by a jury in Wayne County in 1979.

While Nelson took down detailed notes, Sinclair sat there and attentively listened to the details of forty years ago that Williams was referring. He found it very hard to believe that someone would have possibly killed his ex-wife the previous night, slicing her up so brutally, based on a family vendetta from so many years ago.

"Do you have any initial idea of who may have done this?"

"I don't know," Williams stated. "All I know is that I was warned about my life being in danger, and that was the reason why my wife and I had left town and moved to Tennessee. We believed that Valentino's family, including his brothers, were out to get us after the trial. We were warned to get out of town."

"By whom?" Sinclair asked.

Williams hesitated. "Some friends."

At that moment, Sinclair banged his automatic ballpoint pen against the pad of paper and glared at Williams.

"And you're expecting us to buy all of this?"

"I don't care what you buy, Detective. All I know is that those dago-bastards are still out to get me, after all of these years."

"And you guys escaped murder charges because Valentino had a green squirt gun in his pocket? And you were able to plead self-defense based on that?"

"Yes. Our attorney advised us to plead self-defense based on the fact that Valentino was armed."

"With a fucking squirt gun?"

"Well, yes. We didn't know. Hansen had the gun with him at the time, and three shots went off."

"By accident, of course," Sinclair sarcastically replied.

"Yes. The gun Hansen brought along was borrowed, and we only had it to scare him. The gun had a history of jamming, and it went off. Hansen thought the gun's safety was on."

"And three bullets accidentally went into Tony Valentino," Sinclair was reading off of his notes. "Killing him by accident?"

"Well yeah. We didn't mean to kill him."

Sinclair looked at Commander Nelson as the two of them made eye contact. He then looked at Williams.

"Why did you bring the gun with you if you were only going to scare him?"

"Because we had suspected that Valentino was armed, and we didn't want to take a chance."

"After you followed him around, trying to scare him?"

"Yeah, that's right."

Sinclair rolled his eyes in the air and looked at his commander.

"I would say, Mr. Williams, that if all of this is true, you and your friends are very fortunate indeed."

Howard Williams had a confused look on his face.

"Why?"

"Because if you know anything about vendettas, especially in this town, then you would know that you and your friends should have already been killed off by now. That is if this whole story of yours is true."

There were a few silent moments at the table.

"Besides, if you and your friends 'accidentally' killed this Valentino guy, why would someone brutally kill your ex-wife?"

Williams had a blank look on his face.

"When and where did this whole incident happen again?"

"November 1, 1978, on El Camino Drive."

Sinclair smiled at Williams. Being a veteran Detroit Police Detective for many years, he was very familiar with the East Side reputation of El Camino Drive off of Eight Mile Road.

That street always had a very seedy reputation, and he knew that very few people ever committed anything on El Camino and lived to talk about it.

"El Camino Drive, huh?"

"Yes," Williams verified.

Detective Sinclair rose from the table and smiled at Williams, not initially saying a word. As the commander got up as well, they both headed out of the conference room. Before closing the door behind them, Sinclair made a parting statement to Howard Williams.

"Being a former Detroit copper, I have some friends that I need to call and check out your story."

He then paused for a moment, shaking his head.

"El Camino Drive, huh? I would say that you're a very lucky man, indeed."

I was finishing up some paperwork at my desk and trying to survive my throbbing headache. I had just taken three Tylenol at noon. After having a Jimmy John's Italian Sub sandwich, I was still suffering from its remnants. Between the heartburn from the extra hot giardiniera peppers and the aspirin, my head was still suffering. It was just after two o'clock on that Monday afternoon when Commander Riley called me into his office.

"Valentino, we have some company."

"Who?"

"There are some detectives from Ira Township who want to speak to you in the conference room. One of them is a former Detroit copper. His name is Ronald Sinclair. We used to work together when we were both at the Fourth Precinct. There was a pretty gruesome homicide there over the weekend, and he has some questions."

"Really?"

"Yeah," Riley said.

There was a moment of silence.

"Where were you over the weekend, specifically last Friday night?" he asked.

"I was with my boys. They spent the weekend over my apartment. We went out for pizza, and they spent the whole weekend at my place."

Riley looked at me as if to be relieved.

"Okay, good. I feel better."

I was momentarily confused.

"What does this homicide have to do with me, Chief?"

My commander looked at me with a somber look on his face.

"The victim in that homicide was the lady your father was allegedly having an affair with over forty years ago. Her body was sliced up like a pig."

I felt a rush of cold shivers go up to my spine. For several long seconds, I was mute and speechless. I absolutely couldn't talk.

"Don't worry, Johnny. I've known Sinclair for years, and he's a good guy. He's an old school copper, and he's one of us. He just wants to ask us a few questions. He called earlier this morning and said he would be stopping by. I told him I was the lead investigator in your father's homicide investigation in 1978, and I think he just wants to know more information."

I began shaking my head in total disbelief. Someone had brutally killed the lady who was supposedly fooling around with my father over forty years ago, and somehow, a detective wants to talk to my boss and me about it. I just couldn't get my head around all of this at the time.

We both got up from his office and walked over to the conference room, where there were two men seated. Both looked like they were on the older side. One of them looked like a hard-nosed copper from the TV series 'Law & Order: SVU,' while the other one looked like Buffalo Bill. The four of us all shook hands and exchanged pleasantries when Riley began explaining how long he and Sinclair had known each other.

We all sat there like bumbling idiots while Detective Sinclair recounted some stupid story about how the two of them went on a stake-out somewhere on the west side of Detroit. Riley turned red, and I pretended to laugh at how they ended up locking themselves out of their squad car and had to have it towed back to the station.

Sinclair then suddenly turned serious.

"There was a brutal homicide in the Chateau Estates last Friday night. The victim in that homicide turns out to have a connection with the death of your father forty years ago. Her name was Joni Williams Harper," Sinclair started.

"I heard," I politely acknowledged.

"She was there visiting her ex-husband, Howard Williams. He states that he left her alone, sleeping, to go to the party store at about 11:30 pm. When he got back, he didn't notice until almost two hours later that she had been stabbed and butchered up in his bed while he was gone."

I looked at the Ira Township police detective, trying to appear sympathetic.

"His story checks out," Sinclair continued.

"We interviewed the clerk at the party store and the store manager, and he remembers Williams going in there to purchase a six-pack of beer."

I looked at my boss, who was listening attentively.

"The coroner estimated her time of death at about 11:45 pm," Commander Nelson said. He then pulled out some police photographs and passed them along the other side of the table for the Chief and me to inspect.

The color photographs looked absolutely horrific. The victim looked like she had been stabbed over two dozen times, with a large gash going from her sliced-up neck down to her genital area. There was blood splattered everywhere, and something significant and bloody was protruding out of her mouth. I kept staring at the photographs, trying to make out what it was.

"The thing in her mouth is an animal penis, apparently from a horse."

I took every bit of strength to keep myself from laughing as I saw the shadow of a smile appear on Riley's face.

"Wow. So, who do you think the killer is? Sonny Corleone?" Riley snickered.

Sinclair had a smile on his face as well. "Apparently, this was quite a bloody crime scene, and her ex-husband somehow threw himself on the deceased victim accidentally when he discovered the body. He was passed out, naked, and full of blood when we found him in front of his mobile home."

We all looked at each other, trying to find the connection to all of this.

"Williams, the ex-husband, kept rambling about some kind of family vendetta against him. Some family curse that was verbally cast on him at the trial when they were all acquitted for your father's murder. Do you have any knowledge of that?"

At that moment, I got a little angry.

"Considering that I was only six years old at the time? No, Detective. I know absolutely nothing about any kind of family vendetta," as Riley made eye contact with me.

"There was nothing ever mentioned to you?"

"No."

"We found some surveillance records regarding Williams on someone named Rossano

Valentino. Evidently, he was tailing Williams for several weeks after the murder trial in 1979, according to the Detroit police records," Commander Nelson commented.

"So, you guys called up the Detroit P.D. and found surveillance records on my Uncle Ross?"

"Yes," Sinclair answered. "Williams keeps saying there is a vendetta against him by your family and especially your uncle."

"Okay," I felt my temper starting to boil.

"So, what the hell does all of this have to do with the price of eggs?"

Sinclair looked at me.

"There was a green squirt gun found next to her body, similar to the toy pistol that was found next to your father forty years ago."

I felt my whole body turn cold. I could feel the hairs on my neck starting to stand up.

"There was a note too," Commander Nelson said, passing over a copy of the note found at the homicide.

"Our killer is a poet," Sinclair said as I quickly looked at the note:

A warm dark night, All Hallows Eve,
a hunted man went there.
A small toy pistol was all he had,
because his hands were bare.

I passed the note to Commander Riley, who quickly read it and gave it back to the Ira Township detective.

"Looks like the killer is a poet, a real Shakespeare, isn't he?" I coldly observed.

"I still don't understand why a homicide in your township would have something to do with me. I was with my boys all weekend. We were at Buddy's Pizza on Van Dyke Road last Friday night, and then they were all sleeping at my apartment. I'm sure you guys can go there and get the surveillance tapes. So, if you think that I..."

"Oh no, Detective Valentino. We are not insinuating any such thing. We are just here to make you aware of what happened. We hoped that maybe you could shed some light on this vendetta that Williams keeps rabbling about."

"Really, Detective?" I said in a very audible voice.

"Look, guys. I've been a copper with the Detroit P.D. for over twenty years. I know how all of this works. I know how the game is played," I felt my temper starting to boil.

"You guys come over here all nice and innocent, pretending to be our pallies and show us some crime scene photos like they were pictures from a fucking high school yearbook."

I was trying to control my anger.

"Then, you guys start babbling some bullshit about a family vendetta from over forty years ago."

At that moment, Riley grabbed my hand, trying to calm me down.

"This bastard planned, executed, and stole our father away from us when I was only six years old. So, if you're expecting me to shed any tears now because his ex-wife got butchered up with a horse's dick in her mouth...well, sorry, guys, I can't help you."

"Johnny..." Riley tried to quiet me.

"No, Chief. I'm getting fucking pissed here," as I started to get up from my chair.

"These fucking detectives come in here trying to start some shit about my father's murder and his killers over forty years ago. Now

I'm supposed to sit here like a good little altar boy while they drum up some goddamn bullshit about my uncle and a fucking vendetta?"

"Sit down, Johnny…"

"No, Chief!"

"My Uncle Ross is a little old man now. He's eighty years old, and he walks with a fucking cane, for God's sake," I thundered.

"I doubt that he has nothing else better to do than to recreate the murder scene from 'The Godfather' movie on some old, hillbilly whore bimbo," I started to thunder.

At that moment, I was beginning to see red.

"He barely has the strength to hold a knife to cut his potatoes, let alone use one to slice up some old bitch like a porterhouse steak!"

At that moment, I could see the other detectives from the glass wall of the conference room looking at us while I was loudly losing my temper. Detective Sinclair looked at me, his beady eyes piercing through mine.

"How did you know she was a hillbilly?" he coldly asked.

I looked at the three of them. At that moment, I wanted to shove my fist directly down that Ira-hick Township copper's fucking throat.

"Fuck you!" I said to them as I stormed out of the precinct conference room.

I quickly walked over to my desk and grabbed the car keys to my squad car. I knew at that instant that I was leaving Commander Riley alone in that conference room with those asshole detectives. I briefly felt terrible that I was again, leaving my boss to clean up after my temper and my bad judgment.

But at that moment, I didn't give a shit. The last thing I wanted to talk about to any strangers was the tragic loss of my father and how someone finally gave it to the lady who indirectly was responsible for my father's death.

As I sat in my squad car, I held the steering wheel in my hands, thinking about who and how such a murder could have happened. How would the murderer know about how my father died, leaving such a poem at the crime scene? And how would the murderer have known about the green squirt gun? Someone in my family, maybe? My uncles, perhaps? It had to be someone familiar with Dad's death.

But who?

As I pulled out of the precinct parking lot, I peeled the tires as I entered eastbound Grand Boulevard. I was looking to find a watering hole to drown out my anxiety over this whole murder thing. If Joni Williams, my father's mistress, was now dead, she got what she had coming to her, forty years later. I didn't feel one single ounce of compassion or sympathy for that old, hillbilly whore.

Somehow, I ended up in the parking lot of the Crazy Horse Lounge. As I shut off the ignition, a little voice went off inside of me. I had managed to succumb to the very demon that I was struggling so hard to overcome.

My alcohol dependence had always started and stopped in the same way. It was my continuous struggle in trying to deal with the horrific ghosts of my past...ghosts that invariably began with my dead father.

I started my squad car back up, and I pulled out of that parking lot, refusing to concede to my demons.

For one brief moment, I wished that I was the one who had committed that murder.

It had been almost six months since Patrolman Andrew Hacker was on street duty in the Tenth Precinct. His patrol duties were paired with another female patrol partner, Patrolperson Denise Coletta, to accompany him while making the rounds on Livernois Avenue.

Other than some burglaries and some DUI arrests, there wasn't a whole lot of action or crime in the Tenth Precinct. He knew that the precinct commander, Nick Manzie, was observing him, and he had to rebuild his reputation at the Detroit Police Department.

But Patrolman Hacker was still extremely bitter, and he never got over his anger towards Detective John Valentino. He had a small work desk at the station, and Hacker began doing some part-time research.

Rumors were starting to travel around the Detroit P.D. about the 'Water Pistol Killer' and its possible links and connections to Valentino and his father's murder over forty years ago. There was a significant amount of gossip going around about some ancient vendetta that had been put on the exonerated killers and their families back in 1979.

There had been a brutal stabbing in Ira Township the weekend before. There were rumblings regarding the victim and her connection to Valentino and his murdered father. Having remembered Valentino talking about his tragic childhood several times, he recalled the link between his father's murder and the perpetrators who got away.

Hacker's mind started to wander, thinking and pondering how he could make any direct connections between this new killer and his nemesis at the Third Precinct.

"That would be one karma payback I would just love to see," the patrolman said to himself.

He then got an idea one afternoon while sitting at the Tenth Precinct and decided to make a phone call.

"Detroit Crime Records?" answered the receptionist.

"Yes, this is Patrolman Hacker. I would like copies of a homicide record from several years ago, please."

"What records are you requesting?"

Hacker smiled to himself, knowing that he now had a very devious plan in mind.

"Antonio Valentino, November 1, 1978.
Homicide on El Camino Drive."

CHAPTER TWENTY-SIX

A VISIT FROM OLIVIA-SUMMER 2019

I pulled into the parking lot of the Third Precinct on Grand Boulevard in a daze that August afternoon, as though my Crown Victoria squad car had driven itself. I sat in the parking lot for several long minutes, thinking about the green toy squirt gun and the poems left by this "Water Pistol Killer."

The inside of my squad car appeared to be the only form of peace and solace that I could find during that time, as I put both of my hands on the steering wheel and said a quick prayer to myself. I was never much of a Christian, and I certainly didn't pray very well, forgetting most of the prayers that I learned in Catechism. But one of my biggest fears was that the actual killer who was committing these murders was someone very close to me, and for whatever it was worth, I just couldn't figure out who it might be.

I walked into my police precinct and back to my office. I wasn't at my desk for more than five minutes when my desk phone rang.

"Johnny? It's Frank."

"What's the word, Frank?" It was Detective Frank Partridge from the Eighth Precinct.

"Sinclair has been hanging around the precinct asking a lot of questions about you."

"What's his fucking problem?"

I was so involved in thinking about who the actual killer might be, it never really occurred to me Detective Ronald 'Dickhead' Sinclair was actively still considering me as his prime suspect. He had Williams' mobile home actively dusted for fingerprints from the murder of Joni Williams Harper, and he had the crime lab from the Michigan State Police over there pulling that trailer apart nail by nail. Sinclair was following the oldest trick in the book, and it was scaring the living shit out of me:

If you don't have a suspect to fit the crime, make the crime fit the suspect.

"He's been researching your father's murder files from 1978. He has asked for copies of the crime lab regarding the details and the information of the exonerated suspects."

"Well, good. Maybe he can figure out how to make the murders stick and put these guys back in jail forty years later," I smiled and sarcastically replied.

That will never happen, I thought to myself. I knew that the possibility of trying the same suspects for the same crimes after forty years was double jeopardy and would never happen against Jack Hansen. To think that Sinclair was looking for an angle to bring up murder charges again against Williams and his buddies was very wishful thinking.

In double jeopardy, a person cannot be tried twice for the same crime based on the same conduct. Nor can one be tried for two different offenses based upon the same behavior unless the two crimes are defined to prohibit the conduct of significantly different kinds.

Thus, one cannot be tried for both murder and manslaughter for the same killing. But one can be tried for both murder and robbery if the murder arose out of the theft. The defense of double jeopardy also prevents the state from retrying a person for the same crime after he has been acquitted. In our judicial system, jeopardy does not attach until the jury is sworn in a jury trial or until the first witness is declared in a bench trial.

Actions before jeopardy will not bar a subsequent prosecution. For example, if a judge dismisses indictment at a preliminary hearing for lack of evidence, this ruling or determination does not prohibit the government from initiating new charges for the same offense since jeopardy will not have attached at that point.

The possibility of Williams and Johnson being brought up for murder charges forty years later *does actually exist* because the charges were initially dismissed for lack of evidence. Jack Hansen was the only one who was tried for second-degree murder. If new evidence or a new confession would ever be brought up against my father's original killers, since they were never tried, they could possibly be formally charged with first-degree murder again.

But Sinclair wasn't looking for the same justice I was looking for. He was rummaging through my father's murder files to find a connection between myself and this recent murder. Bringing up new charges against Howard Williams was the last thing on his mind.

"Ostensibly, Sinclair is looking to find a reason why someone would so brutally kill a woman so many years after an alleged affair over forty years later. According to him, this murder has the word 'revenge' written all over it," Partridge said over the phone.

"Well, we all know that, Frank. Nice to know that Detective Dickhead is taking his smart pills."

"Yes, but you're the only one who fits the profile."

"I get it, Frank."

I had a good alibi. I was having pizza with my kids when this old broad was violently murdered. That was probably the only genuine reason that was keeping my ass from being arrested on suspicion of first-degree murder and being thrown in Sinclair's jail cell.

"Sinclair has been visiting different horse stables in the Ira Township area."

I had heard through the precinct grapevine that Sinclair was going to all of the different horse ranches and stables in the area, trying to figure out how the killer was able to acquire a dead horse's penis to put into the victim's mouth during the murder.

"I heard that. Maybe if Sinclair keeps watching the 'The Godfather' movie, he might figure it out," I laughed.

It was almost five o'clock that afternoon when I got a surprise visitor. Someone was greeting me with a familiar voice, standing over me while I sat at my cubicle.

As I looked up from my computer screen, I could immediately see who it was, and my heart rate started beating out of my chest. Even my hands were beginning to perspire.

"Well, this is a nice surprise," I exclaimed as I excitedly stood up from my desk.

She smiled as I gave her a quick peck on the cheek. This beautiful girl looked and smelled incredible, as always. The insurance executive then sat down on the steel, folding chair in front of my desk.

Olivia was wearing a tight pair of blue jeans and a white blouse with a stylish blue windbreaker that gave me the impression that she was ready to go to a ball game or do some hard drinking at a local watering hole. We exchanged pleasantries as she was carrying a large handbag, which looked like it had some files inside.

"You don't return my calls, Detective. You must very busy *catching your man...*" she said in a sultry tone of voice. Her expression sounded more like a rehearsed Greta Garbo line from an old 'Mata Hari' movie.

I had recalled receiving one voicemail message from her, but I had forgotten to return her call.

"I've been pretty busy here, Olivia. But this is a nice surprise. What brings you here?"

Olivia sat down on the only steel chair next to my cubicle, showing off those incredibly firm legs and her tight blue jeans.

"I've come here to ask for your help. You being a Detroit detective and all, I was hoping could assist my department."

"Sure," I mindlessly said.

I was still mesmerized by her gorgeous body, so neatly tucked inside her very tight, size five blue jeans. They looked as though they had been spray-painted on.

"I have some insurance claims for some beneficiaries, and I need some personal information on them. If I give you a list of names, would you be able to give me some data and information to help me find and track down these individuals?"

"What kind of information?"

"Full names, addresses, dates of birth, social security numbers, you know..."

"And this is for recent life insurance claims?" I inquired.

"Well, yes and no. We have some old insurance policies that we are trying to locate the beneficiaries of, and we need assistance in trying to trace these potential recipients. The Great Lakes Insurance Company normally goes through great lengths to find and track down these recipients before writing these policies off."

I looked at her for a moment and didn't say anything. Her reasons for my helping her get some personal information initially made sense. She then pulled out several thick files with information claims in each one of them, disclosing the names of each of the beneficiaries she was trying to locate. She then pulled out a summary list of the data she was requiring.

"Here's a list of names whose information I need. If you could get as much information as possible for each individual, I would appreciate it. The insurance company is willing to pay for your time."

"I'm not a private eye, Olivia. And the department doesn't sell information."

"I understand, John. I just want you to know that your time in helping us locate these people is valuable to us, and you would be compensated."

I thought about it for a moment. I didn't see a problem with doing her a favor and helping her find some outdated, obsolete information on a few of her stale life insurance policy beneficiaries.

"I'll do whatever I can to help you, Olivia."

She then handed me a list of about twenty names, with their policy numbers, names of the policy owners, and their dates of death. I would probably have to prepare a spreadsheet with the requested information she needed for these obsolete insurance claims.

At first, I didn't think anything of it. I figured these were administrative issues that she needed help with and that she usually came to the Detroit P.D. to get whatever assistance she might need in these claims.

I then got distracted, still mesmerized by those incredibly tight blue jeans.

I began wondering if her sexy, casual appearance meant that she was interested in more play and less work. I was starting to fantasize. For some reason, I couldn't take my eyes off of her, as she probably knew I was a sucker for a hot, beautiful brunette in a tight pair of blue jeans.

"Can you get back to me in a few days? I need to process these claims fairly soon."

"I'll do what I can, Olivia. I promise."

"Great," she said as we both sat down and enjoyed a few moments of silence.

"So, is there anything I can help you with?" she eagerly asked. Her question sounded seductive.

"Like?"

"I understand there was a gruesome homicide in Ira Township the other night that your department might be investigating."

I wondered how the hell she had even heard that information, let alone ask me about that particular murder.

"Well, yes. The Ira Township police are busy investigating it, and they are looking for our help in cracking the case."

A few moments of silence, as I could see the wheels spinning in her head.

"I heard that this homicide the other night was related to your father's death many years ago."

"How did you hear that?"

"I know a lot of people at the Detroit News. One of the reporters, Justine Cahill, was mentioning how the victim had been brutally stabbed and murdered."

"Evidently, the lady who was killed was allegedly having an affair with my father before he was shot to death by her husband and his friends in 1978," I casually mentioned, still staring at her tight jeans.

"And the Detroit P.D. are now reopening this case?" Olivia inquired.

"I wish it were that easy, Olivia. We are only assisting the Ira Township detectives in investigating it to see if there are any clues as to who the current killer might be."

"I see." I could tell she knew a lot more information than what she was letting on.

"Do you usually hang around news reporters?" I suspiciously asked.

"Only the one's snooping around for insurance claims. One of the reporters contacted our company, wondering if there had been any claims made on the victim," she said.

At that moment, I wasn't sure if she was telling me the truth. Why would the homicide victim, who was a resident in Tennessee, have an insurance policy claim from a Midwestern company like Great Lakes? Olivia was getting her information from somewhere, and I immediately knew she was trying to pump information out of me regarding this gruesome homicide.

Another silent moment.

"So what time are you off, Detective?"

"Well, I have a few things here to wrap up, and..."

"You know, the best way to a girl's heart is through a great pizza. Do you have a favorite place?"

"Well, my boys and I happen to enjoy Buddy's Pizza on Van Dyke and Twelve Mile Road," I suggested. "We go there every Friday."

"Hmmm...is that like New York-style pizza?"

"No, not at all. We've been going there for years. It's definitely Detroit style pizza."

"Well...to tell you the truth, I heard about this place, Louie's Pizza on Dequindre and Nine Mile Road. I've heard that place is pretty good too," Olivia replied.

"Now that is Detroit style pizza!" I exclaimed.

"They serve deep-dish, square pies with lots of cheese and tomato sauce, and then loaded up with pepperoni mushrooms onions, or whatever else you like. It has an old-fashioned Italian ambiance, with the fiaschi bottles wrapped in straw baskets hanging all over the walls. It's a lovely place," I excitedly described in detail.

I looked at her for a moment, waiting for her to jump at the chance to go to Louie's.

"Really?" she replied.

"But since you've been hanging out in Chicago, maybe you would have a craving for a Chicago style pizza instead," I reasoned.

"I like Chicago-style pizza except for the thin crust. I'm a deep-dish girl."

"I've never met a pizza that I didn't like, so I would be a very biased judge. But having New York pizza a few times, I can certainly say that Detroit pizza is better," I replied.

She was crossing those gorgeous legs, all wrapped up in those very sexy blue jeans and a black pair of Zanotti shoes, bouncing her right leg on her left knee while making her statement.

"Pizza is positively the way to a girl's heart," she repeated.

"Hmmm, sounds like somebody wants some pizza," I observed. "So, is it Louie's or Buddy's Pizza tonight?"

"Louie's it is," she exclaimed.

Louie's Pizzeria is a small, quaint pizzeria on Dequindre Road in Hazel Park that had all the makings of a memorable, intimate dinner date. It has been around the Detroit area since the 1950s, with its checker cloth tables and old school ambiance.

Louie's was one of those Italian restaurants where you would expect 'Angelina the Waitress' to be serving your table while Louie Prima was singing love songs in the background.

I threw a few papers into my small briefcase and packed them up for the evening. It was now apparent that I had a pizza date with a beautiful insurance executive.

We both took her car from the Third Precinct, and she did the driving. There was already a long line when we got there, just past six o'clock. It was usually crowded almost every night there, as it was practically six-thirty when we were seated at a small, checker cloth table.

We had a lively conversation on the way over as she talked about her job, her friends, and her healthy lifestyle. Olivia was telling me a little about her nationality and her background, as her father was French Canadian, and her mother was Italian. Although she only a half-breed, she always considered herself an Italian girl first.

"You do realize, Johnny. I will need an extra hour at the gym tomorrow for this pizza tonight."

"And this is my problem, how?"

"It is your problem because I don't think you'll want to be dating a fat Italian girl."

I smiled to myself, thinking that she was actually considering being my steady girlfriend.

"It will be well worth it. The deep-dish pizza is to die for, and I promise you, the dough will melt in your mouth," I assured her.

We ordered a couple of O'Doul's beers, which are non-alcoholic, and the waitress brought over some freshly baked bread and some baked garlic, chopped into a small dish of virgin olive oil mixed with some parmesan cheese. I thought it was nice that she indulged in drinking a non-alcoholic beverage like myself in order not to make me feel isolated.

"So, Johnny…what's new with this murder investigation in Ira Township?" she began to inquire again. I thought that it was weird that she was so interested in what was going on with that homicide.

I started to give her a progress report on the 'Water Pistol Killer' investigation, along with the poem that was accompanied by the victim's body and how the victim was killed.

"Who came up with that name? The 'Water Pistol Killer'?"

"That was the moniker that the Detroit News used in their article about the murder last week."

She asked me some more particular questions regarding my father's homicide in 1978 and how his murderers ended up getting exonerated. For some strange reason, Olivia seemed to be extremely interested in all the details of Dad's murder forty years ago.

She asked about the symbolism of the green squirt gun.

"What does that mean?" she asked.

"Evidently, the murderers pleaded self-defense because my father found my toy water pistol in his truck on the night of the murder, so he put it in his pocket to make his killers believe he had a weapon," I explained.

She thought about it for a moment. "And the horse's penis? Isn't that from 'The Godfather'?"

"Yeah," I smiled, "But I don't know what that's about."

"Maybe the 'Water Pistol Killer' is Francis Ford Coppola?" she joked.

Laughing, I suggested, "Or maybe Robert DeNiro."

"No. He didn't come around until 'The Godfather, Part 2." Olivia laughed.

"But why would the killer go through all the trouble of inserting a horse's penis into the victim's mouth?"

"The killer clearly is trying to send a message," I replied.

"A message to whom?" Olivia asked.

I thought about it, "I don't know."

"Maybe a message to the original killer who planned your father's murder."

"You mean Howard Williams?"

"Yes," she nodded. "There is a lot of symbolism there. If you're going to investigate this, find out what the killer is trying to say, between the poem, the toy water pistol, and the horse's 'catzo' in the lady's mouth."

I was momentarily amused by Olivia's use of the Italian slang word for 'penis.'

"I would agree, except I am not the one investigating this murder," I reminded her.

Olivia took a long sip of her cold beer, then looked at me intensely.

"Well, Johnny, it sounds like you have only two choices here."

"Really? And what are those?"

"You're either going to have to help them find who the real killer is or wait for them to pin this murder on you," Olivia observed.

"I've been involved in a lot of criminal homicide investigations, and I can tell you objectively what's going through their minds. Right now, you're probably their only logical suspect."

"Now that's a ballsy statement," I retorted. At this point, I didn't know if I should be grateful for her honesty or angry at her realistic insinuation.

"Think about it, Johnny. You're the only one who has the motive, the ability, and the means to pull off that kind of murder. You satisfy all three of the criteria for committing a homicide. If I were you, I would be playing nice with these Ira-hick Township detectives. I would be doing everything in my power to help them with this investigation."

I silently glared at her for about ten seconds. As much as I hated to admit it, I knew damn well that she was right.

The waitress brought over another round of cold beers along with our pizza, which was nicely baked with green peppers, onions, and pepperoni. The pizza looked and smelled heavenly.

As we were both devouring our first slices, I continued to tell her about the evidence that was found at the crime scene and the fact that their star detective, Ronald Sinclair, used to be a veteran cop with the Detroit P.D.

"Really?" she replied, reaching for another piece of pizza. For some reason, the sound of her voice sounded like she was getting disinterested.

I was devouring my pizza and contemplating her advice regarding my cooperation with the Ira Township Police Department. Throughout the whole meal, she was rubbing her shoeless foot up against the calf of my leg.

"Are you a runner?" she asked.

"Not anymore. I used to run a lot several years ago before I threw out my back."

"You have huge calf muscles," she observed. She seemed to be rubbing her leg against mine even more intently, and I was starting to get a little aroused.

"Johnny, tell me why you got divorced. Was it mostly because of the drinking?" as she was taking the last sip of her O'Doul's beer.

"Mostly. Being a detective with the Detroit P.D. didn't help either. Marina spent a lot of time alone at home with the boys, and it took a toll on her and our marriage."

She was smiling as the waitress brought over another cold one. I suddenly felt her foot rubbing up harder against my leg. Olivia was glaring at me with those sultry brown eyes, and she was rubbing her shoeless bare foot up against my right thigh. It was taking all of my psychological strength to keep myself from getting very excited.

"Do you always rub your bare feet up against the legs of coppers?" I asked, trying to keep my voice from quivering.

"Only the ones I'm attracted to," she mischievously replied.

"You know, Detective..."

"You're not going to call me 'Johnny' anymore?"

"Yes, Johnny," as she was continued to rub her bare foot up against my leg and in my crotch. "I would love to go for a nice, long walk on the Detroit Riverfront. It's a beautiful night."

"The Detroit Riverfront? Now?" I replied.

"Well, yes, it is a beautiful night. What better way to get to know each other than a nice, romantic walk along the Riverfront, with a wonderful view of the city?"

She stopped and pressed her foot up hard against my crotch.

"You're not afraid of walking around the Riverfront at night, are you?"

I almost answered her in a falsetto voice. "No," as I shook my head.

Great. There I was at Louie's Pizzeria, trying to finish my pizza and beer with her bare foot rubbing hard between my legs. I was trying to figure out how the hell I was going to gracefully get up from the table and go over to the Detroit Riverfront without totally embarrassing the hell out of myself.

I suddenly grabbed her barefoot.

"You going to have to stop doing that," still holding her left foot, "before I make a scene, and we both find out how ticklish you are."

"You wouldn't dare," she playfully replied.

"Try me."

There I was, with a beautiful, classy brunette, making a hard pass at me while I was trying like hell to ignore her advances. My sixth sense was talking to me, and I knew that ignoring her was going to be a very challenging task, indeed.

She smiled at me with those alluring brown eyes as she withdrew her foot. This girl was drop-dead gorgeous. I could tell she was teasing me to see how I would react to her advances. There was a part of me that just wanted to jump over the table and make incredible love to her in the middle of the pizzeria. But I knew I had to control myself, realizing that I wasn't eighteen years old anymore.

I had to be a responsible adult. I had to be a gentleman. I had to try like hell to control myself.

We both finished our pizza and beers, allowing myself to calm down as I paid the waitress. We then got into her car, and we made our way to the Detroit Riverfront. I figured we would walk around the new parks, restaurants, and cafes that were now available there in front of the Detroit River.

I was having the time of my life.

CHAPTER TWENTY-SEVEN

JACK EDWARD HANSEN-SUMMER 2019

The sun was out on that warm Sunday morning in August as Jack Hansen sat outside on his backyard patio, reading the morning paper. His wife, Barbara, had just brought him his second cup of coffee that morning, as he was perusing the Columbia
Examiner. He was peeling it apart and reading it section by section.

Sitting outside on his patio every morning was a daily ritual for Hansen. He had recently retired as an electrician for a local contractor he had worked for in Columbia, South Carolina, and had recently purchased a townhome in Beech Island. He and his wife had raised four children together during their forty-seven-year marriage and now enjoy their nine grandchildren, ranging from the ages of two to fifteen years old.

At the age of 68, Jack was retired and finally doing what he enjoyed doing the most: Absolutely nothing.

He had enough pension and social security income for him and his wife to live comfortably in their new townhouse on Beech Island. When his wife wasn't babysitting their grandchildren (which he refused to take part or participate in), they spent their time taking long walks, going out for dinner twice a week, or fishing together at the nearby lake.

Considering where he had come from and what he had left behind forty years ago, Jack Hansen was now living a charmed life. He grew up on Hamburg Street in the Von Stueben neighborhood on the East Side of Detroit, near

Gratiot Avenue. He graduated from Osborn High School in 1969 and was immediately drafted into the Army for a two-year stint in Vietnam.

After serving his country and being honorably discharged, he married his high school sweetheart, Barbara Addison, and continued to live with his parents on Hamburg Street. Hansen got a job as an electrician apprentice, while Barbara worked as a hairstylist at a local beauty salon. They continued to struggle to put enough money together to buy their own home someday.

But by the time Jack had been discharged from the Army in 1971, he came out of his combat unit mentally and emotionally scarred. Hansen had an acute case of post-traumatic stress disorder.

With all of the bloody combat he had seen and experienced during the Vietnam war, Hansen overcompensated his psychosis with frequent drinking, gambling, and drug use. Those bad habits, along with his violent, uncontrollable temper, started getting him into some trouble with the law. He did a short stint at Jackson State Prison for trying to rob a gas station and was sentenced to three years. After doing nineteen months, he was released on good behavior and had now met a new set of friends.

He had encountered Howard Williams and George Johnson while he was in Jackson State. They had frequented the horse track in Hazel Park, and Williams covered their bets on the sportsbook. He was running the numbers for the Licavoli Family on the East Side at the time, and Hansen and Johnson's many bets on college and professional football were starting getting them in trouble.

By the middle of 1978, Hansen was into Williams and the boys for over five thousand bucks. He became desperate and borrowed four thousand dollars from his mother-in-law to pay off a large portion of his balance, along with the 'vig.'

So, when Howard Williams approached Johnson and Hansen to help him with 'a situation' where he would cover 'a G-note of their markers,' they both jumped at the chance. They were desperate and would do anything to get out from under 'the boys.'

That decision came with very tragic, horrific consequences and changed the lives of everyone involved. It would all come down on Halloween night, 1978.

Howard Williams asked Jack Hansen and George Johnson to help him 'rough up' someone who he believed was sleeping with his wife. He asked Hansen to borrow a gun from someone and bring it along that night in case 'things got crazy.'

Williams and Johnson parked their cars in the parking lot of Fourteen Mile and Van Dyke. Hansen picked up his two friends in his 1970 Oldsmobile and went over to where Howard's wife worked the afternoon shift.

As the three of them waited in the parking lot of the Ford Assembly Plant on 23 Mile Road and Mound, Williams had brought along a twelve-pack of Stroh's Beer and a large bag of pretzels to drink and pass the time. The three of them then patiently waited for Joni Williams and her boyfriend to finish their shifts at 11:00 pm.

By one o'clock in the morning on that Halloween, the three of them were enjoying several beers at the Blue-Ribbon Lounge. They had accomplished their task.

And their hunted victim, Tony Valentino, was lying face up in a pool of blood on El Camino Drive.

But the next day, the three of them were sitting in jail, having had been arrested by the Detroit Police Department on murder charges. It was then that Jack Edward Hansen had realized the ugly truth about the events that they had gotten themselves involved in.

His so-called friend had used him.

Howard Williams primarily knew of Hansen's violent, unstable temper and his PSTD syndrome. He played it to his advantage. He allowed Hansen to be the only one handling that borrowed weapon, the .25 caliber Pic-DeCauter automatic pistol, as he was the first person to turn himself into the police.

He immediately insisted on taking the 'paraffin test' at the police station the next day, proving that he did not handle the murder weapon. Williams stood in the background that evening while Johnson and Hansen roughed up Valentino. He watched them manhandle him, grabbing him by his shirt collar before Hansen fatally shooting him three times.

When Hansen's wife Barbara had realized what had happened on that Halloween night, she was hocking jewelry (including her wedding ring) the next day at a pawn shop on Gratiot Avenue. Barbara needed to come up with the money to retain an attorney for her husband.

Jack Edward Hansen was being held on criminal charges of first-degree murder without bond.

Williams and Johnson were eventually released three weeks later. But Hansen's homicide charges were reduced to the murder of the second degree, with the prospect of 25 years to life in prison. He spent the next five months locked up in the Wayne County Jail.

It was the legal skills of Hansen's high-priced, politically connected attorney, Mark Abdo, that effectively secured his freedom. Hansen's pleas of innocence and self-defense successfully influenced the jury into acquitting him in March 1979.

When Jack and Barbara Hansen were forced to leave Detroit in May 1979, they were penniless. They and moved to Columbia, South Carolina, to live with her parents. They then settled down and had started a large family. Jack went into psychological rehabilitation. He got help for his PSTD, his drinking, his gambling, and his drug abuse. He later joined the IBEW Union Local 379 and worked as an electrician for several construction and development companies for almost forty years before retiring on his sixty-fifth birthday.

For all definitive purposes, Jack Hansen had cleaned up his life. His ugly, Detroit past was long gone and distantly behind him. As far as he was concerned, what happened on El Camino Drive in 1978 had occurred at another time.

Jack Hansen's dark past was a very distant memory.

As the retired senior citizen was reading the newspaper, Barbara came out to the patio with a tray of fresh, English muffins. As they made small talk about their upcoming day, Jack gave her the lifestyle section of the Columbia Examiner, displaying the want-ad section. He took out his ballpoint pen and circled a particular personal ad and smiled, giving it to his wife.

"How would you like to go back and visit some friends in Detroit?"

"Huh? Why?"

Hansen then eagerly pointed out the ad to her.

Barbara Addison Hansen glared at her husband for a few long seconds before she emphatically said the word 'No' several times.

"I will never go back to Detroit. There are too many dark memories there, and I have no desire to relive any of them. As far as I'm concerned, that city doesn't exist."

Jack looked at his wife, still smiling.

"Why would you want to go back there? Every terrible thing that's ever happened in your life happened in Detroit. Do you miss being used then going to prison for murder? Do you miss those shady friends that used you and took advantage of you?"

Jack tried to reason with her.

"They're long gone, honey. Besides, we can't continue to hide away from our past."

Barbara was quiet, now only glaring at her husband.

"Come on, honey. It's been over forty years. It would be fun," he said, still pointing at the personal ad.

"No, Jack. That town still has horrific memories for us, and I don't have any desire to revisit those."

"But Barbara, we grew up there. We went to school there. We started our lives there. It's just for the weekend, honey. We can't hide forever."

Barbara began to stare out at the beautiful horizon of the South Carolina countryside. On a clear day, they could see the Atlantic Ocean from their townhouse, perched high above the pristine, coastal beaches.

She then grabbed the newspaper and read the personal ad out loud:

Looking for All Graduates of
Osborn High School-Class of 1969
Fiftieth Class Reunion
Detroit, Michigan
Colony Club Detroit
2310 Park Avenue
Detroit, Michigan
Saturday, September 30
Please respond: www.osborn1969reunion.com

Jack looked at his wife with a huge grin on his face. He was suddenly looking forward to seeing all the friends that he had grown up with on Hamburg Street and the Von Steuben neighborhood. He was thrilled at the opportunity to see his classmates from his high school years.

For the first time in ages, Jack was actually excited about something. He was eager to visit the hometown that he had grown up in, to see people he hadn't seen in a very long time.

But most of all, he wanted to confront the bad memories of that Halloween night that had changed his whole life. He tried to reassure himself that he had grown beyond the horrific events of that evening in 1978.

Barbara then made a shadow of a smile to her husband. She would do anything for the love of her life, even if it meant going back and revisiting their personal demons in the Motor City.

"Find a hotel in downtown Detroit, honey. We're going to our high school reunion."

It had been over forty years. For him, the bad memories had faded. The people associated with those events have long gone. And after all that time, Jack Edward Hansen was confident that there was no longer or a dangerous vendetta against his life.

The Osborn High School 1969 Fiftieth Class Reunion Committee had wanted their event to be an overwhelming success. They had been planning this affair for over two years. Because many of their graduates were scattered across the country, the committee decided to put a personal ad in all of the major newspapers nationally. They put out emails, set up Facebook and Instagram pages, and put together a sophisticated, interactive website.

All the members knew that, with the average age of their alumni at 68 years old, many would probably not be around for their next reunion. They were committed to find and account for all 486 graduates of their high school class. The members put down a large deposit on the banquet hall, as they were anticipating that most of their alumni, along with their spouses, would attend.

That same personal ad was posted in the Detroit News on June 15th and ran consecutively in the Sunday edition for twelve weeks. A week before the class reunion, 514 alumni and their guests had purchased their dinner tickets for the Colony Club-Detroit for that upcoming Saturday evening.

An exciting weekend for their former students was planned. All the alumni would be at the football game between Osborn and Denby High Schools on that Friday night for Homecoming. There would be a 'Memory Lane' event during the day on Saturday, where all the alumni would have brunch in the high school cafeteria and then visit the classrooms and hallowed halls of their beloved school. And after the reunion dinner dance at the Colony Club, a picnic at Metropolitan Beach would follow on that Sunday afternoon.

The Reunion Committee had well-publicized their alumni get together, and they all anticipated it would be a runaway success. All the alumni names that were attending were posted on their website, making their guest list on that Saturday night public knowledge.

Osborn High School 1969 alumni Jack Edward Hansen and Barbara Addison Hansen would definitely be in attendance.

But on that September weekend, someone else had also become aware of Osborn's class reunion.

The police station in Ira Township was rather quiet on that Friday afternoon, as Detective Ronald Sinclair was sitting at his desk, trying to finish some police reports. He had several minor crime cases that he was working on, but the gruesome murder at the Chateau Estates was clearly on his mind.

He had read the police reports from the homicide of Antonio Valentino several times, and no matter how many different ways he tried to slice it, it always came out the same:

Detective John Valentino was the prime suspect.

It all made sense to him, and every time he tried to give the Third Precinct detective the benefit of the doubt, the facts and evidence from the crime scene kept pointing back at Valentino.

Sinclair had talked to several other Detroit P.D. personnel and found out about John Valentino's Third Precinct suspension. Commander Riley was clearly having concerns about his detective's anger and behavior problems. Sinclair had also discovered Detective Valentino's drinking troubles and that he was an alcoholic.

A veteran detective with a bad childhood, a terrible temper, and a drunk? For Sinclair, this was starting to become an open and shut case. Valentino clearly wanted to take revenge against his father's killers, and perhaps, decided to start with his father's old girlfriend from over forty years ago. Who would be more successful in fulfilling an old family vendetta than a troubled, drunken cop with anger issues?

"Have some mail for you here, Ron," the dispatcher said, as she placed several envelopes on top of Detective Sinclair's desk.

The Ira Township detective shuffled through the several pieces of mail when he noticed an envelope addressed to him with a return address, stamped from the Detroit Police Department in the Tenth Precinct.

As he opened up the letter, there was a cut-out picture of a green squirt gun, along with a handwritten, yellow sticky note:

Look no further than the Third Precinct for your Water Pistol Killer. I have some information that may help your investigation. Call me.

Patrolman Andrew Hacker- Detroit P.D.

Why would Sinclair be receiving a note from a patrolman from the Tenth Precinct? It didn't make any immediate sense to him.

But Sinclair wanted to make sure that he left no stone in this investigation unturned. If this copper had some information regarding this case, he was certainly interested in hearing it.

Especially if the informant had some trustworthy information that would lead to the arrest and conviction of Detective John Valentino of premeditated, first-degree murder.

At that moment, Ira Township Detective Ronald Sinclair picked up his desk phone.

CHAPTER TWENTY-EIGHT

AN INTIMATE EVENING-SUMMER 2019

Olivia and I had been walking along Detroit's Riverfront that August evening for almost two hours. It was a warm, romantic summer evening, where the stars were visible, dancing across Detroit's downtown skyline.

We stopped at the Riverfront Café and ordered some cheesecake and cappuccinos. Olivia and I talked and discussed so many different subjects, and I was immediately smitten with her easy-going demeanor and her casual attitude. Olivia had the ability to make me feel comfortable around her, and I found myself being completely unashamed. We talked about everything and anything that evening.

I talked to her about my difficult childhood without my father, and she discussed her personal background as well and the problematic relationship she had with her dad. Olivia disclosed that her mother and father had divorced when she was in high school. She and her brothers had a hard time getting along and staying close to one another, as her parents seemed to continue to take their anger out with each other long after their divorce.

Olivia was an intense Detroit Red Wings fan, and she had season tickets for the upcoming hockey season. Her family had been season ticket holders for over thirty years, going back to when they were playing hockey at Olympia Stadium. Olivia was raised in a fanatical hockey environment. She had three other brothers who played high school and college hockey, and she had been around the sport all of her life. She even traveled to some of the Red Wings away games when they corresponded with her out of town business trips.

I told her that I had only gone to a few hockey games my whole life. I was more of a Detroit Tigers baseball fan, having gone to Briggs Field to see my first Tigers game when I was in the fourth grade with the other safety boys from my class. We then promised that we would take each other to a Red Wings and Tigers game.

It was just after eleven o'clock before we arrived at her condominium on Jefferson Avenue. Her eighteenth-floor apartment overlooked a beautiful view of the Detroit River from her balcony. The lights from the Ambassador Bridge were shining brightly and in full view from her condo. I was mesmerized by the downtown skyline, with Windsor, Canada glimmering its bright lights on the other side.

"Can I get you anything?"

"No, Olivia. I'm fine. Between the pizza and the cheesecake, I don't think I'll be eating for a while," as I sat down and made myself comfortable on her couch.

The décor of her condo was quite eclectic, with large, framed movie posters of famous American movies in French. There was even one from my favorite silent film, 'The Son of the Sheik' with Rudolph Valentino, a distant, wanna-be relative. Her furniture consisted of a large, black, eight-piece leather sectional, several black swivel chairs, and some hanging lamps that accented the room décor nicely. Her wall to wall flooring was that of Italian Travertine marble throughout and blended well with the living room fireplace.

The high-level view of the city's skyline was breath-taking as she opened the balcony sliding door to allow a quiet, summer breeze to rush into the room.

"I need to excuse myself for a moment," after she turned on the television, where "Late Night with Jimmy Fallon" was still on. I watched her go into her bedroom, and after about ten minutes or so, reappeared wearing a long, off-white, satin bathrobe.

"I couldn't wait to change out of my clothes," she apologetically said.

"I don't know about you, but I need a drink."

Olivia must have temporarily forgotten that I couldn't consume alcohol, so I reminded her to give me a Diet Coke.

"I'm sorry, Johnny, I forgot."

"That's okay. You go ahead and pour yourself some liquor. I don't expect you not to drink because of me."

She walked into the kitchen and poured out two Diet Cokes, then put a splash of rum in her drink. Olivia then brought both glasses over to the couch where I was sitting.

"Salute," as we both made a toast to our good health.

At that moment, she had on a Creed Fiorentina perfume that smelled totally amazing. She was sitting extremely close to me as we were both gazing at Jimmy Fallon interviewing some young, insignificant guest that I didn't recognize. By then, she was sitting so close to me that she was practically sitting on my lap, while her mesmerizing perfume was doing the trick in getting me excited.

Olivia then started kissing my cheek, my neck and began unbuttoning my Polo shirt. She was then rubbing her hand up and down my chest while I was struggling to keep from spilling my Diet Coke. We started intensely kissing, and she pulled off her bathrobe.

Olivia was wearing a black, see-through negligee and sheer, black thong underwear that looked incredibly sexy. Her soft skin, along with her strawberry lip gloss, was impossible to resist as she was rubbing her hands up and down my unbuttoned shirt.

She then got up and pulled my arm, and I followed her to her room. We couldn't have been in her bedroom more than five seconds before she assaulted me, unbuttoning my shirt as I eagerly undid her top and black bra. We were wildly undressing each other like two high school teenagers. She stood there naked, showing off her unbelievably well-shaped body. Her abdomen looked like an athlete's chiseled six-pack as if she spent all of her spare time doing sit-ups and core exercises.

"You must spend a lot of time in the gym," I commented.

"Only when I'm bored," she joked, as she continued to kiss me on my stomach and my chest.

Her breasts were perfectly shaped, as her rosy nipples seemed to protrude with every kiss that I implanted on her chest. She was sun-tanned and very well-toned, as I placed wet, long kisses along every inch of her curvaceous body.

We were completely naked on top of her bed when she guided my body on top of hers, and her legs were now wrapped around my waist. I was so excited, and I wanted to make love to her so badly.

I teased her for about ten minutes or so until I finally pulled myself off of her.

"Johnny, what's wrong," she asked.

"Nothing, honey. I haven't made love to another girl except for my wife. Right now, at this moment, I'm nervous, and I'm just not ready."

We both looked at each other for about thirty seconds or so without saying a word. Olivia then pulled me close to her, and she hugged me as hard as she could.

"I understand, baby. I really do," as she continued to kiss me up and down all over my body.

We continued our intense caressing and kissing for what seemed like hours. The curtains and windows of her bedroom remained wide open the whole time, overlooking the Riverwalk shoreline and all the fantastic skyscrapers lined up and down the Detroit River coastline.

I wanted so much to make love to Olivia. But I wanted to feel the same passion and emotion for her while making love to her the same way I did while making love with Marina. I loved the intense emotional feeling that I had whenever I made love to my wife, and I wanted that same feeling with Olivia.

I know I was asking too much of myself, and I was probably just putting more unnecessary pressure on my feelings. I never learned just to screw or just fornicate. Maybe I was too old-fashioned in that way. I learned to make love to the only girl I ever loved in my whole life, and I wanted that same feeling when I made love to Olivia.

She was very understanding, maybe even sympathetic. At that moment, she must have thought that I was this chivalrous, gallant gentleman that put his heart before his zipper. But at that moment, I just couldn't allow myself to fall that deeply in love.

I just wasn't ready.

But it felt terrific to lay next to Olivia, and I felt myself falling deeper and deeper into that emotional abyss. We fell asleep in each other's arms that night, hoping that the sunrise would never come.

As I closed my eyes, I felt utterly uninhabited. I felt totally fearless. I was unashamed to sleep next to Olivia, now the only other girl I had ever laid next to except for Marina.

On that steamy summer evening, I would have given anything for it never to end.

Chapter Twenty-Nine

The Colony Club-September 30, 2019

It was just past midnight on that late Saturday night when I had put on my pajama bottoms and a tee-shirt to get ready for bed. It was a cold, late September evening, and I had just gotten home from a night out on a date.

I had gone out with Olivia to the movies in Grosse Pointe earlier, and we both decided to go home early. We had gone to the Woods Theater to see "The Irishman" with Robert DeNiro and Al Pacino, and it was a great movie. But it was also three hours long, and I found myself dozing off several times sitting in that theater.

We were both tired, as it had been a long week for both of us. I took her home to her condo downtown on Jefferson Avenue, and she started with a gentle, warm good night kiss. Then the kissing got more intense. We probably then spent another good twenty minutes mashing and grabbing in front of her condominium building. Olivia and I had been dating for several months now, and although we had gotten into some pretty hot and heavy necking sessions, we still hadn't gotten intimate yet.

To be quite honest, I wasn't in any hurry. I was still pretty torn up emotionally over my failed marriage and broken relationship with my ex-wife, Marina. Even though Olivia and I had been going out for a while, she sensed my emotional hesitation and didn't seem to be in any rush. The guy rule of 'three dates and in bed' didn't apply here, and I was okay with it. Besides, I was still struggling to stay sober and didn't want to get distracted by regularly going out, wining and dining her. I didn't want to become tempted to start drinking again.

Olivia was very understanding about my drinking problem. Whenever we went out to dinner, I would usually have a non-alcoholic beverage, and she was okay with drinking Diet Sodas or Arnold Palmers.

I usually slept with the television on, which had a timer to turn off automatically after a few hours. Reruns of 'Blue Bloods' was on cable TV almost every night, so I usually managed to fall asleep with Tom Sellick's voice going through my head. I couldn't have been sleeping for more than an hour when my police cellular phone loudly went off.

"Hello?" I could barely talk, still groggy.

"Johnny? It's Frank."

"Hey Frank," being half asleep, it didn't register in my head who was calling me.

"There's been a double homicide downtown here in Fox Town. You need to come down here."

I then realized it was Detective Frank Partridge, my old partner, and police pallie. Frank seldom ever calls me, especially on homicide investigations, so I was curious.

"Okay, Frank. Where?"

"Colony Club on Park Avenue. You may want to get here as soon as you can."

There was a moment of silence, as I didn't like the sound of his voice. It sounded urgent. Having known and worked with him for so long, and it seemed almost accusatory.

"Okay. But what happened?"

Another silent moment.

"Do you recall those homicide police reports that you've been reading up on and investigating? You know, the ones about your father's murder?"

"Yeah?"

"We just found one of the murderers and his wife in their rental car in the parking lot of the Colony Club. Two bullets each to the back of the head. The parking valet called it in."

I went into total shock.

"Oh my God," was all I managed to say. "Who?" For some reason, my mind was drawing a blank, and I couldn't remember the names of my father's killers.

"The victim's names are Jack and Barbara Hansen. They had just attended their class reunion party at the Colony Club over an hour ago. We only know that this is the same guy because I remember you telling me about them when we were out a few weeks ago and remembered that one of them lived in South Carolina."

Another silent moment as my mind began racing.

"This guy's ID checks out. We just ran a background check on him, and it's the same guy."

I then remembered his full name. "Jack Edward Hansen, Beech Island, South Carolina, correct?"

"Yep. That's him," Partridge said.

"Are you sure, Frankie?"

"Just hurry up and get down here. I'm calling you out of courtesy, Johnny. Expect a lot of questions when you get here."

I groaned out loud, knowing now that the top brass was looking more closely at me now, especially since that gruesome homicide at the Chateau Estates on Marine City Highway last month.

And now, this murder happens.

I must have whispered, 'Oh my God' under my breath a hundred times.

"Okay, I'm on my way."

As I was ready to hang up, I heard Frank still talking.

"Oh, Johnny? Just for your info, there was a green squirt gun and a sealed letter at the crime scene. It looks like we've got a serial killer on our hands."

I listened intently, still numb from this sudden information.

"Not a poem, I hope."

"I'm afraid so, John. Hurry up and get here!" he abruptly hung up the phone.

I threw on my pants and a sweatshirt and jumped into my squad car, taking Ten Mile Road to the Ford I-94 Expressway. Within fifteen minutes, I was on Park Avenue at the Colony Club parking lot, across the street from the Park Avenue Hotel. The whole lot was tapped off with yellow crime scene tape, and there were at least ten Detroit P.D. squad cars surrounding the perimeter of the area. I counted at least three EMS ambulances there, even though there were only two victims, and the whole city was crawling with patrolmen, detectives, and top brass. It looked like a downtown party, and for a few seconds, I felt honored that I was invited.

Frank Partridge was waiting for me next to the entrance of the parking lot, trying to intercept me away from the other detectives.

"What's up, Frank? What's going on?"

"Get ready, Johnny. These detectives are asking a lot of questions, and most of them are going to be directed towards you."

I felt a cold shiver go down my spine as Frank said those words. I started to feel as though that, because there were similarities between this double homicide and the murder in Ira Township last month, that I was going to be the Intel Unit's special boy. I boldly walked over to the white, late model Cadillac CTS where the murder took place.

The rental car was parked near the corner of the parking area, up against the wall next to the adjacent building surrounding the lot. There were other vehicles parked around the crime scene vehicle, and several other bystanders from the party were standing around, anxious to volunteer their information on the victims and what they remembered that evening.

"What was the occasion?" I asked Partridge as we walked together towards the vehicle.

"Osborn High School's Fiftieth Class Reunion. They had over five hundred attendees, and both victims were members of their class."

I walked closer to the Hertz rented vehicle, as the police department CSI was now examining in detail the crime scene. I got a good look at both victims, as the husband was slumped over the steering wheel, the back of his head full of blood. The wife was also slumped, at an angle lying next to her husband, blood coming out of her mouth. Based on the position of the dead bodies, it looked as though the husband was shot at point-blank range in the back of his head. The wife probably got a good look at the killer, as her head seemed to be turned, with the two bullet wounds entering the left side of her temple.

"Looks like the killer shot both of them from the back seat," I observed. "Was the car unlocked? Was there forced entry?"

"No, it looks like the killer somehow jimmied the passenger door open, then probably waited for the victims while hiding in the backseat," Frank hypothesized.

"Or maybe he just waited for them to come out, and then he forced his way into the car at gunpoint? Are there any security cameras?" I asked.

"There is one on the other side of the lot, but as luck would have it, it wasn't working at the time."

"What do you estimate as the time of death?" I asked Frank.

"Probably around 11:20, maybe a little before. One of the party guests said the reunion was breaking up after the band stopped playing at 11:00 pm. Many of the guests were hanging around socializing in the grand ballroom of the Colony Club. None of the guests heard or saw anything, and the valets were too busy retrieving cars to see what had happened," Detective Partridge summarized.

I took a good look at the husband, slumped over his steering wheel. Studying his face, he looked exactly like the mug shot that was made of the victim over forty years ago. Although he was now bald and many years older, his aged face and features accurately resembled the pictures of my father's killers in his police file.

He was wearing a dark blue suit jacket, a light blue shirt, and a striped tie. His wife was red-haired, combed up in a bun, and had on a white satin, short-sleeved dress. She looked older, probably in her late sixties. Her overdone makeup and her dark red lipstick blended well with the excessive blood that was seeping out of her mouth.

She had been shot in the left temple and another bullet hole directly in her forehead. Blood was splattered over the front of her dress, where the husband's bullet wounds were both from behind to the back of his skull. Both victims had clean, direct shots.

I glared at Frank. "Looks like a clean kill."

He then looked back at me, "Don't let the detectives hear you say that," he said nervously.

As I was assessing the crime scene with Frank, another familiar detective was gazing at me from the other side of the car. He was getting ready to approach me.

"What's Detective 'Dickhead' doing here?" I asked Partridge. He must have immediately known to whom I was referring.

"They called him up from the Ira Township Police Department since they still had an ongoing investigation on that mobile home murder last month. There could be a relationship between both murders. He's been snooping around asking a lot of questions."

Partridge paused for a moment. "I remember this guy from the Eighth Precinct. You described him correctly, Johnny." He was referring to my moniker.

"This guy's a real piece of work. He's probably watched too many 'Columbo' reruns."

I came to later find out from Commander Riley that I had another nemesis involved in these murder investigations. He had mentioned, through his communication with the Ira Township detective, that my old partner, Andrew Hacker, was blowing into Sinclair's ear.

During my months of working with Hacker, I had mentioned my thoughts about investigating my father's homicide forty years ago and how I thought the investigation should be reopened. He may have picked up on my disdain and possible desire to take my revenge out on these former, acquitted killers.

I recalled talking to him about it one evening while we were at the Crazy Horse Lounge after work. I remember the two of us sitting at the bar having way too many drinks, and I probably started shooting off my mouth.

Since being demoted to a patrolman in the Twelfth Precinct, Hacker now had it out for me. He had confirmed to Sinclair of my verbal desire to 'take out' my father's murderers.

Detective Ronald Sinclair walked around from the other side of the crime scene and approached me.

"Detective Valentino? It's so nice to see you again," as he extended his hand out towards me.

I thought twice about shaking the hand of this two-faced bastard. I had not seen or talked to him since our cozy little meeting at the precinct office with his Commander and Riley. I looked at him and gave him one of my fake smiles.

"Looks like our 'Water Pistol Killer' has struck again," he observed.

"Why?" I pretended not to know.

He then held up a clear evidence bag, which he acquired from CSI. It contained a green plastic toy squirt gun that was left at the crime scene.

"This was on the front seat, between both victims," as he gave the evidence bag back to the investigators combing the crime scene for prints.

There was another moment of silence as he then gave me a copy of the 'love poem' that the killer left as well. It was in a white envelope, and according to Sinclair, it was left on the dashboard in the car. It had been neatly opened. While holding it up in the moonlight, I read its contents out loud:

To scare his assassins, to force them away,
they wouldn't leave him alone.
Their rage and anger became no match
for a woman, not his own.

"Wow," was all I managed to say.

"Looks like a continuation of the last poem that was left by the killer at Chateau Estates," Sinclair stated.

Frank and I looked at each other. There was no doubt that this double homicide was related to the first murder last month. The stanza of this poem, put together with the first stanza from the initial crime scene in Ira Township, was pertaining to my father's murder forty-one years ago.

"Detective Valentino, I now have to ask: Where were you tonight? "Sinclair inquired.

I immediately pulled out my cell phone and dialed Olivia's phone number. After a few rings, she answered.

"Hey, Olivia, sorry to bother you."

"Johnny…is everything okay?"

"Just need you to vouch for me. Going to pass the phone over to Detective Sinclair."

I gave Detective Dickhead my cell phone as he walked several feet away with it, interrogating Olivia. After a few minutes, he nodded his head as he passed the cell phone back over to me.

"Okay?" I asked him.

He looked at me and nodded his head, then confirming that my alibi checked out. With Olivia still on the phone, I apologized to her, briefly telling her of the situation, and promised I would call her later.

"Please take care of yourself, honey. I'm worried about you," she lovingly said over the phone.

"Call me later," she said as I pushed the end button.

"Have you been dating her long?" he asked.

"Is that any of your business?" I sarcastically replied.

"A few months, maybe."

He then smiled, taking a few moments to respond.

"I'll bet she likes poetry," he snidely observed, winking his eye.

"Not really, Detective. Other than 'roses are red, violets are blue,' we don't recite much poetry."

By now, I was getting myself ready to kick the living shit out of this 'Ira-hick' detective. Sinclair only gave me a dirty look.

"Have you ever been to Ira Township?"

"Can't say that I have, Detective," I answered.

"We have very some very comfortable jail cells in our new police station. As a matter of fact, the jail cell toilets are brand new and have never been used before. You would probably really enjoy your stay there."

I began counting to ten under my breath, biting my tongue. I was trying so hard to control my temper.

Sinclair continued to make eye contact with me, then pulled a cigar out of his front pocket. He bit off the end and lit it up, puffing it intensely, while standing right in front of me. He was now blowing his cigar smoke in my face.

"Let me guess. You watch a lot of 'Columbo' reruns on TV," I observed.

Ignoring my comment, the 'Ira-hick Township' Detective only scowled at me.

"How does the rest of that poem go?" Sinclair sardonically asked.

"Roses are red; violets are blue.
There are three dead bodies now.
And we'll be watching you."

He then turned and walked away, back to the crowded crime scene.

"Looking forward to it, Detective," I shouted, making sure everyone heard me.

What an asshole!

It was as though he was trying to convince himself that I was the perpetrator of this murder. He seemed to have a look of disappointment on his face when he handed me back my cell phone after talking to Olivia.

Frank was still standing next to me throughout the whole time Sinclair was making his rude, blatant insinuations. We began walking over to the other side of the parking and over to the Park Avenue Hotel across the street.

"Detective Dickhead is trying his best to tie me into these homicides. Do you believe this shit? Even after he talks to my date tonight, he's still trying to make a connection," I said to Frank.

"Do you blame him, Johnny? You're the only one in the whole world who has a motive. And with your personal problems and you're now snooping into your father's murder files, reviewing those police reports and all, it certainly makes a lot of sense."

By then, we were walking into the lobby of the Park Avenue Hotel, far away from the crime scene and the various police and firefighters that were still lingering outside.

I noticed Frank suddenly stop and look at his shoes. He then quickly walked over to the concierge and wiped down his black Allen Edmond shoes with a Kleenex, then deposit the tissue in his pocket.

"What's wrong?"

"Oh, nothing. These are brand new shoes, and I've already gotten mud on them."

I then stopped dead in my tracks, and I looked at Frank straight in the eyes.

"I didn't kill anyone, Frank."

"I believe you, Johnny. But you can't tell me that the thought never crossed your mind."

I only looked at him, trying hard not to reply. I didn't want to confirm any of his assumptions.

"I'm not feeling any pity for these victims, Frank. With that old bitch getting sliced up like a pig last month, and now these two, I'm not going to pretend I'm feeling any sympathy for these hillbilly bastards."

Frank then put his hand on my shoulders.

"Keep your feelings to yourself, Johnny," he advised.

"And please make me a promise. You are going to try very hard to control your temper and watch your back. This guy is looking for an excuse, and he's probably gonna put a tail on you. Be aware of your surroundings."

He paused for a long moment.

"Don't be going over to the gun range for target practice any time soon," he smiled.

"I'm going to be on duty, Frank. What the hell is this guy gonna do? Sit on my lap? Ride with me on my crime investigations?"

"Who the fuck knows, Johnny. These 'Mayberry Hick- Coppers' are capable of anything," he said.

"Just watch your back, John."

With that, we gave each other a brief hug, and he then walked out of the hotel lobby and back over to the crime scene. Partridge would be involved with the Intelligence Unit in investigating this crime scene and its two victims.

As I walked out of the Park Avenue Hotel and back to my squad car, I started thinking about what Frank Partridge had said.

He was right. Of all the potential suspects in these 'Water Pistol Murders,' I was the only one so far who had the motive, the experience, and the ability to pull these murders off. If I were investigating these murders and had to come up with a list of suspects, I guess I would probably put myself on the top of the list.

Whoever the killer was, that person was going out of his way to let everyone know that this was in retribution for my father's murder forty years ago. These murders had the words 'payback and revenge' written all over them.

But I didn't do it, which made me even more suspicious as to who did. Could it be someone in my family? Could it be my Uncle Rossano? He's almost eighty years old now. Would he have the ability after all of these years to commit a murder? Although he is in good shape for his age, he doesn't have the physical strength or the desire any longer to take out his revenge against his brother's killers.

Could someone else in my family have hired someone to kill my father's murderer and his alleged girlfriend? My uncles? My sisters? My friends? Who else would have the motive *and* the ability to pull this off?

I didn't have a clue, and the thought of who this killer might be scared the living shit out of me. All I knew at that moment was that I had to investigate these murders myself personally. I needed to come up with my list of viable suspects in these three brutal homicides.

Or, as Sinclair suggested, I'll be in 'Ira-hick Township' sitting in their brand-spanking-new jail cell.

CHAPTER THIRTY

IRON MOUNTAIN, MICHIGAN-FALL 2019

Iron Mountain, Michigan, is a sleepy small town in the Upper Peninsula, located less stone's throw away from the Wisconsin border. It has a population of fewer than 8,000 people and is known for its pasties (a popular Michigan delicacy), Bocce Ball Tournaments and World Cup Ski Jumps. There is a large Italian population that immigrated and settled there over one hundred years ago to work in the iron and copper mines located in the area.

It is the revered hometown of MSU's basketball coach Tom Izzo and former NFL coach Steve Mariucci. It's a place where the Midwestern winters are so brutally cold and snowy; you need a pair of snowshoes to walk out to your mailbox. The significant, deep accumulation of snow seldom ever melts before the end of April. And the most popular means of winter transportation in this town are either snowmobiles, sleigh dogs, or a herd of reindeer.

When George Johnson was banished from Detroit over forty years ago, he decided to move back to where he was originally from
and where his parents lived. The small upper peninsula town was one of the furthest points in Michigan, away from the Motor City. He married a local Italian girl, Arcangela Maria Riggio, a few years later, and started a large family. The small Midwestern town was a great place to start a new life, and George Johnson embraced the opportunity. He finished his apprenticeship and became a licensed local plumbing contractor, G.F. Johnson & Sons Plumbing, Inc.

His past life as a former convict and accessory to murder was in the distant past. So far distant that he never even disclosed his past skeletons to his wife and family. He never considered or talked to anyone about his dark checkered history.

George Johnson had found a safe haven in Iron Mountain. After forty-plus years of living a clean life in the upper peninsula, he ultimately convinced himself that his ugly, dark history had occurred in another life.

George Johnson was now a respected member of his community. He went to Catholic mass with his wife and family every Sunday morning. He was a member of the Iron Mountain Rotary Club and a former grand knight with the St. Anthony's Parish Knights of Columbus. He and his wife ran the local food bank there twice a week and contributed to almost all of the worthy causes within the Iron Mountain community.

Johnson has just recently retired from his plumbing contracting business, having turned it over to his two sons, Michael and Thomas. His two daughters, Sarah and Sofia, had graduated from Marquette University and became registered nurses. His youngest daughter took on a job working at St. John's Hospital on Seven Mile Road in Detroit and was engaged to a cardiologist there. They had been living together in the Grosse Pointe area for a few years until they set a date for their fall wedding.

Their planned nuptials were to be quite extravagant, with their wedding mass at St. Paul's Catholic Church in Grosse Pointe.

The old, brick stoned gothic church was set back on Lakeshore Drive, looking over the calm waters of Lake St. Clair. Their wedding reception would be at the elegant Roostertail in downtown Detroit, facing off of the Detroit River.

The young couple planned for their wedding guests from the upper peninsula to stay at the Detroit Marriott Hotel at the Renaissance Center. Their elegant, upscale wedding was set for the last Saturday of October.

George and Angela Johnson had assisted the engaged couple with all of their wedding plans, even hiring a professional party planner to help them out with their big day. They were excited to marry off their youngest daughter and wanted her wedding day to be nothing less than perfect.

George's criminal past was so far behind him that even he didn't think twice about setting foot back into the town where he was warned to stay away. The year 1978 was a distant millennium in the past. As far as he was concerned, George believed that all of the players that were involved in that Halloween tragedy had long gone away, disappeared, and were completely forgotten.

But George Johnson was gravely mistaken. He had hugely miscalculated the horrific ghosts of his forgotten, disregarded past. Living in Iron Mountain, he was far away from any of the recent crime news regarding the 'Water Pistol Killer.'

Up to that time, there had been three homicides and two bloody crime scenes. They both had the commonality of a green water pistol and a white sealed envelope with a poem left behind at both of the murder scene locations.

The Detroit Police detectives and their Intelligence Unit had been working overtime, trying to catch a break in capturing this murderous killer, to no avail.

Detective Frank Partridge had been spending long hours on that murder case that had occurred a few weeks before. He had interviewed Howard Williams, one of the El Camino assailants over forty years ago, but he had an airtight alibi. He was having drinks at the Crazy Horse Lounge and could be seen on surveillance cameras sitting at the long bar, drinking, and enjoying lap dances from all of their exotic young strippers.

Partridge and his Intelligence Unit were collaborating with the Ira Township Police Department as well in searching for this murderous felon. Detective Ronald Sinclair was convinced that the same killer committed the murders at the Chateau Estates and the double homicide at the Colony Club.

Despite Detective Valentino's protests, Rossano Valentino was interviewed as well. His 'Uncle Ross' was asked to come down to the Detroit P.D. Thirteenth Precinct and answer a few questions. After spending three hours of intense questioning and verifying his location at the times of both of these homicides, both detectives ruled him out. His age and his valid excuse checked him off of that suspect list.

Both detectives were clueless as to whom could be the killer perpetrating these murders. They both interviewed Rosanna and Lucia, John Valentino's sisters, who both had reliable accounts of where they were at the time of the killings. His two uncles were also asked to come in for an interview at the Ira Township Police

Station. Both of his uncles, Mario, and Aldo, had severe health issues, having neurological and coronary heart problems. Both were in their early eighties and were far too old and frail to have physically committed these murders.

The crime scene at the Chateau Estates was analyzed and investigated for two weeks after Joni Williams' murder. It had to be cleaned up and detailed, with all of his bedroom furniture replaced by the insurance company. Williams needed to live elsewhere for an extended time with his sister living nearby. Howard Williams needed to mentally cope with the intense crime that occurred in his mobile home, knowing that he was the intended victim.

The Colony Club parking lot had several outdoor cameras, but neither was of any assistance in videotaping the killer or the murder. All of the adjacent businesses either didn't have working cameras or weren't useful at the time or location of the shooting.

Both Sinclair and Partridge had no other clues, no other leads, and no other additional suspects.

Every way the two detectives cut up and analyzed the facts, they both came up with the same potential suspect on top of their list:

Detective John Valentino.

Frank Partridge begrudgingly met up with his close friend several times. He asked him not to take it personally but that he was only doing his job as a detective and that he had no doubt that his former police partner was innocent.

He asked Valentino to come up with the actual proof of when and where he was at the time of both murders. He produced canceled movie tickets from the Woods Theater on the night of Hanson's murders. He also created the credit card dinner receipt from Buddy's for his Friday pizza night with his two young boys on the night of Joni Williams Harper's murder. Valentino had reliable accounts on the night of both killings, and Partridge and Sinclair were clueless.

The only thing that they both agreed upon was that John Valentino had a powerful motive to commit both of these murders. How he was able to perform them with reliable, substantial proof of his physical whereabouts stumped both veteran detectives.

That last week in October, Mr. and Mrs. George Johnson made the trip from Iron Mountain to Detroit and arrived at the Detroit Marriott in the Renaissance Center on that previous Thursday before the wedding. There was an elegant rehearsal dinner planned at an exclusive downtown restaurant in Corktown on the following Friday evening. The Johnson's wanted to be on hand to assist their daughter with any last-minute arrangements and details.

As was the Catholic tradition of St. Paul's Parish, a wedding announcement was published in the church's newsletter and posted on the vestibule of the church. It was also published in the Lifestyle section of the Detroit News:

> Mr. and Mrs. George Johnson of Iron Mountain, Michigan, announce the engagement and wedding of their daughter, Sarah Elena Johnson, to Dr. David Scarborough, son of Dr. and Mrs. William Henry Scarborough of Grosse Pointe Shores.
>
> Their nuptials will be at St. Paul's Catholic Church in Grosse Pointe Farms on Saturday, October 26th, at 2:00 pm. Fr. Thomas Bryson will be presiding.
>
> Wedding reception at The Roostertail in Detroit will follow.

The invitations had been mailed out that previous summer to the families and friends of both the bride and the groom. As is the custom nowadays, the nuptials were posted, broadcasted, and announced on the internet and all-over social media. Over three hundred guests had responded and were expected to attend.

But somewhere out there, someone very essential to this gathering was extremely disappointed.

The 'Water Pistol Killer' hadn't received a wedding invitation.

CHAPTER THIRTY-ONE

THE DETROIT NEWS-FALL 2019

The newsroom at the Detroit News on West Fort Street was especially loud that Wednesday afternoon, as everyone was trying to make their news article deadline for the morning addition. There was a Domino's Pizza box from lunch sitting on the corner of Justine Cahill's desk as she was busy working on her latest assignment. Only three pieces were left, as the cold pizza were remnants of the lunch that she and three other employees had devoured at noon.

The veteran investigative reporter was far too busy to snack at her desk and take a break from the fact-finding article she was working on. For some reason, although it had been a slow, newsworthy month of September in the newsroom, she was swamped. She had been covering some of the recent negotiations between Fiat-Chrysler and the automobile union.

In light of the recent embezzlement scandals that had been discovered in the auto industry over the last couple of years, Justine Cahill was covering the results of the arrest and sentencing of those involved by the Justice Department. But she was abruptly pulled off by her editor over the weekend to cover some recent murders that had been occurring in the metropolitan Detroit area.

Assistant Editor Dave Stover had a considerable amount of faith in his 'roving ace reporter.' As a long-time investigative news sleuth, Justine Cahill had just celebrated her fiftieth birthday. She had been a veteran reporter for the Detroit News for over thirty years and never worked for another paper. She originally got her job with the newspaper as a copy girl in the summer of her junior year at Wayne State University and had never looked for another job since.

Justine was a divorced mother of two grown-up girls, both with productive careers in something other than journalism. Her oldest, Brittney, 25, was a legal receptionist for a law firm downtown and was living with her boyfriend in an apartment in Corktown. Her youngest daughter, Bridget, 22, had just finished a sales and marketing degree at Michigan State and had started a job with Oracle's sales office in the suburbs. She had a comfortable home in suburban Birmingham, which was probably the reason why her youngest daughter was hesitant to move out.

The Detroit News reporter was an attractive, dirty-blond haired lady with light freckles and blue eyes that revealed her distant Irish roots. She had a proclivity for pizza and Italian food, which was probably why she had so much trouble losing those last twenty pounds, no matter how hard she worked out. She wore her red, horn-rimmed glasses most of the time on the edge of her nose, which let everyone in the newsroom know that she meant business.

Stover's confidence in Justine Cahill was not without merit. She had broken several big stories within City Hall, including the recent sex scandals with the city's former mayor, Kwame Kilpatrick. He was charged with perjury, obstruction of justice, and official misconduct stemming from a sex scandal and his handling of an $8.4 million settlement of a whistle-blower lawsuit against the city. Her tenacity in probing into the financial transactions that evolved from all of City Hall's key players was to her credit for her investigative determination. Many insiders believe that the scandal would not have been uncovered if it was not for her persistence and resolve in getting the facts in that case.

She also assisted in the investigation of the auto union embezzlement schemes that had occurred with the United Automobile Workers and the Fiat-Chrysler automakers. Cahill was instinctive in following the players involved in upper management's misuse and misappropriation of funds from the UAW's employee training facilities.

Justine Cahill had now been assigned to investigate the 'Water Pistol Killer' murders by her editor after a husband and wife had been found dead in the car at the Colony Club last week. She had started the investigation and written an article on the murders last Monday, discovering that there was a commonality of a green squirt gun and stanzas from a poem left at each crime scene.

But her investigation into these recent murders had now become very frustrating. Starting with the brutal stabbing of a Tennessee woman in Ira Township and now the double murder of a South Carolina couple at the Colony Club over the weekend, she was not coming up with a whole lot of new facts regarding these homicides. She only knew of the circumstances of the murdered couple Saturday night, and she had only recently discovered the poem stanzas and the green squirt guns left at the scene of both crimes.

For some strange reason, these Detroit City coppers weren't talking.

Her desk phone suddenly rang.

"Justine Cahill," she answered.

"Justine, come into my office for a minute. I need an update on those 'Water Pistol Killer' murders you're working on," Stover demanded.

"Okay, Dave. Anything else?" Justine asked as she was looking at her watch.

It was almost three-thirty, and she had a six o'clock deadline to meet.

"Yeah, is there any pizza left?"

"Three cold slices."

"Bring them in here before someone else devours them."

"Okay, Dave," Cahill nicely answered him. She did not appreciate being talked to like some kind of cafeteria waitress. She also knew that Stover was never one to leave precious pizza leftovers around in the office for very long.

Her assistant editor was a tough, no-nonsense, pull-no-punches kind of guy who always went to bat for his reporters whenever they were jammed up on a story. He was a six-foot, five-inch, 320-pound University of Michigan former linebacker, and he was a good boss to have on one's side.

He was always there to push for her and 'pinch-hit' whenever she needed to get something past the editor when covering a news subject. She had worked for him since 2009, and they had developed a mutually respectful relationship over the many years of working together.

Justine walked into Stover's office, carrying the half-empty Domino's Pizza box and her notes from her recent story.

"Nothing like cold pizza in the middle of the afternoon," Justine smiled, placing the pizza box on top of Stover's already dirty, disheveled, inordinate desk.

It was crowded with papers, files, scattered books, faxes, documents, lunch bags, and a McDonald's drink cup, which was probably from yesterday's lunch.

The assistant editor didn't even bother to greet her, and he immediately raided the used pizza box with its valuable contents.

"So, what's new with the 'Water Pistol Killer'?" Stover had managed to ask her a question while shoveling most of those three cold pieces into his mouth.

"Not a whole lot, Boss," Justine replied.

"Please don't choke in your office while on my watch. That wouldn't look good on my resume."

Stover picked up his day-old, extra-large Diet Coke in the McDonald's drink cup and washed down the three consumed slices. The assistant editor managed to devour his afternoon snack as if he were a starving Doberman Pincher in front of his dog dish.

"Listen here, my little Irish lass. Stop being a smart-ass and trying to change the subject. I expect an update on these murders for tomorrow's morning edition."

"Good luck with that one, Boss. It's pretty hard to get an update and write a story when none of the coppers at the Detroit P.D. or Ira Township aren't talking."

Stover coldly looked at his reporter.

"You're not trying hard enough."

"Bullshit, Dave. I was at both the Eighth Precinct and the Ira Township police departments yesterday and this morning. Nobody wants to talk to me."

"Do you blame them? Your showing up at their precinct would be like Lesley Stahl from '60-Minutes' waiting for an interview in their waiting room. I wouldn't want to talk to you either."

"Thanks, Boss. I love you too."

"Your reputation precedes you, my dear Justine," the assistant editor smiled.

"Everyone at City Hall is still 'm-f'ing you since you broke that story and sent Kwame to federal prison."

They were both silent for several moments as Justine began to smile.

"Did you call me in here to suck up? Isn't it supposed to be the other way around?"

"As a matter of fact, Justine...yes, it is," as he was dusting off the breadcrumbs from his black pants and his freshly coffee-stained white shirt.

"Would you rather be writing sleepy union articles and interviews regarding the two-year contract negotiations with General Motors and the United Auto Workers this month? Come on, Justine. I'll bet you'd have a lot of fun with that one."

"No thanks, boss. I like reporting on homicide investigations in this city. It will give me lots of material when I start writing Agatha Christy-style murder mysteries."

"Stick to your day-job, Justine. Tell me where we are in this investigation."

Justine Cahill pulled out her notes and starting reciting facts in the case.

"We know that Jack Edward Hansen and his wife, Barbara, were both in town from Beech Island, South Carolina, for their fiftieth-class reunion at Osborn High School."

"Osborn High School? No shit! We used to play football against them when I went to Denby High."

"May I finish?" Justine asked as her boss was busy reminiscing.

"They had checked into the Marriott Hotel near the Colony Club on Thursday afternoon and went to the homecoming football game at Osborn High against Denby that Friday night and..."

"Really? Who won?"

"Who fucking cares?" Justine loudly responded, now getting annoyed with her boss.

Dave Stover was now smiling from ear to ear.

"Note to self," he said as he scribbled on his notepad. "Osborn-Denby football score."

"Stop interrupting me, Dave," she angrily demanded as she looked again at her notes.

"The Hansen's had dinner and stayed at the reunion party until about 11:15 pm, according to the restaurant manager, who remembered them leaving."

"The parking lot manager was out valeting cars and didn't see who had assaulted the couple when they got into their car Saturday night. He saw the husband slumped over the steering wheel of their Cadillac, with blood splattered on the windshield when he notified the manager, and they called it in."

"Who were the Cadillac license plates registered to?"

"Rental car from Hertz."

"No surveillance cameras in the parking lot?"

"Nope. There are two cameras on each corner, and neither one of them was working at the time."

"Was there an apparent break-in to the vehicle by the killer?"

"No sign of forced entry."

"Hmmm...that seems odd," Stover observed. "How did the killer get to the victims?"

"They're not sure. The detectives think the killer assaulted them outside of their vehicle before assassinating them in their car."

There was a silent moment as the assistant editor was deep in thought.

"Who's the investigating copper?"

"Detective Frank Partridge, from the Intel Unit at the Eighth Precinct."

"Were you able to get any additional information from him on this case?"

"Very little. He didn't want to go on record, as there was a lot of missing and suspicious information that they were still looking into and had no comment on."

"Really? How did you find out any information about the squirt gun and the poem?"

"I have a connection with one of the patrolmen who was at the crime scene last Saturday night. He confirmed the squirt gun and the stanza from the poem, same as the murder of that Tennessee lady over at the Chateau Estates on Twenty-Six Mile Road."

Stover smiled at Justine, looking almost amused.

"A killer who writes poems and plays with squirt guns. How interesting!" He gulped another swallow of his probably stale and flat Diet Coke.

"If this serial killer isn't fucking sick, I don't know who is."

Stover looked at his star reporter,

"Do we know what was in the poem?"

"Nope."

"Do we know if there were any prints of DNA evidence at the crime scene?"

"Nope."

"Do we have an idea why a killer would be leaving a poem and a squirt gun at both crime scenes at the Colony Club and the Chateau Estates?"

"No, we don't," Justine replied.

"Who is the investigating detective at Ira Township?"

"A guy by the name of Ronald Sinclair. He used to be with the Detroit P.D. a few years ago. I had a run-in with him on another homicide several years back, and he was rather cold to me last month when I tried to interview him. When I called him this morning, he only said that there were some common elements in both homicides."

"Well, that's an understatement. Are any of these detectives calling this a serial killing yet?"

"Come on, Boss. You know the police are never quick to label any homicide as serial killing. That usually comes from the media. They are probably pissed at me for labeling the murderer as the 'Water Pistol Killer' in my last news article."

"And what are we supposed to call him? The Squirt Gun Poet?" Stover laughed.

They both smiled as Stover was becoming familiar with Justine Cahill's frustration.

"Why are these coppers acting so tight-lipped? What are they hiding?" the assistant editor asked.

"That's a good question, Boss. My source at the Eight Precinct didn't have any answers for me," the reporter summarized.

"Sounds like we're pretty far away from a decent news article for the morning press."

"Thanks, Boss. Now you understand my frustration. For some reason, the Detroit P.D. and especially these investigating detectives have very little to say about the commonality or the motives of both of these homicides," Justine said as she shuffled her notes.

"Usually, coppers and detectives are anxious to get their names in the papers."

"What are they hiding? Who are they protecting? Why aren't these coppers coughing up more information about who the killer might be?" Stover asked Justine.

The two of them sat there for several moments in silence, as if they were both waiting for that old Domino's Pizza box to magically throw out some answers to their pertinent questions. After several long, silent minutes, Justine had a thought:

"I remember a homicide that happened on the East Side several years ago when the Detroit coppers weren't cooperating either. It turned out that one of the detectives at the Seventh Precinct was the prime suspect in the murder of his ex-wife. We didn't get any answers out of them until an arrest was made, and they had definite, irrefutable evidence to make an arrest."

"Yeah," Stover commented, "I do now remember that case."

Another silent moment.

"Who in the Detroit P.D. would have an interest in killing a down south woman from Tennessee and an older couple from South Carolina, and leave a squirt gun and a poem at each crime scene?" Assistant Editor Dave Stover asked.

"It would make sense, Boss. Both murders were both done as though they were professional killings. The perpetrator in both of these murders definitely knew what they were doing."

Stover suddenly sat up in his chair.

"A revenge killing, perhaps?"

A light went on in Justine's head as she smiled, still fumbling with her notes.

"That would make a lot of sense."

"Justine, do me a favor? Go through our database and find any articles from any local homicides. Go back fifty years or more if you have to. See if you can find any media articles involving anything unusual or any props from the murderer, especially any poems or a squirt gun."

"Got it, Boss."

As Justine got up from her chair, Stover gave her another directive.

"Do me a favor and get rid of this empty pizza box for me."

Justine smiled, refusing to be no longer pushed around that afternoon.

"You can handle that, Boss. Besides, it looks good on the corner of your desk, next to your McDonald's lunch bag," she sarcastically answered as she left his office.

Justine Cahill decided to work late, spending the next several hours that afternoon researching old homicide articles on the computer and the internet. No data or information from anything relating to a poem or a squirt gun seemed to come up until she went as far back as the year 1978.

In an article that was published on November 2, 1978, she read about a murder of a victim by the name of Antonio Valentino, age 41, from Warren, Michigan. He had been killed on El Camino Drive in Detroit after leaving work at the Ford Assembly Plant in Sterling Heights. The article mentioned that he had been shot three times and that a 'green toy squirt gun' was discovered at the crime scene. Following up on several other articles that had been written about the Valentino murder, she found another headline that raised her eyebrows.

It was published on March 20, 1979:

Suspects Acquitted of Warren Man's Murder

The news article went on to discuss the successful trial defense of the suspects, Jack Edward Hansen, and how the other two accused men, Howard Williams and George Johnson, were initially incarcerated but then released because they didn't fire the weapon in the murder. The news article went on to state that his killers accused the victim of having an affair with one of the murderer's wives.

Because the victim had a 'green squirt gun' in his pocket and the borrowed pistol used in the murder had a history of jamming, all of the accused perpetrators were released and exonerated from second-degree murder charges.

The article went on to mention an averted potential scuffle in the courtroom between the victim's brother and the acquitted killers after the trial, swearing an Italian vendetta to 'get even.'

And now, two of the people involved in this murder case over forty years ago were brutally killed over the last two months. Both victims had a toy water pistol left as a souvenir at the crime scene. Both victims had a four-line poem stanza left next to their bodies.

She now went on the Detroit Police Department faculty listing at each precinct. Justine researched the internet for a few more hours before finding the name of the very person who fit the 'modus operandi' of the suspected 'Water Pistol Killer:'

Third Precinct Detective Sergeant John Valentino.

CHAPTER THIRTY-TWO

THE ROOSTERTAIL -OCTOBER 26, 2019

It was a gorgeous fall afternoon, as the autumn sun-splashed the Lake St. Clair shoreline with warm, Indian Summer weather. St. Paul's Catholic Church in Grosse Pointe Farms was filled with over three hundred guests on that Saturday afternoon, as the organist played 'Here Comes the Bride' in splendid, grand fashion.

George Johnson, as the proud, teary-eyed father, slowly walked down the aisle with his youngest daughter Sarah as she gleamed with joy to meet her husband-to-be at the altar. The sounds of the pipe organ filled the majestic old church, with its French Gothic Revival style architecture and its antique stained-glass windows.

Both sides of the aisle were filled with wedding guests, as more than one hundred people had made the long, seven-hour trip to be with the family that had stood as a pillar of their community.

The Town of Iron Mountain had rolled out a going away party for the young girl they all watched grow up. Many of their citizens remember little Sarah as a tomboy, playing softball and powder-puff football with the other girls in town. There were 'Best Wishes Sarah & David' signs posted all over Iron Mountain. Everyone was excited to see the young, twenty-six-year-old registered nurse marry the man of her dreams and live happily ever after.

As the father of the bride kissed his young daughter at the altar, he turned and shook hands with his future son-in-law.

"Take good care of my little girl," he said with tears in his eyes as he took his place in the front pew next to his wife.

Fr. Thomas Bryson did the honors of marrying the young couple, as they both stood there in front of the altar. Eight couples stood up in black tuxedos and yellow chiffon dresses as they stood witness to Dr. & Mrs. David Scarborough taking their wedding vows.

The whole church erupted in applause as the two were formally announced as husband and wife. They all filed out of the church as the wedding guests and church attendants waited for the young couple to leave the vestibule. They were then showered with rice and confetti for good luck.

The parents, along with the bride and groom and wedding stand-ups, posed for pictures in front of the church altar. Sarah and David lovingly held each other as they posed for the wedding photographs in front of the majestic church overlooking the lake. It couldn't have been a more picturesque day for the young couple. The beautiful lakefront setting offered a scenic, romantic background for the young newlyweds, anxious to start their new lives together.

After an hour of picture taking, the whole wedding party climbed into a rented stretch limousine and went to Belle Isle to take more pictures in front of the beautiful fountain, a famous landmark of the Detroit River.

By six o'clock, the newlyweds and the accompanying wedding party arrived at the Roostertail on Detroit's Riverfront. The amazing waterfront ambiance, along with the city skyline views, made the wedding venue a perfect choice for the young couple to celebrate their wedding vows on that late October day.

Wedding guests began filling the elegant dining room, holding champagne flutes, and enjoying hors d'oeuvres and finger food appetizers. Each guest table was adorned with large, towering flower centerpieces filled with white gardenias, Waterford porcelain china, Baccarat crystal goblets, and gold-plated silverware.

The twenty-four-piece orchestra began playing soft, dinner music, with the "Theme From a Summer Place," putting all of the guests into a romantic, celebratory mood.

The head table was long and decorated with several towering flower arrangements, as each standup from the wedding party took his or her place at the table. Endless toasts and nuptial congratulations were made by the best man and maid of honor as the white tuxedo-clad waiters began to serve dinner.

The wedding feast consisted of New England clam chowder, Caesar salad with chicken, salmon with filet mignon, baked, breaded artichokes, red potatoes, asparagus wrapped with bacon, and escargot as a portion of the appetizers. The wine was plentiful, as the 'exclusive reserve' chardonnay and pinot noir kept getting poured into glasses of every guest by the several waiters serving each table.

There were desserts and a long coffee table afterward, with a large assortment of chocolate cakes, cheesecake, and several different flavors of ice cream.

The bride and groom had their first dance to their favorite romantic song, while Mr. and Mrs. Johnson kept a close eye on all of the waiters and the dinner guests that they were serving.

After the chocolate mousse desserts were served and finished, the orchestra began playing several old songs from the seventies, which got all of the wedding guests in a slow-dancing mood.

As the Daddy-Daughter dance took place in the middle of the dance floor, Sarah began to dance with her father very closely, as he had a hard time dancing with tears in his eyes.

"Thank you for this wonderful day, Daddy. And thank you for everything that you've done for me," Sarah gratefully said, trying to keep from sobbing with joy.

George Johnson, with tears in his eyes, only smiled and kissed his youngest daughter on the cheek. He continued to hold his daughter tightly as they finished dancing to the Paul Anka song "Times of Your Life."

As George sat back down at the table, the orchestra began playing 'Love in Blue,' followed by a beautiful rendition of 'Moon River.' Angela Johnson kissed her husband on the cheek as a show of gratefulness for graciously and so generously paying for his daughter's over-the-top wedding.

George Johnson had not held back or spared no expense in marrying off his youngest daughter on her wedding day. She was the last of his children to get married, and he wanted to give her the celebration that she had so much deserved.

George and Angela Johnson tended to ignore the needs of their youngest daughter throughout her childhood. At times, they seemed to pay more attention to their daughter

Sofia and her brothers, as Sarah's demands as a little girl managed to get overlooked.

Sarah had been a good, obedient daughter to the two of them, and they wanted to express their love, their gratitude, and their generosity to the little girl who went from girl's baseball and Barbie dolls to becoming an ICU nurse at St. John's Hospital. She was now a registered nurse, married to an established cardiologist, and they couldn't be happier.

As everyone began twirling on the dance floor, George excused himself to go to the men's room.

"I'll be right back," he said to his wife as he kissed her on the cheek.

He got up from the table and walked across the dance floor, over to the men's room in the vestibule near the ballroom's grand entrance. When he walked into the large restroom, he immediately noticed that there was no one else in either of the bathroom stalls or in front of any of the urinals.

As George Johnson entered the bathroom, someone was sitting on a red velvet chair, waiting for him to go inside. The stranger followed him into the men's room, making sure that no one else was in there. Noting that Johnson was sitting on the toilet in the last stall, the stranger withdrew a Smith & Wesson 9mm handgun and quickly screwed on the silencer.

The intruder then kicked down the locked stall door.

George Johnson, relieving himself and sitting on the toilet, was utterly startled. He gazed into the eyes of his killer.

"Who the fuck are you?"

The killer replied, "Valentino's Ghost."

Two bullets were then fired directly into Johnson's forehead.

Blood suddenly spattered all over the toilet and the marble-tiled bathroom floor. He quickly slumped off of the commode and thumped loudly onto the floor, his head momentarily hitting the steel wall of the stall. His blood started completely gushing out of his head like a fountain, spilling everywhere on the commode stall walls and the marbled floor. The murderer then placed a green toy pistol next to Johnson's body, along with a white, sealed envelope.

The killer quickly exited the men's room, completely undetected. Walking rapidly out of the restaurant, the murderer climbed into a black Ford Escape and started the engine. Within minutes of the murder, the elusive perpetrator exited the parking lot and had disappeared from Detroit's prestigious Roostertail.

Detective Frank Partridge was at his West Side home, sitting on the couch on that Saturday night with his wife, Patty. He had just arrived home late from his Saturday shift. They were enjoying some popcorn, jokingly bantering as they were shuffling through the cable TV channels. He suddenly heard his police cellular phone loudly go off in the kitchen.

"Will that phone ever leave us alone?" his wife asked.

He shook his head.

"One day, we may get a Saturday night to ourselves," he replied.

Frank walked over to the granite kitchen counter, and before answering it, he noticed it was from central police dispatch. Answering his phone, Patty saw Frank immediately covering his eyes.

"Oh shit!" he loudly exclaimed.

He quickly grabbed his Detroit police jacket and his gun holster and ran out of the house without barely saying goodbye.

"There's been another murder," he only said as he jumped into his squad car. His wife looked out of their front picture window as her husband hurriedly left the house to rush to the scene of the crime.

The police dispatcher described the victim as an older man in his late sixties, shot twice in the head in the men's bathroom. The victim was described as the father of the bride, shot and killed as he was celebrating his daughter's wedding at the Roostertail.

A cold chill ran up the detective's spine as he said a prayer to himself while he was driving downtown to the Detroit Riverfront.

He prayed that it wasn't the same killer they had been chasing from the Colony Club and the Chateau Estates murders. He prayed that it wasn't the 'Water Pistol Killer' and that this wasn't another serial killing.

But most of all, he prayed that it wasn't Johnny Valentino.

CHAPTER THIRTY-THREE

SAVED BY THE PIZZA BOX

I was lying down on the couch on that Saturday night, flipping through the TV channels, as it had been an extremely exhausting day. We had been working on a series of car thefts that had been going on in the East Side. A portion of our day was spent interviewing suspects.

Detective Mike Palazzola had been assigned to temporarily be my street partner at our Third Precinct until Commander Riley could find another partner for me to beat up and send to the hospital. We had been in correspondence with the Detroit Crime Scene Investigations Unit and had lifted the fingerprints from several of the abandoned stolen vehicles. We were now on the verge of making an arrest.

Anthony and Dario were staying with me that weekend. My boys were in the other bedroom, playing video games, and I was hoping they would eventually fall asleep. They had to hang around the apartment all day today while I had to go to work at the precinct. Although Anthony had just gotten his driver's license, he did not have a car and was still not permitted to drive alone.

When I got home at five-thirty, we ordered Jet's Pizza and just hung out here watching TV. Dario then got bored and started playing video games in the bedroom, while Anthony and I talked for a while until he crashed about an hour ago. It was a dreary day for both of them, and I promised that I would make it up to them and take them to breakfast, to the shopping mall, and maybe the movies tomorrow.

As I looked around my apartment, I was thankful for the way my life was finally coming together. My apartment was now well furnished, with a brand-new Sony 48-inch flat-screen television and a black leather sectional couch that I was able to purchase on credit from Art Van Furniture. I was thankful for the salary advance that Commander Riley gave me to help me get settled, and I was putting some money into my savings account again. My credit cards were slowly getting paid down, and I wasn't hanging around the Crazy Horse Lounge on Eight Mile Road anymore.

I hadn't had a drink in three months and was devoutly committed to attending my Alcoholics Anonymous meetings at the Emmanuel Lutheran Church on Nine Mile Road. We got together every other Wednesday night at 7:00 in the basement hall of the church. I was making good friends with others there at the meetings who were going through the same struggles.

We were asked to keep a daily journal of our personal battles of trying to stay sober, and I decided to write two or three descriptive paragraphs about what I was feeling or going through each day. During those AA meetings, we were asked to read several highlights from our diaries and discuss some of the setbacks or personal victories that we were going through over the prior two weeks.

I know it sounds corny, but I was actually enjoying it. I was never much of a writer, but putting down my thoughts about my anger, my frustrations, and my troubled feelings became a new experience for me. It was very therapeutic.

I was so used to grabbing a bottle of scotch whiskey every time I got the urge; I never truly understood the reasons for *why* I was drinking.

Dr. Elaine Trafficanta, the police psychologist, began seeing me regularly as I was finally starting to accept the concept of being in therapy. I was becoming more agreeable to exploring my troubled feelings using psychoanalysis rather than exploding and losing my ferocious, violent temper.

Dr. Elaine was becoming more beneficial and helpful to me mentally. I began listening to her constructive advice instead of psychologically blowing her off and sexually fantasizing about her gorgeous, magnificent body.

I was seeing Olivia once or twice a week, and we were dating somewhat steadily. I wasn't quite sure if she was dating me exclusively, but to be quite honest, I really didn't care. As much as I liked and enjoyed being around Olivia, I wasn't in love with her. We were becoming better friends than we were lovers. It wasn't for anything that she had done or said, as we got along very well whenever we talked or got together on Friday or Saturday nights.

The real reason was that I was still deeply in love with my ex-wife. I had the boys over my apartment every other weekend, and we usually went out for pizza on Friday nights and spent the rest of the weekend either hanging out here at the apartment or going out shopping or to the movies.

I missed being a full-time husband and father. I would often try to get bits and pieces of information on how their mother's life was going without me and with her live-in, shit-head boyfriend.

"We don't like him, Dad," my son Dario had said to me on several occasions. He and his brother Anthony were not happy with their mother or her relationship with her boyfriend, Tom Pratt. He seemed to spend more time laying on the couch in the family room, more interested in watching Agent Gibbs on 'NCIS' reruns, then having a decent relationship with Marina and the boys.

"She's getting fed up with him, Dad. It won't be long," Anthony said to me last weekend, which was music to my ears.

Both of my sons were predicting that their mother would eventually toss her lazy lover out on the street very soon. From the information I was secretly receiving from my kids, there was definitely trouble in La-La Land. I came to find out a lot of information that my boys were happily volunteering, and I didn't feel guilty at all for the way I was covertly receiving my data.

I had met him several times when I went over to the house to pick up the boys. Looking at him closely, I couldn't figure out what the hell she saw in him.

Tom Fucking Pratt was a Chrysler Auto Worker in his late fifties, who had been twice divorced with several full-grown children. He was around six feet tall and had an enormous protruding stomach, probably from all the Coney Island hot dogs he devoured every day.

He sported one of those 1970s mustaches that were once in style for older men, and he had a full head of Elvis, jet-black hair. I knew it wasn't a hairpiece, as the boys would have jumped all over that right away.

Tom Pratt took meticulously good care of his hairstyle, looking at himself in the mirror and neatly combing it every chance he had, according to the boys. His hair was never out of place.

It didn't take a genius to figure out that he spent a lot of time dying and coloring his excessive mane. He probably went to the Earl Schieb body shop once a week for the $49.95 paint job.

I came to find out that his five kids wanted nothing to do with him, and he didn't have much of a relationship with any of them. After hearing several detailed, blow-by-blow reports on some of their intense, frequent arguments, I figured that it was only a matter of time before Marina threw him out the door.

Having known Marina since Cousino High School, I knew her like the back of my hand. I knew it was only a matter of time before their 'hot and heavy fling' completely fell apart.

Marina needed a man who would give her the attention she deserved, no matter how small or minuscule it was. An older man who spent more time on the couch eating Coney Islands and watching TV wasn't her idea of a close, intimate relationship.

Every time my boys came over to my apartment, a sigh of relief came over both of them. It was as though they couldn't wait to escape the tense atmosphere that this Tom 'Asshole' Pratt was bringing into their house. They were volunteering information about the week's past events and how little Tom Pratt did around the house except lay on the couch and watch some TV crime show reruns.

I decided to play it cool and not say a word. The last thing I needed was for my ex-wife to accuse me of brainwashing my boys. Whenever they began bitching and moaning about their mother's boyfriend, I would always take the high road. I would only give them my famous 'Father Knows Best' look and tell them:

"As long as your mother is happy, that is all that's important."

Of course, they believed the sincerity of that explanation for all of about three seconds.

I knew that Anthony and Dario were bragging to their mother about how their father wasn't drinking anymore and was going to therapy once a week. The feeling of pride that they were communicating to me whenever we talked about the improvements that I was making in my life was an incredible incentive for me. I was feeling better about myself, not being as angry and depressed with my life. I truly felt like I was doing better, and I knew I had to stop drinking for them.

Regarding their mother, I was just sitting back and enjoying the show. I was feeling like I had a front-row seat at a Broadway play, eating popcorn while her relationship with this strange man, who was living in my house and sleeping in my bed, was finally falling apart.

I was spending a lot of time gloating and laughing at myself. It seemed as though Marina had gone from an 'alcoholic' to a 'food-a-holic,' who probably spent more time working the remote control and eating french fries and Coney Islands than he was with her. And with me not drinking anymore, she was hopefully feeling some sort of remorse.

But only in my wildest dreams could I ever hope that Marina, the only love of my life, would ever come back.

It was almost 10:00 pm, and I was thinking about going to bed when the front door buzzer went off.

"Who is it?"

"Detective Ronald Sinclair, Ira Township Police."

What the fuck was he doing here? I thought to myself. I pressed the unlock button and buzzed them in, hearing several sets of loud footsteps coming up to my second-floor apartment. I stood by the door, holding my breath while there was a loud knock.

As I opened it, four coppers were standing in front of me. There was Detective Dickhead along with his Commander Paul Nelson, Detective Frank Partridge, and another Detroit patrolman, Jack Pearson.

"May we come in?" Frank politely asked.

"Do I have a choice?"

The four of them filed through my door and into my apartment, and I immediately felt overwhelmed. I couldn't remember the last time so many people were in my small two-bedroom apartment at the same time. Two of them sat down on my brand-new Art Van black leather couch, while Patrolman Pearson and Frank Partridge continued to stand.

"To what do I have this honor?"

"Johnny, we need to talk," Frank said.

No matter what Frank said or how he said it, I knew that our friendship was strong enough that he would always take my side. Frank Partridge was doing his job, and in a way, I was lucky that he was on the front lines of this investigation.

Detective Partridge had to give the appearance of looking objective and independent to the other detectives and coppers involved in this investigation. Only a few people in the Third Precinct were aware of my prior street partnership with Frank Partridge several years ago.

"The 'Water Pistol Killer' came to revisit us today," Detective Dickhead loudly exclaimed. He sounded almost excited, as I could hear an 'oh-goody-goody' tone in his voice.

"Where?"

"The Roostertail on the Riverfront. The victim was one of the 'perp's' in your father's murder years ago."

"Which one?" I asked.

For a quick second, I was hoping it was Howard Williams.

"George Johnson. The guy who moved up north to Iron Mountain and was a plumbing contractor."

I remembered reading that Johnson was one of the guys who roughed up my father, according to the police reports, but he wasn't the one who actually pulled the trigger.

"Really?" I only said, trying to sound sympathetic.

"He and his family were at a wedding reception for his daughter at the Roostertail. Someone followed him into the bathroom and put two bullets in his head," Frank explained.

I sat down on my dining room chair and tried to catch my breath. I didn't want to sit next to the Ira Township policemen, and I kept looking into Frank's eyes while he was talking, trying to read what was going through his mind.

These serial murders that were going on against the perpetrators of my father's death forty years ago seemed like something out of the Twilight Zone. I was utterly clueless as to what was going on or who this killer was. For a moment, I was beginning to wonder if the actual 'Water Pistol Killer' was attempting to frame me for the murders.

"The killer left us a few gifts, as always," Sinclair stated.

"The green water pistol and a 'love poem' from Shakespeare."

I was totally shocked, and Frank started showing me some pictures from the crime scene taken on his cell phone. The murder scene looked quite bloody, as there was an older man with his pants pulled down to his ankles, slumped on the bathroom floor with his bald head covered in blood. His feces was covered all over the toilet seat and around the stall, with blood splattered on the back wall. The poor bastard didn't even get a chance to flush before he was killed.

Frank then showed me the poem, which he took a picture of at the crime scene:

He tried to push his enemies far,
but their rage could not be broken.
A gun was drawn, and bullets flew,
their threats had now been spoken.

"Wow, this guy is quite a poet," I only managed to say.

The other coppers began to look at me as if I was their prime suspect.

"Where were you around eight o'clock tonight?" Detective Dickhead eagerly asked, pretending he was Sargent Joe Friday from Dragnet.

"Right here, watching TV with my boys. They're asleep in the other room."

"Really?"

"Really. I got home from the precinct around five-thirty, and we ordered a pizza and hung out here at the house," I quickly explained.

All of the coppers looked at each other, but I could see a sigh of relief coming from Frank.

He looked over on the kitchen table, as the Jet's pizza box with four slices of pepperoni pizza were still leftover, cold, and uneaten. He walked over to the table and looked at the credit card and delivery receipt that was still attached and stapled on the box.

"He's in the clear, guys," Frank said, as I could recognize a tone of relief coming from his voice.

"Why?" Detective Dickhead demanded to know.

"The pizza box delivery receipt is stamped at 7:55 pm, and his signature is on the credit card slip attached here on the box."

I immediately looked at him and smiled. Frank Partridge nodded his head at me, making sure 'Columbo' wasn't looking.

Saved by the pizza box, I thought to myself.

Sinclair got up from the couch and looked at the receipt on the Jet's pizza box. The look on his face said it all. Both he and Commander Nelson were clearly frustrated and disappointed, knowing that I had a reasonable explanation about where I was.

It would have been difficult for me to be at the Roostertail downtown shooting the victim while I was signing for a delivered pizza at my apartment at the same time. It was quite apparent that their investigation wasn't going very well, as they were not coming up with any more viable suspects other than myself.

It completely baffled me that the 'Water Pistol Killer' had been able to commit these murders and escape all three crime scenes, without any trace of any DNA evidence or any images of any surveillance cameras located in the areas around these murders. I started thinking about these gruesome murders over and over again.

This killer has to be a fucking professional.

The 'Water Pistol Killer' was either just that good, or the detectives on this case, and Partridge included, are just that lousy.

"Has CSI been at the crime scene?"

"Yeah, but they weren't able to lift any prints in the bathroom stall. The killer was probably wearing gloves," Frank replied.

"Whoever this bastard is, he's gotta be good," I said out loud.

That comment didn't go over very well and got a dirty look from both the Ira-hick Township coppers. Everyone then got up from my couch, and they filed their way out the front door.

"Sorry to disturb you, Detective Valentino," Commander Nelson politely said. At least he was respectful and courteous.

Everyone else nodded their heads at me as they were leaving. Frank made eye contact with me, letting me know that he would probably be calling me later on.

“Don’t go on any vacations,” were Detective Dickhead’s only parting words, letting me know that I should probably hang around town in case they needed to get in touch with me again. Or try to arrest me.

“Sure thing, Columbo.”

Everyone filed out of my apartment as I was left alone in the kitchen, trying to make sense out of all of this.

Who in the hell was avenging my father’s death if it wasn’t me? I felt as though I was indeed the only person in the world who wanted to retaliate against the perpetrators who were involved in my father’s death forty years ago.

But why go after Johnson? He was probably the least guilty of the three offenders. He didn’t pull the trigger, and he certainly didn’t plan the murder.

Why kill him in the bathroom stall at his daughter’s wedding? Whoever the killer was, had to have something very deep inside of them that was far more intense and far more extreme than any anger or emotion that I was feeling or pent up inside.

Someone out there on the street was angrier at my father’s killers than I was.

Chapter Thirty-Four

Great Lakes Insurance Company-Fall 2019

Jefferson Avenue was bustling with people, trying to avoid the pending rainstorm that had been predicted by all of the weather channels that afternoon. The darkened skies cast a long shadow over the Renaissance Center in downtown Detroit on that early November day.

On the thirty-sixth floor, the CEO and President of Great Lakes Insurance Company was sitting at his office, overlooking the Detroit River. On a clear day, he could easily see Windsor, Canada, from his desk. He had been an insurance executive with the company for over twenty-seven years, and he worked his way to the top spot within the company.

James P. Moran started as a junior life insurance salesman after receiving his bachelor's degree in marketing from Wayne State University. His intention when he joined the insurance company was to make enough money to support his newly married wife, as they were expecting their first child.

He went on to acquire his master's in business at the University of Michigan and eventually obtained his law degree from the University of Detroit. He worked hard, learning the art of making the deal and played by the rules. After moving through the ranks, he never thought that he would someday be sitting in the executive's chair of the largest and most established life insurance company in the Midwest.

At fifty-two years old, he now looked back on his fruitful career at the company with gratitude and pride.

Being at the helm, he had constructed a management team that has helped him navigate the highs and lows of the current economy. Having weathered the recent recessions and bull markets, Moran has been able to triple the company's net worth during his tenure in charge. The company's board of directors has credited his successful leadership as the reasons why their insurance company has enjoyed such a long string of prosperity.

But James Moran looked beyond the Detroit River over to Windsor on that day. He was extremely concerned about a pending problem that was now looming over the company.

His internal auditors have revealed some unusual transactions and trends that have been brought personally to his attention. The large reserve accounts for dormant insurance policies and claims have been getting a significant amount of activity over the last six months. Insurance policies that were dormant and classified as inactive were oddly being cashed in by their policy beneficiaries.

These life insurance claims, now totaling over twenty million dollars, were unusual because all of these policy claims were cashed out and sent to various blind trust accounts rather than sent personally to their specific beneficiary's home addresses.

His chief financial officer, Olivia Laurent, had dismissed the internal audit team's unusual findings as an 'economic trend' that many estate tax attorneys and financial planners are now encouraging their clients to do when receiving these substantial proceeds. Laurent proclaimed that, because of the pending changes in the federal estate tax laws, that these payments to these various trusts were becoming a popular means of deferring any pending income taxes while settling the financial estates of the decedents.

It was an explanation that Moran initially excepted. But when his senior internal auditor, John McCafferty, brought the issue up directly to his attention, the CEO became concerned. Moran began to slowly realize that some unusual transactions were going on under his CFO's supervision.

McCafferty had discovered some peculiarities. There were some suspicious similarities in the ways and means to which these trusts had been opened and created. The registered agent of these trusts was actually to the same individual at a local law firm and address registered to a post office box.

Was it possible that several of these insurance claims were being settled and created by the same law firm specializing in estates and wills? Upon further investigation, the name of this individual was non-existent.

These were unusual transactions that, over the last three months, had totaled over five million dollars.

He had asked McCafferty to spend more time investigating these odd financial circumstances covertly, behind the back of his chief financial officer. He wanted the auditor to ascertain and verify that this strange trend of old insurance policies being cashed out and disbursed was not the result of any suspicious, criminal activity.

McCafferty submitted his report to the CEO three days ago, and his findings were not favorable. The chief internal auditor now believed that there had been a significant amount of collusion and questionable activity in the way these life insurance claims had been getting administrated, processed, and paid out. All of these claims were conveniently being handled and signed off by the company's CFO, Olivia Laurent.

James Moran had now decided to contact the authorities, believing that there may be a severe issue of embezzlement going on within his company.

Moran liked Olivia and had always trusted her judgment. He felt that her unscrupulous honesty throughout her years with the company was never in question. But over the last twenty-four months, her behavior and reasoning had now become extremely erratic.

The CEO had remembered the much-publicized 'Pedophile Priest Murders' that were going on in Chicago last year and how his company was involved in the underwriting of those broad insurance policies of those defrocked Catholic priests back in the 1970s. He trusted Olivia to make the right decision in signing off and paying out on those policies, totaling almost twenty million dollars in claims.

But when she suspiciously disappeared last year for three months, taking some accumulated vacation time and some long-needed time off, Moran became concerned. He had heard through the office grapevine that her romantic relationships and her personal life were considerably affecting her job performance. Her business decisions regarding her administration of those life insurance claims had now become suspect.

As Moran sat in his chair looking out the skyscraper's glass window, there was a loud buzzing on his desk phone.

"Mr. Moran, your two o'clock appointment is here to see you," his administrative secretary, Linda Menard, announced.

"Thank you, Linda. Please send him in."

After several moments, Linda had opened the door for the gentleman whom Moran was expecting.

The CEO rose from his desk and introduced himself to the stranger from the U.S. Treasury Department.

"How do you do, Mr. Moran," the dark-haired, slim, and trim stranger replied. He was tall, a little over six feet, and was built as though he spent all of his free time working out at the gym. He was tieless, wearing a crisp white shirt, dark suit jacket, and gray slacks. Sporting a mustache and goatee, he had a dark complexion and was unusually handsome. The gentleman looked as though he could pass for a Hollywood extra rather than a federal employee.

"I'm Treasury Agent Carleton, from the Midwest Office of the Internal Revenue in Detroit," he announced, displaying his federal badge. He then presented his business card, disclosing his offices located nearby on Woodward Avenue.

"Please, call me Jim. Let's forget the formalities. Make yourself comfortable," as he directed him to sit down.

Treasury Agent Carleton sat down in front of him on one of two of his comfortable, black leather chairs.

"May I offer you something?"

"You're too kind, but no, thank you. We just had lunch in Greektown."

"Which restaurant?"

"I met my district manager at the Parthenon."

"Oh," Jim Moran replied. "Their gyros sandwiches are amazing."

The agent crossed his legs and smiled.

Special Treasury Agent Anthony V. Carleton had been with the Internal Revenue Service for almost twenty years, going directly to work for them after he graduated from Central Michigan University in 2001. He was specially trained and became an expert in financial fraud transaction audits and forensic accounting within the service. Three years ago, after being promoted through the ranks, he became a field agent supervisor with the Federal Treasury Department.

Carleton's specialty was now the head auditor of suspicious financial activities and the investigation of potential white-collar criminals. His examinations centered around large corporations, and he headed a team of experienced forensic auditors from the Internal Revenue Service. They could quickly dissect and analyze suspicious, fraudulent, criminal activities within any large corporation. Carleton had an impressive record of catching and helping prosecute a long list of white-collar criminals and corporate embezzlers over the years.

"I trust you received the reports from my internal auditor," Moran started the conversation.

"Yes," Carleton answered, "Thank you for sending those. My associates and I went through those reports, and we agree with your concerns."

Moran silently sat at his desk while the federal agent recapped the summary of suspicious activities that had been included in the internal auditor's examination summaries. After his recap, the CEO expressed his concerns.

"I hope that your audit team can examine these transactions with as little disruption to my company as possible. I initially do not want my CFO to know about this outside federal investigation. How will you handle this?"

"My associates and I will come in and make copies of all of her computer hard drives and files after hours. We will probably conduct most of the examination at our offices on Woodward. Any fieldwork will be done after hours, presuming that you will be able to assist us with this."

"Well, that may be an issue. We will have to enlist the help of her associate, Ms. Cindy Jankowski, to assist you in getting whatever information you may need."

They were both silent for several long moments.

"And you're certain that you can conduct all of this fieldwork after hours?"

"As long as we have access to all of your systems and computer files within your accounting department."

Moran reiterated, "Your discretion in conducting this investigation is imperative. I do not want Ms. Laurent to become suspicious or discontinue her covert activities."

"I agree. I'm certain that if we can receive the help and assistance from one of your staff personnel that we will be able to keep this investigation confidential."

There was another silent moment.

"What we initially do is tell the accounting staff that we are outside auditors conducting an independent audit so that they don't become suspect at the onset," Carleton explained.

Moran looked at the federal agent.

"I am still hoping that none of this is true, and all of this turns out to be a financial misunderstanding."

Carleton looked at the CEO.

"Activities like these are usually criminal ones, Jim. It is highly unlikely that at this level, that your CFO, Ms. Laurent, can logically explain these unusual financial activities. Our initial problem will be tracing the ownership of those blind trusts and the financial transactions that have gone through them."

"You're probably right. I'm just hoping beyond hope that none of this is true. She has been a hard-working, stellar employee of this company until recently," Moran said.

The federal agent looked at the insurance company CEO.

"We can start this audit as soon as this Monday."

Agent Carleton rose from his chair, and the two of them shook hands.

"Looking forward to working with you," Moran exclaimed.

With that, he escorted the treasury agent out of his office and out to the lobby.

"You have my card, Jim. If you have any questions, please don't hesitate to call me."

They shook hands again, and Moran watched the agent leave his office. When he returned to his desk, he called his administrative assistant into his office.

"Linda, contact Cindy Jankowski to come into my office immediately, please."

"She is currently in a meeting right now."

"Well, have her come in here when her meeting is finished."

It wasn't until after four o'clock when Cindy Jankowski entered his office.

"Cindy, I've hired an independent accounting firm to conduct an audit of our claims department, and I am hoping that you can stay after hours for a few days and assist them. This is for our bankers as they are looking to ascertain and independently verify our assets on our balance sheet. I trust that you can be discrete about this, as I do not want Olivia or the rest of the accounting department to know what is going on. I trust that you can keep this financial audit discrete."

Cindy sat at the chair nodded her head.

"Not a problem, Mr. Moran," she replied.

Cindy Jankowski did not think much about it at first. But when she returned to her desk, she gave the situation more thought. She had been with the company for over ten years, and she was never asked to stay after hours to assist some independent auditors from an outside accounting firm.

But she was also asked to keep this audit 'on the down-low.' No one was to know in accounting, including Olivia. Being that Olivia was her boss and one of her best friends, she knew that keeping this quiet and 'on the down-low' would be difficult.

Something big was about to come down, and she was fearful that Olivia was right in the middle of it.

CHAPTER THIRTY-FIVE

BARRICADE-LATE FALL 2019

The TV set was blaring as Howard Williams was sitting at his trailer home at the Chateau Estates. He was lying on the couch with several empty beer cans lying on the floor. As was his routine, he was falling in and out of drunken consciousness. A half-empty bottle of Jack Daniels was on the coffee table.

And on the floor, within his reach, was a loaded, Colt .38 caliber pistol.

It was another cold, blustery November night. Williams had passed out, drinking his usual twelve-pack of Old-Style beer and taking long swigs from his whiskey bottle. Since learning of the cruel deaths of Jack Hanson, along with his wife and now the recent killing of George Johnson, the next victim seemed obvious.

It didn't take a Harvard genius to figure out that he was on top of the 'Water Pistol Killer's' victim list.

Needless to say, Williams was scared for his life. He spent each day locked inside of his trailer, being vigilant of everyone and anyone that drove around in his trailer park.

It had been a few months since the gruesome, bloody murder of his ex-wife, Joni Williams Harper. After returning to Detroit, experiencing Joni's death, and then hearing about the killings of his former friends, Williams now realized there actually was some truth to the 'vendetta,' the Italian curse that had been placed on him and his friends in 1979.

Howard Williams was now afraid, terrified, and fearful. His surviving brothers and sisters, who lived in the area, had advised him to move back to Hermitage, Tennessee, and leave Michigan once and for all.

But realistically, Williams could no longer afford to do so. He had blown the $77,000 inheritance that he had received upon his brother's death several months ago, paying cash for a new truck and paying off several old debts.

Until he had heard about George Johnson's murder at the Roostertail last week, he was spending a majority of his time and money at the Crazy Horse Lounge on Eight Mile Road. The continuous hours of drinking JD on the Rocks and exotic lap dances had taken a considerable toll on his finances, and he could no longer afford to go out.

His pension benefits had dwindled due to the advance loans that he had taken against them for the purchase of his mobile home. He had no savings left and was living on whatever income he had coming from social security.

Williams considered selling all of his assets and moving, but it would only be enough to get him by at a new location somewhere else temporarily. He would lose too much money liquidating his trailer, his truck, and his car. And he didn't have the money to move his mobile trailer home to Tennessee, as the costs to do so were exorbitant.

Howard Williams now only had two choices: Stay in his paid-for mobile home in Chateau Estates and be vigilant or move back to Hermitage and eventually become homeless.

He decided to be attentive and become ready to defend himself. He wasn't going to spend the rest of his life being fearful.

He went to the gun shop that week and purchased a used Colt .38 caliber pistol with whatever credit he had available on his credit card. He would keep it holstered on his person at all times, Williams figured. He had acquired a concealed weapon license, allowing him to do so in the State of Michigan.

His mobile home would now be his fortress. He went to the Home Depot store and purchased an additional deadbolt lock for his entrance door. He installed a motion detector light for the outside of his trailer. He screened his calls and accepted no visitors to his home unless he knew them.

If the 'Water Pistol Killer' were after him, he would be ready to defend himself.

It was almost six o'clock on that Wednesday evening when there was a loud knock on his entrance door. Williams was immediately awakened from his deep, drunken stupor and grabbed his pistol. He got up and looked out of the curtains of his window. He didn't know who the visitor was, but he did realize that it was a police car.

"Who is it?"

"Detective Sinclair and Commander Nelson, from the Ira Township Police."

At that moment, Williams had figured that it was safe to open the door.

"Yes?"

"We would like to speak with you for a moment, Mr. Williams," the detective said.

Williams let them in. The two cops entered his home, and Detective Sinclair was immediately overtaken by the terrible stench in the room. Williams had not cleaned his mobile home since Joni's murder, and the accumulated filth from his garbage, liquor bottles, and empty beer cans was extremely overwhelming.

Apparently, Williams was even afraid to take his trash out to the scavenger dumpster located several hundred yards away from his mobile home.

Sinclair and Nelson found two empty chairs in the living room and sat themselves down.

"What can I help you with?" Williams demanded to know. He was still 'half in the bag' and in a semi-drunken state, having been drinking most of the day.

"Mr. Williams, I'm sure you've been hearing reports in the media about the 'Water Pistol Killer' that's out there targeting the alleged suspects from the Valentino murder in 1978."

"Yes, I've heard about it. I told you when Joni was killed that they're after me, those Dago bastards."

Sinclair looked directly at Williams.

"I don't know who you're referring to."

"You know damn well who I'm talking about," Williams loudly said, slurring his words.

"The brother of that bastard that was fucking my wife...what's his name, something Valentino..."

At that moment, he couldn't recall Tony Valentino's brother's name.

"We talked to the brother. He's over eighty years old now and sickly. We don't believe that he's a threat or a suspect in these homicides," Commander Nelson explained.

"But we do believe that it would be in your best interests to leave the trailer park for a while until it's safe for your return. As you know, George Johnson, Jack Hanson, and his wife were both murdered by, who we believe, is the same killer. It would make sense that you might be the next victim," Sinclair tried to explain.

At that moment, both of them realized that Williams was barely coherent. With the empty beer cans and liquor bottles scattered around his living room, it was evident that he spent most of his time being drunk.

Williams looked at both of them.

"I'm armed and ready," he said as he disclosed his holstered weapon.

"Did you get a conceal and carry permit for that gun?"

"Yes," as he slowly pulled out his wallet, then rummaging through cards and dollar bills that were neatly stuffed inside of his billfold. After a few moments, he found the newly issued conceal and carry card, showing it to Sinclair.

"Well, Mr. Williams, we are both advising you to leave and go elsewhere until it's safe for you to return. We cannot guarantee that you will be safe staying here in your home," Commander Nelson reiterated.

"Don't worry, officers," Williams said loudly.

"I'm ready," pointing to his gun.

"I don't think you're carrying a gun is going to keep you safe. We believe that this killer is a professional, and you're being armed probably won't do you any good," Nelson advised.

"You can't kick me out of my own home!" Williams said loudly. He was now slurring his words so badly that he was barely coherent and understandable. He was staggering in his chair, swaying back and forth, struggling to stay attentive.

With that, both the Ira Township officers realized that this visit was a colossal waste of their time. At this point, Sinclair could no longer stand the stench in William's trailer. He handed Williams his business card, then pulled out his handkerchief to cover his nose and mouth.

"You were advised and warned, Mr. Williams. Have a good day," as they both hurriedly exited the mobile home.

The old hillbilly watched both of them get into their squad car and leave.

Howard Williams began to chuckle to himself. He had plenty of food, liquor, beer, and water in his refrigerator to keep himself barricaded. He also had his new Colt .38 pistol to protect him and keep him safe.

He was more than ready now for the "Water Pistol Killer."

Chapter Thirty-Six

New Year's Eve-2019

It was a cold, frigid day on New Year's Eve, as the freezing wind from the brutal winter weather had dropped down to minus 18 degrees without the windchill. The small furnace in the mobile home at Chateau Estates could only accommodate moderately cold temperatures. With the paper-thin, scantly insolated walls of the trailer home, one could see their cold, frosty breath indoors.

Howard Williams had been sleeping with his winter jacket on for the last three nights. He was cursing to himself about why he even bothered to leave the comfortable climate of Tennessee to live in these brutal, Midwestern temperatures.

The southerner had been holed up in his trailer home for the last two months. He had been very vigilant the whole time, ordering his groceries online and being very careful of where he went and who was around him. He seldom went outside, and when he did, he brought along his weapon with him. He would only leave his trailer to start his truck or his car. Otherwise, he had been bunkered down the whole time.

He had not heard or read anything about the 'Water Pistol Killer' in a while, and he began to wonder if it was safe for him to go out again.

Williams was now going stir crazy. He had not left his home to visit his sisters and brothers, and he didn't leave his trailer at all. The smell and stench of all the garbage were now even bothering Williams. He knew that he had to eventually clean up and throw out all of his amassed rubbish, beer cans, and empty liquor bottles that he was collecting in his home.

Tomorrow was New Year's Day, and the beginning of a new year, he thought to himself. As a New Year's resolution, he would resolve to clean out his trailer and do his best to keep it tidy. He would clean it out the next day.

Having spent the whole Christmas holiday all alone, he was now going insane from the loneliness of being by himself and not being around people. Williams was a social person, and living like a hermit was not his style.

Tonight was New Years' Eve, he said to himself. He will go out to the Crazy Horse Lounge and celebrate the new year. He was not about to spend another night all alone.

That evening, Williams got himself dressed and threw on a hefty dose of Polo cologne to cover up the stench on his clothes. He was now about to go out and celebrate New Year's Eve.

The music was playing loudly in the bar, as the exotic dancers were barely dressed in very sexy, see-thru holiday attire.

The old man was so excited to be around people again that he began talking and bragging to the surrounding customers sitting at the bar about how he had 'beaten' the 'Water Pistol Killer.'

After doing several shots of Jack Daniels, Williams was soon drunk, and he felt it necessary to shoot off his mouth at the popular strip bar.

"Those other assholes that were killed...they were just stupid," he told one of the bar patrons that he had just met.

"When you catch another man doing your old lady, you gotta be careful. You gotta plan things. You gotta make sure that somebody else takes the rap when you decide how you're going to kill the fucking bastard," he loudly explained.

"Man, I tell ya," he said to the stranger sitting next to him.

"That son-of-a-bitch thought he could just fuck my wife and get away with it," he loudly said at the bar. He was obviously talking about Tony Valentino.

"But we all killed that bastard. And when they tried to nail us on murder charges, we pleaded self-defense!"

Dolores, the bartender, was slinging drinks at the bar that night. She couldn't help but overhear that the old hillbilly was bragging. She momentarily stopped serving drinks to listen to what he was saying.

"Do you know how we beat those murder charges?" he loudly exclaimed, talking directly now to the bartender.

"No!" Dolores replied, loudly breaking into his boisterous conversation.

"Tell us, how did you guys beat those murder charges?"

Williams started laughing.

"That dago son-of-a-bitch tried to fool us with a toy water pistol in his pocket!" he laughed.

"But that Valentino-dago-bastard got what he had comin'."

He took another long drink from his JD on the Rocks.

"We shot that bastard forty years ago!" he bragged. "Back in 1978!"

Williams was nodding his head and smiling as if to be reminiscing about a pleasant, past experience.

"My buddy Jack put three bullets right into his fucking head, man."

He then made a gun hand gesture with his right hand.

"BANG, BANG, BANG," he shouted out.

Dolores now completely stopped what she was doing. Remembering that Detective John Valentino used to be a good patron at the bar, she was stunned. She now realized to whom he was referring.

"Howard, keep your voice down."

"NO!" he loudly screamed at the bar.

Several bar patrons were now attentively listening to what was coming out of Williams's mouth.

"THERE AIN'T NOTHIN' BETTER THAN WATCHIN' ANOTHER MAN DIE!" he laughed out loud.

"Dolores, give me another one!"

The young man, who was probably in his late twenties, was barely listening or interested in what the old hillbilly was saying sitting next to him. But he was now getting annoyed with the old drunk, spraying his words while bragging about a crime he so notoriously committed so many years ago.

"Get the fuck outta' here, old man."

"Fuck you," he said to the young kid.

At that moment, Dolores looked at the young man and shook her head, pointing at her temple.

Rather than starting trouble, the young, dark-haired kid shook his head and got up. He quickly settled his bar tab. He then pointed his middle finger at Williams and then walked out of the bar.

The drunken hillbilly looked at Dolores, still laughing and bragging.

"Ain't nobody gonna fuck with me," he said to the bartender as she went about her business.

"I got me this here gun now," he told one of the dancers as he handed her a twenty-dollar bill for another lap dance.

By then, it was almost midnight, as the announcer began counting down the New Year.

"Five-Four-Three-Two-One, Happy New Year!" as confetti came sprinkling out of the ceiling ducts of the bar lounge, covering all of the patrons. The dancers started passing out New Year's kisses to all the men sitting at the bar, as Williams received several kisses from the dancers.

"Happy New Year, Howard," Dolores said as she had walked from behind the bar to kiss him on the cheek.

Williams, now loudly slurring his words, pointed his finger at the bartender.

"Nobody's gonna fuck with me," he loudly said again, smiling.

Several drinks and four exotic lap dances later, Williams began the process of leaving the Crazy Horse Lounge. It was now almost one o'clock in the morning. The old hillbilly at that moment was so drunk that he had urinated all over himself in the men's bathroom. He now had such a bad odor that none of the girls wanted to dance for him anymore.

He was now stumbling in the parking lot. He had almost fallen a few times while he was walking, tripping on some ice banks in the middle of the lot. It took him several long minutes to locate his black Cadillac CTS.

Fumbling with his keys, he found the Cadillac fob and unlocked his car in the freezing cold. He then sat inside of his vehicle for several long moments, bobbing back and forth in the driver's seat. The old man was desperately trying to focus his eyes, attempting to get his bearings. The drunken bar patron was too intoxicated to drive.

Howard Williams then pressed the ignition button.

The customers who were still sitting at the bar of the Crazy Horse Lounge saw their drink glasses suddenly start rattling on the bar's countertop. The music from the dance floor became momentarily inaudible as everyone looked at each other, completely startled. It felt as though an earthquake had suddenly hit Eight Mile Road in the middle of Detroit. The thunderous, deafening noise unexpectedly shook all of the bar customers.

There was an incredibly loud explosion coming from the parking lot.

CHAPTER THIRTY-SEVEN

NEW YEAR'S DAY-2020

My son, Dario, and a few of his friends were fast asleep in the spare bedroom of my apartment, while two of Anthony's buddies were sleeping on the couch in my family room. Anthony was sleeping on the other side of my king-size bed while I was struggling to fall asleep. The previous night was New Year's Eve, and the boys had planned to have several of their friends over for a year-end party. Their mother had plans to go out with her boyfriend somewhere for a New Year's celebration, so I was stuck chaperoning the boys and their teenage friends at my place.

I really didn't mind. As a matter of fact, I rather enjoyed it. There was no alcohol, of course, so we celebrated opening up bottles of non-alcoholic cold duck (which tastes like grape juice) at midnight. With my alcohol addiction problems, being home with my boys drinking grape juice on New Year's Eve was the best place for me to be.

My sister Lucia had called me earlier and asked me if I had any plans for New Year's. She was concerned that I would be alone. I explained that I would be with my son's chaperoning their teenage New Year's Eve party.

I had recently quit smoking as one of my New Year's resolutions, and I was using one of those medicated nicotine patches to assist me in stopping. I also got a suggestion from Dr. Elaine about keeping hard candy, chocolate, or menthol cough drops around every time I had the urge to light up a cigarette.

Needless to say, I had already gone through a full bag of cherry cough drops.

I had met Olivia at the Grand Trunk Pub on Woodward Avenue at three o'clock for a late lunch and to wish each other a Happy New Year the day before. She had plans with several of her girlfriends to go out to Greektown (her favorite place) in downtown Detroit where they had party reservations. She had asked me to come along, but I had committed to my sons to help them host their New Year's party at my house, so I regretfully declined.

We had spent most of the evening playing card games, while some of them were in the other bedroom playing on Dario's video games. Several of their little girlfriends came over, and I popped for several pizzas from Jets. The girl's parents (along with a few boys) had come to pick them up around 12:30 am.

There was probably a total of almost twenty high school kids in my small, little apartment. Ryan Seacrest from 'Dick Clark's New Year's Rockin' Eve" came on the television to count down the Times Square Crystal Ball. When I was reminiscing to some of the kids about how we used to celebrate New Year's watching the same program many years ago, the only comment I got was:

"Mr. Valentino, who's Dick Clark?"

The party didn't break up until around three o'clock in the morning.

Before going to bed, Dario came up to me and kissed me on the cheek.

"Good Night, Daddy. Thank you for everything tonight. My friends had a great time."

He paused for a moment.

"I love you, Dad."

I melted right then and there on my leather couch. It made the whole night with my boy's totally worth it.

I was still awake, tossing and turning in bed, when I got a text on my police cellular phone. It was from Frank Partridge:

Johnny, Happy New Year. When you get this, call me.

After a few minutes, I received another text from him:

You got your wish.

What the hell was he talking about? I laid in my bed for about a half-hour more, wondering what Frank could have possibly been referring to. I didn't want to call him back right away as I knew I would then be forced to run out of my apartment and go to wherever he was directing me to go.

It probably had something to do with the "Water Pistol Killer," and to tell you the truth, I just didn't want to deal with it at that hour. Besides, I had all of my sons and his friends sleeping over at my house, so I couldn't very well run out and leave all of them alone.

I didn't want to turn on the television and wake up the boys sleeping on my couch, so I got up from my bed. I took out my regular Apple iPhone and starting perusing the internet. I usually looked up the Detroit News headlines, and in bold letters was the early morning headlines:

One Man Dead in Eight Mile Car Explosion

The article went on to describe that a car explosion had occurred at the Crazy Horse Lounge on Eight Mile Road and that the victim was identified as Howard Williams, 67, of Ira Township, Michigan.

There was a picture posted of the crime scene, which looked like the remnants of a Cadillac, burned to a crisp. There were also several black garbage bags staked around the lot, which usually means that the victim's body was dismembered.

The Detroit Police had the parking lot of the popular strip club taped off with yellow crime tape as the victim's blown up body parts had been scattered across the parking lot.

I did not want to call Frank back at that hour. Pretending that I was in bed and sleeping on New Year's Day was a great excuse not to call him back right away.

It was almost six o'clock when my curiosity got the best of me.

"Happy New Year, Frank."

"Happy New Year, Johnny. You got your wish."

"What are you talking about?" I said, pretending to play stupid.

"Howard Williams was blown up in his car in the parking lot of the Crazy Horse Lounge a few hours ago."

I wanted to jump up and scream with exuberant joy, but I decided to play it cool and pretend to be somber. I didn't want to make my excitement too obvious.

That old hillbilly finally died the violent death that he so much deserved. Getting exploded apart into a million pieces in the parking lot of his favorite strip club was far too good for him.

Of course, I couldn't say any of that to Frank Partridge. But he knew what I was thinking.

After a few silent moments of respect for the worthless dead, we continued the phone conversation.

"I'm supposed to ask you where you were a few hours ago; otherwise, I would be very neglectful of my job."

"Not a problem Frank. I was here at home, supervising a New Year's Eve party for a bunch of high school kids. About six of Dario and Anthony's friends are still at my house sleeping."

"Good," Frank replied. "You have lots of witnesses. But get ready for a bunch of questions from Detective Dickhead."

Surprising how these nicknames and monikers for others tend to stick, I laughed to myself.

"What the hell is he doing on Eight Mile Road?"

"He seems to be an interested party. They never closed the case from the first murder in Ira Township, and he feels obligated to come into the city and snoop around."

A few more silent moments.

"Does this fucking guy have anything else better to do?"

"You're the one who calls him 'Columbo.' You tell me," he laughed.

Another quiet moment on the phone.

"Don't you want to know if it was the same killer?"

"Only if the killer left you another green squirt gun for a present. Although I wonder how the bastard would have done that, blowing up the car and all," I observed.

"The killer was clever. It was left nailed in a plastic bag on an oak tree adjacent to the parking lot."

"Really?"

"One of our detectives found it not far from the crime scene."

"What? No poetry?" I smiled.

"Oh, yes. Sealed in a nice white envelope, right along with the green squirt gun."

"I can't wait to read it."

"I took a picture of it. I'll text it to you."

"Wonderful. I look so forward to reading this killer's creative poetry."

Frank laughed over the phone.

"I gotta tell ya', Johnny. This one is my favorite."

At that moment, I walked over to the coffee pot in the kitchen and started a pot of coffee, which I so desperately needed.

"Any camera surveillance?"

"Yeah, and that's what's interesting. There wasn't anyone lurking around Williams' car to plant the car bomb while it was parked at Crazy Horse. Our investigators think it was planted in the car well before he drove it over to the Crazy Horse, and then it was detonated either by timer or by remote control."

"Where are you now?"

"I'm at my precinct office, doing some paperwork. I left the Crazy Horse about a half-hour ago, while CSI was doing some clean-up and some investigating. Intel is over there now."

"Oh, I see. What was Dickhead doing?"

"He was still there on Eight Mile Road, trying to look important. He was assisting me as we were interviewing everyone that was still at the bar. We talked to the bartender, Dolores, who said that she knew you."

Great, they brought poor Dolores into this mess, I thought to myself.

"She said that she overheard Williams bragging at the bar about how he and his friends had killed your father back in 1978."

"That mother-fucking, son-of-a-bitch," immediately came loudly out of my mouth.

At that moment, I was sure I had awakened a few of my son's friends sleeping on the couch.

Frank chuckled.

"Better get it out now before Dickhead calls you into his station to interview you. You know that's coming."

"Yeah, I know. He can't seem to get the notion of my not being the killer out of his head."

I was now pouring myself a cup of coffee, wondering how I was going to function on only a few hours of sleep. I was especially worried about my temperament if I was going to get called into the station to talk to one of the detectives.

No booze, no cigarettes, and no sleep was never a good combination for me.

"Well, I'm stuck here at home with my boys and their friends. What time do you think all of this will happen?"

"I'm sure Detective Dickhead will be calling you this morning. Get ready."

"Thanks, Frank," as I hung up the phone.

I poured myself another cup of eye-waking Mrs. Folger's coffee, and my iPhone suddenly beeped with a text message from Detective Partridge.

It was the crime scene poem that Frank took a picture of and sent over to me. I had to admit, this killer's poetry was getting better and better:

> His lifeless body, soaked in blood,
> from a battle, he couldn't survive.
> His spirit now one of many ghosts
> ...of El Camino Drive.

Very clever, I thought to myself. This killer definitely has some literary talent. For about three seconds, I was hoping for another murder to occur as I was enjoying this killer poets' rhyme and prose so much.

A few hours had passed that morning while I sat at my kitchen chair, periodically dozing off with another full cup of black coffee in my hand. Anthony then got up to grab a drink of something cold out of the refrigerator.

"Is everything okay, Dad?"

"Yeah, son. Everything is fine. I may have to go to work for a few hours. Any idea what time everyone will be getting up?"

"Depends what time you'll have your famous pancakes ready," he smiled.

That was my clue from my very smart, very sensible oldest son. Prepare one of my famous, legendary pancake breakfasts.

Wake them, feed them, and get them the hell out of here.

CHAPTER THIRTY-EIGHT

BANG, BANG, BANG

It was almost three o'clock in the afternoon on New Year's Day, as I pulled my squad car into the drab, snowy parking lot of the Crazy Horse Lounge. It had just started snowing that afternoon, and the strong city winds of Eight Mile Road were creating a frigid windchill. The cold January breeze was turning the balmy, comfortable temperature of 26 degrees down to a minus 10 degrees that afternoon.

My son and his friends enjoyed their sleepover and my hospitality so much that they all didn't leave my apartment until almost noon. I was playing short-order cook, having to run out to Kroger's to pick up some more eggs, pancake batter, and breakfast sausage.

I was probably enjoying my parent and supervisor role more than they were. I had not felt like an actual father in a long time. Making memories with my boys and their friends was something that I knew I would always cherish that morning. It was so enjoyable talking and socializing with all the young teenage boys about football, parties, fast cars, and girls.

Detective Ronald Sinclair (aka Dickhead) of the Ira Township Police and Detective Frank Partridge of the Eighth Precinct were at the parking lot of the Crazy Horse, and they were practically waiting for me.

Detective Dickhead had called me earlier that morning and politely asked me if I was interested in helping them in their probe and investigation into the parking lot car bombing. Being that I had a great alibi the night before, he was following the Italian proverb, 'keep your friends close, and your enemies closer.'

He figured he couldn't charge me with a crime anytime soon, so he probably thought I should hang out with them so he could keep an eye on me. They were still cleaning up, examining, and investigating the car bomb explosion that had killed Howard Williams very early that morning.

"Happy New Year, Valentino" were the first words out of Dickhead's mouth as he approached me and shook my hand.

"Thanks for coming out and assisting us."

"My pleasure," I lied.

Truthfully, I was somewhat resentful of having to miss watching the Rose Bowl with my sons, who were still back home at my place.

As I was standing there talking to Sinclair, I noticed Partridge supervising the tow truck as they were picking up what was left of Williams' Cadillac CTS. There were still various puddles of frozen blood scattered around the parking lot on the ground and some of the snowbanks. The victims' body parts had been appropriately gathered up and taken to the morgue. The other patrolmen were still trying to assess the damage the explosion had caused in the parking lot area. Several other parked cars were also damaged by the blast and had to be towed as well.

"How do you think the car bomb was detonated?" I asked Frank as he walked over to me and shook my hand.

"The investigators think it was probably by some remote-control device, so the killer had to be close by," Partridge replied.

"The killer was probably sitting at the Dunkin' Donuts across the street."

"Yeah, right. Probably eating donuts and drinking coffee," I remarked.

"The car was still in park, according to the investigators, so he probably had just started up his Cadillac when the car bomb exploded," the detective observed.

I followed Detective Partridge around the parking lot, looking for clues, as the light snowfall was beginning to cover up all of the bloodstains that were scattered around the parking lot.

It had been a long time since I had been involved and investigated a car bombing. The last one was at an adult bookstore on Seven Mile Road and Hayes back in 2012, and that one had the words 'mob hit' written all over it.

The victim, Santino "Sonny Bad" Badalamenti, was into the Licavoli Family for some large unpaid juice loans totaling over $250,000. When he couldn't pay the vig, he conveniently decided to start blowing off his weekly juice payments to 'the boys.'

In the world of finance and big business, that usually isn't a good idea.

The 'Licavoli Bank and Trust' included a revolving line of credit loan with 'reasonable' finance charges discounted ten points from their standard prime rate of 35%. The loan repayment and amortization schedules called for timely payments of usually $10,000 in cash a week.

Of course, their mortgage loans are usually cross-collateralized by taking a first position on the real estate of the borrower's business property (ahead of the bank, of course). Their security would also usually include the house, cars, equipment, and in Sonny Bad's case, his elaborate adult magazines and porn inventory.

And finally, a formal recorded mechanic's lien on Sonny Bad's pathetic, miserable fucking life.

Even the coppers in the Seventh Precinct were happy that he was erased and aced out of the way. There were no tears in the neighborhood that his sleazy adult bookstore was finally shut down.

I had talked to the Licavoli underboss, Caesar Giordano, regarding that murder. After several lengthy conversations, he told me off the record that Sonny Bad's killing was a huge favor to the community and that he had it coming for a long time. It turned out that Sonny was running a 'drug store' out of the back door of his adult book shop. He had a meth lab in the back and was pedaling cocaine, heroin, and some juicy, prescription opioids, supplied from several of his hospital and drug company connections.

After talking to Caesar Giordano several times regarding that murder, I came to know him as an upstanding guy and a gentleman. He expressed his condolences on the loss of my father some thirty years later. He also mentioned his family's connection to Howard Williams back in 1978 and how upset Don Licavoli was about my father's meaningless, cold-blooded death.

"We strongly encouraged Williams and his buddies to get the hell out of town after that trial, or someone would have taken them out."

"I wish you would have," was my reaction to Giordano when he explained his connection to him.

"I wouldn't worry, John. Williams and his friends are going to get what they got coming.

Maybe not now, but someday," he said to me back then.

Remembering my conversation with Caesar Giordano several years ago, back in 2012, it would only make sense that they could very well be the 'Water Pistol Killers'.

The Licavoli Family could be responsible for the murderous deaths of Joni Williams Harper, Jack Hanson, and his wife, George Johnson, and now finally, Howard Williams, the man who planned my father's murder. Those victims ignored their street order to stay out of town by coming back to Detroit after being exiled. They defied their 'deportation orders' by coming back to Detroit.

Their disregarding and snubbing the Mafia's directive in staying out of town was more than enough motive to connect the Licavoli Family to these gruesome homicides.

If anyone knows anything about the Detroit Mafia, you don't ignore your walking papers and come strolling back into town uninvited.

The Licavoli Family has always been well recognized and established for their discreet, professionally executed murders. Their hitmen have always been well known for their skilled use of stealth .25 caliber silencers, their intricate car bombs, sharp serrated knives, and their very competent butchering skills.

If the Licavoli's are involved in these brutal murders, I was certainly not about to instigate or volunteer any information to the Detroit P.D. The last thing I would want to do is tip off Partridge, Sinclair, or the other Intel police detectives about the possibility that these five murders could all be mob hits.

Although Don Licavoli would probably be happy to take the credit, I don't believe they were involved with any of these homicides. 'The Boys' don't go running around leaving green toy squirt guns and elaborate poetry at their crime scenes.

As far as I was concerned, the 'Water Pistol Killer' was doing me a huge favor and saving me the trouble of killing these pathetic bastards myself.

After spending a delightful New Years' with my boys and their friends, I was a little annoyed. I was disappointed that I had missed the gory, horrific murder scene on that very early morning. As much as I wanted to personally dole out my own brand of justice on my father's chief murderer, I would have enjoyed seeing Howard Williams' ruthless body splattered all over the Crazy Horse parking lot. But of course, I couldn't verbalize my actual thoughts and feelings regarding that callous, hillbilly son-of-a-bitch.

"Has anybody interviewed the bartender?" I asked Detective Partridge.

"I talked to her for a bit this morning. She's opening up the bar in a half-hour for her customers who want to watch the Rose Bowl, so you should be able to talk to her."

"Is she in now?"

"Think so. Somebody just saw her pull up."

I walked inside the bar, and it felt weird not having been there in several months. Since giving up the juice, I found it easier to stay away from the dark, ominous gin mills that I visited so often in my past.

My eyes were still adjusting to the darkness of the bar when I heard someone yelling out my name.

"What's up, Johnny?" Dolores said as she quickly came from around the bar to hug me.

"You look great, John. What are you doing these days? We don't see you anymore."

"I'm cleaning up my act, Dolores. I'm working out at the gym three times a week, and I'm only drinking grape juice now. I even quit smoking."

"No, shit?" Dolores looked shocked.

"What else did you do, join the monastery? We all miss you," she said as she gave me another hug.

"You look great," she complimented.

After spending so much time drinking at the bar and blowing all my money on lap dances, I'm sure they missed the donation of my weekly paychecks.

"I hear Howard Williams was here last night for New Year's Eve."

"Yeah, Johnny. What a piece of work he was. He was really shooting off his mouth last night, pissing off a few of the customers."

"That's what I heard."

"A young kid was sitting next to him that he really pissed off. They almost got into it before he flipped the old man off and walked out of the bar."

"Did you happen to get his name?"

"Yeah...he paid with a credit card, so I'm sure I can pull up the transaction."

Dolores then went behind the bar and pulled out the credit card summary of all of the transactions from the night before. As she was looking at the machine, she continued talking about how drunk and belligerent Williams was.

"Yeah, Johnny, that old hillbilly was pretty drunk last night. I almost wanted to stop him from leaving, as he was staggering out the door. There was no way he was gonna make it driving home last night."

"Well, he didn't make it home."

A few more minutes had passed as she found the credit card receipt.

"Here it is. His name is Jeff Radzinski, and his receipt with the tip was $89.54."

"Thanks, Dolores, make a copy of that for me, and I'll give it to the detective outside. They'll give him a call and interview him," I said to her.

"Can I get you anything?" she politely asked.

"No thanks, dear. I better get outside and see what else they're coming up within this homicide. Part of the parking lot is still going to be closed for a few more hours."

"No problem, Johnny," as she sat down at the stool on the other side of the bar.

"Boy, I gotta tell ya, the way that Howard was shooting off his mouth about how he and his friends had killed your father forty years ago. I was getting angry, just listening to him."

"What exactly did he say?" I had to ask.

She paused for a moment.

"He said something to the effect of 'there ain't nothin' better than watchin' a man die,'" she brazenly said, completely unabashed.

"Then he put his hand up, shaped like a gun and said 'bang, bang, bang.'"

Dolores was making the shape of a pointed gun with her right hand.

"He was bragging that his friend Jack put three bullets into the man that was fucking his wife, and how he had the pleasure of watching him die."

Upon hearing all of that, I was starting to get extremely angry under my breath. That hillbilly bastard had the nerve to brag about killing my father in public, shooting off his mouth in front of a bunch of strange people in a damn strip bar.

I thought about it. Maybe this was a divine act from heaven. Perhaps the remote-control device for that car bomb was being operated from some distant location in the afterlife, with my father, Tony Valentino, gleefully pushing the button.

"Doesn't that anger you, Johnny? That hillbilly piece of shit had it coming, ya know?" she paused, taking a sip from an ice-cold beer she had poured herself from the bar.

"Especially after the way he was talking about your Dad and all," Dolores said.

There was a long moment of silence.

"And then saying those disrespectful words in the middle of bar... 'bang, bang, bang'!" she repeated.

I walked over to the exit door and smiled at Dolores. Making the gun sign with my right hand, I confidently answered her loudly:

"Bang, bang, bang...BOOM!"

CHAPTER THIRTY-NINE

AN IRS INVESTIGATION-WINTER 2020

The commotion of taxpayers walking in and out of the Internal Revenue Service office that February day was distracting as U.S. Federal Treasury Agent Anthony Carleton was sitting at his cubical, trying to finish his audit report.

The downtown Internal Revenue Service office is located in the Ally Detroit Center, still commonly known as the One Detroit Center, located at 500 Woodward Avenue. The elaborate, forty-three story granite skyscraper is considered the tallest building in the City of Detroit and the second-highest in Michigan. The IRS office occupies three floors of the upscale office building, and Carleton's cubical is located next to the Taxpayer Assistance section of the department.

Agent Carleton had been working on a special audit for the Great Lakes Life Insurance Company for the last six weeks and was being pressured to submit his reports to his field office supervisor by the end of the week. The district attorney's office at the U.S. Department of Justice was put on notice that a felony at the insurance company had been committed, and they needed his reports to begin their formal indictment.

He had a few loose ends to tie up, but otherwise, he knew that the Treasury Department had a 'prima facia' case of embezzlement, misappropriation of funds, and fraud against the insurance company's chief financial officer, Olivia Laurent.

They had spent several long nights mirroring the financial transactions within the company's file server and computer systems. Carleton personally examined the dormant life insurance policies for which significant insurance claims had been made, to the tune of $5,731,000. These monies had been claimed through fraudulent beneficiaries of these dormant policies, where checks were drafted and disbursed to the insurance policy beneficiaries.

Unfortunately, these beneficiaries never received their funds. The checks were cashed at various banks, using fake bank accounts and personal information to open these accounts. The monies were deposited, then siphoned out through cash transactions into a bank account in the Grand Cayman Islands, with the names of the blind trusts to which several foreign entities were the signers. After 'following the money trail,' Carleton was able to trace the final destination to a single Swiss bank account that received these funds, opened under the name of Olivia Laurent.

As Anthony Carleton was writing this report, he couldn't help but smile to himself:

This person is a corrupt, financial fucking genius.

The veteran Treasury Agent was impressed. It would have taken the Treasury Department years to unravel all of the misappropriated policy payouts and the money laundering trial of opened savings accounts, foreign bank accounts, and international holding companies that Laurent had set up to acquire and embezzle these funds.

If it wasn't for Carleton's keen intuition and his experience in auditing these foreign transactions, Laurent might have gotten away with this elaborate financial scheme.

She had set up enough roadblocks and detours, using pseudo blind trusts and foreign corporations to distract and throw off any competent forensic accountant.

"Follow the money" was an old audit cliché that Carleton never lost sight of, and this was Laurent's downfall. Had she not used the money so quickly, she would have probably never been caught. The ultimate destination for these embezzled funds ended up in a Banco di Roma account in Italy. This account was owned and maintained by her mother, using her maiden name, Rosina Colavito, who was still an Italian citizen.

If Laurent had only allowed the Italian government to assess taxes on the money sitting in the account and allowed the funds to remain dormant in the bank, her intricate scheme would have probably never been discovered.

Laurent had purchased an ostentatious villa in the region of Tuscany, near the town of Barga, nine months prior. She had paid for it in cash, to the tune of 1.5 million Euros, under her mother's name. If it weren't for the cooperation of the Italian government in monitoring these cash real estate purchase transactions, Carleton would never have made the connection.

Carleton also found several business trips that Laurent charged to the insurance company to Miami, Florida. Because of her financial responsibilities and job duties there, she was able to escape and take a five-day journey from Hollywood International Airport in Ft. Lauderdale to Leonardo DiVinci Airport in Rome. After meeting her mother there, they withdrew the stolen funds from the bank. The two then closed, furnished, and maintained their newly acquired, Tuscan villa.

The federal agent, once again, smiled to himself. Olivia Laurent was going to be in prison for a very long time.

Carleton was also in the process of assembling criminal charges on two accessories to this elaborate life insurance fraud.

The first person was Rosina Colavita Laurent, Olivia's mother, who lived in a modest house in Sterling Heights. The 78-year-old senior, if she pled guilty, would probably get sympathy from the courts and do very little prison time, if any at all.

The other accessory would be a Detroit police detective from the Third Precinct. He had assisted Laurent in assembling and acquiring all of the personal information for these policy beneficiaries. Carleton, while assessing Olivia's emails, found several correspondences to a Detective John Valentino of the Third Precinct.

Apparently, Carleton figured out that Valentino had provided Olivia with this personal information, which included social security numbers, addresses, mother's maiden names, discrete data, and other information to assist the corrupt financial officer in opening these fake bank accounts.

Carleton became very suspicious of the assistance Laurent had received from the Detroit police detective. Having heard of this detective before, this outstanding criminal fraud investigation gave him the excuse to go over and interview Detective Valentino in person.

It was time to take a ride that afternoon to the Detroit P.D.'s Third Precinct.

"May I help you?" Desk Sergeant Jeanine Zupo asked the federal agent.

"Yes, I'm here to see one of your detectives, John Valentino. Is he available?"

"Certainly. May I have your name?"

"Yes. Agent Anthony Carleton from the U.S. Treasury Department," he replied, displaying his federal badge.

Unconcerned, the desk sergeant called the detective on his desk phone. Within ten minutes, the detective came to the front desk to greet the agent. They both shook hands, as the street detective was unaware as to why he was receiving an unannounced visit from a federal agent.

As the two of them made small talk, Desk Sergeant Zupo made an immediate observation.

"Are you two related?" she asked, immediately noticing the uncanny, similar resemblance of the two men.

Both men were remarkably handsome, were both similar in height and build, and had the same pattern of graying hair. Both men had olive skin complexion and had the same mannerisms. The only difference being that Agent Carleton sported a well-trimmed mustache and goatee with horn-rimmed glasses. Valentino was clean-shaven and looked a little older than the agent, although probably not by much.

Agent Carleton smiled to himself while the detective smirked at the desk sergeant.

"Yeah, right," Valentino laughed.

He then tried to be cordial to the federal agent.

"May I offer you some coffee? I need a strong cup to survive these late afternoons."

"Certainly," Carleton accepted.

They both walked into the precinct cafeteria, and Valentino poured a black cup of coffee for the agent. Making small talk about the weather and the horrific hockey season the Detroit Red Wings were having, they both walked to the precinct conference room and sat down. The precinct detective figured that the federal agent was there to investigate another crime that both he and his partner were involved.

"Are you here for the Hernandez case?"

Valentino was referring to a bust that he and Palazzola were investigating regarding a DUI where the driver had over $160,000 in cash stashed in the trunk of his car.

"No, Detective. Actually, I'm here to talk to you about another crime."

"Really?"

"Yes. Do you know an individual by the name of Olivia Laurent? The CFO for the Great Lakes Insurance Company?"

"Eh...yes, I do."

"What is your relationship with her?"

The detective paused for a moment.

"We've been dating for the last several months. Is there a problem here?"

Smiling, Carleton pulled out some files from his briefcase, which he had brought along.

"We have evidence that you have given some personal information from your department's confidential data files to Ms. Laurent regarding some outstanding life insurance claims. Sensitive information, including social security numbers and personal addresses, credit files, maiden names, and driver's license records."

Valentino sat at the conference table, frozen. He had trusted Olivia that she needed this information to track down these beneficiaries to refund their cash surrender values for these stale policies. He had no idea that she was using this information for fraudulent purposes.

There was a long silence at the table as Valentino buried his hands in his face. He then finally looked up at the agent.

"What has Olivia done?"

"Your girlfriend has managed to embezzle an exorbitant amount of money out of her company."

"How much?"

"Let's just call it seven figures."

Detective Valentino groaned out loud.

"Believe me, Mr. Carleton. I had no idea what Olivia was up to. I was never made privy to any information regarding any devious schemes or purposes for that information that she requested. She assured me that it was for locating dormant insurance policyholders and their beneficiaries."

The federal agent decided to play a little hardball with the Detroit detective.

"You do realize the fraud penalties that go along with aiding and abetting a fraudulent scheme such as this one. You may be in prison for eight to twelve years for helping your girlfriend. Did you receive any compensation or anything else in return for this information?"

"Not a dime."

Carleton looked at Valentino. He was no longer able to hide his excitement any longer.

"Detective, did you have a father who was killed in 1978? And was his name Tony Valentino?"

The third precinct detective looked at the agent.

"Yes."

"On El Camino Drive?"

"Yes. Why?"

Agent Anthony Carleton smiled at the detective, as he was unable to control his enthusiasm. He then extended his hand to the detective.

"*Welcome to the family, Bro!*"

Johnny Valentino went into shock.

"What?"

"You and I have the same father. We are brothers."

John practically dropped his coffee cup, which was still filled with hot, black coffee. He looked at the federal agent, who was still smiling.

"What the hell are you talking about."

Still excited, Carleton then began reciting the story that was told to him twenty years ago by his mother. Until that point, Anthony Carleton was always told that his birth father and mother were engaged to be married when he was tragically killed. It wasn't until he was married and had started a family that he learned the truth about his biological father and that Tony Valentino was already married with a family of his own.

This all came as a total shock to Johnny. He began to sweat and get very anxious, not knowing how true this story was.

"How do I know all of this isn't bullshit?"

Carleton grinned.

"Well, for starters, my name is Anthony Valentine Carleton. My first and middle names are after my biological father, Antonio Valentino."

Johnny was still shaking his head in disbelief.

There were several more moments of silence as the detective was trying to absorb all of this.

"Look, John. I understand that this is a lot to get your head around. You're going to need some time to absorb all of this."

Still, in a daze, Johnny nodded his head.

"In the meantime, presuming that you didn't receive any compensation from Olivia Laurent regarding the disclosure of this private information, I will see what I can do about talking to the Department of Justice's office."

More silent moments.

"As far as I'm concerned, you were an innocent victim in this scam, John. And that is what I will say to the DOJ."

John Valentino only sat there, still silent. Anthony Carleton rose from the conference table and, grabbing his briefcase, walked toward the door.

"You were used, John. I suggest you keep Ms. Olivia Laurent at a very safe distance, if any, at all. She's not a very nice person," he suggested.

A moment of silence as John still sat there in a daze.

"Take care of yourself, Bro," the agent said. "We'll be in touch."

Anthony Carleton then left the precinct, with Johnny still sitting at the conference table, in a complete and total trance.

Was all of this true?

Could his father have had more than one girlfriend, and did he impregnate someone before his death?

Did his mother know about this illegitimate child before she died? Did his sisters know?

Who could he talk to and verify this story?

Later that evening, John Valentino was sitting at a Starbucks coffee shop on Ten Mile Road and Gratiot. He was eagerly waiting to speak to the only person that he knew who could verify this story.

Several minutes after he arrived, an older man with a cane walked into the Starbucks and ordered a double espresso. He then sat down across from Johnny.

"Hello, Zio," Johnny said as he stood up and kissed his uncle's cheek.

"I don't understand how you kids can come in here drink the coffee in this place. It's total garbage!"

Ross Valentino was feeling all of his eighty-one years as he slowly steadied himself into the small, confining wooden chair and darkly stained table.

Johnny didn't allow him to even get comfortable in his chair before he verbally assaulted him.

"Who is Anthony Carleton?"

"Who?"

"You heard me, Zio. Who is he?"

Rossano Valentino sat there for several long seconds, still drawing a blank.

"He says he's my brother!"

The older man sat at his chair, thinking long and hard until an embarrassed look overcame him.

"Oh, so you have met him?"

"Yes, I've fucking met him!" Johnny said loudly.

"Yes, as a matter of fact, this bastard child of my fathers could literally end up throwing me in fucking jail," he angrily stated.

Johnny then explained the situation regarding the embezzlement scenario with Great Lakes Insurance and the girl he was currently dating, Olivia Laurent.

After several long minutes, Uncle Ross smiled at his nephew.

"Well, I guess we have family in some high places."

"This isn't funny, Zio. How could you let me go around my whole life without knowing that I had a half-brother out there in the world somewhere?"

Ross then defended himself.

"Do you know how many ladies, how many fucking girlfriends your father had? God only knows how many other bastard children there are out there."

"Zio, this guy is definitely my half-brother. He even looks like me. The precinct desk sergeant even picked up on it, asking if the two of us were related."

Ross looked at his nephew.

"I'm sorry you had to find out this way. I was there at the coffee shop when your father met this lady. It wasn't until months later, after your Daddy was killed, that I found out that she was pregnant. I remember asking her if she needed anything, and she said no."

Another silent moment.

"I remember when the baby was born over forty years ago, and that was the last time I had heard anything. She never contacted us."

"You could have at least told me, instead of my getting fucking broadsided like an asshole this afternoon."

Ross Valentino's eyes widened.

"Johnny, do you realize how many girlfriends your father had? Your father couldn't keep his dick pants. Your poor mother suffered from your father all the years they were married. And yet, she still loved him, unconditionally."

"This lady even came to your father's funeral, and I realized right away who she was. But she never started any trouble with our family or especially your mother. She never asked us for anything."

John looked at his uncle.

"Who else knows about this? Do my sisters know?"

"No, I don't think so. I never mentioned anything to your aunt. And nothing was ever said to your sisters that I know. I'm certain that your mother never found out, or she would have approached me."

"Great."

The two of them looked at each other as Uncle Ross began to smile.

"Well, look at it this way: You have another person in your family now that is a part of your father. You now have the brother that you always wished for."

John shook his head and smiled.

"I guess we'll be putting out some extra chairs for Christmas Eve."

They both chuckled as John got up to leave, while his uncle gingerly followed him out the door. The older man was still carefully maneuvering his walking cane.

Uncle Ross kissed his nephew goodbye. And then before entering his car, he eagerly asked:

"Is your brother at least a nice guy?"

"I don't know, Zio. I guess we'll find that out when he throws me in jail."

CHAPTER FORTY

THE TRUTH IS DISCOVERED-WINTER 2020

I was sitting at my desk that early February morning, drinking my black Dunkin' Donuts coffee and eating an onion seed bagel with cream cheese. I had gotten into my office early at the Third Precinct, wide awake from a night of complete sleeplessness.

I was still trying to digest the information that Agent Carleton had passed on to me the day before, along with the elaborate scheme that Olivia was operating out of her life insurance office.

Although I was shocked, I must say I wasn't surprised. I had always denoted a sneaky side of Olivia that I just couldn't trust, no matter how much I tried to do otherwise. I couldn't put my finger on it, but I noted a side of her that was a little insincere, and it made me very cautious about trusting her.

She wanted so much for me to get emotionally attached to her so that she could probably take advantage of me even more than she already had.

I was so disappointed in myself. I should have realized that she was using me as a detective to acquire this private information for her own benefit. But for some stupid reason, I believed her. I should have known better, being a detective and all.

I had learned in my forty-eight years of life not to trust anyone. I wanted to call her. I wanted to tell her off and let her know how I was finally wise to her.

I was so tempted last night to tie one on, as the thought of running over to the party store and grabbing a whiskey bottle off the shelf crossed my mind several times. I had no booze. I had no cigarettes. I had nothing that I could use to calm my nerves the night before, and I was utterly alone.

I then remembered Dr. Elaine's advice. I put on my running shoes, some jogging pants, and a sweatshirt with a hoody. I then went out running for an hour, putting in over six miles at a decent clip. I was back at my apartment by 8:30 pm, now too exhausted to feel lonely or depressed.

I hoped the exercise would knock me out once I crashed in bed, but I was wide awake and watching TV by 1:30 in the morning. I watched several episodes of 'Blue Bloods' and 'Chicago PD,' then old reruns of 'Mr. Ed' on MeTV.

By then, it was 5:00 am, and I still couldn't close my eyes. I kept thinking about Olivia. I kept thinking about Agent Carleton. I kept thinking about what a fucking scumbag my father was.

Over and over and over again.

A little brother named Anthony. I just couldn't believe it. I could have used a little brother to lean on when I was growing up. When I was struggling with the loss of my father, the man that I worshiped and put on a pedestal, having a brother would have helped. I idolized my father, no matter how rotten he treated and betrayed my mother. I could have used a little brother to play baseball with, to kick around a soccer ball, to toss a football with, and call at any time of day or night.

With all the drugs and alcohol that I did in high school and into my adulthood, I could have used a little brother. He might have followed me around with a baseball mitt or a football and looked up to me. Someone to grow up with, to spend my fatherless childhood years. Someone to help me look after my mother and my sisters.

Maybe it would have been nice to have a little brother to help me carry the cross of anger and resentment all these years against my father and his adulterous stupidity.

"Your father couldn't keep his dick in his pants."

What an incredibly fucked up legacy my father left not only for my sisters and me but for poor Anthony Carleton. He never learned the truth about what an asshole his father was until later in his life. He didn't even want him to be born.

Anthony said that my father told his mother to get an abortion, and he would just wash his hands of it all.

I just couldn't sleep anymore. I then took a shower and got dressed. After hitting my usual Dunkin' Donuts stop, I was sitting at my desk at the Third Precinct at seven o'clock in the morning.

I had not talked to Olivia in a few days, and I knew I was overdue to hear from her. We usually returned each other's phone calls and tried to stay in touch, even if we missed not speaking with each other for several days. I remembered her telling me she had to make some business trips back and forth to Miami on business, and there were times when we went a week or more without talking to one another.

When Carleton told me about her Italian investments, it suddenly all made sense. There were times when I called her, and she didn't answer the phone. And when she did, she sounded distant, as if she were talking from a remote part of the world.

I slowly realized how much she had used me and what a complete idiot I was. I started thinking about her past relationships with the priest and the Chicago detective.

At that point, I went onto the internet and the police computer and did some intense digging.

"Chicago P.D., Sixteenth District."

"Yes, this is Detective Valentino from the Detroit Police Department's Third Precinct. I'm looking for Detective Philip Dorian. Is he available?"

"Let me check," the desk sergeant said.

A few long moments on silent hold passed when someone finally answered the phone.

"Detective Dorian," said a deep voice on the other end.

"Yes, I'm Detective Valentino from the Detroit P.D. I wondered if you were available to answer a few questions."

"Questions regarding what?"

"Questions regarding someone by the name of Olivia Laurent."

There was a very long silence on the phone.

"Hello? Hello? Detective Dorian? Are you still there?"

"Yes," he finally responded.

"I wondered if I could..."

"How did you get my name and number?" Dorian abruptly asked.

"You were the lead investigator in the 'Pedophile Priest Murders' in Chicago two years ago. Your name was splashed all over the papers. You were also injured in that investigation. All of the detectives in our Detroit Police Department know who you are."

"Yes, but…how did you know that I knew Olivia?"

"She revealed your name in a few conversations that I had with her when she was mentioning..."

"Please tell me you're not dating her!" he rudely interrupted me.

"Excuse me, Detective Dorian. I never said that I…"

"Look, whatever problems she's into right now, I don't want to hear about them," he rudely interrupted me again.

At that moment, I started getting pissed.

"Look, Dorian, I didn't call you to start an argument with you. She's being investigated right now by the Treasury Department, and she has managed to pull me down with her," I loudly interjected.

Dorian started to laugh.

"I'm not surprised."

A few moments of silence while I gathered my thoughts, and he began to calm down.

"Could you tell me how she was involved with your 'Pedophile Priest Murder' investigation?"

"She had her own investigation going on with Intel behind my back, and then we all came to find out that she may have been involved with the Monsignor who was later accused of planning the murders."

"Monsignor Kilbane?"

"Yes, that's him. I came to find out that our relationship was another way of her pumping information out of me and assisting Kilbane."

"Really?" I said to him as we began finally talking civilly to one another and comparing notes.

"We can't prove that Olivia was involved in the scheme. But I'm shocked that she had the guts to return to Detroit," the Chicago detective exclaimed.

Another silent moment.

"What is she into now?"

"She's been cashing in old and stale life insurance policies."

Dorian laughed again.

"Let me guess: She got you to help her get some information from your database."

I was startled. "How did you guess?"

"Nothing from that bitch surprises me."

"Well, the Feds are hot on her tail right now. I'm just praying that she doesn't pull me down with her."

Suddenly, Dorian began to sound amiable and sympathetic.

"Well, listen, Valentino. If there is anything you need from us, please feel free to call. I would love nothing more than to see that conniving bitch locked up in a prison cell."

"I appreciate the offer, Detective. I'll keep you posted," I replied. There were a few more quiet moments on the telephone.

"If you want some good advice, get away from that deviant whore as fast as you can," he loudly advised.

"Thank you, Detective. We'll be in touch," as I hung up the telephone.

I knew right then and there that I had to take control of the situation and probably take Dorian's advice. At that point, I could only hope that Agent Carleton would do as promised and put in a good word.

With everything else going on in my life, I didn't need to be involved in some fraudulent financial scam with Olivia.

I then picked up my phone and sent a short and sweet text.

It was a sunny, bright afternoon, as the water from the Detroit River glistened with the reflection of the urban sunshine. Olivia Laurent was sitting in her living room, staring out of the eighteenth story window of her Jefferson Street condominium. She was very deep in thought.

She was informed the day before by the CEO, James Moran, that she would be on unpaid leave and suspension, pending the outcome of the federal investigation that was being conducted in her office. It seems that the board of directors of the Great Lakes Insurance Company had been made aware of her questionable transactions and the cashing in of the various stale life insurance policies over the last year.

She had just met with the criminal attorney that she had hired, and he has been in contact with the Department of Justice. Olivia was ordered to surrender her passport and that she should be expecting federal charges in the form of a formal indictment from the district attorney's office within the next week.

Olivia continued to stare out of the window, her eyes filled with tears. Her life was now a total mess. Because of her greed and pride, she had let her dishonesty and ability to manipulate people get the best of her.

She now was looking at being formally indicted by the Department of Justice for criminal embezzlement, grand larceny, and probably, tax fraud. With her knowledge of the law, Olivia knew that the judge, in this case, once she was arrested, would throw the book at her. She was looking at doing some serious prison time.

At that moment, there was a loud beep from her iPhone, letting her know that she just received a text.

It was from Johnny:

Olivia,

Got a visit from a treasury agent regarding your illegal, fraudulent activities. Thanks for getting me involved in your criminal schemes. Nice to know that I was being used.

Please lose my number and stay away.

John

Olivia read the text several times and began to cry. She was genuinely sorry that she had gotten Detective John Valentino involved in acquiring the information she needed to process those fraudulent insurance claims. She tried to return the text and apologize, but it wasn't going through. It was evident that Johnny had immediately blocked her cell phone number.

She had developed strong feelings for John Valentino during the several months that they were dating. He was kind, sincere, respectful, and fun to be around. Valentino reminded Olivia of a broken bird on the mend. She felt as though it was up to her to help him heal from his ruined marriage and recover from his drinking addiction.

In a way, Olivia felt responsible for saving John from himself. But most of all, she wanted to help him mend and repair his broken heart. Olivia was being very patient and didn't push John into having a hot and heavy sexual relationship.

His ex-wife hurt John immensely, and he wasn't ready to jump into another intimate relationship with someone else. Olivia was okay with that. With enough time, friendship, and intimacy, she hoped that John Valentino would eventually see that Olivia was the right partner for him and that they could have a permanent life together.

She hoped that with her new Italian villa in Tuscany, that she could make a new life for herself and, hopefully, include John Valentino in it.

But she had now been caught, and Olivia felt ashamed. Her devious intentions had been brought out in the open, exposed to everyone in the whole world to see.

Her name and her life had now been ruined. Her fellow employees, including Cindy Jankowski, no longer wanted any part of her. She had no more friends to call. Her mother wasn't returning her phone calls, either.

There was no longer Philip Dorian, Joseph Kilbane, or especially John Valentino to help her emotionally.

Olivia had taken out a bottle of Jim Beam Whiskey earlier that afternoon and had already consumed several whiskey shots. She walked back into the kitchen and fixed herself another drink.

With three fresh ice cubes, she splashed more liquor into her drink tumbler and walked over to the balcony. She was now standing outside, looking down at the Jefferson Avenue traffic, eighteen stories below.

Olivia was holding a black rosary in her left hand as she continued to cry to herself loudly. Perhaps, she thought, the small statuette of that man hanging on a wooden cross, connected by fifty-nine beads, was the only friend she had left.

She felt so desolate, so alone. Olivia hated herself for her criminal actions. She had used everyone around her, and she had now completely ruined her life.

"Play by the rules," her father had always told her while she was growing up.

"Nothing comes for free," he would always say to her.

Olivia was always looking for the simple shortcut, the 'easy button' to fix her personal and financial problems. This whole scheme began because she didn't know how to control her credit card spending habits, and she was in tremendous personal debt. With time and patience, the business executive could have fixed her financial problems. But she got impatient. And greedy. Olivia Laurent had destroyed her life. There was nothing for her to live for. She gulped down her drink, then put down the empty glass tumbler on top of the outdoor coffee table. Climbing onto the balcony railing, Olivia balanced herself just long enough to look down at the traffic below.

Taking one long deep breath, she closed her eyes.

CHAPTER FORTY-ONE

WELL DESERVED BEATING-WINTER 2020

The cold February windchill on that day was minus twenty degrees below zero. The frosty, blistery air was quickly converting our previously mild climate of the last few days into the cold wintry weather that everyone in the Motor City was accustomed to.

I had stayed late at the precinct on that Tuesday night, trying to close out a few investigation files, when my desk phone rang.

"Valentino here,"

"What's up, Bro?"

I didn't recognize the voice, and for several seconds, I didn't put two and two together.

"Who is this?"

"This is Federal Agent Anthony Valentine Carleton, if you must formally know. May I have the pleasure of speaking with Detroit Police Detective John Valentino?"

I started to smile.

"I'm sorry, Anthony. I'm still trying to get my head around the fact that I have a little brother now."

Carleton started to laugh out loud.

"Well, I was hoping we could lose the formalities and talk the way brothers do if you're okay with that?"

"Sure," I said, amused that this federal agent was not only going to be my friend but a little brother as well.

"So hey, dude? What's going on?" I said in a Motown tone of voice.

"Well, Bro, I have some good news."

"Okay. Let's hear it."

"The Department of Justice has completed their investigation and are now assisting the Great Lakes Insurance Company in filing a claim against the estate, so you're off the hook."

"Oh, really? So, I won't be going to jail?"

"Nope. I talked to my supervisors, and I was able to delete your name from my audit reports. So, you won't be going on any long fishing trips anytime soon."

I took a deep sigh of relief. I had felt like a huge elephant had been lifted off of my shoulders.

"That is great news," I confirmed.

"I thought we could get together for a beer, you and me, tomorrow night at Roger's Roost on Schoenherr, near my house to celebrate. Get to know each other better, ya' know, like brothers and all..."

"Sure, Anthony. That sounds swell. What time tomorrow night?"

"Seven-thirty or so. We'll have a few drinks."

"Sounds great," I said.

I then asked him to clarify something that he had said that didn't make sense to me.

"What did you mean by 'filing a claim against the estate'?"

There was a moment of silence on the phone.

"You mean you didn't hear about it?"

"Hear about what?"

Another silent moment.

"Olivia Laurent killed herself the other day. She jumped off of her condominium balcony."

"Oh, dear God," I initially reacted.

I intermittently put my desk phone down and began to rub my eyes. A cold shiver went down my spine, and I needed a minute to recover and catch my breath.

I had not heard about any suicide on Jefferson Avenue, and I since I had sent that text to her, I was completely unaware of what was going on or what Olivia was doing.

I picked the phone back up.

"Johnny? Are you there?"

"Yes, Anthony, I'm here."

"I didn't realize you didn't know, John. I'm sorry. Are you okay?"

I thought about it for a moment.

"Eh, yeah, I'm okay. We had just broken it off, so I wouldn't have heard anything."

"Well, I'm sorry you had to hear that news from me. Nobody deserves to die or kill themselves, right?"

"Yes, Anthony. You're right."

"Okay, Bro. We'll see each other tomorrow. Take care," he quickly hung up the telephone.

I began shaking my head. As mad and as angry as I was at Olivia, I never expected that she would kill herself. She seemed like she was too much of a narcissistic sociopath to allow herself to take her own life.

I thought about her, sitting at my desk in silence for several long minutes. I then grabbed my things walked outside to my squad car. I was a little relieved, as this was the first time I had heard an update on this insurance fraud case.

As I was driving on West Grand Boulevard on that Tuesday night, my mind began turning over how fortunate I was to dodge a bullet in that DOJ investigation. I also tried very hard not to think about Olivia killing herself anymore. The only good distraction for me was to think about food.

It was past 6:30 pm, and I had been so busy at work that I didn't have a chance to stop and eat lunch, so I hadn't eaten all day. I was contemplating where I was going to go when I got the urge to stop at the McDonald's near my home on Kelly Road.

"Welcome to McDonald's. Can I help you?" said the loud voice on the speaker.

"Yes, I'll have Quarter Pounder with Cheese, fries, and a large Coke, please."

A brief moment, then she repeated the order.

"Anything else?"

"No, ma'am," I answered the female voice, which sounded African American.

"$9.59, please pull up to the next window."

I had previously checked my wallet, and I had over fifty dollars in cash, so I knew I could afford a trip at McDonald's this time around.

As I pulled up to the window, the attendant was an older lady who looked very familiar. She looked like she was the manager.

"$9.59, please," she said.

I immediately recognized who she was.

I pulled out a twenty-dollar bill from my wallet and handed it to the attendant.

"Keep the change, ma'am. I owe you this."

The older lady looked at me and smiled but had a confused look on her face.

"You gave me some food a few months back when I didn't have enough money to pay. I'm just paying you back," I said with a smile.

The McDonald's manager looked at me, not recognizing who I was or realizing the good deed she had done for me a few months back.

"I'm sorry, sir. We don't accept tips."

"No, it's not a tip. It's just a way of saying 'thank you' from someone who was down on his luck."

She then smiled at me, trying to study my face and where she had seen me before.

"That's for the next person who needs help," I said, as she handed me my Quarter Pounder meal with French fries and a large Coke.

We both smiled at each other as I put my food order on the front seat and pulled out onto Kelly Road towards my apartment.

I was already munching on the French fries and was just about to pull my car into the parking lot when my cell phone went off. It was my son Anthony.

"Hello?"

"Dad, Dad...please come over here, hurry!" My son was frantically crying over the phone.

"Anthony, what's wrong."

"Mom's asshole boyfriend is beating her up downstairs. He's hitting her and breaking things and throwing things at her and on the floor!" He was crying out loud and almost out of breath.

"Please, Dad! Come over here...NOW!"

My son had barely finished the sentence before I flipped my squad car sirens on and pulled out of my parking lot. I must have been going almost 100 miles an hour down Kelly Road. My McDonald's drink cup and spilled all over the front seat, and the French fries were scattered all over the floor. I was taking turns hard, trying to get to my ex-wife's house on Balfour Street in Harper Woods as fast as I could. I was probably there in less than five minutes on what was usually a fifteen-minute drive.

I knew my sons were probably hiding upstairs, so I had to open up the side door by myself. I tried to open up the front door, but it was locked and deadbolted. I pushed and kicked it in with my foot and hit it as hard as I could with my shoulder, breaking the deadbolt and swiftly damaging the door frame.

As I went flying into the kitchen, Tom Pratt was busy throwing objects at my ex-wife, who was bloodied up and crying on the floor of the kitchen, curled in the fetal position.

I swiftly grabbed Tom Pratt by the throat and pushed his head up as hard as I could against the wall. He started resisting me, hitting me on the side of my face with his right fist.

Big mistake, Asshole!

I began frantically hitting his head with my right fist while pinning him up against the wall with my left hand. His face and his nose were taking a pounding. As I extended my left arm against his neck, I took out my gun and began hitting him on his face and head with the butt of my pistol, totally dislodging his face and mouth.

His face was so bloodied up and beaten that he couldn't stand up on his own two feet anymore. I was still holding him up by his neck, practically choking him, while I continued to pistol-whip him with my right hand. I must have been pounding hard on him for a good, long five minutes. His body was pinned up against the wall, with my holding him by his throat while I was hitting him as hard as I could.

"Johnny, don't kill him!" I heard Marina yell out from behind me.

At that moment, I finally let go of him as he completely collapsed on the floor. His head was cracked wide open, and blood was protruding everywhere on his face, his nose, his mouth, and all over his shirt.

Tom Pratt was lying on the floor and practically dead from the intense beating. By that moment, the boys had come downstairs to see what had happened to their mother. She was bloodied up on the left side of her face, swollen and beaten as though she had been hit in the face several times by this asshole.

I looked at her boyfriend on the floor. He looked like he was dead and wasn't breathing. I bent down and couldn't feel a pulse. At that moment, I called 911.

"This is Detective Valentine here. Send a bus over here right away, please," as I gave them the address. Within five minutes, the Harper Woods Police Department, their fire department, and two ambulances arrived at the house.

"What happened?" one of the coppers demanded to know, as I explained the situation.

By that moment, two paramedics came in to take Tom Pratt's vitals and assessed the damage that he had suffered. He was still barely alive, but his pulse was quite faint and barely beating. At that moment, two of the Harper Woods coppers brought me outside and had me sit in their police squad car while they assessed the damage, both to my ex-wife and her boyfriend. They immediately took away my weapon.

As it turned out, Pratt had been drinking heavily that evening. After making a few demands for him to get off the couch, Pratt physically went after Marina. She saw him trying to lunge at her from the family room over to the kitchen where she was standing. Marina didn't have enough time to grab something to protect herself as he began wailing on her with his open hand and fists.

As the paramedics put him on a stretcher, three more squad cars from Harper Woods and another Detroit squad car pulled up behind the police unit I was sitting in. As I was patiently sitting in the patrol car, an all too familiar 'angel' popped his head through the window of the back seat where I was sitting.

"Valentino, I am getting so fucking tired of bailing your ass."

It was Commander Riley.

I had heard later that the Harper Woods Police Dispatcher had notified one of the nearby Detroit squad units that were patrolling on Eight Mile Road. That unit informed the Detroit Police Dispatcher, who was given the address on Balfour Street, of the domestic violence altercation. When Riley heard the Balfour Street address over the dispatch, he knew right away, something was up and that I was probably involved.

Needless to say, after about two hours of curbside drama and several squad cars from Harper Woods and the Detroit Police, they all finally disbursed. I was released from the Harper Woods Police squad car.

I was standing on the sidewalk with Commander Riley and another copper.

"Why didn't you call for backup, Johnny? You're such a dumb shit. Do you realize you almost killed that guy?" Riley asked.

I was reticent, and I tried not to say anything. Truth be told, I was still in shock. Knowing that if I not gotten to the house sooner, there was a good possibility that Tom Pratt would have killed Marina right then and there on the kitchen floor.

I looked at Riley.

"What would you have done in my shoes, Chief?"

We both looked at each other. Then my precinct commander smiled.

"The same fucking thing you did."

At that moment, Marina came outside. She had several white bandages on her face and her forehead. Marina had refused to be taken to the hospital. The cuts and bruises she received on her face didn't seem to require stitches, according to one of the paramedics.

Marina came down the front stairs in front of the house and quickly rushed into my arms, crying profusely and holding me tight. At that moment, I started crying as well, and for several long minutes, we were both crying in each other's arms.

"I'm so sorry, Johnny, I'm so sorry," she kept saying. Marina was crying so hard; she could barely get the words out of her mouth.

I held her tight and tried to console her, telling her that everything was going to be alright and that she was safe now.

"I'm so sorry, Johnny. I'm so sorry for what I did to you. I'm so sorry for breaking up our family. I'm so sorry for abandoning you. I pushed you away when you needed me the most.

I was so damn mean to you...I'm sorry Johnny...I'm so, so sorry," she kept crying.

I only held her as tightly as I could, as my shirt was completely drenched with her tears.

"Your husband is a hero, ma'am. It's a good thing he was here when he was," one of the patrolmen said to Marina.

At that moment, Anthony and Dario came outside, and they put their arms around both of us. They, too, were crying, as Anthony kept saying, "Thank you, Daddy, thank you."

For ten minutes or more, the four of us were a family unit, holding each other so tightly that nothing could have separated the four of us away from each other. We were all standing on the sidewalk, crying in each other's arms, holding each other as tightly as we could.

At that moment, all of the bitterness, all the anger, and all the hatred that I had been carrying around in my heart had suddenly escaped me. The boys kept saying, 'I love you' to myself and Marina, over and over again.

I felt the weight of over one hundred pounds of anguish had been lifted off of my shoulders. For the first time in more than four decades, I felt the joy, the blissfulness, and a total feeling of love come into my heart and soul. I was utterly overwhelmed with peace and contentment, and it was exhilarating.

Then Marina looked at me with her big brown eyes, her bruises and bandages still covering her left eye, and said those words to me that I thought I would never, ever hear from her again.

"I love you, Johnny."

At that brief moment, we were now once again...a complete family.

CHAPTER FORTY-TWO

MEETING ON EL CAMINO-EARLY SPRING 2020

It was a cold March morning on the West Side of Detroit, as Joseph Riley was sitting home with a cold. He had been off of work for a few days, and the coughing and sneezing became so bad that he had been bedridden at home.

Commander Riley had been taking some over the counter cold medication over the last several days that wasn't seeming to work. He was about to make an appointment to see a doctor for his intense coughing and sneezing.

Riley was lying on his couch that morning, watching 'Good Morning America' when he received a text on his cell phone:

I need to talk. Meet me at 2 pm on El Camino Drive – Johnny.

He looked at his phone and realized it was John Valentino. He had always had a fondness for John since that morning that he had lost his father when he was only six years old. Riley looked after him as if he were his own son.

John Valentino was still having difficulties staying sober and dealing with the issues of getting divorced from his beloved wife. He was struggling to adjust as a single, part-time father. He had taken Joe Riley into his confidence several times over the last several months, and Valentino knew that he could trust the precinct commander with whatever was bothering him.

Riley wanted Johnny to stay sober in the worst way, knowing what he had personally gone through in his own life. Riley committed himself to help Detective Valentino at any cost, and he knew that John had finally trusted him with his issues.

But why meet at El Camino Drive? Maybe John was feeling melancholy about his father's death again. It wasn't uncommon for Johnny to drive over to El Camino Drive in front of the very house that his father was murdered. John would mention to Riley that he would spend hours upon hours there, wishing and hoping that his father's spirit could somehow speak to him there.

Riley encouraged Valentino to embrace his Catholicism and go to Mass on Sundays. If John wanted to speak to his father's spirit, he suggested, he should do it through God.

Joseph Riley had learned to embrace his religion after he lost his beloved wife, Elena, to breast cancer several years ago. Going to daily mass at seven o'clock in the morning brought him the peace and reflection that he needed in dealing with the personal loss of his wife, for which he continued to beat himself up.

Riley only wished for that peace to come to John Valentino, so he realized that this meeting at El Camino Drive would be a reflective one.

That early afternoon, Joseph Riley left his home on Tracey Street on the West Side and drove over to El Camino Drive. As he pulled up his car, he parked it in front of the very house that Tony Valentino was murdered at some forty years ago. The wood-sided house was now boarded up and abandoned, as several other homes in that dilapidated neighborhood were now vacated and in dire need of repair.

Riley sat in his squad car for several long minutes until a black Ford Escape pulled up behind him. Assuming that it was John

Valentino, he casually unlocked his passenger door and waited for Johnny to get in.

When the door was opened, Riley was startled to notice that it wasn't Valentino.

"Good Afternoon, Commander."

The passenger, wearing a black mask over his face, drew out a Beretta 9mm handgun pointed it up against Riley's head.

"I need your weapon, please."

Riley withdrew his gun and handed it to the assailant.

"Don't you know better, Commander?" the assailant asked.

"Who are you? What the hell are you talking about?"

The stranger paused and then smiled.

"Don't end up on El Camino Drive."

Wearing gloves, the stranger then used Riley's loaded .40 caliber Smith and Wesson and shot him on the side of the head with his gun. The blood and brain matter from being shot at close range splattered across the squad car windshield and on the closed driver's side window.

The assailant then put Riley's gun into his right hand with his finger on the trigger. He withdrew a white envelope with John Valentino's name typed on it and placed it on the dashboard. The killer then shoved a plastic Walmart bag with some contents under the passenger seat.

Locking the car door of the squad car, he quickly got back into the late model Ford Escape, with its black, darkened windshield, and drove away.

Another body lay dead, slumped over his steering wheel on El Camino Drive.

CHAPTER FORTY-THREE

SUICIDE ON EL CAMINO -MARCH 15, 2020

The traffic on that chilly, March afternoon was quite heavy at that time of day, as we were coming back from a domestic violence incident. I was on an investigation with my partner, Mike Palazzola, driving south on Gratiot Avenue when my radio had gone off.

It was the middle of March, and it had been almost two and one-half months since the "Water Pistol Killer" had struck and killed his last victim on New Year's Eve. I had not heard or gotten any more additional information from either Detectives Frank Partridge or Ronald Sinclair.

From the information I was getting, they had hit a stone wall in their probe and investigation. None of the DNA evidence that was coming up from the blown-up wreckage of Williams' car was turning up any hard evidence. The surveillance cameras from the crime scene didn't indicate that anyone had tampered with his car in the parking lot before the explosion. And none of the evidence acquired from either the murders of George Johnson, Jack Hansen, or Joni Williams Harper pointed to anyone relevant or any direct positive clues or essential subjects.

I had talked to Partridge a few times, and he sounded frustrated. He was under a lot of pressure from his commander at the Eighth Precinct to solve this case, as they had now asked for the help of the Federal Bureau of Investigation to assist him in locating any potential subjects.

I was doing better personally, having completely stopped drinking and going to my AA classes on Wednesday nights every other week. I was working out regularly and trying to stay away from eating all of the unhealthy crap that isn't good for you, especially fast food.

I had not had a cigarette since the holidays. Although I still had the urge to light one up with my coffee, I didn't let the lack of nicotine bother me as long as I was on those nicotine patches. Friday night pizzas were probably the only vice that I still had left, and that was only because my sons enjoyed going out to Buddy's Pizza whenever they stayed with me on the weekends.

Things at the Third Precinct were a little unusual, as Commander Riley hadn't been at work all week. The desk sergeant, Jeanine Zupo, didn't think anything of it at first, figuring that he probably either had caught the flu (which was going around) or had a bad cold. But by yesterday, the desk sergeant approached me:

"Johnny, have you heard from Commander Riley at all?"

"No, should I?" I asked. By now, the whole precinct must have figured out that I was Joe Riley's special boy.

"Just wondered. He hasn't called into work in a few days, and no one has heard from him."

There was an anxious look on her face. I then decided to go over to Riley's house and check on him.

He lived on the West Side of Detroit, off of Eight Mile Road and Schaefer near Oak Park, in a little house on Tracey Street. The neighborhood was racially mixed, but local coppers from the Twelfth Precinct kept it under control and well patrolled.

When I had knocked on his door, there was no answer, and his squad car was gone. Palazzola and I peered into his home and in his garage, but there was no sign of him or his vehicle.

I called back the desk sergeant.

"We're at his house, and there is no sign of him," I reported.

"Maybe you should knock on some of the neighbor's doors and see if anyone has seen him."

"Okay," I agreed. "We'll knock on a few."

We split up and took a few houses on each side of the street and interviewed a few of the neighbors, letting them know that we were doing a well-being check on Joseph Riley, who lived at 20202 Tracey Street.

No one had seen him at all, except for one neighbor who saw his squad car leave the house early the day before.

We were still on his driveway, standing outside of our squad car, when we got a call on the radio.

"John, we just got a call from another squad car on El Camino Drive. One of our squad cars is parked there, and there's a dead body inside."

"A dead body? Who?" I asked.

There was a long moment of silence.

"It's Commander Riley's squad car."

At that moment, my heart fell to my stomach. I felt intense pain as though someone had stuck a knife inside my gut.

I doubled over immediately, and I started puking whatever was inside of my stomach from lunch. Detective Palazzola helped me for a moment until I could get my bearings and then helped me over to the passenger side of the car.

"We need to rush over there," as he flipped the sirens on, and he started driving down Eight Mile Road.

Every terrible thought was rushing through my head as I was wondering what the hell could have possibly happened to the man who was not only my boss but my mentor and life counselor.

It probably wasn't longer than twenty minutes before we had arrived on El Camino Drive. There were several other squad cars parked there, and several other detectives were surrounding the parked Detroit PD car.

I looked at the driver's side of the car, and there was blood splattered all over the driver's seat and window, with Riley slumped back, blood protruding from the side of his head.

There, of course, was Detective Frank Partridge, who rushed over to me as I was next to Riley's squad car.

"Johnny, I'm sorry," he said.

"Frank, what happened?"

"From what we can tell, this was a suicide. It looks like Riley used his revolver and put a single bullet into his head about a half-hour ago. One of the residents heard the shot and came outside, then called it in."

He looked at me and, knowing that I was going into mild shock, held me up and trying to keep me from collapsing.

I tried my best to control my tears and to keep myself from falling apart. Palazzola had his arm around my waist as they both escorted me away from Riley's body.

"Why would Riley kill himself?" I asked them loudly.

Frank looked at me, trying to explain what was going on gently.

"Commander Riley had been on anti-depressants for a long time, and he started taking some opioids for some severe back pain that he was suffering from over six months ago. We found a couple of vials of pills in his glove box."

"Are you sure this is suicide?" I asked.

"The car was locked from the inside, and he's still holding the gun in his right hand when we got here. There was no forced entry and no other sign of another vehicle. No tire prints, no footprints anywhere around the Commander's squad car."

I stood there, trying to absorb all of this information.

"He probably went off his meds and started hallucinating while still hooked on the opioids," Partridge hypothesized.

Several moments of silence as the other patrolmen were gathering information at the suicide scene.

"Johnny…Riley left a note here for you."

He then handed me a white envelope, with my name neatly typed on top of it.

I hesitantly opened the envelope with my finger and read the note.

A letter was neatly typed as follows:

Dear Johnny,
I just couldn't do this anymore, and I only want to be back with my Elena again. I'm just letting you know that I have always loved you as the son I never had.
Good luck with your life, as I'll be watching you from afar.
I did all of this for you.
La vendetta è stata compiuta.
Joe Riley

Along with the suicide note was a typed copy of the poem, each excerpt from every murder put together in its entirety:

El Camino Drive

A warm dark night, All Hallows Eve,
a hunted man went there.
A small toy pistol was all he had,
because his hands were bare.
To scare his assassins to force them away,
they wouldn't leave him alone.
Their rage and anger became no match
for a woman, not his own.
He tried to push his enemies far,
but their rage could not be broken.
A gun was drawn, and bullets flew,
their threats had now been spoken.
His lifeless body, soaked in blood,
from a battle, he couldn't survive.
His spirit now one of many ghosts
...of El Camino Drive.

We all looked at each other as I was reading the note to myself several times, over and over.

"What's that last part in Italian say?" one of the other detectives asked.

"Probably something to the effect that the vendetta has been accomplished," I guessed.

Frank Partridge looked at me with that gazed look of his, as though he were wondering if I knew anything at all about any of this.

At that moment, I saw Sinclair's' Ira Township squad car park alongside my vehicle as we were all trying to absorb all of this.

"Well," Frank said. "I guess we now know who the 'Water Pistol Killer' is."

I glared at Partridge and Palazzola. Sinclair was then coming out of his vehicle and getting briefed by the other patrolmen about the suicide.

This whole thing just didn't make any sense. Commander Riley, for as long as I've known him, wasn't the suicidal type.

Although I had heard that he was on meds, I assumed that was mostly for his minor health issues, like cholesterol, blood pressure, and occasional back pain. The fact that he was taking anti-depressants and was hooked on opioid medication was a total surprise to me, and no one else was aware of this.

Commander Joseph Riley, who was the epitome of personal strength and confidence to not only me but to the rest of the Detroit Police Department, suddenly decides to kill himself on El Camino Drive? His dead body is locked inside of his squad car with no prints, no sign of struggle, and a copy of the El Camino Drive poem neatly folded with a suicide note addressed to me?

Riley made no indication to anyone that he was contemplating 'acing' himself and committing suicide. His behavior before his death did not point to a manically depressed individual thinking about killing himself.

I just wasn't buying it.

Riley's squad car was dusted for fingerprints, which of course, only revealed his own. When they checked under the passenger seat of his squad car, they found a plastic Walmart bag filled with three green, plastic squirt guns. There was also a receipt from Walmart, dated July 30, 2019. It was for the purchase of eight green plastic water pistols, for $26.00 apiece, or a total of $223.08, including taxes. These toy pistols were, of course, paid for in cash.

My mind automatically did the math, and it just didn't add up. If there were four murders, and four green squirt guns left at each crime, and three squirt guns were found under Riley's car seat, that left one missing.

Where was the missing squirt gun?

The murderer was careful to make sure that none of the items had any evidence, fingerprints, or means of identifying who the purchaser was. There was no evidence as to who had purchased the toy guns or, for that matter, murdered the other victims.

So why would Riley kill on my behalf? Did he love me like a son so much that he would kill my father's murderers for me and then check out?

Why?

Palazzola and Partridge were discussing the details of Riley's suicide to Detective Sinclair for several minutes while I stood there staring at my lifeless commander and boss, slumped in the front seat of his squad car. His blood was drenched all over his head, his face, the windshield, and all over the driver's side window.

But it just didn't add up. If this were a homicide, who would want to kill Commander Riley and why?

I was literally talking to myself next to Riley's squad car, asking myself the very questions that any detective would be asking.

Sinclair, Palazzola, and Partridge were all on the same page with this incident, and to them, Commander Riley being the 'Water Pistol Killer' made a lot of sense.

Commander Riley, according to the other detectives, had this perverted sense of parental obligation to me to avenge my father's killers and put my life back on track. They concluded that fulfilling the vendetta that my Uncle Ross declared on his brother's killers over forty years ago would be Riley's way to fix my problems somehow.

But did Riley see it that way? Other than making sure that he had my back, he never mentioned anything about my being the 'son he never had.' He only stated that my father's murder was a gross miscarriage of justice back in 1978.

But to assume now that Riley would kill on my behalf and then kill himself?

The murder mystery of the 'Water Pistol Killer' was now solved, all wrapped up in a cute little bow, according to all of the investigating detectives.

If a dead man could talk...

CHAPTER FORTY-FOUR

RILEY'S FUNERAL

The Ides of March made the cold winds almost unbearable on that dark Monday evening. Bagnasco Funeral Home on Harper Avenue was filled with people going in and out of the funeral chapel to pay their respects. The funeral home was a long-established undertaker on the East Side and had been around for generations, serving the Italians and other prominent nationalities in the Detroit area.

It had been a very long few days. Commander Joseph Riley did not have any living next of kin to speak of, so everyone assumed that I would take charge of his funeral. I was suddenly responsible for setting up and arranging his funeral services, choosing his casket, and finding him a cemetery plot.

Knowing that he was a devout Catholic, I called the pastor, Fr. Richard Connelly, over at St. Casimir's Catholic Church in Riley's neighborhood and made the solemn preparations with him. Fr. Connelly and the Bagnasco family were very helpful in assisting me with the arrangements. They all said that they would even wait for payment until I could coordinate a meeting with Joseph Riley's attorney and plan to sell off his assets and paying for his funeral.

Two Detroit policemen were standing guard in their full, formal regalia, watching over Joseph Riley in his dark brown casket.

Several other police and patrolmen came over and stood beside me in front of the funeral chapel, as over two hundred mourners had filed past the casket to pay their respects.

At about 8:00 pm, I took a break from greeting all of the mourners and went downstairs to the funeral chapel cafeteria and use the restroom. When I arrived back at the funeral chapel, my two sisters were both there kneeling in front of the casket.

Instead of interrupting them, I decided to take a seat towards the back of the chapel. As they were both praying over Riley's casket, my sister Lucia went into her purse and pulled out an envelope. She then placed it inside of Riley's coat pocket as a memento to be buried with him.

What the hell was she putting in his casket? I was perplexed, and I shook my head in disbelief.

I greeted my sisters without saying a word. They then sat in the back of the funeral chapel and waited for the Catholic priest to pray the rosary after the wake.

At the end of the chapel service, final prayers were made for the dearly parted. I gave some of the floral arrangements to a few of the mourners who stayed for the final prayers and rosary. We then all greeted each other one last time before leaving Riley's casket in the funeral chapel.

My two sisters left the chapel and began walking towards their cars in the parking lot. I caught up with my sister Lucia, who was about to unlock her Lexus and leave.

"Lucia, do you have a minute?"

"Hey, Johnny...what's up?

"What did you put into Riley's casket?"

"A card with a nice poem that I wrote for him."

I was perplexed at that moment.

"Why, Lucia? That seems so silly?" I replied.

"No, it isn't. He was a wonderful man who appreciated poetry and literature. I thought it would be nice to write a poem for him to read in heaven."

I looked at her for a moment.

"Why would you put a card with a poem inside of Riley's suitcoat pocket in the casket?" still concerned.

Lucia laughed. "It's just a memento from our family, something for him to take into the afterlife with?"

I then got a little annoyed.

"Are you kidding? There was a 'Water Pistol Serial Killer' out there, leaving poetry next to dead bodies, and you think a poem is a lovely memento to put in Riley's casket? Everyone already thinks he's the killer. What is wrong with you?"

"Lighten up, Johnny."

"Lighten up my ass! Everyone thinks Riley is the 'Water Pistol Killer' and a fucking poet!" I raised my voice.

"And now you're sticking a poem in his casket because you think it's cute?"

Lucia then started to raise her voice.

"I wrote that poem as a reflection of thanks for his love for our family. Did you forget Johnny?" she stated loudly.

"That man sent us birthday cards when we were kids. He checked on Mom after Dad was killed, and he always looked after you. That man was practically your surrogate father while you were out drinking it up and being mad at the world. He avenged Dad's killers when the court system let them off the hook," she reiterated while standing in front of her Lexus with the car door open.

"Joe Riley loved you, Johnny. He looked after you. You owe him your life."

There were several moments of silence.

"The poem is just a reminder of the love that we all had for him, too," Lucia reminded me with tears in her eyes.

At that moment, she began to hug me tightly, as I could feel my sister's wet cheeks rubbing against my face.

"Will I get to read this poem?" I was starting to calm down.

"Someday," she replied.

Another silent moment.

"He killed for you, Johnny. He killed for us," she said while holding me hard.

She then pulled herself away from me and looked at me directly.

"No more bad dreams, my little brother. No more nightmares. The bad people who killed Daddy are all dead. They are all gone," talking to me like I was still six years old.

She then hugged me again.

"I'm so proud of you. You've gotten so strong, and you're no longer trying to destroy yourself. I'm sure Joe Riley was proud of you too."

By then, there were tears in my eyes, and I was having trouble trying to keep my composure. I kissed my big sister on the cheek.

"Will you be at the funeral tomorrow?"

"Of course. We will both be here for you."

She then got into her car and drove off.

I was now standing alone in the parking lot, crying my eyes out.

It was hard for me to understand at that moment, but I now realized that I had lost my very own guardian angel. This man, who was my precinct commander, my boss, also continued to look after me, to save me from myself.

Perhaps, he actually did love me.

Maybe, I thought to myself; *I indeed was his son.*

The black Cadillac hearse pulled up in front of old St. Casimir's Catholic Church on that bright, sunny morning. The shadow of Riley's casket was reflected on the brick cobblestone entranceway of the church as a long line of Detroit Police squad cars were parked behind the hearse.

Mourners were beginning to assemble out front as the organ music was loudly playing 'How Great Thou Art' and could be heard from outside.

It was a little past ten o'clock, as Father Connelly was standing in front of the old, wooden doors with two altar boys in front of the old catholic church. He was holding a bible and an aspergillum, which is used by the priest during mass to bless the body.

The bell tower of the church frequently rang its bells precisely every hour, on the hour. Instead of the bells ringing for the current hour of that morning, it only loudly rang six times:

One ring for each victim.

Riley's casket was draped initially with the City of Detroit's flag, escorted by six police officers as pallbearers dressed in full uniform, including myself. The pall, a holy garment used to drape over a casket during a Catholic funeral, replaced the city flag as his coffin was wheeled into the front of the church.

Detective Frank Partridge approached me before the funeral mass and gave me a big, tearful hug.

"I'm so sorry for your loss," my old partner and my best friend said.

"Thanks, Frank," as I tearfully hugged him back.

Both of my sisters then came up to me and kissed me on the cheek. They had brought along my uncles, Ross, Mario, and Aldo, who all felt obligated to offer their condolences. Each of my uncles was walking with either a cane or a walker to keep themselves from falling.

I took off the white gloves and followed the casket to the front of the old, antiquated church surrounded by beautiful, ornate stained-glass windows and dark walnut trim. The canter was now singing the 'Ave Maria' in a loud, glorious voice, and the traditional song seemed to reverberate and echo off the walls of the old, renaissance cathedral. The pews were all filled with police officers, family, and friends, and there was standing room only for those who wished to witness the ascension of Joseph Riley's innocent soul.

As I looked around at all the people in the church that morning, I couldn't imagine one single person at that mass who believed that Riley was indeed the 'Water Pistol Killer.'

Murder and suicide were not words in Riley's vocabulary. It wasn't in him, and he wasn't a murderer. And Riley certainly wasn't the type to point a gun at his head and check out. Being that Riley was a devout Catholic, he would have never broken a commandment and committed the ultimate cardinal sin.

Joseph Riley was a kind, caring, loving man with a gruff exterior and a huge heart. It didn't matter how much he disliked a person or a situation, and he would have never allowed himself to play judge, jury, and executioner and take another's life.

'That's only God's decision,' he would say.

Joseph Riley wasn't a murderer. He wasn't an executioner. And he certainly wasn't irrational enough to kill himself.

I knew in my heart that someone else had committed those six murders, and yet the Detroit P.D. and Intelligence were now putting the 'case solved' stamp on all of these homicide files. They had now plastered Joseph Riley's name all over those unsolved murders, signed with his own blood.

According to them, Riley was doped up and irrational under the intense medication and suffering from the aftereffects of being on opioids for too long. His obligations to look after me since I was a little boy only reinforced the police department's theory that Riley was true, the 'Water Pistol Killer.'

I looked up at that large, rosewood crucifix suspended over the church while Fr. Connelly preached the gospel and said a short sermon. I kept shaking my head, still in disbelief, as my eyes were drenched with tears.

I turned my head and looked behind me, mentally counting all the people attending Joe Riley's funeral mass. All of the church's pews were full, with dozens of people standing in the back of the church.

Joseph Riley was, obviously, a cherished man, and we were all grief-stricken. We were all emotional. We were all looking up to the church's articulate rafters, surrounded by a foray of anonymous saints, trying to figure out who had really done this.

Who could have possibly made a larger than life man like Joe Riley lower himself to a self-inflicted gunshot wound in the middle of the day on El Camino Drive?

Suppose my father had only known forty-two years ago that his irresponsible, immoral actions would lead to other things. His selfish behavior would be the catalyst for a long line of misery, alcoholism, manic depression, a suspected suicide, and several bloody murders, starting with his own.

We were all praying in front of God that morning, looking for answers. Nobody in that church knew the truth about what happened to my father's killers, my father's alleged girlfriend, or Precinct Commander Joseph Riley. Not a single person praying in those church pews knew who the real executioner was.

No one in that church except two.

CHAPTER FORTY-FIVE

A RECONCILIATION-SPRING 2020

The parking lot of Buddy's Pizza on Van Dyke Road was filled with cars on that Friday night in April, as everyone on the East Side must have had a taste for Buddy's deep dish, square pizza. I pulled up with my two boys in the car, who were telling me several times about how hungry they were and how they hadn't had enough to eat for lunch at school.

My sons were definitely growing teenagers. Anthony, who was finishing his junior year at Notre Dame High School, was already six feet tall and starting to bulk up some muscle. Besides playing baseball, he stayed after school three times a week to work out with the '220 Club'. That's an active weightlifting group that earned its name from anyone who was able to bench press a full rack of weights on the universal weight machine, or two hundred and twenty pounds.

Dario, who was only five feet, six inches tall, was finishing his freshman year at the same school. He was slowly approaching his growth spurt and had an appetite that would rival any NFL linebacker. Between the two of them together, Marina was complaining about going through three hundred dollars of groceries a week. She needed every penny of my child support money to bring to the grocery store and keep our growing boys nourished and well-fed.

Dario had recently quit the freshmen baseball team, so he was getting a lot of grief from his older brother, who had made the varsity team and was playing first-base.

"I didn't like the coach, Dad," was his reason for quitting. With his inherited quick-trigger temper, it was probably better that he resigned.

"How bad could he be, Dario?"

"How about Mussolini?"

"Really? What the hell do you know about Mussolini?"

"We were studying about him in History class last week. From what we were reading, he was a real piece of work," Dario explained as we were walking through the parking lot and into the entrance door of the restaurant.

"Dario, 'Il Duce' would shoot the train conductors when their trains arrived at the stations late," I patiently explained to my youngest son.

"Well, exchange the words 'trains' with 'baseball,' and you've got the same thing," reasoned my aspiring-politician-youngest-son.

At that moment, the hostess found us a booth next to the window overlooking Old Thirteen Mile Road. Buddy's Pizza was always an East Side staple, with its green, white, and red décor and straw cantina wine bottles hanging everywhere.

The Detroit-Style pizzeria began at Six Mile and Conant Streets on Detroit's East Side in 1946, when square-shaped pizza was first introduced. The pizza was first baked in blue steel pans borrowed from the local automotive plants, and the original owners were able to produce a very light and crispy crust, which is now known as Detroit-Style pizza. It has been a popular eating place with its unique brand of old-style Italian food.

"Dad, Dario is exaggerating. He's not that bad."

"Oh, bullshit, Anthony..."

"Dario, watch your mouth," I interjected.

"No, Dad. Seriously. He had us doing laps around the baseball diamond for an hour after we lost our first game to Brother Rice last week."

"That's because everyone on your team is so damn fat that you guys can't even steal any fucking bases," said my oldest son.

"Enough, Anthony."

I only laughed to myself, realizing how much I missed talking, laughing, and bantering back and forth with my two sons.

For me, getting together on the weekends for Friday night pizzas was never enough. I now needed my family fix with my sons seven days a week, as being a weekend father just wasn't cutting it.

With the many months of being separated from my wife and now divorced, I was now feeling remorseful. I regretted all of the nights I spent drinking at the bar while my wife and kids were home having dinner without me. It took the loss of my wife and family to realize how good I had it.

There was nothing for me at those bars every night after work. There was nothing for me at the Crazy Horse Lounge. My pot of gold was sitting at my kitchen table every night after school, with my young boys telling their mom about what they had learned in school that day. My final salvation, from now on, was to have my sons with me as much as possible, to watch them grow up and get older.

To watch them bring their friends home and experience life through their eyes. To view them go to their high school proms and graduate from high school. To watch my boys go off to college, join a fraternity, and eventually find jobs and start their careers. To experience, they're getting married and having families of their own. These are the things in life that every man needs to experience and treasure, above and beyond anything in a whiskey bottle or a crystal glass tumbler. Or perhaps, someone sitting on a bar stool, waiting for you to buy them a drink.

These are all the valuable jewels of life that some men need to travel through hell and back to find. Some men never realize that their complete and total life's treasure hunt starts and ends in their own backyards.

Some people never get it. Some people never understand. I was just sorry that it took a nasty divorce and an excessive amount of legal fees to some overpriced law firm in Southfield to figure it out.

"So, how is your mother?" was the way I usually started out the conversation on Friday nights.

"She is doing better, now that Tom Asshole Pratt moved out."

I smiled to myself.

"Man, Dad. Did you clean his friggin' clock or what? You sent him to the hospital. Mom said he was in there for four days," Dario said.

"Did you guys help him pack his bags?" I gloated.

"Yeah, we should have thrown his shit in the back of the ambulance when they scooped him up and brought him to the hospital," Dario suggested.

"He's not the first guy Dad has sent to the hospital," Anthony interjected.

"Yeah, Mom said you beat the fucking shit out of your partner for calling you a 'dago-drunk'," Dario reminded me.

"Okay, Dario. That's enough."

Both of my boys sat in the booth and smiled at me with pride. They knew that I had chased down and slain the devil out of their house.

"Losing one's temper is a sign of a very weak man, boys. Beating someone up and sending them to the hospital is not a good thing. It's nothing to be proud of."

"Yeah, well...you do it so well, Dad," Dario observed.

The last thing I wanted to teach my sons was that it was okay to lose one's temper and violently take it out on some poor asshole that so greatly deserves it. That wasn't a lesson worth passing on to the next generation.

About the time that our extra-large square pizza with pepperoni and mushrooms arrived, we received a surprise visitor.

Well, at least, she was a surprise to me.

"May I join all of you," a very familiar face approached our table.

"Okay," I said out loud. "This is a nice surprise."

I later came to find out that Marina had texted Anthony and Dario earlier to see if it was alright for their mother to join us for dinner.

Marina was wearing a white, pleated skirt, white blouse, and a dark blue sweater with a bright blue belt. Her outfit went well with her Zanotti high heeled shoes, looking as though she was ready to go out on a date. Marina looked absolutely stunning.

The familiar smell of her perfume started to bring me back into a trance of a time long ago when our family enjoyed Friday pizza nights together.

As she sat down next to me across from our boys, I ordered her a glass of her favorite Pinot Noir. We all took a slice of pizza and laughed out loud, enjoying the special moments of being a family together once again. It was a reminder of the many Friday pizza nights we used to all enjoy together as a young family years ago.

When the kids were little, when we both had less gray hair, wrinkles, and in our younger years, we all enjoyed our Friday nights as a tightly knit household.

Before the fights, before the anger, before the lawyers and all the motions for discovery, there was a family and a special night where two people with their two children got together to laugh, love, and enjoy deep-dish, square panned pizza.

"I have a surprise for you," she said after we finished dinner.

After I paid the waitress, we all walked outside onto the parking lot.

There parked in front was my 1966 Corvette Stingray Convertible. It had been newly painted in its original black color, with the top down, looking sleek and as shiny as ever. The car needed a be painted and partially restored before, and it was on my list for many years to do it when I had the time and the money.

"I had Vince over at the body shop finish painting and restoring the car for you. The boys found the keys to the storage unit, and they helped me bring it to the body shop," she smiled with pride.

"Do you like it?"

"The car is gorgeous, honey," as I kissed her on the cheek.

By that moment, Anthony and Dario strategically walked away from the two of us, obviously to play with their all-too-important-cell phones. As we both stood there in front of my Corvette, Marina grasped my hand.

"You can keep your car in the garage if you want. There's room for it," she suggested.

I thought about it for a moment.

"That would be great. I won't have to deal with the hassles of going back and forth to that storage unit."

At that moment, Marina put her arms around my neck and kissed me. It was probably the most passionate kiss I had ever received in a long time.

"Come back home, Johnny. There's room for you too."

She had suddenly said the words that I wished she would say for a very, very long time. I couldn't count the number of dreams and fantasies that I had thinking about what it would be like if my ex-wife ever wanted me back home again. I missed my wife, and I wanted nothing more than to be her husband again.

But then I thought about her old boyfriend, and how I sent him to the hospital too. At that point, I still didn't trust myself or my temper.

I was still a former alcoholic with horrible anger issues and a sour, fatherless childhood. I had now stopped drinking, and I was doing much better about controlling my anger. But I was still struggling with my bitterness.

The last thing that I wanted was to walk back into my old house and step back into my former life as a new man. I couldn't just pretend that none of my past demons that caused the drinking, the anger, and the violent episodes would never come back.

And what was stopping Marina from getting upset or angry with me and running off with her girlfriends to the bar? Would she come home again with another boyfriend, as if it were a new puppy from a pet store?

I was conflicted. I was still hurt, and I was extremely apprehensive. I knew I had to take an emotional risk. But for some reason, standing in front of Buddy's Pizza next to my freshly painted Corvette wasn't the right place and time.

"Marina, I love you," I said as she held me as tightly as she could.

"I have always loved you. You are the only girl I have ever loved. You are the only girl that I have ever been with," I confessed.

"When I take my last breath in this life, I want you to be next to me until that very last second," I declared.

"But I don't want to rush into anything right now. I want to make very, very sure that I am and will always be the husband and the man you deserve," as tears were starting to well up in my eyes.

"I want to make sure that all those terrible demons from El Camino Drive have forever gone away. I want to make sure that they never come back."

Marina looked at me as tears were starting to stream down her face.

"We both need some time, Marina. Time to heal from all of the hurt and pain that we have suffered and inflicted on each other for such a long time."

By that moment, Marina was copiously crying, as the boys who were standing nearby. They began looking at both of us, wondering what was going on.

There were several long minutes of silence as we both composed ourselves so that we could present ourselves to our children.

She then gave me another long kiss.

"Let's switch cars. You take your Corvette sweetheart home tonight and come over for breakfast in the morning. Deal?" she asked, putting on a brave smile while kissing me on the cheek.

"Deal," I smiled.

She handed me the Corvette keys, and I climbed in. As my old car started right up immediately, 'my girl' couldn't have sounded any better.

Marina got into my car with the boys and started it up. Before putting it into drive, Marina got back out and came over to my Corvette, leaning her arms on my car door.

"I'm going to have the house painted," she said, which initially startled me.

"I am going to sell our old bedroom set. Then you're going to come with me to the store, and we are going to pick out some new furniture for our bedroom. And I am going to throw out that old couch immediately," Marina smiled.

She then kissed me one last time on the cheek.

"I am going to get our house ready for your homecoming," Marina exclaimed.

"And when the day finally comes when you do come back home, I promise I will never, ever let you leave," she beamed as she wiped away the tears from her eyes.

"See you in the morning."

Marina winked her eye and got back into the running car. Slowly, she pulled away onto the bustling traffic of Van Dyke Road.

As I adjusted my seat and looked into the rearview mirror, I noticed that my eyes were still red and wet. But not from any tears of sadness caused by any of El Camino's horrific demons.

These were tears of joy.

CHAPTER FORTY-SIX

THE STERLING INN –LATE SPRING 2020

The rain puddles in the parking lot of the Sterling Inn were starting to turn into small, miniature ponds on the black asphalt, as it had been torrentially raining most of that spring day in May.

A black, late model Ford Escape pulled into the sparsely occupied hotel. It was almost seven o'clock that Wednesday evening. The daylight hours of spring were getting longer, with the picturesque Michigan sunsets occurring much later at night.

A tall man dressed in a button-down shirt and blue jeans then got out of the car and walked into the hotel office. He was extra careful not to get his Allen Edmond shoes soaked in the standing water of the parking lot. He shut off his cell phone and police radio as he was off duty for the rest of the evening. He was about to check-in to their usual hotel suite.

Frank Partridge had again lied to his wife Patty about his whereabouts. He told her that he was working the night shift and would be on patrol most of the evening. He probably wouldn't be home until very early in the morning.

Frank and Patty Partridge had been married for almost twenty years and had three beautiful daughters, a lovely house on the West Side of Detroit, and all the niceties of a loving, caring family. Frank's home life was something that any man would have envied, as his wife was one who was always thoughtful, loyal, and faithful to her husband.

But Frank Partridge, at the age of forty-two years old, was not a happy man. Since losing his mother to cancer two years ago, his emotions in dealing with her loss has thrown his private life into a tailspin.

At this point in his life, Frank Partridge should probably have been nominated for an Academy Award. He went from being a loving husband and father to a viable, award-winning actor. He was performing the part, pretending to be happy and still be in love with the same girl he married when they both were only twenty-three years old.

With the death of his mother and losing his father seven years prior, Frank felt like an orphan. He no longer had the love and support of his always loving parents, and it put pressure on his marriage.

Deep down inside, Frank Partridge wanted the hell out.

On that late spring evening, Frank had booked a hotel room at the Sterling Inn on Fifteen Mile Road. It was his usual meeting place once a week with this lady, who Frank now considered his soulmate and the girl of his dreams.

"Good Evening, Detective Partridge," the young, female innkeeper greeted him.

"Good Evening...our usual suite, please."

"Certainly, sir. That will be $175.00."

Frank reached into his pocket and paid cash, as usual, for the same deluxe suite he and his girlfriend occupied every Wednesday night for the last ten months. The elegant suite included a king-size bed, a bar stocked with several liquors, a large bathroom with a shower, and a very sizable jacuzzi.

He usually brought along their favorite choice of red wine, the 2018 Belle Glos Pinot

Noir, some healthy snacks, and several bags of munchies, which they often enjoyed most of the evening.

Their usual routine was to spend the next several hours being intimate, sometimes ordering pizza or carry-out food, and sleeping in each other's arms for most of the evening. By four-thirty in the morning, after they would both shower together, Frank would return 'home from work,' while his girlfriend would return to her house in Grosse Pointe to let the dog out.

That Wednesday evening in May was no different. Frank gained the key to the Sterling Inn's deluxe suite and went back into his car to acquire his bags of food and refreshments, bringing them up to their suite.

At this point in their relationship, it was safe to say that Frank Partridge was in love with another woman. This female was everything his current wife Patty was not. Although this new lady was almost ten years his senior, she was his dream girl. She was smart, educated, beautiful, and shapely. She had a professional, upscale job, and she had already raised her children.

But most of all, this lady was divorced. And with her recent divorce settlement, she had enough money and assets to be secure and comfortable for the rest of her life.

The only reason why they didn't meet at her house was that her youngest son still lived at home and would not react well to his mother having an intense relationship after getting divorced that prior spring.

Also, Frank was very familiar with her family, and his being at her house would create a very uncomfortable situation.

Frank Partridge knew that he couldn't have it both ways. He knew that he would eventually have to file for divorce and move on with his new love and his life. He had promised his girlfriend that he would file with his attorney and move out after the summer.

At seven-thirty that evening, there was a loud knock on the door as Frank unlocked the deadbolt and opened the hotel room entrance. His girlfriend was standing there, dressed for the evening.

"Hello, baby," she purred in a sultry voice.

The dark-haired beauty was wearing a long black raincoat, long black leather boots, leather gloves, and her usual black mask. Underneath her long black overcoat, she was barely clad in a dominatrix black leather outfit, complete with her dark 'goodie bag' filled with her sadistic sex toys.

This was the way Frank liked it. He had always fantasized about having a sadistic dominatrix whipping him and having her way with him in the bedroom. He enjoyed the intense whipping and beating before, during, and after they had very rough, very physical sex.

The dominatrix immediately pushed Frank onto the bed, and without saying a single word, began tearing his clothes off. While he was naked, Frank let her take out her usual steel handcuffs from her dark bag and cuffed his hands onto the headboard.

Removing her black raincoat, she then had her way with him, flogging him with her leather whip across his bare legs and stomach. After about twenty minutes of this rough foreplay, she reached into her bag and pulled out a condom. Placing it on his penis, she began to tease and make love to him for what seemed like hours, yelling profanities at the Detroit detective.

"I want you, baby. Fuck me hard," he was shouting as she kept bouncing herself up and down on top of him until he could no longer control himself.

After several long minutes of more flogging, Frank was exhausted and in complete pain. His buttocks were bleeding from the continuous thrashing she resumed on him, as their hour-long sadistic, erotic sex session had finally ended.

Frank Partridge was fatigued, and with his eyes barely open, he said the phrase that he often said to his girlfriend as she removed her mask:

"I love you, Lucia."

Lucia Valentino smiled and nodded her head. She acknowledged his intense love for her as he had always done whenever they were together.

"Let me wipe you down, baby," she softly said, and she went into the bathroom.

She came out with a wet washcloth and wiped down Partridge, almost giving him a sponge bath there in the king-size bed while still handcuffed. She removed and neatly disposed of the used condom.

Frank enjoyed the wet massage, as she thoroughly soaked his body with soap and warm water.

Still wearing her outfit and black gloves, she excused herself and went back into the luxury suite bathroom to change out of her costume, like she usually did. She typically put on a sexy piece of clothing or lingerie that Frank habitually bought for her as a gift.

But this night was different.

Lucia Valentino had been seeing Frank Partridge for over a year, and she was well aware of his marital status. They had met at a family party last spring, and her brother briefly introduced the detective to her. She later accepted Frank's telephone number that night when his wife wasn't looking. The Eighth Precinct detective had promised her several times that he would file for divorce from his wife Patty later that summer, and Lucia played along.

Truth be told, Lucia didn't give a fuck.

She needed the veteran Detroit detective for another, more important purpose.

While they were initially dating, Lucia learned that Frank Partridge was a certified explosives specialist, long-range rifle marksman, and gun expert while he was in the Marines. He was extremely talented when it came to using any weapon, be it a rifle, a handgun, a serrated hunting knife, or planting a remote-controlled, detonating auto explosive.

As a Detroit detective, she knew that he could plan, perform, and get away with almost any murder that she wanted. Lucia also knew that once Frank had fallen deeply in love with her, that she could control and manipulate him. At that point, he would probably do anything that she asked:

Including murder.

After her mother died, Lucia decided to take up the vendetta that had been neglected and abandoned by her Uncle Ross. She didn't want her brother Johnny involved because she knew that he would be the first person that they would suspect. She needed to summon revenge against her father's alleged girlfriend and his murderers, without her brother Johnny's knowledge.

The only way that could happen is if she enlisted an expert killer to do it for her. She had to make sure that the murderer was capable of successfully killing Joni Williams Harper, Mr. and Mrs. Jack Hansen, George Johnson, Howard Williams, and finally, Commander Joseph Riley. And she had to make sure that her brother had a valid and verifiable alibi at the time of every single murder.

When Frank Partridge declared his unwavering love for Lucia, she knew that she had him exactly where she wanted him.

Lucia asked him to perform the ultimate acts of love. She demanded that he murder her father's killers and to make sure that Partridge did it without her brother's knowledge, suspicion, or involvement.

Their Wednesday night rendezvous encounters at the Sterling Inn became detailed planning meetings for the killings of the people who assisted in murdering her father.

Lucia and Frank would usually have their rough sex sessions first. Then they would spend the rest of the evening putting together their plans for their vigilante justice against Williams, Hansen, and Johnson.

Because Lucia felt that none of this would have ever happened if Joni Williams Harper hadn't seduced and enticed her father into sleeping with her, Lucia figured that she had to be the one who would violently and brutally be eliminated first.

Detective Frank Partridge was more than happy to kill for his soulmate, knowing that her adoration would be the only love he could ever need. Her mesmerizing charm and ravishing beauty would sustain him for the rest of his life. Partridge loved Lucia so much; he was more than willing to kill for her.

It was Lucia's idea that the murder of Joni Williams Harper included a severed horse's penis inserted into her mouth. She called a local butcher, paying him five hundred dollars to acquire the animal anatomy, and of course, his silence. She wanted to make sure that Joni was choking on a horse's penis while the killer fatally stabbed her.

It was Lucia who had discovered that Jack Hansen was in town for his fiftieth high school reunion last September, and she planned and scouted the parking lot of the Colony Club. She then enlisted Partridge into depositing two bullets into Jack and Barbara Hansen's heads after celebrating their high school reunion. The Ira Township Detective, Ronald Sinclair, didn't bother to notice the victim's splattered blood on Frank Partridge's shoes at the murder scene.

And Lucia Valentino wanted to make sure that George Johnson had the pleasure of escorting his daughter down the aisle at her wedding. She made sure that the young bride had her final dance with her father before going into the men's room and getting brutally shot in the head while sitting on the toilet with his pants down last fall.

She then convinced Detective Partridge to plant the automatic detonating explosive under the chassis of Williams' Cadillac at his trailer home one evening before New Year's. Lucia wanted the pleasure of pressing the button when Howard Williams came out of the Crazy Horse Lounge.

She smiled with delight as she watched his Cadillac explode into a thousand pieces with Williams inside while she sat at the Dunkin' Donuts parking lot across the street drinking her large coffee...light cream, extra sugar.

And of course, she needed to make sure that Detective Riley was 'the patsy,' who took the complete and total blame as the 'Water Pistol Killer' last March.

Lucia had typed Riley's suicide note to her brother John on her computer after work. She made sure her creative prose, her poem 'El Camino Drive,' was included with Riley's suicide note.

She felt very proud of herself, knowing that her creative writing classes at Macomb Community College had come in handy. She also knew about Commander Riley's total love for literature and poetry.

Lucia Valentino had taken revenge against her father's killers and the married lady who ruthlessly instigated it all. And she made sure that a replica of Johnny's squirt gun was left at the scene of each murder.

Frank Partridge was head over heels in love with Lucia, the new love of his life. And for her love, he was willing to do anything for her. Having learned his assassination skills in the Marines, he was more than happy to practice the talents he had so capably acquired for his new soulmate.

Lucia went into the bathroom. She then changed out of her dominatrix outfit, being careful that she didn't leave any fingerprints or any sign of her presence there in that hotel suite.

There were now only two people in the whole world who knew who the real 'Water Pistol Killer' really was.

And as far as Lucia was concerned, that was one person too many.

She put on a pair of blue jeans and a black tee-shirt. Still wearing her long black boots and leather gloves, she came out of the bathroom, holding her dark, goodie bag.

"Hey honey, how come you're not wearing that black Victoria Secrets lingerie outfit that I bought you last week?"

"Not now, baby," as she stood there, putting on her long black raincoat.

Frank stared at her, still handcuffed to the king-size bed.

"Lucia, where are you going? Aren't we going to open up that bottle of wine?"

"I'm not in the mood, Frank," she said, as she then reached into her dark, goodie bag.

At that very moment, veteran detective Frank Partridge suddenly realized that he had made three very stupid, very fatal mistakes:

He allowed himself to date and fall in love with his best friend's sister.

He then let Lucia Valentino convince him to blindly kill for her several times.

And worst of all, he permitted her to handcuff him to that king-size bed on that wet, spring evening.

Frank now realized what was about to happen. As he lay there naked, he was completely and utterly helpless. He began to break out in a cold sweat and started yelling, screaming loudly and uncontrollably:

"YOU FUCKING BITCH!" he vociferously shrieked as his final last words.

While he was still screaming, she shoved the last green toy water pistol that she had in her possession into his mouth.

Johnny's big sister then pulled out a Beretta 92 MM gun from her dark handbag and screwed on the silencer. Lucia was now smiling as she looked at her soon to be ex-lover straight into his eyes.

She had now memorized and loudly recited the last stanza of the poem she had composed:

"His lifeless body, soaked in blood,
From a battle, he couldn't survive.
His spirit now one, of many ghosts
...of El Camino Drive."

The dominatrix excitedly inserted the gun clip and cocked back the chamber, making sure that there was now a 9mm bullet inside. Standing from across the bed, she wanted to make sure that she was far enough away. She didn't want to splatter any blood on her expensive black Athleta raincoat when she fired the first round.

Lucia was now about to use her brand new Beretta semi-automatic black pistol.

EPILOGUE

This fictional story was inspired by actual events.

On El Camino Drive, a factory auto worker was hunted and gunned down by his two killers, Howard Stiles and Jack Harrison, many years ago. He was accused of allegedly having an affair with Stiles' wife, Joan Stewart Stiles. They both worked together at the Ford Assembly Plant in Sterling Heights, Michigan.

The forty-one-year-old man was unarmed, having only his son's toy water pistol to fool his potential killers into believing he could defend himself. Jack Harrison, after a brief scuffle, shot him with three .25 caliber bullets into his head.

He left behind a wife and three children.

At a preliminary hearing, Stiles was released after spending three weeks in jail because he was able to prove that he did not pull the trigger.

Harrison had his criminal charges downgraded to second-degree murder. Taking the legal position of self-defense and claiming that the borrowed pistol had jammed up, Harrison was later acquitted at his trial in Macomb County.

After his acquittal, Jack Edward Harrison moved to Beech Island, South Carolina, where he died peacefully on November 27, 2019, at the age of 79.

Stiles and his wife Joan were initially divorced, and she moved to Hermitage, Tennessee, where she started a new life selling real estate and later remarried.

When her second husband died, the two reconciled. She died of Alzheimer's disease on May 27, 2013.

Howard Levoy Stiles, the man who initially planned the murder, died July 5, 2017, at the ripe old age of 91.

He is now buried next to the woman whom he so devotedly killed for.

Made in the USA
Monee, IL
28 June 2023

37839619R00267